The Mist
In Crest Hill County

Vernon Clay

Brick Publishing
7616 Jamaica Ave, Woodhaven, NY 11421

Book Cover Design © 2016 by Tiffany Hunter

ISBN-13: 978-0692733639

ISBN-10: 0692733639

DEDICATION

To My Grandmother, and for all those who wanted, but didn't have the chance, to say one last goodbye...this is for you – Annie Mae Hodges

Chapter 1

Part I

Until this day, no one knew where the mist had come from, or for that matter, where it had eventually departed. It slid into this little roadside town, and forever changed the lives that lived there.

The town was known as Crest Hill County, a population of a little more than thirty-thousand, where a small, kind, and diligent people lived. A town where there resided one Grandmother – the mother of them all – Jenna Reed; a citizen so wise in years, and so long in stem, that some thought it was the beating of her heart that kept this town alive.

Crest Hill County used to be filled to the gills with visitors of all types, traveling its old road, which spanned at least 30 chickens lengthwise as some might have said. A single road which once brought people from many walks of life, until they built a certain interstate, which carried more traffic, and more people, away on a new road filled with new dreams, and even newer directions, leaving Crest Hill County now with a present road that now only carried memories.

But to all things, there comes a time for change.

Just outside of town, something happened to the ground, and it opened up and unfurled like a yawning beast. Steam, dew, a mysterious mist of some sort had erupted, as if the earth itself had gone into a sweat. It placed a light, wet blanket upon the air, where the wind slowly carried it northward, just fifty miles from town. It traveled strangely, on a day where there was no wind, towards a town which bordered no coast; the simple town of Crest Hill County.

The town however, sat unawares.

The people however, continued their lives.

The clock however, proceeded to advance time.

Nothing changed.

But before nightfall placed its open palm on this town, things would begin to change...many, many things.

Part II

It's not often that a Pastor and his mistress can occupy the same room. Unless of course, one of them is dead.

Pastor Luther Reynolds sat in his office contemplating. He was to be the orator of today's funeral; a most difficult job. Normally funerals were like popcorn; it took no forethought to digest either. Today it was different.

But today, as most of the town gathered to this service, in a year that oddly saw many of such services, Pastor Luther Reynolds was lost for words. He leaned back in his chair; thick dark hands embraced each other as they lay across his rotund belly.

The office door opened, and a tiny head peered in. A mane of curly blonde locks bounced like springs, followed by a woman of even tinier statue.

Pastor Reynolds slowly looked up, adjusting his glasses. "Lisa, it is so good to see you. How are things out there?"

"They seem to be running along smoothly, Pastor Reynolds, but..."

"Is there another concern, Lisa?"

She cleared her throat, in an almost unheard, dainty sort of way. "The congregation is a bit concerned about you, Pastor. You were not out front to shake hands with the mourners as you normally do."

He nodded. She was right, but when a mind is troubled, a lot of routines become askew. "I know, Lisa, I know. This is a most sensitive matter, as you can realize."

Lisa stared at the floor as if her thoughts were etched in the wood. Yes, it was very sensitive, she contemplated. The affair. It shook the whole town, but it was seldom talked about, because some things were allowed to transpire without verbal assurances. "Very well, Pastor. I'll let you know when you're needed." And with that, Lisa McNally slid her tiny golden head back to where it had come from.

Pastor Reynolds began to realize something ironic about his known discretion...

Suddenly the door opened again, breaking his thoughts.

Lisa reentered. "I'm sorry, I forgot to tell you that you wife has not yet arrived."

He exhaled, "Thank you, Lisa."

"Very well..." and she left.

Yes, Pastor Reynolds thought, his wife. The ironic thing about this town, and the lurid affair he's been transfixed with, was that not only did his congregation know, not only did the town murmur about it amongst themselves, not only did all who heard the tale behind the telling forgive Pastor Reynolds, but barring the woman his wife was, they also completely understood.

Part III

Mrs. Erica Ross didn't ask for much out of life. She didn't ask for a huge home, luxurious clothes, or even the perfect father for her children. True, Erica Ross didn't ask for a great many things.

But perhaps she should have.

Erica Ross should have at least asked that the father of her children stick around a while after the birth of their second child. He went out for a bottle of milk nearly 3 years ago, yet to return.

She should have asked for her first home to be a little bit closer to town, instead of on its outskirts, where a few years ago a twister snatched her picket fence dream up and away like a scene from The Wizard of Oz. She was now lived in a mobile home, only slightly closer.

She should have rested more on a certain Sunday morning, when she had decided to take her son Eric Jr. into town with her. She was exhausted after working ten straight nights at the diner. She hadn't noticed he wasn't wearing his seatbelt, until after she realized her blink had turned into a nap, and the car had overturned into a ditch. The doctor said his neck had broken in two places.

Lastly, Mrs. Erica Ross would have asked her best friend to live just a little while longer. She would have talked with her more about this scandalous affair. At first she thought it wrong, but that was until she looked into Maya's eyes, the blueness of them vacant, her soul was in a place that no one could reach, and she realized that she was looking at an action that denoted true love.

Maya knew it.

Erica knew it.

The estranged wife knew it.

The whole town knew it.

And because they knew it, the town of Crest Hill County forgave them.

Here, outside the church, on the day of Maya's funeral, Erica sat in the small garden area to the back of the church, the magnolias and tulips casting a soft, sweet scent to her senses. She sat watching her son, Timothy, coloring in a coloring book. She had been so caught up in her own ocean of thoughts, that she hadn't felt the hand on her shoulder, until the accompanying voice rang out.

"You heading into the church, Erica?"

She looked up to see Lisa, her appearance calm, almost angelic as the sun cast a halo around her golden tresses. "I suppose. I didn't want to be one of the first to go rolling up in there. I didn't want to hear any of the questions."

Lisa took a seat beside her. She noticed her son and waved at him. "Hey there, Timothy, what'cha doing?"

Timothy looked at her, his smile broad. "Just doing some coloring, Mrs. McNally"

Lisa leaned forward slightly, gently resting her elbows on her thighs. "I can see that, and you're doing a mighty fine job at it, from what I can see."

"Thank you, Mrs. McNally."

"You're welcome, Timothy." She leaned back. "You doing a mighty fine job at raising that one, Erica. I would be proud of him."

Erica glanced at her son, the only remaining one, and knew that she was. "Yea, this one is turning out to be a fine young man." She could see Timothy feign a grin in his obvious eavesdropping. "Unless of course, we happen to be talking to him about cleaning up his room."

"Mom!" Timothy protested.

Erica smiled sheepishly at him, and waved a teasing finger in his direction.

Lisa whispered in Erica's ear, "So when are you going to go in there and take a look at your best friend? I really thought you would have been one of the first to view the body."

"Now, why would you think something like that?"

"Because it's what Maya would have wanted."

The silence that followed that statement became so prevalent, that Erica could hear Timothy's crayons scratch against the pages of his coloring book.

"I guess I'm just not good at these things, Lisa."

"Hell, who is?"

For one fleeting moment, Erica stared at Lisa. To Erica, the closest that Lisa had ever come to cursing was once, when saying "shoot". This was when she was cleaning choir robes and had accidentally mixed the colors with the whites.

Lisa stood, placing her hand once again on Erica's shoulder. "There's no shame at what Maya got herself into. No Shame at all. So listen, you just take your time, and go in there to see your best friend, and let this town see that there is no shame in true love.

And with that, Lisa simply turned and walked away.

Ten minutes later, Erica followed, her head held high.

Part IV

"Will you be wearing the ruby or the opal shoes today, First Lady?"

Mildred looked up into the vanity mirror, seeing the housekeeper staring at her from the open doorway. Mildred quickly returned her attention back on her own reflection, "We'll go with the ruby, Tilly. Might as well add a little color to this drab affair."

"Very well, very well," Tilly said, as she began to leave.

Mildred glanced up at the now empty doorway, and her mind did a quick flashback on what Tilly had been wearing; black silk dress, modest jewelry, and gray lace ups, with brown nylons. Nothing too high brow, she thought, but questionable.

"Tilly!" Mildred shouted, as she heard the rhythmic thud of the girl's heels as she returned to the door.

"Yes First Lady," Tilly addressed, breathing heavily.

"Don't tell me that you're going to this funeral too."

Tilly's eyes roamed, as if perplexed at the question. "Why yes. I knew Maya very well and…"

Mildred raised an open hand, "Spare me the flashback, my dear. Just go and bring me my shoes."

"Of course," she said, and was once again walking down the hall.

Mildred looked back upon herself in the mirror, staring down at the collection of lipsticks she had lined up on the counter like tiny colored soldiers. It was taking her the longest time to get ready for this...this *affair*, for lack of a better word. She closed her eyes and laid her head in the palms of her hand. She was not sure how she was going to survive this. Everyone in this fuckin' town was going to this damned funeral, she thought. To be in this sort of position where her husband presided over a funeral of his mistress, in a town that appeared to condone such behavior, and a wife that was really trying to make sense of it all; not the affair exactly, but how this would interfere with her social and financial state was appalling!

She could feel her hands forming into fists, and she closed her eyes tighter. This had to be handled carefully. She was not used to exhibiting such a weak position, but what would the town think if their First Lady did not attend this service? Would she be thought of as vindictive by not being at her husband's side? Was she not a woman of God? Was she not supposed to appear above this? What harm could Maya do now? What retribution was there in the deceased? She had to go, but not really to pay her respects to a woman she could really care less about, but because the town was going to be there…and if not for the town, she would not have been able to afford the lovely ruby shoes that Tilly would be bringing her

In fact, she should have already brought them, but she didn't hear her walking back at all. Mildred opened her eyes, and the name of her housekeeper sat on the tip of her tongue, but those words rolled back into her mouth like spent saliva, for on the vanity top, only inches from her, were her ruby shoes. Mildred quickly spun around. Odd woman, that Tilly, she thought.

She picked up the shoes; their red sheen glistened so that Mildred could catch a glimpse of herself on its hide. She lightly placed them on the floor, her actions slowed, and her movements deliberate. She was not about to hurry for this function.

The only reason she was going to this circus was to show the citizens of Crest Hill County, who was still the Queen of this two-bit town. She could feel her prestige begin to slip a little in the last few months when this shameful act of her husband's was at its peak. Those she passed on the streets, had not cringed in her shadow, and Mildred realized that her power had somehow been diffused. The First Lady demanded a certain amount of fear, of respect, of a tiny amount of public cringing for God's sake.

In truth, Mildred had grown quite bored with her husband, and like the town, she almost welcomed his affair which gave her more time to herself. The town had admired her resilience.

But that respect had been waning of late.

"Will there be anything else, First Lady?" Tilly asked, as she peeked her head within the doorway.

Instantly, Mildred had thought of a hundred different duties that needed attending to, but this anxious child, with the forlorn look, and the mousy voice, was not something that Mildred wanted to endure at this moment. Her absence would serve this house well.

"No, Tilly. You may go."

And before she could intake another breath, Tilly's face retreated, and all that Mildred heard was the patter of a tiny pair of charcoal gray lace ups trotting down the stairs, and out the door.

She looked in the mirror again. This death of Maya, this odd little death, was going to be a thing to deal with. A time like this would should have lifted the First Lady back to her Grand Significance, but Maya's death was on the verge of being lifted to a grander, legend-like pinnacle: From Adulteress to Awe-Inspired.

Even in death, the affair seemed to continue, she pondered. She would have to walk into this funeral, and take back what belonged to her...

...Respect.

Part V

Jenna Reed parted her curtains and looked out unto the clear skies. In the distance, she could see the wide stretch of town known as Crest Hill County. In Crest Hill, Jenna, along with her husband Nathan resided in one of the few homes that remained on *the* Hill, which *is* Crest Hill. Oil dykes used to litter these hills like pieces of a chest board. It was at those times that this town boomed with populous, and it was an investment that Jenna's parents had the wherewithal to invest in when the land appeared only good enough for an acre of string beans.

But as is always the case with the Black Elite, they were still black. Jenna's parents had the smallest amount of land in those times and were the lower class of the rich because of it, and as is customary, when the blacks move in, no matter how small the amount, the whites slowly began to move out especially since the oil dried up. Jenna, through it all, has always remained very modest in her living, and in her wealth. She was old enough to know that when her parents left her this estate that it would be a hard fight to keep it...and it had been. But now that fight is over.

Jenna looked out unto the town, a gorgeous view, and could see the steeple of the church, just before the bell rang, announcing the funeral for Maya Ohlms.

"Tilly should be at the church by now, you think?" Jenna said.

"I'm sure she is, Jenna. She was pretty close to Maya," Nathan said behind her, as he nibbled on a few pieces of fried green tomatoes. During this light lunch, he had given up the mind over matter of convincing himself that this was actually chicken fried steak. "I might soon be joining Maya in the hereafter if you keep feeding me like this. Sure could use a cheeseburger."

"Quiet. You know the doctor told you to watch your weight."

"As I remember, he told you that. I only sat by as an uninvolved bystander."

"Well, serves you right. How did you think you could lie to the doctor about you not touching any greasy foods, when we both could smell the bar-b-que on your breath?"

"It was a holiday for God's sake."

"The date of the death of your childhood puppy is not recognized as a legal holiday, Mr. Nathan Reeds."

"Humph!" Nathan grunted.
"I heard that," Jenna said, her attention still on the township. She squinted as she looked beyond the church, out unto the crest of the community and its many homes, its many people." There seems to be some low lying clouds out there in the distance.

"Using that snoop-o-vision again, Mrs. Jenna Reeds?"

She laughed in spite of herself. "You're the comical one, aren't you?"

"I do what I can. Now what about this cloud you talking about?"

"I just see the hint of it hovering just beyond the cemetery. I find that a might peculiar, considering the heat of the day, and how something of that nature should have been burned off long before morning got started."

"Then it would appear that the universe is also being comical."

"It would appear so."

Jenna however, didn't think the situation comical at all. Nature had been somehow altered, and that this could not be an ordinary mist, or haze, or whatever it was. It did not appear to be falling from the sky, as much as it appeared to be rising from the ground.

"Did you want to go out to the funeral, Jenna?" Nathan asked, as he moved his fork around his plate, positioning his vegetable army.

Jenna continued to look out unto the horizon, shaking her head. "No Nathan, not this one. There is a lot attached to this funeral that I would rather not bare witness to at this time. I loved Maya, as we all have, but her passing has put a hole in this town, that I am afraid has not yet been realized."

"And what do you think needs to be realized?" Nathan asked.

"Now that, Mr. Reeds, we will have to wait to see," and with that, Jenna let the curtain fall back over the window.

Chapter 2
Part I

Lisa stood by the church's entrance, shaking hands with those that entered; performing the duties that were usually best left to the Pastor, who unfortunately remained somberly in his chambers. The church bell had rung, announcing that the services would commence very soon.

"May be the first time I've been to a funeral, and not a cloud in the sky," said a voice that almost startled Lisa.

A hand was thrust out, and she followed it up past a hairy arm and broad shoulders, to the handsome features of Benny Martinez; whose light skin would belie his Costa Rican heritage, and his voice which was all New York, all Brooklyn Heights.

Benny's other hand was being held by his lover, Harold Baines; a simple white boy from Ohio.

Lisa smiled, for she could remember a time when this would cause a stir; not here in Crest Hill, where there was a lot more scandal to be had than the union of two men.

Lisa looked up at the sky too, "Not all funerals carry a cloud of despair Benny."

"Well, Maya always carried the sun in her pocket. How's she looking, Lisa?" Benny asked; his eyes saddened pools of sepia.

Lisa looked back into the church, along the purple carpet that led to Maya's elegantly displayed purple casket. From here, Lisa could see the white gloves hugging Maya's hands as they lay across her midsection. Benny recommended a close friend of his to do the makeup. It was his final gift to her.

"She's beautiful, Benny," Lisa said.

He smiled. It was all he really wanted to hear. "See, I told you," he said, tugging gently at Harold's arm.

"Yes you did, baby, yes you did," Harold replied, winking and mouthing the words, 'Thank You' towards Lisa's.

Lisa held out her hand towards the entrance, "I think you boys need to just come in and find your seats. I'm sure the Pastor will be quite expressive during this service, and I want you to be comfortable."

Before Harold and Benny walked out of sight, Harold said, "What does it mean when someone this good is allowed to pass away, Lisa? What does it mean?"

Lisa lowered her head, "I wish I had an answer for that, Benny. I really do." She turned away from the couple for a moment, jolted at the desperate tone in Benny's voice. It was not long ago that he'd buried his ex-lover Jason; a good man, who left too soon. "I'm sure it will all make sense when this movie of life is over."

He solemnly strolled inside. Lisa wished she could do something for him, but this town had become used to the act of grieving, and there were a lot of them today. The church was full. The Parking lot revealed that with nary a space left for another car. She was about to close the doors.

But then something caught the corner of her eye.

A dust cloud was moving in the distance.

Soon there was the glint of a car's windshield.

The scent/sweet smell of a woman's perfume.

Then she could see clearly the white hull of a Lincoln, as it pulled forward into the only parking stall left; the one reserved for the second commander-in-chief of the church. The First Lady, Mildred Reynolds. Her late arrival was obviously an attempt at making an entrance.

Lisa looked frighteningly at Mildred.

Mildred looked at Lisa amusingly - almost able to read her mind. *She is wondering what I am doing here, and it frightens her*, Mildred thought – and it was a very valid fear.

She took a deep breath as she let the car idle to a stop. Then she checked her glove compartment, fiddled with the radio, examined herself in the vanity mirror, adjusted the shoulders of her black-*sequined* dress, and dabbed a little more perfume on her hot spots. She then retrieved her clutch and pulled out a stick of gum.

She examined it.

She pulled the wrapper off meticulously.

She nibbled on it like a squirrel.

She remained amused also, at Lisa standing there, watching her impatiently, holding the door open, allowing Mildred to do her dance, take her time. Mildred knew that Lisa would remain at that door until she got there; even if day turned to night, and summer turned to winter. This was why she liked so very much being the First Lady – games of intimidation were very amusing.

Finally, Mildred popped the last strip of gum in her mouth, and pulled the handle on her door. It made a most silent *"click"* noise.

That was more than enough din to animate Lisa. "Good afternoon, First Lady," Lisa shouted, enthusiastically.

"I suppose, Lisa." Mildred responded, as she slithered from the car, and meandered in Lisa's direction.

"Everyone is seated already, but the casket is open for those who can't stay, and want to quickly view the body. It's also a little too crowded to have the whole town crammed up in here.

Mildred's eyes suddenly began to blink for a sporadic minute. "What was that dear?" she said, placing a hand on Lisa's shoulder. "I'm sorry dear, my mind was on something else, but I am sure what you just said was pretty important. But you just stay strong my sister-in-God, for we have to remain resilient in times such as these."

Lisa had to whisper a quick prayer for the un-saintly thoughts that ran through her mind. Yet still, she was curious as how to best bitch-slap a First Lady, and get away with it. "I suppose you're right First Lady," Lisa responded absently.

Mildred patted her shoulder, "Of course I am dear," and leaned forward to see what the situation was like within the church. She knew it was full, just from the body heat that had met her at the door, but how full she had no idea. It was a press so tight, that there was no indication of where bodies stopped and separated. She lightly coughed, as if clearing her throat, and waited.

Slowly the necks began to turn, eyes began to veer in her direction, whispers followed, and slowly, very slowly, there rose an air of reverence – one she had been anticipating. Calculating the right moment, she reached into her purse to pull out a tissue, and began to dab at her eyes. "She is going to be missed, Lisa. Her spirit had warmed us all, even though her flesh still struggled with sinful acts."

"Excuse me?" Lisa blurted accidentally, still trying to absorb this display of emotion her First Lady was exhibiting.

Mildred proceeded. "I just have to think about the woman's soul at a time like this, and not the actions of her flesh. The flesh has always been weak, since the days of Adam and Eve."

Lisa tried to grin, smile, and do something with her lips besides bite at them for what she heard. "Yes…of course, First Lady. Do you think we should be going in now?"

"No." Lisa was taken aback at the suddenness of the tone. Mildred continued, "I would feel better if you allowed me to go in alone – you can close the door when I get close to the casket, and save some of the Lord's good air conditioning."

"Of course, First Lady. I apologize for not letting you have your moment, if that is what you were thinking. I just wanted the services to…"

"No need for apologies, Lisa. This is a very trying moment for us all, and none of us are really thinking clearly."

"I suppose you are right, First Lady, I suppose you are right."

"Of course I am," and with that, Mildred proceeded into the church, looking out unto the purple runway that lead to the purple casket, as if it were laid out just for her.

The walk was a simple one, slow and careful, with tiny steps as if she didn't want to walk at all. Then she picked up her pace, and began to stroll a little.

Then she paused.

Then she stammered.

Then she walked again…but only a bit slower.

It was as if she were being pulled back by emotions that were bigger than her.

A reaction her church was not used to witnessing.

The congregation was stilled. Murmurs could be heard erupting between the pews. Mildred could hear them; sounds of bewilderment and amazement. The church lights were hot against her as she moved closer to the casket, her dress sparkling like tiny paparazzi cameras, her shoes showed brightly from beneath her black dress, their ruby splendor shooting from beneath the hem like some alien tongue licking the carpet as she walked.

Then she reached the casket, her head slowly bowing as she viewed the body of Maya Ohlms, her ears listening to the fluctuation of the crowd's timber. She could feel their concern, as if at any moment she would lurch forward and strangle a body that was already dead. She would not…

…although a few days ago, she did entertain such a thought.

What she'd decided upon was for something a little less dramatic, albeit wholly unexpected. She stood there for a while, staring unmoved at this white woman with the flawless skin the color of an ocean brushed beach sand, and lips the color of ripe grapefruit, with those tiny hands covered in lace, sleeping the forever-sleep in her long lashes like palm leaves resting at the end of her lids. She looked to be taking a short nap.

No mistaking, Maya was a beautiful woman. This South African woman who could in fact claim two races at once, two cultures, two homelands. This woman who caused a Pastor to fall from Grace in a slow decline that took two years. She looked down at this mistress and smiled an almost hidden smile…just before she fell upon the body.

"Maya! Oh my God! Who would take such an angel from among us? A saint!"

The murmurs rose.

"I am soooo sorry!"

Her knees buckled, collapsed against the side of the casket, moving it slightly.

People stood up, some inhaled sharply, others sat wide-eyed.

"I forgive you, I forgive you, just come back!"

Hands touched her shoulder, whispers and warm breath fell against the back of her ears; sounds of consolation.

"No, Noooo!" she sobbed, trying to nudge these helping hands aside.

More feet shuffled along the runway, traipsing in her direction, and more hands gently embracing her.

"First Lady, it will be fine…" - "Is there something we can do?"- "You shouldn't have had to go through this…" - "You're so brave for being here…" - "We are here for you," …and the litany went on.

The voices came and went, and Mildred's anguish multiplied. Her legs gave way again, falling backwards. She was on the precipice of fainting.

Tears began to flow.

More hands arrived to sooth her.

Her throat clogged with emotion.

She had to practically be carried to her seat, as a swell of people surrounded her, held her hand, squeezed her shoulder, and hugged her softly. She lowered her head into her palms, and beneath her sobs came the slightest of chortles.

There was only one thing that Maya took to the grave, which Mildred had been bent on reclaiming...

...Respect.

Part II

Pastor Luther Reynolds had no idea of the antics begot by his wife just outside his door. He sat quietly at his desk in his chambers, drumming his fingers, and listening to the silence which resounded as thick as cotton candy around his ears.

His thoughts were on Maya.

His mind troubled with past transgressions and indiscretions, battling between loyalty and morality, sprinkled heavily with grief, as it traveled back, back, back to a moment still fresh in his recollection.

"...and don't look so worried, my dear," Luther said, as he looked out *upon the open road he traveled. "These people don't bite."*

Maya sat beside him, two Bibles stacked neatly on her lap. She watched the cascading of a few raindrops on the windshield, their image splayed as the car picked up speed. "I'm sure they may not be biting now, but you never know...fresh meat is always worth trying out, and once they smell my fear, they'll be on the attack, I just know it.

He smiled, "This is not Silence of the Lambs, and if they are going to make a meal out of anyone, I believe I would make a much better selection than you."

She looked at him with a slight grin, "Yea...they might even have enough for leftovers too."

They both laughed.

The two of them had been on their way to the Marin Institute, which was about two hours from Crest Hill County. The Marin Institute was a maximum security prison, and four days out of the month, Pastor Reynolds would go there to pray for the inmates, and to converse with those on death row. He attire was untraditional, donned in the latest Hip Hop attire, baseball hat pushed down on his head, wearing jeans and gym shoes, face slightly unshaven. He also brought in a small stack of porn magazines; which won him much respect among the inmates.

This was the first time he had brought Maya along, and in truth, she was the only one to actually accept the offer. This was not something anyone, faithful or not, was cut out to do, for sometimes the inmates, their language, their desires, their past sins, were something not anyone could listen to with an empathetic ear.

This was also a time that Pastor Luther Reynolds, could escape from the mundane and insanity experienced by his wife. He loved her, but in the game of love and marriage, for years, he had been the only player. The tragic thing was that it was the town of Crest Hill County that his adoring wife really hated, not necessarily him, but she had yet to learn that difference.

"I feel so honored to be doing this," Maya said, her pink lips pulled into a strained smile.

Luther nodded, "Yes, it is an important work that we do, Maya, and it is I who is also honored. The First Lady is not too keen about such duties of this nature."

"Yea, I hear that the First Lady isn't keen on many things."

"She does have that reputation, I'm afraid."

"My ears are only attuned to people's positive attributes, Pastor."

"Then maybe you should meet our First Lady. You could be better than me in finding some," Luther said, as heavy rain began to fall. He quickly turned on the wipers.

Maya laughed to herself at his comment, as she picked at her nails, "I am sure that the First Lady has some redeeming qualities, seeing how well she was able to find such a redeeming Pastor."

Luther smiled at this, and glanced at Maya, who was still picking at her nails, but looked up at him for a moment, her eyes very serious. That was the moment he felt something pass between them like a simple wind. He reached out to grab her hand, nothing alarming or beguiling, but friendly. "That was very kind of you to say," he said, releasing her hand. "Sometimes gossip can be what it perceived on the surface, but most times, she's not what people make her out to be."

"None of us are Pastor, none of us are," and while his hand rested between them, Maya reached over to lightly place hers atop his.

Pastor Reynolds glanced down at his own hands now, clasped together, palms sweaty, his wedding band glinting from the office lights, his nails pristinely manicured by Tilly. He once again, thought about Maya's hands, sitting atop his, sitting within his, like chocolate and vanilla cake batter swirling together. Sweet.

The piano music played, which announced the services were already in progress. Luther nudged himself away from his oak desk, the ghost of his sweat leaving a wet impression where his palm pushed off.

Nervous. That's exactly what he was feeling at this moment. The piano was an instrument that Maya played, and hearing it, brought in the reality that he was not going to wake up, that he was not daydreaming, that she was actually gone, sitting in a casket donned in a color primarily reserved for grapes and dinosaurs.

She had touched his heart like a pebble touching the ocean, and still the ripples were shaking him.

Standing at the door, Luther looked back at his desk, scattered papers signifying his frustration at trying to capture the right words to describe a woman that was beyond mere words.

He decided to forgive such banal exercises, and to simply open his mouth and let the words write themselves.

As he opened the door, he could feel the sweat and tears of the church explode across his face like popped bubblegum, and a gust of wind disbursed the papers on his desk; some fell to the floor, and others to the trash bin - sooner or later in life, we all reach our ultimate destiny.

I may have my sermon, after all, he thought.

Part III

Mildred left in the middle of Pastor Reynolds' eulogy, to take a piss. Such powerful words the church had not heard in such a long time about someone so new to town; such accolades, such honor, such an irony. He had not praised The First Lady in this manner in quite some years. Many may have wondered if the restroom was in her car, because that is where she headed, locked door, speeding tires – she didn't say *what* restroom she wanted to use, so she figured one very far away from that church would do. No one could blame her. Under the circumstances, many wondered why she waited as long as she did.

The One Star Church of God was built when Mildred and Luther were dating, and its bells rang loudest when they decided to exchange vows there. Their union was powerful, and their love strong. It was said that it would take a streak of white lightening from the heavens to break such a bond.

Then came Maya.

Maya: The Missionary who was only supposed to be passing through town. The missionary pastor had been privileged to speak, her fellow missionaries had the chance to praise, and the choir a moment to sing, at this Spirit-Driven sanctuary named: The One Star Church of God. It was amazing.

The people were kind, and the town reminded her of one in Florida where she grew up – but not where she was born. Maya was from South Africa, she gained citizenship in the United States very young, becoming a true Afrikan American. She fell in love with Crest Hill County, as if it had been waiting for her, and she decided to stay.

That is when she began to know Mildred – her opposite in many ways: Mildred hated this town, while Maya loved it. Mildred soon resented being married; her life going in a mundane circle like the band around her finger, while Maya wanted a new simple life, and someone to share it with. Mildred was dark like the peel of a ripe plumb, and Maya light like the skin of a fresh peach. Mildred was a church mother, the First Lady, living richly for God, and Maya a missionary, a humble servant, living poorly for God.

They both loved a Pastor, who was caught in the middle of a situation that his heart and dignity could not divide.

++++++

"You want some macaroni and cheese, Pastor?" Lisa said, as she stood behind the long row of picnic tables, serving the mourners at the repast. It was held at the back of the church in the courtyard, and every now and then a breeze would cool the dryness in the air.

Pastor Reynolds looked up at Lisa, staring into her eyes and arched eyebrows, which were pressed together in question. He realized, as he held his plate out, that her expression, a strained one at most, must have been a reflection of his own. "Sure, some macaroni would be nice, Lisa. With this figure, I can't let anything go to waste."

Her face softened at his attempted humor, "I wish others were feeling the same. This is quite a showing of folks, and that was one of your longest services, but no one seems to be very hungry, Pastor Reynolds."

Pastor Reynolds nodded. "Grief can be a bitter meal, and can fill the belly twice as much, Lisa."

"True, Pastor," she replied, as she lumped a spoonful of macaroni on his plate.

"That was well said, Pastor."

Pastor Reynolds turned to see Jenna Reed directly behind him. She wore a simple white chiffon dress that ran to her ankles and closed at the neck. Near the shoulder were pinned a few pink carnations. She turned, and her long stringy hair, caught a hint of wind and fluttered about her face. She pulled the gray strands behind her ear. She held out a plate with nothing on it but a few diced vegetables.

"Lisa, can you give me a modest spoonful of that macaroni," Jenna said.

Lisa looked at her almost empty plate, and then back along the assortment of food that lined the tables, and then back at her plate again, "Are you sure, Jenna. We have plenty here."

She laughed. "Honey, this is for Mr. Reed. I will be back at this table with two plates for myself. No need for this food to go to the flies."

Lisa sighed, "You are so right, Jenna. Good to see you're still of good spirits," and she placed a dollop of the food on her plate.

Jenna turned to the Pastor, "And I hear you gave a mighty powerful sermon for our fair Maya, Pastor."

"He sure did," Lisa interjected.

Jenna's eyes looked sternly at Lisa. She never really liked her, and her saint-on-overload attitude; it sometimes came across a little crass. "Yes, I heard that," then she turned to the Pastor, "and I understand that the burial was quite the thing to see too, with the doves and the high school band playing."

"Oh, it was such a splendid spectacle, Jenna. Such a sight, you would love to have witnessed," Lisa said.

"Riiiiiiiight," Jenna said, without turning to face Lisa, and when she did, her finger was directed to the far end of the tables, "Now, correct me if I am wrong, but isn't that that bad little Herman Mills ducking under the table over there, taking food with his hands? I could have sworn he was playing out near the pond only minutes ago. Disgusting!"

"What," Lisa said, turning to look, her eyes squinting, "I thought I had seen that little devil's food during the service, but wasn't sure." She turned to bow her head to both Jenna and the pastor, "If you will both excuse me for-"

Jenna waved her hand, interrupting Lisa, "Naw, you go ahead, and take care of your godly duties, Lisa."

As she marched down to the end of the tables, a serving spoon raised in her hands, Pastor Reynolds spoke, "Now you know that wasn't saintly, Jenna. You know little Herman Mills and his two brothers are off at camp this summer. His parents are gonna think Lisa crazy, when she finally accosts them about their son."

Jenna placed a hand on the Pastor's shoulder, "At camp you say? Imagine that."

"Now let us walk away from here before she comes back, vexed at your little charade."

Jenna looked to be contemplating, "Seeing Lisa vexed, may be just the thing to stick around for, but I do need to get these vegetables to Nathan."

As they walked, Pastor Reynolds spoke, "Yes, about the burial, very odd. There was a low-lying mist hanging about the place, and it seemed to cover the whole cemetery. Very odd considering it was the middle of the afternoon."

"I did happen to see that this morning. I'm not really sure what it means though."

"Is it supposed to mean something, Jenna?"

Jenna eyed the Pastor, "Doesn't everything mean something? Am I that many years past your senior, to know that little pearl of wisdom?"

Pastor Reynolds smiled, "Now you know I know better than to answer a question such as that one."

They had reached the picnic table where Nathan sat, hands on his chin, elbows on the table. Jenna replied to the Pastor, while placing her husband's plate on the table, "I am sure glad to see that we have such a wise man shadowing our pulpit," she said in jest, as she turned to Nathan, pushing the plate closer to him with the tips of her fingers, "Here, this is for you, and the macaroni was a treat, so try and eat it all, will you Nathan?"

Nathan, dressed in an open white dress shirt, with a bow tie hanging off one of the lapels, smiled at Jenna, his bulbous cheeks like light bulbs pressed into his skin, "Thank you Dear," he said, as he began to run his nimble fingers through the assortment of vegetables selected for him.

Jenna had turned towards the Pastor, who was still standing holding his plate of food, and appeared to begin to speak, but turned back towards Nathan, "What did you say to me?"

He looked nervously up at her, his eyes redirected quickly back into his plate, "Nothing."

She leaned over the table, both palms flush against the wooden surface, "You said, Thank You…that is what you said, Mr. Reed!" She then reached across the table to grip his jaw within her hand. "Exhale!"

Instead, Nathan inhaled.

"Do it!" Jenna demanded.

He tried to snap his head back, but Jenna held firm. Then as his eyes rolled back into his head, Nathan exhaled, and macaroni flew from his mouth.

Jenna snatched her hand back so fast, that there was a snap within Nathan's neck. "I knew it! You have been chomping on hot links, and a little bit of that potato salad heaped in mayo."

Pastor Reynolds, who was still in shock at this whole scene, stood unmoved, "Is there some sort of problem that I can help with, Jenna?"

"Nothing that a syringe full of pig lards wouldn't cure, Pastor."

"I'm sorry," Nathan expressed, wiping his mouth with the back of his hand. "I mean no harm. A man gets mighty hungry with all this food about."

She slapped the table so hard, that Pastor Reynolds would swear that the folks in China felt the tremor. "Quiet, you silly old fart! I'm just trying to lower the eulogies that the Pastor will have to do this year. He is not going to have the time to preside over an old man's suicide, just 'cause you are bent on tryin' to kill yourself in an ocean of grease. He just don't have the time."

"It's okay, Jenna," the Pastor said, finally taking a seat at the bench. "Now, I suggest you go and get yourself something to eat, revive yourself, and I'll talk to Nathan about this."

Jenna pointed an accusatory finger at Nathan, her eyes on the verge of tears, "You just want to worry me to death, that's all you want to do. Do you hear me Mr. Reed?"

He smiled. "Yes Mrs. Reed…to death," and he winked at her.

She turned to the Pastor, "See him flirting? Right there in front of a man of the cloth, no less."

Pastor Reynolds smiled, and watched as Jenna turned her head from the pair, to keep from smiling herself. These two were made for each other. "Now go and feed yourself, Jenna, and leave this to me."

Without turning, she began to walk away, "I think I will," and as she slowly moved farther away she said, "You crazy old fool."

Pastor Reynolds watched her walk towards the food table, and then turned to look at Nathan, "Now you know better than to do that, Nathan. You have been very bad."

"I know Pastor," Nathan said.

"Good," he began to eat out of his plate, his mouth instantly filling up, "Now consider that your verbal punishment," and with that, he continued to eat.

Part IV

Mildred drove back to the cemetery, when the sun was just bowing its head upon the town, wiping tears with one hand, steering with the other. For some reason, her whole head was like a sponge, because she could not wipe her tears fast enough.

Although she did have to leave the funeral; caught between a most unnerving set of feelings: love, hate, betrayal, grief, pride, jealousy, commitment, and confusion – it was most of all the confusion that seemed to fuck her up completely.

"Why in God's name did you have to go and die, Maya? Maybe I should have shut my trap, let you two carry on in your supposed secrecy. Do you realize the predicament you've put me into?"

Mildred listened to the silence of the engine as if it were about to speak in an unknown tongue. But Maya was dead, and it was the town that seemed to be turning in its own grave. How could one woman effect so many?

It was nearing 7pm, and Mildred did not want to be caught out and about when the sun decided to finally bid this day farewell, so she pressed the gas pedal a little more, watching the oak lined roads pass by her a little faster…if only she were brave enough to keep the pedal pressed, right on out of this dead end town. She began to slow down when she witnessed light traces of dew kissing her windshield, the fog appearing heavier the closer she approached the cemetery known as Morning Glory. Gravel crunched under her tires as she pulled into the parking lot. She sat in her car thinking…thinking...thinking about the last time that she saw Maya.

That lingering moment when they talked and Mildred cussed her out…

"I'd been expecting you'd be coming sooner or later," Maya said, opening the door to Mildred."

She walked in, or some might say she strode in, with long wide steps, on the tips of her toes, like an ostrich bounding through the oasis. Mildred stepped into Maya's home, as if the floor was made of water, and she was Jesus Christ.

"Good afternoon Maya, I figured you might be expecting a visit from me too. Rabbits can always smell the Fox; however the Fox is always the one to make the first move."

Maya closed the door behind Mildred, her simple sundress catching the last of the wind before it shut. "And am I to assume, you are the Fox, Mildred?"

Mildred turned her hot gaze towards Maya. "That would be First Lady, to you Maya," she said positioning herself in the center of the living room, the sun's rays beamed on her through the crosscut design of the windows, like spider webs made of light. "And yes...you are the Rabbit."

"Very well, First Lady *Mildred*," Maya said, as she walked past Mildred to the far end of the room, to sit on an antique chair crested there, its lining white edged with a delicate embroidery. Next to it was a small end table, and lying atop it was an open Bible and large coffee cup, steam twisting from its rim. "You may have a seat if you like."

Mildred was plucked. It brought her to an emotional boiling point to be directed to sit, instead of being offered. As she turned towards the large sofa, she could look out the window, along the yard, beyond grassland containing two fruit trees, out unto a few more houses, a school, fountain, and beyond that out unto many more homes, and finally the church steeple. She realized Maya was far from town, almost alone in her tranquility, her welcomed solitude. It smelled of apples and baby powder in here. Maya loved this damned town so much that its very spirit, its aromas engulfed her cocoon surroundings, Mildred thought.

"See something out there that you like, *Mildred*?" Maya said.

Mildred breathed deeply, calming herself at the blatant disrespect of her title, before turning back upon the Rabbit. "Nothing at all," her gaze purposely lingering upon Maya.

Maya sipped at her drink, turned her blue eyes down towards her open Bible, and flipped a page, "Must be that mirror you're holding up to yourself," she whispered.

"Excuse me?" Mildred said.

Maya slowly looked up, "I'm sorry, did you say something?"

Mildred smiled, and slowly took a seat on the sofa. She had to remain resilient to the mistress of her husband, for after all, that is all she really was, an African Snow Queen in search of a Kingdom. "Maya, we have some things that need to be discussed, and I don't have all day to-"

"Yes, yes, I understand, and am sure that you do have some things to discuss, and I will do my best to abide, *Mildred*."

"For one, I do not like you referring to me by my first name, especially when…" she paused. Something was amiss here, she thought, and noticed Maya's cup shaking in her hands as she held it to take another sip

"I can quite understand your concern, First Lady Mildred, but you have actually caught me at a bad time. I have to get ready for the Bible Study today, seeing as tomorrow is Sunday."

Mildred remained silent.

"You do understand what I am talking about, don't you First Lady Mildred? Maya continued, "This is really pressing because I have to play at the church tomorrow, and I have not even gone over my music sheets."

"Of course, I understand my dear," Mildred said, as if she were unaware of the words that were escaping her lips, "Of course, I understand."

Maya reached out to pick up the Bible and place it in her lap. There was redness in her cheeks; she was flush, as she glanced at Mildred, before putting her attention back on reading the Bible.

…or at least that is what she appeared to be doing.

Mildred smiled. It was a slow grin at first, which turned into a most interesting shape, as if the lips were not used to doing such a thing.

"I understand that there is a situation that is connecting us that really needs to be addressed," Maya said, her eyes still perusing the pages, "And I am aware that there needs to be something-"

"No." Mildred said softly, but sternly.

Maya paused in her reading, her fingers stopped midway as she lifted a page, "I realize that we-"

"No." Mildred said again, in the same timbre.

Maya said nothing this time, as her features were drained of the little color that filled it only a moment ago. She placed the Bible back on the table, then palmed her cup in both hands. "I need to go and get some more tea," she said, about to stand.

"No! Don't you move!" Mildred said. She looked at this white woman with the power to bend the knees of a Pastor. She began to understand.

"Excuse me?" Maya said.

"You love him that much, don't you." Mildred said. It wasn't a question.

Maya was visibly shaken. She remained silent, but it was obvious that it took all the strength she could summon to keep her aqua tears from falling.

"You love him that much that you would sit there and try to piss off your First Lady, upset me, and have me to storm out of here."

Maya's lips became stern, her shoulders pushed back, her face taut, like a perturbed child, and still she said nothing.

Mildred crossed her legs, leaned back, and shook her head, "Clever Maya, even for a rabbit. To have me stomp out her here, not wanting to talk to you at all, forgetting to speak my mind, forgetting to face this situation I have been dealt with, and wish you good riddance. Yes, I must say, that was one clever ruse."

"I think you should be leaving, First Lady," Maya said, her lips so pressed together, that they appeared as one.

"What, no *Mildred*, this time? You not wanting to use my first name now? Has the Fox actually found another fox, but in Rabbit's clothing?"

"No, First Lady," Maya finally said, "The Rabbit just learned how to think like a Fox." She began shifting her empty cup from one hand to the other, "And, so where does that leave us?"

Mildred stood. "Where does that leave us? Is that what you asked me? Where does that leave us?"

The silence within the room was the loudest thing to be heard, and even the slow rustle of the leaves outside could not surpass its sound; it was a silence so thick with emotion that the very walls began to cry out, creaking, just to hear its own voice.

And then it was broken.

"You are going to stop seeing my husband."

Maya's lips parted…if only to inhale.

"This charade was amusing at best, Maya, but the town, the town my dear, is acting as if it is the norm. It is not the norm. Do you hear me? It is not the norm."

"But you care nothing for him," Maya spat from her throat as if dislodging a wedged pit.

"That's true, Maya, but I like the bones that dog brings home."

"But what about love, First Lady?"

"What about it, Maya? It would appear that I should be asking you that question. How is it to love, and to make love to my husband?"

Maya lowered her head. "You can leave now, First Lady."

Mildred stepped forward again, "Oh can I? First you try to anger me so that I may end up walking out, and now you tell me to actually get out. Maya, you need to get your own act together. Fucking with my husband is one thing…"

Maya looked up at Mildred, stunned at her language.

"…but fucking with my coins is quite another. How can my husband's flock grow when his sermons can't be believed? An adulterous man cannot preach on how adultery is a sin. How can I sit at the head of a Woman's Bible League, asking for donations, from a church that seems mired in damnation? How can I keep gas in my nice expensive car, diamonds on my finger, and a wonderful home and housekeeper, if the white woman from the black country is stepping in shit, tracking it through my life, and calling it rosy?"

"I get the picture, First Lady," Maya said.

"No dear, you are getting out of the picture. That is what you're going to be doing. Today, right now, and until the end of time. It stops." Mildred took one more step forward; a foot from Maya. "You can now lower your head and keep it that way. I'll let myself out."

Two weeks later, Maya was dead.

Mildred sat in the parking lot, at another spot reserved for the First Lady. Why not? Her husband was the Pastor, a section just for her was befitting.

She looked up, and in the distance, she could see the many tombstones, flowing up and over following the wave of the ground. The fog, the smog, the mist, dew, whatever it was, still hovered above the ground, like stretched cotton balls. Amidst its cloudy surface, was a vast shadowy darkness moving within.

"Very strange," she said to herself. The thickness covered the windshield in moisture. She activated the wipers to clear it away.

"Can I help you?"

Mildred turned to see an old white man staring at her, glasses swinging by a thin metal chain that rested from his neck. He stood not too far from Mildred's window, silent in his approach. He bent forward, eyes squinting, to get a good look at her.

She rolled down her window, "Carl?" Mildred asked, a bit unsure, as the haze dimmed her vision. "Is that you scaring an old woman?"

"Yes ma'am. First Lady, is that you sittin' in that car? I knew I heard somethin' out here." He placed his glasses on his face, "Forgive me if I startled you."

Carl looked behind him, and scratched his head, "She's straight ahead, First Lady," he said, raising his arm to point in the distance, "Out at the highest ridge over there."

Mildred looked in that direction and could see the small hill; the sun appeared to be sitting directly upon it. "I see it, Carl."

He turned back to look at her, "You are planning on paying your respects, correct?"

She nodded. Carl had been the caretaker of Morning Glory Cemetery so long, that Mildred expected him nothing short of a mind reader when it came to visitor's needs. "Yes, that is exactly what I am going to do."

"Mighty fine." He had on a nylon jacket, but there was a leather coat that seemed to be hanging across his arms. He stretched it out towards, Mildred, "Well it is a mighty wet out there, so you should be thinking about wearing this. You can bring it back when you are done."

Mildred turned off the car's engine, and opened her door, "That is mighty kind of you, Carl. I think I might be a little while in doing what I have to do."

As she walked towards him, she turned her back on him so that he may place the coat across her shoulders, "And what might you be doing, First Lady. Should I get you a sandwich from the kitchen?"

"Yes, that might be a good idea. It takes some time for a woman to realize that she has to humble herself, and finally ask another woman…for forgiveness."

Chapter 3

Part I

There is a saying in Crest Hill County, Two-years old, which states, *"It's hard to keep a secret from the eyes that guard Crest Hill."*

That saying was thought to be a silly one, sprouted from a horrific accident that took the lives of many. Some of the unmarked graves within the Morning glory Cemetery were those of children. Children that perished in an accident caused when a tanker truck filled with oil lost control on the hill, careening down and into a school bus. The explosion was massive.

That accident also involved a postal truck that was coming in the opposite direction of the school bus. Mail scattered for miles, and so did the many secrets of others. Love letters, divorce papers, medical results, and financial statements. The town was awash with the private information of others.

And that is how the saying originated; and what followed was a great unwavering grief. Life, a most treasured thing, was suffocated now by Death; causing those that were forced to live without their loved ones, to wish for death. There is a feeling, a type of residue, which sticks to the living when a loved one has passed.

Mildred was dealing with this residue, with the disappearance of her younger brother Eric, the only man that made her life here at Crest Hill County bearable. He loved this sorry town, the wife he had here, and the two children he fathered. He loved this town mostly because of the family that surrounded him; Mildred included. But he (and her) were really too big for such a simple life. They longed for larger adventures.

Chicago, or their closer neighbors like Springfield is what they craved; but family, work, and community cast a shadow a of reality they could not escape.

"You doing fine, First Lady?"

Mildred looked up to see Carl there, his presence although a bit unnerving was always welcome. "I'm doing fine, Carl. Was just thinking." Mildred was sitting on a stone bench, watching the sun slowly begin to fade behind Crest Hill, the mist in the air looking thinner as darkness loomed.

"Eric, is it?" Carl asked, nodding his head, as a wisp of his thin sandy brown hair licked across his forehead. He carried a broom in his hand, while he swept under the bench.

Mildred smiled, reflecting on his subtle foresight. "Yes, actually I *was* thinking about Eric."

"I assume you have already paid your respects to Maya?"

She looked up at him. "Yes, I have done that as well, Carl. This night I think I have thought about many things."

"As we all do at some time or another, First Lady." He finished sweeping, "but I will leave you to do your thinking in private now."

"I appreciate that, Carl."

Mildred continued to listen as Carl walked away, the soles of his shoes echoing as the sun began to settle. She was sitting in the spot known as Prayer's Court. She sat on the first of the benches, at its tip, and behind her the tiny benches spread out in the shape of a pyramid. It was a place to come to when you wanted to pray.

Not long ago, many of the town's citizens crowded these benches to the point of exhaustion – filling the seats many times over. That oil truck plowed into the school bus, hitting that mail truck on a street filled with people. Many mourned because of what was lost, of the many who were missing, and some, because of the mail truck and the secrets that littered the pavement like fallen confetti.

And so became the legend that was Crest Hill County, for in this town, secrets had a way of coming back to you.

Sitting here at the Praying Court, Mildred thought about her brother (stepbrother in fact), who was lighter and prettier than her because of the pretty white woman her father ended up marrying after her mother left. They quickly bonded as children and into adulthood, until now, when Eric seemed disappeared.

For some reason he left his family, and he left his sister. This town with its boring town folk, but amazing wealth, and loyal church-goers; it was the one reason she felt trapped here, in a lifestyle she could not escape.

He left with only the clothes on his back and a platinum watch given to him by Luther on his wedding day. She could still remember the last time she saw it, so many years ago.

Twirling
Swirling
Curling…

…around his index finger like a miniature hoola-hoop.

"I was thinking about leaving this town, Mildred," he said, his light sandy hair (a trait from his mother), had a splattering of water droplets in it as he walked from the pool.

"Oh be quiet," Mildred said, with her eyes closed as she lay on a lawn chair, her hair pushed back into a bright pink bathing cap. "You know you love that wife of yours a little too much. And don't get me wrong, because I think you did the right thing, saving those children from a lifetime of bastard-dome."

He slapped her thigh, "You quit saying that about your nephews."

"Don't you dare have those rug-rats calling me *auntie*. You know I'm not too fond of that word, or your wife for that matter," Mildred said.

"You two need to start playing nice. She's your sister-in-law now."

"She's too mousy, Eric. You know I hate weak women, and for you to marry one is beyond me. And as for you leaving...you know I would miss you too much, so quit teasing me with threats like that."

He clutched the twirling watch it in his palm. "Really Mildred, would you miss me if I left?"

She could sense seriousness in the tone. "Like air, Eric…like air."

"Well, you can still breathe, Mildred, my older sister. This boring life just isn't for us; we like the adventure of newness."

"We just like the adventure of living," she finished.

Eric nodded, "Yea, we like living."

…and the next day, Eric was gone.

For weeks, Mildred was gone too, if only in her mind, for she could not believe Eric had left her.

Her anger became an outward reflection of her inward scars. She blamed Erica. Eric and Erica, the former cuteness of their mirrored names was now a sour taste on her tongue. It had a flavor that was too close to the only one she truly cared about in this one-church town.

So it was here, at the Praying Court, within Morning Glory Cemetery, that she came to speak to a brother that had not contacted her since his leaving more than three-years ago. Alive? Dead? Dying? She had no idea.

"I'm leaving now, Carl," she said, standing and running her palm across her hair.

"Very well, First Lady," came the voice, and right behind it came the man, folds of warm breath swirling about his cold lips.

"I'll escort you back to your car."

Mildred nodded. "Great, I appreciate that."

As they began to walk, Carl turned to glance back at where she had sat, "One moment, First Lady."

Mildred watched Carl's slightly hunched form, ease behind the stone bench to reach for something.

"I think you've dropped something, First Lady."

"I did?"

"I believe so," he said, returning with his fists clenched.

When he opened his hand, Mildred almost fainted. She plucked the object from Carl.

"Does it belong to you?"

She thought her heart was crawling up through her ribcage, pushing at the back of her eyes as she gazed upon the watch; one that she knew was the same one her brother once wore.

"Is everything okay?" Carl asked.

"No," she replied, "No. I believe that everything if far from being okay."

Part II

Erica reached into the cabinet, pulling out the bag of marshmallows she'd stored there. "You know you have to go home sooner or later, Pastor Reynolds," she said, placing the bag beside two cups of hot chocolate.

The Pastor grinned. Yes, as much as that home cost, the least he could do was to visit it on a constant basis. "Yes Erica, you're right."

"I do want to thank you for all your help in getting me back home. Something told me to check that tire. I knew it was looking a little low a few weeks ago, but I had forgotten all about it. I'll return your spare as soon as I get to the tire shop next week."

The Pastor remained quiet, his eyes burning into the tile along the kitchen floor.

"Pastor?" Erica said, digging her hands into the marshmallow bag, and sprinkling the contents atop the hot chocolate. "Are you going to be okay?"

The Pastor jerked his neck, as if he just realized he was not the only one in this room. "I'm sorry, Erica," he said, watching as Erica brought the drink to the table. Faintly, he could hear noise coming from Timothy's room, from either a very loud television, or very violent video game. He admired the young, and their ability to distract their minds at will. "This has been a pretty overwhelming day."

Erica sat across from him, blowing at the top of her cup. "This day has turned out to be a lot of things. With the lives that Maya touched in this town, being overwhelmed seems like such a mild statement."

Pastor Reynolds traded his glare from the kitchen floor, to the immediate dinette table, as he absently pushed a thick finger through the handle of his cup. "I have a feeling you are right, and I also have a feeling that with it, this town may undergo a severe reckoning," he said, bringing the cup to his awaiting lips.

Erica was too late in warning him, for the liquid had barely touched his lips before he sprayed it from his mouth. "That is *hot* chocolate, Pastor."

He whipped his mouth with the back of his hand, "I am so sorry about that. I must seem like a fool."

A silver napkin holder was in the center of the table, and she reached for one, and wiped the table. "There have been a lot of deaths you've had to deal with in these last few years. The tragedy of the school bus alone was something that this town is still getting used to. It is understandable how you are reacting today."

"It is true, a lot has been asked of your faithful Pastor...but," his voice suddenly cut off. He sat there for a moment, and raised his hand towards Erica, as if to regain his composure. "I'm sorry, my mind is constantly racing it seems." He shook his head, "I just can't stop thinking about her, you know." He coughed, and moisture slowly pushed itself out on his eyelids. "I loved her very much, Erica. I really did."

Suddenly it felt as if everything from pecans to cashews had caught themselves in her throat. She sipped at the hot chocolate, feeling the knot subside a bit. "We know you did, Pastor…and we know you still do."

She let the Pastor continue to think. The silence of the room was broken only by his breathing, as if he had his own bushel of nuts to keep down. She watched as he spun his cup on the table, the marshmallows knocking against the sides. She looked down at her own cup, the marshmallow and the chocolate fighting for space within a cup they both owned. She was brought back to the moment she last saw them together, when Pastor Reynold's sat hovering above Maya's lifeless body…

… Erica could not remember ever being able to run that fast in all her life.

She had been at a neighbor's home down the road from Maya, when there was a knock on the door and her phone rang. Pastor Reynolds was trying to talk, but his words were covered in such a blanket of misery, that she could not understand a word he was saying. At the door was a child, Erica noticed him as one of Timothy's friends. He said something about an ambulance was at Maya's, and that the Pastor was already there. The police were blocking off the driveway and something very bad had happened because the Pastor was crying in the doorway, not wanting anyone to come near him, the home, or anything.

The next thing Erica knew, she was suddenly running down the road, having forgotten that she'd left her car at her friend's; going so fast it was as if the road had been pulling her along. She would have run directly into Maya's home, had not the regal arm of an officer barreled into her chest.

"Slow down ma'am, I can't let you go any further."

"What are you talking about, Peter," Erica said, suddenly recognizing the officer. "What's going on here? Why the ambulance? I just heard that something was happening here. Did Maya get hurt?"

Peter said nothing, and his eyes had been telling a story that Erica did not want to unravel. That's when she noticed the yellow police tape, and two EMT's standing near an empty ambulance. *They were waiting for someone,* she thought.

"I'm sorry Erica, but we're still investigating the house. I hate to tell you this…"

And for some reason, Peter never got the opportunity to do just that, because when Erica looked into Maya's home, the door opened just enough for her to see Pastor Reynolds sitting on the sofa, a phone hanging limply in his hands, another officer standing next to him with his arm on the Pastor's shoulder, was when the pieces began to fall into place. Both gentlemen were looking down, as another EMT kneeled on the floor, struggling with a black bag he was slowly trying to close; that she saw two bare feet, white as pressed paper, toes painted in a dark purple, that she finally realized what Peter must have been struggling to say.

"No! No, I don't understand. Who is in that house? Where is Maya? Why is the Pastor in her house, and who is that on the floor?!"

"I think you should step over to the police car, Erica. I'll explain what I know to you."

"I don't want to have to go to any police car, Peter. You need to let me in there - you have to. That's my best friend's home. Let me talk with the Pastor."

"Erica!" Peter shouted, stepping between her and the view of the house. "You have to step back, so we can finish what we need to do here so we can have some answers for you. I know this is hard…"

"But who is that person on the floor! Who…" she found the words would not come out. "I told her not to wear that hideous looking toe polish. I told her." She rested her head upon Peter's shoulder, peering over it, watching how empty the Pastor looked, how hopeless.

"Maya!" she tried shouting, just before her legs turned to papier-mâché.

"You still have problems with those stray cats around here?" Pastor Reynolds said.

Erica blinked rapidly. She was back in the present. "Excuse me. My mind took a little vacation. What were you saying about the cats?"

There was a noise outside, and I thought it might have been those stray cats chasing their dinner again. The sensory light came on, but it's just flickering now," Pastor Reynolds said, pointing towards her window.

Erica could see the light flickering off the window, and her first thought was, *how dirty those windows were*, and her second thought was how the sensory never came on before when cats roamed about. "I've been meaning to get that fixed too. I'm so used to someone here taking care of these things."

"You should head to the hardware store sometimes. Errol's son teaches ladies small hardware tips every other Saturday. I'm sure they can teach you to change a light bulb," Pastor Reynolds said, holding back a smile, and taking another sip from his cup.

"Funny. You just make sure you keep the hot chocolate inside your mouth this time," she said, noticing the noise of static coming from the light. It was at that moment, she realized Timothy's room was awfully quiet. *He must have turned off that television*, she thought.

"Well Erica, I am going to head back home," Pastor Reynolds said, pushing back his chair.

"I understand, it's late, and you need some rest I'm sure. Thank you for the car."

"Don't mention it," he said, as he drained the cup, and turned towards the door.

Erica stood, and walked in his direction, placing a hand on his back, "You call me if you want to talk, Pastor. It's always good to have someone to express yourself with who's also in your corner."

He spoke with his back turned, "Yes, I would appreciate that. I am sure I'll need a friendly ear from time to time."

"Good, because that is what friends do, and I consider you a friend, Pastor."

He turned to face her. "Great. Then maybe you can start calling me Luther."

"I can do that," she said, stepping in closer to him. She hugged him, and whispered in his ear, "I can do that...Luther. I want you to have a good night, and get some rest, okay."

He stepped back, grinning. "I will, Erica. You have a blessed night as well, and I will be along sometime this week to see about putting a new light in for you." He opened the door, looked out at his car, and stopped as he was heading down the stairs. "Yea, you're going to have to do something about those cats I see."

Erica ran to the door, and under her window, where her small flower garden stood, there were a couple that had been trampled. "Someone must have had another litter. I will speak with you later tonight, if it's not too late, just to make sure you're doing fine."

"I'm sure I'll be okay but feel free. Goodnight."

"Goodnight," Erica said, as she closed the door.

After placing the empty cups in the sink, she pressed an ear to Timothy's door. She could faintly hear the sound of the television. "It's late,

Timothy, and I can hear that television. You should be getting ready for bed, young man."

There was no reply.

Erica rapped on the door, "Timothy, do you hear me?"

She heard a small noise again, but as she heard it, realized that it wasn't the television. "Timothy?" she called and pressed her ear to the door again. She closed her eyes, and what she picked up from within, was not the noise from the television or computer, but a tiny voice calling out, "Mom."

She quickly opened the door, and warm air enveloped her. She looked across the room and saw that the window was open letting in the balminess of the day.

"Now Timothy, why do you have that window open, when you can clearly feel all my air conditioning going to waste?

Timothy said nothing. He was sitting at his computer desk; his chair pushed back and monitor blaring though the dark room. Erica stared at the orange light coming from the optic lens representing his web camera. This appeared to have Timothy's full attention. In addition to this, the television was showing some action adventure movie of some sort; with flashing cars, and explosions.

"Timothy Ross, do you hear me talking to you?" Erica asked.

"Yes, mother," he said, voice very monotone.

"Then why do you have that window open as if I am not paying the bills around here?" She walked closer to his desk.

"Someone came by today...they knocked at my window."

"What!" Erica said, looking back at the opened window. "What are you talking about? You mean someone came by your window tonight, while I was out there talking with Pastor Reynolds?"

He nodded. "He said he would be back."

She stood there, not knowing what to say. She dashed towards the window, shutting it tight. Whoever it was must have been the one to set off the sensor lights. "Don't open the door for strangers, Timothy. You have to come to me whenever something like this happens. Where did this person-"

He cut her off. "This wasn't a stranger, mom." He said, still staring into his computer monitor.

She looked out the window, not really hearing what he was saying, but trying to think about what she had to do next. If there was someone out there, then they very well could still be running about. She turned to address

Timothy, but her eyes veered slightly towards the monitor that had him so transfixed.

"Oh my God!" she said, shocked at what she saw.

Timothy must have been taking snapshots of himself with his web cam when this stranger came knocking at the window, because there was a still picture of him, looking startled, directly into the camera. With the angle of the camera, and the darkness of the room, Erica was barely able to make out a face in the background, outside the window, looking in. She moved in closer, just to be sure. The shadows were deep, and the light from the monitor and television set an eerie glow on this person's features, but Erica knew them all too well.

"Mom...Daddy said he would be back to visit you tomorrow."

Part III

Benny ran his fingers along the picture, as he sat on the toilet. He was not using it, but sitting there in his underwear, holding an old picture, his finger tracing the edge of the wallet-size image: an image that held a stream of golden locks, blue eyes, and a "character mole" near the chin. Being at Maya's funeral reminded him of another death that was just as close to him; that of Jason Colby, his former and now deceased lover.

"I'm gonna take the spaghetti out," said the voice beyond the door. "I know it's late, but I am getting considerably hungry."

"That will be fine, Harold. I'm a bit hungry too, and the spaghetti sounds perfect," Benny replied. He opened his wallet and placed the photo behind his driver's license. He then took a few slow breaths; anxiety was getting the better of him, as it always did when he was thinking about Jason. *Too bad you can't bury the guilt along with the body*, he thought.

Benny lowered his forehead into his palm, his fingers getting intertwined within the thin brown strands of his wet hair, his eyes directed at the floor, but staring into nothingness.

"Do you want cornbread, or the sweet rolls?" Harold said from the kitchen; the sound of pots could be heard clanging against the stovetop.

Benny rose slowly and pushed his hair back as he stood in front of the mirror. He grabbed the face towel that hung above the sink, dried his hands, and pressed his fingers into his eyes; drying them too. "The sweet rolls sound good," he shouted back at Harold. He turned around, where his silk robe was hanging, grabbed it, and strapped it on. He closed his eyes, letting the touch of the silk caress his body, ease along his flesh, calm his nerves, bring him back into the reality that he now lived; a reality with a new lover, and a new relationship that he was beginning to doubt should have ever existed.

His emotions felt like broken glass under his skin.

When Benny stepped out of the bathroom, tiny plumes of steam following behind him, he could see Harold on the sofa, his head dogmatically buried in the ledger book that held the constant changing revenue of the salon they both owned: Snips n'Clips. His head was down, and his hair tussled forward, the tips of his locks touching the pages he read. "What were you doing, digging out your pores with a toothpick?" he said as he looked up.

Benny went to the kitchen, to check the boiling pasta on the stove, "You know I got that new shower head, and that water is sooo therapeutic."

He lowered his head back into the ledger, "The spaghetti will be done in another minute or two. Can you put a little more olive oil into the water for me?"

"No problem," Benny said, opening the cabinet. "I see you are once again back at work, even when you are at my place."

"I'm sorry about that, you know how I got that Business-Gene in my DNA, and just can't seem to stop working. Why don't you come over here and sit next to me, so I can work on some other business."

Benny gingerly poured the olive oil across the pasta, "How can you even make such a statement when you didn't even look up from that ledger book to tell me that."

He looked up, smiled, and slowly closed the book.

"That's more like it," Benny said, closing the pot, and walking over to the sofa. He flounced atop it and swung his legs on Harold's thighs. "You might as well tell me how things are looking. Will I have to start buying off-the-rack?"

"Nothing that drastic. We actually made a pretty good profit this month."

"I'm not surprised, with all the people in the shop whose hair we had to do, so they would be able to look their best for the funeral."

Harold began to guide his hand along Benny's legs, watching as Benny leaned his head back and closed his eyes. "It has been an exhausting week, but I think everyone just wanted to look their best for Maya."

Benny huffed. "As if Maya is looking down at those folks telling Jesu how amazing folk hair looked at her service. Most of them needed a makeover from the neck down, not up."

Harold slapped Benny's legs, "Stop talking like that. Those thrift-store folks are the ones that know how to save money on clothes, so they can pay us to style their crops."

"Well, I wasn't talking about their taste in currency spending, just their taste in clothes," Benny said, laughing slightly before placing a palm over his eyes. "I'm gonna miss her, Harold. I'm gonna miss her a lot."

"I know," is all that Harold could offer, as he listened to the stammered breath of his lover. "I think this whole town is going to miss her in some way. I too am going to miss her…a hellova lot," he said, as he lifted Benny's legs to stand, and placed them back on the sofa. "I'm going to check the food."

Benny turned to look at Harold, as he walked towards the kitchen. Benny knew he was not good at talking about death.

"You okay with corn on the cob?" Harold asked, as he stirred the pot.

Benny sat up on the sofa. "Sure, that sounds good," he said, as he began to open the ledger book. The profit did look very good, he thought.

"Knock, Knock,"

Benny looked up to see Harold hitting the baking pan filled with sweet rolls against the counter, loosening them. He looked up to see Benny staring at him, "Sorry about that. I forgot to dust the pan with flour. The rolls are sticking."

Benny barley heard him.

"Knock, Knock"

Benny's thoughts were suddenly filled again, with noises, with recollections, with memories.

"Knock, Knock…

His mind going back in time, to a time, when he was dealing with the thought of Jason not coming out of his coma, as he stood in this living room wrestling with emotions. Harold had dropped him off at home after he visited and talked to a comatose Jason.

He could remember standing in that living room, feeling twisted in his emotional reality.

…there came a knock at the door…a knock from a past memory.
Knock, Knock!

When he'd opened it, there stood Maya in the threshold, holding what appeared to be 20 boxes of Turtles Candy, stacked up to her nose, "They were a lot cheaper than flowers."

"Glad I renewed my dental insurance," he said, as she walked past him.

He stood shirtless, pajama pants on, and a yogurt and fruit in hand.

Maya became a much needed distraction of late, because all he had been able to think about was the multiple fracture wounds of Jason's broken and unconscious body. He also could not stop thinking about the guilty fact that he had been cheating on Jason with Harold. But now, as he continued to visit Jason, he felt as if his feelings had changed again. He felt as if he were falling back in love with Jason.

His heart was dramatically divided, and a divided heart, though filled with love, was at its center, still a broken one.

"I was thinking about stopping into Snips n'Clips next week to try out a new style," Maya said, as she began to place some of the chocolate boxes into the refrigerator.

Benny smiled, "Oh, really? Have you been looking in Elle Magazine again? I told you about having us recreate those glamour styles on your head."

"No silly, I was actually looking in the Ebony this time."

"Now I know you are crazy," He said, closing the door, and walking in her direction, spooning yogurt in his mouth.

She tossed a box at him, "Be quiet. You know you love the challenges that I bring to that salon of yours."

He caught the box with one arm, and quickly placed the bowl of yogurt on the coffee table, then opened the box of chocolates, and began to pick through them. "I know the constant drama that you bring to the shop…and you are right, I do love it. What I don't love is how you are ruining my diet right now."

"Well I'm going to ruin it some more. You want a beer with that? I know you are only half Costa Rican, but as I understand it, you guys want beer with everything."

"I would tackle you right now, if you were not so right about that. I am sure you know where to find it in the fridge." He turned towards his reclining chair, as he sampled the Turtles Candy. Only a few of his friends knew about the connection he and Jason shared regarding this treat. It was the one thing that they shared at Turtle Bay in Hawaii when they met. Benny could still remember sitting on that cruise ship and slipping the candy into his mouth after their initial introductions. Jason sat there on the bridge of the ship staring at both Benny and the chocolate in his hand – declaring finally that the chocolate looked very delicious. Benny tried unsuccessfully to suppress his grin, and finally said, "I can guarantee that everything you see is delicious, but right now, you'll only get to sample the chocolate. And slowly Benny offered another piece from a small tin he was carrying. Before the night ended, there were many treats tasted that night.

"Are you reminiscing?" Maya said, bringing him a tall Corona.

He sat and stared at the candy, as he replied, "Yea, I guess I am. Things are looking so bleak, that all I can do is think about what we had meant to each other.

She slid around the chair and sat in his lap, then softly kissed his cheek. "I know it's tough babe, but I'm here for you."

"I appreciate that, but really," he began, unlocking his eyes from hers, "But you are crushing the Turtles!" he said, tugging the box from between them.

She flipped out her tongue, and then reached in to grab herself a piece.

"Thanks for coming over, Maya. I needed the distraction, really."

She nodded, and at that moment, it was she that appeared a bit distracted. "You know...Mildred wants to speak with me. A little *Coming to Jesus* meeting, as she puts it."

He knew that could be a serious situation, especially coming from a woman who, if she ate Jesus whole, would still have less Jesus in her than anyone. "What do you think she wants, Maya?"

"The same thing Jason would want to talk about, if he knew that Harold was around."

That response hit him deep, because if it came from Maya, there was a deserved feeling of truth in it. He and Maya had a connection with each other, a commonality as many rarely had; they were people who not only didn't resemble the heritage they displayed, they were both caught up in relationships filled with secret desires and social shame.

"Okay, good point Maya, but really, what are you going to do? Mildred is the Pastor's wife."

"Honey, I know who Mildred is. I have been spending most of my time here in this town trying to avoid her as best as I could, but I knew that this time would have to come sooner or later...and to tell you the truth, I am not sure what I am going to do besides just meet the woman."

Benny could see that she was breathing a little harder; she was more nervous than she was letting on. He reached up to place a hand along her back, rubbing her gently there. "Then maybe it is better not to think about something like that now. We all know Pastor Reynolds deserves better, and I think you would be that better, but Mildred would never leave him. I guess you know all of this, and I am sorry to be bringing it up."

"I'm a little sorry you are too, Benny," Maya said rather harshly, and hopped up, and headed towards the stereo. "Can we play something a little faster paced than this tear-jerker music?"

He decided not to breach the subject again. "Sure, just open the cabinet at the bottom and pick something you like.

She looked around. "I love that man, Benny," she began to say, "And I know that some things just are not going to be realistic when you have feelings like this, but they are feelings, and I am feeling them, so what else am I to do…" she popped a CD in the player – it was Gloria Gaynor's "I Will Survive."

Benny smiled. "I guess that is pretty appropriate," he said, placing the box of candies on the coffee table, and walked up behind Maya. He moved her silky red hair from behind her, and laid it gently on her shoulder, while he hugged her.

She allowed it, and felt herself fall into his chest. "I dedicate it to both of us. I think we both can use a little surviving."

He nodded, his chin rubbed into the back of her neck, "I know about loving someone too Maya. I am in love with two men right now; one who may be dying, and the other who makes me feel alive. The hardest thing is that the one that I am falling faster for is the one that is dying. I can't tell Jason I cheated on him with Harold, and I can't tell Harold that I am falling in love again with the one we cheated on."

"And I can't tell this man I would want him to leave his wife and sacrifice the wrath of a God we both believe in who says such a union would be wrong." She began to cry.

Benny said nothing, and let his own tears fall, as a song played on that was to become a mantra to them both.

Knock, Knock, Knock…

Benny was brought back to his place, the scent of dinner was strong, and his stomach turned with excitement.

Knock, Knock, Knock...

Harold was hitting a spoon against the counter. "It's time to eat baby!" He said merrily. It wasn't often that Harold cooked.

"Great..." Benny began to say, as the phone rang.

"I'm going to wash my hands, but if you can lay the plates on the table, I can serve you."

Benny smiled mischievously. "You know I would like that," he then addressed the phone. "Hello?"

"You can be such a bad boy," Harold said as he stepped into the bedroom to use the bathroom.

"Hello?" Benny repeated, to what sounded like silence on the other end of the phone.

He then heard some breathing.

"Listen, I am going to hang up this phone if you-"

"Benny?" said the other voice.

Benny became silent.

"Benny? Is that your voice? It is you, isn't it? You have the same number...I was surprised to have remembered it."

Benny stuttered as he spoke his next words, "Jason...is that you?"

Part IV

Mildred stared at the door, while she sipped on her cognac. The house was bathed in candlelight, but still she could see the slow turn of the door handle. It would not be long now, she thought.

Only 30 minutes ago she was crying. 1 hour ago she was cursing. 2 hours ago she was in shock - so many emotions and only one body. It was a wonder her skin didn't just unravel from around her shoulders and settle at her feet. She truly felt she had come undone.

The door opened, and Luther stood there, eyes tired, fishing around in his pants pockets. He pulled out his keys, examined them, then placed them back. She sipped at her drink again, noticing that he had not yet observed her, and also mystified at the fact that a man would put house keys back in the very same pants that he would eventually take off later that night. No wonder they can't find things around the house, she thought. A waste of time such an effort was; something like men themselves, just a waste of time.

"Mildred?" Luther questioned, seeing the dark figure on the sofa, in its dark regalia.

"Has it been that long, that you have forgotten what your wife looks like?"

"You're not funny," he said coldly, taking off his suit coat, and draping it across his arm. "You are not funny at all."

"Wasn't trying to be," she said, as she reached over to the lamp stand, and picked up a large bottle to replenish her glass. A bucket of ice was there too in case it began to warm.

"Are you drinking? Mildred, what's going on? How long have you been sitting there in the dark waiting on me?"

"A lifetime."

He looked at her rather curiously, as he walked closer, tossing the coat across the back of one of the felt lounge chairs near him. He ignored her last comment. "I was at Erica's place, consoling her a bit." He sat in another chair across from her, only then noticing the fireplace and candles.

"Humph! I'm sure you were."

"Excuse me? What do you mean by that?"

This time, she ignored his question. "So, how is my sister-in-law doing; the woman who ran my brother away? How was your visit to yet another woman that has been a prick in my side?"

He quickly stood. "You're drunk. I'm not talking to you in this condition. You're sitting here in the dark, half naked in your black see-thru get-up, talking gibberish, on the day that I've had to preside over a funeral that has quite frankly, drained me of any amount of energy to deal with you right now."

She nodded. "Is that how your come to deal with every situation these days, Pastor Reynolds? You run and hide from them?" She sipped, "Some Man of The Cloth you are."

"And is this how a Woman of The Cloth deals with hers, by swimming beneath the waters of a drink, drowning in her own juices?"

"How eloquent."

"How pathetic," he said, and began to walk out of the living room.

"Don't you walk out of here, Pastor Luther Brian Reynolds. Don't you dare walk out of this room."

He stopped, perspiration shot out along his back, he could feel his shirt sticking to him as his anger continued to boil.

"You are going to turn around and sit your ass down. I refuse to be the enemy of your past discretions. Do you hear me? Do you understand that, Pastor Luther Brian Reynolds?"

As he turned around, Mildred was standing, her lingerie was very thin, and the mesh material revealed more than he had every wanted to see of his wife; as it hinted at a pair of breasts and a darkened womanhood that had been denied him for most of their marriage – at least denied him any sort of pleasure, with the act always begun at her discretion, her moment of loneliness. The candles cast an eerie glow about the room, and especially towards her, where her eyes sparkled as brilliantly as the rock glass in her hand, as if he were facing the demon inside his wife instead of the wife he knew so many years ago. She had on her best jewelry; the diamond necklace and tennis bracelet his parents had left him, the diamond wedding ring and band shown amazingly crisp as it was meant to, polished nails like brushed silver, and the scent she wore, like falling into a botanical garden.

He knew what this was all about. Her competition was dead, and she was goading over the corpse. She and her mesh clothes; its tiny specks reflecting like stardust. She with the elixir of dragons in her hands as if it were nectar from The Tree of Life. Her smile casting through like a row of freshly painted pillars in her mouth. He knew what this was all about…she was in need, feeling that feeling of hers, wanting to ebb the loneliness within her thighs.

Tonight, unfortunately, it was not going to work, and he could sense that she realized this too.

Fury formed in his eyes. "No Mildred. Remember you are the one that had a hand in Maya's death. I don't care what it looks like to everyone else, or what it doesn't look like, I know that you are responsible, and you know it too. The motive? I could think of a hundred of them, but they all confuse me somehow."

"I know what you are thinking Luther, and even if it were all true, what did you expect to happen differently? Did you think I should have just stood by while you had your little Afrikan affair? Is that what you think I should have done?"

He lowered his head. "No. I expected you to act as you always do and continue to not love me as you always have."

She froze. She looked at his lips as he started to raise his head. She wanted to make sure that he had been saying those words, that they in fact did come from his direction, because the truth of them side-swiped her.

She sipped again, reaching her hand out to the chair, inviting him there, as she walked back to the couch, where she immediately sat and poured herself another drink.

"So where does that leave us, Luther? What is to become of us now that your *distraction* is gone?"

He took her invitation, and slowly sat in the chair, his body bent forward, his arm bracing himself, unsure if he wanted to continue this dialogue anymore. "*Maya* was not a distraction, Mildred Pricilla Ross-Reynolds."

Her lips grimaced. "Try not to use that name in this house too often, Luther."

He smiled at her in the firelight. "You mean yours?"

"I mean both." She tilted her head towards a small round table that was in front of her. She pushed it with the tips of her toes. There was a glass on it, its cubes sliding in the warmth of the room. "Maybe you need to have a drink Luther. This glass is for you. Perhaps it can help you get that dreaded monkey off your back."

He could only stare at her and the glass - he really did want to have that drink. She leaned forward, with bottle in hand, and poured him one.

"There is another matter that I need to talk with you about tonight, before we sit here and stare each other to death in hatred."

He continued to say nothing, even as she handed him the drink.

She sat back down, "Now, now Luther, surely even caged monkeys bother to speak to one another when occupying the same quarters."

He sipped on the drink. The burn of it made him close one eye. "I'm sure they do, Mildred…or they just sit around tossing shit at each other."

She smiled. "I see you already like the drink. It seems to have at least worked in relaxing your tongue muscles."

"What is the other matter you want to discuss, Mildred?"

"It has to do with my brother, Eric. I found something of his and…"

Mildred paused as she appeared to collect her thoughts, and Luther looked at her, still thinking about what she had started to say; Eric was a name he had not heard in their household for quite some time.

In between this silence, the phone rang, and Luther being nearest it, answered, "Hello?"

Mildred shook her glass, her eyes distant, as if she were grateful for the disturbance.

"Erica, slow down. What's wrong?" Luther continued, his voice becoming more urgent.

Mildred began to shake her glass louder upon hearing Erica's name.

Luther pressed a finger to his other ear; his eyes went from anger at Mildred, to confusion concerning the phone call, to a wide-eyed fear.

She stopped shaking the glass.

"Are you sure? I mean, of course you are. Yes, obviously, I understand. Oh, it isn't?"

Mildred leaned forward, and whispered, "What's wrong Luther?"

He pulled his finger from his ear, to point it to the ceiling, requesting a moment of silence. "Okay, you try to get some rest, and make sure Timothy is doing fine. We'll talk in the morning. You be careful, Erica. You have been through a lot."

He slowly hung up the phone, as if he didn't want to break the connection.

"What did she want?" Mildred asked; her tone more angry than curious.

Luther turned his head in her direction, but his eyes were still looking away, as if he was still raptured in the phone conversation he'd just had. "She wants to see us tomorrow…or shall I say, we are going to over there tomorrow."

Mildred finished her drink, and sat back, "We are? What are we going over there for? To hold her hand while she mourns for Maya?" She said, starting to reach back for the cognac bottle.

"No, Mildred," Luther said, his voice rising. He then took another sip, trying to calm himself. "This is serious, Mildred. Erica said that the spirit of Eric is sitting on her sofa…and he wants to speak with us."

It would take 18 hours for the scent of cognac to finally leave the house from the bottle that Mildred dropped when she heard this news.

Chapter 4

Part I

The fog was still there, Jenna noticed, peering from her window as she chewed a piece of toast. It was well after 10am, and both Nathan and Tilly still slept, their internal sun always in chronological conflict with the celestial one. She could feel the heat of the day beaming through the windowpane.

And that fog; hanging out there near the edge of town like a loose skirt. She squinted at it, as if that action alone would bring her some clarity.

"Good morning, Grandma."

She turned, seeing Tilly still caught in a yarn. Normally her granddaughter would be working at Mildred's place, not that she had to work at all with the silver spoon she received from Jenna, but even a grandmother needed to teach her grandchild a little humility, and what better place to learn it than to be a paid housekeeper under one of the most cantankerous women she knew; Mildred Ross, The First Lady.

It was a good thing that Tilly loved the small job, and even Mildred eventually accepted the arrangement, as it promoted her image of being treated royally; an act her husband was faltering of late.

"Hey baby, how are you this morning? Glad you have a day off from The First Lady, 'cause I made some morning *Eggs Scrambled* for you. They're on the stove," Jenna said, directing her finger in that direction, and in one twist of her wrist, brushed bits of toast from her lips.

Tilly's eyes widened. "They sure do smell good, Grandma," she said, heading towards the stove, and the large skillet still steaming atop it, "And where is Grandpa? Did you leave him in there still sleeping? Marriage must still be spicy, the way you keep putting him to sleep, and treating him with your famous Eggs Scrambled. I can only wonder what you kids are doing each night."

Jenna turned back to the window, "We were up all night stickin' pins in your voo-doo doll, young lady, but the head of it is so hard that we keep bending the steel."

"Grandma, you are too funny," Tilly said, as she grabbed a plate from the counter.

"You gonna be laughing real hard, when I decide to do a Tilly Scramble," Jenna said, glancing over her shoulder at her granddaughter, and noticing her attention was more focused on shoveling eggs into her plate.

"What did you put in them this time?" She asked.

Jenna looked back out of the window, "You know even I am not sure what I put in my *Eggs Scrambled*, but whatever it was, it cleared out two shelves from the fridge."

Tilly said nothing, as she dug her fingertips into her plate, and stuffed her breakfast in her mouth. "You want some coffee, Grandma?"

"Sure baby, and maybe you can get yourself some eating utensils while you're at it." Jenna replied, observing Tilly in windows reflection. "Don't make it too strong."

"I know, I know," Tilly said. "Whatcha looking at?"

"There's a fog hanging out there. I guess it came on overnight. There wasn't anything like it at the funeral, was there?"

"No. It was a clear of moisture at the church, unless you account for all the tears. Even Mildred was balling, falling all over the casket."

"Really," Jenna said, spinning around to make sure she heard correctly. "Mildred? The First Lady? Pastor Reynolds didn't mention that at the repass."

"Maybe because she left before he finished the services."

"Figures. The one funeral I don't go to, and it has the most excitement."

"Yea, it was pretty dramatic." Tilly said, stuffing in another helping, before rising to go to the coffee pot. "But now that you mention it, there was a little bit of fog at the cemetery. More drama, I guess."

Jenna nodded. "And I haven't seen any traffic coming into town either. It must be unusually thick.

"Really, no traffic, this early in the morning? Mark said that there was to be some delivery trucks coming into town for the supermarket today. You haven't seen them?" Tilly said.

Jenna could hear the percolation of the coffee maker. "No, as a matter of fact I haven't. I hope it lifts soon. Can't have folks miss out on any groceries." No grocery trucks, Jenna thought. No paper delivery trucks, or flower trucks, or even the gasoline trucks. It was all very disconcerting.

"I see you back at your crystal ball again this morning," announced another voice, "Maybe we should just attach a duster to your forehead, so at least you can clean the windows while you're at it."

Jenna turned around, to see Nathan emerging from the bedroom. He was limping towards the kitchen table. "Glad you could finally crawl out of bed, Old Man."

"And I can also smell some Eggs Scrambled, Old Lady," he looked Tilly's way. "And how is my Grandchild?"

Tilly was standing, hunched over her plate. She smiled at her Grandpa, and took a few steps to her side, to kiss him on the cheeks. "Doing good, Grandpa. I got some coffee warming up for you. You want me to fix you a plate?"

He looked at Jenna, his eyes forlorn. "Should she, Old Woman?"

She gave a half grin, her eyes still focused on his legs as he rubbed them, "Sure, consider it a treat, Old Man."

"Really?" he replied, as he began to rock the chair like a child, it's legs tapping gently against the tile of the kitchen floor.

"Really," Jenna repeated, watching his legs with concern. "You watch yourself in that chair. You know how that leg seems to always find trouble."

He slowed his momentum, and focused his attention on Tilly, his hands wringing, and tongue lapping at his lips.

Jenna continued to stare at that leg. She remembered that second injury as if it happened only yesterday, instead of little more than a year ago. It was a time that she remembered Maya the most; *this white woman with the African ancestry, had showed her more love on that certain day than many of the people in this town had shown her for years.*

She remembered the time, and the snow casting its frosty whiteness about the town like a blanket of cotton. That was when Nathan, being ever so cheap, decided to shovel his own steps instead of one of the local Middle School children. He walked out on those front steps, carrying a shovel that must have been his own family heirloom; made of a cast iron so heavy that the weight alone could crush most ice cover. It took only seconds before he took two steps, his legs slipped from under him and crashed his butt on the edge of the stair, while the edge of the shovel fell sharply against his knee cap.

He cried like a baby from the ambulance, all the way to the doctor's office, where it was announced that his cartilage was torn – yet again – and he would have a limp. But first, he would have to stay off the leg for a few weeks while it set in a cast. This meant, that while Tilly was in college, Jenna would have to cater to Mr. Reeds every whistle & whim.

Thankfully, a gift came a few days later, named Maya, baring groceries.

"You didn't have to do that Maya," Jenna said, wiping her hands on her housecoat. "Don't you have to be at choir practice this morning?"

Having already dropped the grocery bags on the kitchen table, Maya started unpacking them. "Don't be silly, Jenna. I'm only the piano player, not the lead singer. Those folks can wait for me a little while longer."

"Well, I do appreciate it. The doctor said it may be a month before he's back on his feet, but he may continue to have a limp." Jenna walked toward the cupboard, pulling out a glass. "You want a little something to drink? I got some orange juice, lemonade, water…"

"Maya brushed her hair back with her hands, retying the red polka-dotted scarf she'd wore, while her sandy blonde hair curled about her shoulders. She wore a light red sweater with navy blue pants and black boots. A winter wind pushed through the house at them both, and Maya realized she'd left the door open. "I'm sorry about that, Mrs. Reed," she said closing the door.

Jenna was pouring herself some lemonade, "That's okay. You have to watch that door. The latch comes unhinged in the winter months. But the offer is still on the table; did you want something to drink."

Maya turned to look at Jenna; her usually warm features had become worn. Her eyes hung down like loose rags. "If I get thirsty, I'll get something for myself. You just sit down, lady."

Jenna allowed Maya to take her to a seat in the kitchen; she hadn't really noticed how sore her muscles had become until she stopped moving. Just beyond the kitchen, across a small hallway, was another room, sectioned off by a pair of smoky-glassed sliding doors, and beyond that was the drawing room, where a large wall-mounted television was playing above a round wooded dinette table, two loveseats and a sofa, black stereo system, and a rather large tranquility fountain.

The television caught Maya's attention, as did the small quilted comforter folded neatly beside the sofa. "Been sleeping on the sofa, I see," Maya said, as she reached to open the freezer, and pull one of the shopping bags closer.

"Well, Nathan's knee is mighty sensitive, and I tend to toss and turn sometimes. Tilly is at college this semester, and that sofa is the only place I can hear that old man, and still manage to get me some rest."

Maya continued to fill the freezer with food. "So, the doctor says a month, maybe more?"

Jenna only nodded.

"Well, that's why I said I would bring over a couple of things on my way from the market. These are some meals I made, so you don't spend all your time cooking. I got you a few housecleaning items, a small personal coffee pot to carry from room to room with you, or you can just leave it on in Nathan's room in case he gets thirsty. I also got a few books and crossword puzzles for both of you.

Jenna didn't know what to say, but this gesture seemed to let all the air out of her lungs at once, and she sighed heavily, overcome with emotion. Jenna wasn't the type to ask for help, even when her husband was in such pain, with an injury that brought back too many memories. This girl was truly a missionary, she thought, as a tear escaped her eyes. "I'm sorry, I guess I'm just a little bit tired," she said, brushing the tear with her finger.

Maya walked over to her and reached into another grocery bag that was sitting on the table. It was a box of tissue, "Thank God, I saw these on sale just today." She slid the box under Jenna's chin.

She quickly grabbed one and dabbed at her nose. "I don't know what is wrong with me. That man has been like a baby these past few days, and he can be so demanding. It has been so long since he's needed me like this, and I feel out of practice, I guess."

"And you love him," Maya said.

"What?" Jenna questioned.

"And you love him. Makes you wonder if you should be kicking him for needing so much or kissing him for making you feel so needed."

She chuckled lightly at this. "You damned right…I suppose."

Maya reached over to place a hand on Jenna's shoulder. "Well, I do know a little bit about love, as you may know."

Jenna watched the hand as it retreated, then looked up at Maya, as she folded a few of the empty shopping bags. "I suppose then that the rumors about town have finally passed by your ears?"

"I suppose they have. But as I say, things happen for a reason, even the things we least expect," her eyes were focused on the Nathan's closed door at the end of a hallway leading towards the kitchen.

Jenna was lost for words. She scooted her seat back, attempting to stand, "Surely I can help you with putting this stuff away."

Maya held up a stern hand, "No. You sit there, and try to enjoy just watching. I will need to head to the car for a minute. I got some new pillows for your room. I'm sure Mr. Reed is using a few of them to hold up his leg."

"Thanks Dear, and please call me Jenna," she said, reaching for her forgotten glass of lemonade. "I just hope his knee heals right. That man's knee saved my life you know."

"You'll have to tell me that story one day," Maya said, as she tucked the shopping bags under her arm, and headed for the back door. "Oh, by the way, I think I will just stop by here for a few days, to make sure you haven't worn out that poor sofa."

Jenna looked back into the drawing room, noticing the way the cushions were pushed unevenly upon the frame. "Maybe that will be a good idea, unless of course you happen to have a new one in one of those shopping bags."

"Nope, sorry, all I had was a little miracle," and she was out the door.

...could you manage to pull that alligator out your rear, and answer the door old woman," Nathan suddenly yelled, his dropped fork clattered against his plate.

Jenna looked around, bringing herself back to her present surroundings. She looked cross at Nathan. Suddenly a frantic hammering at the door distracted her attention. "We have a doorbell!" she said, running through the small foyer. "And you better use it!"

When she opened the door, Mark stepped in wearing a red cap twisted backwards atop his head and brushed past Jenna. "Is Tilly here? I need to talk to her."

Jenna walked up behind the young man and slapped him on the back of the head, knocking off his hat. He clutched his head, fingers gripping his wayward hair. "Hey..." he said as he spun around, only to now recognize Jenna, "Heeeyyyy...Mrs. Reed. I'm sorry."

"You should be," she replied, brushing past him with a forceful pat of her shoulder. "You know better than to be storming in here like that, Mark. Now pick up that hat and keep it off your head while in my house."

He replied, visibly still out of breath, "Sorry, Mrs. Reed."

Tilly was standing at the kitchen sink, and placed her empty plate in it, "Mark, why are you here so early? We're not supposed to meet until this afternoon."

He licked his lips, as his breathing slowed.

"What you breathing so hard for, boy? You gonna drain the color right out of your skin," Nathan said.

"That's not funny, Granddaddy," Tilly said, giving Nathan a cross look. Mark was from Creole descent, ivory complexion, and wavy black hair so thick that on extremely humid days he could pluck it out into an afro. Nathan was always making fun of him.

Nathan focused his attention back on his plate, subdued laughter mixed with the spittle.

"What's going on," Tilly said, as she walked closer to Mark. Why are you out of breath?"

"I parked on the street – car was getting hot – and ran up here as fast as I could." He glanced at the rest of the family, before settling his eyes back on Tilly, "Something is going on in town, at the grocery store…something really weird."

"Weirdness just walked through that door, interrupting my breakfast," Nathan blurted out.

"Quiet, old man! Let the boy talk. Can't you see the poor child is rattled about something?" Jenna pulled a chair out from the table. "Did you want something to eat, Mark? There's plenty."

The boy shook his head, and stared at the floor, saying nothing for the moment, just licking his lips, and then suddenly, he looked up at Tilly. "Turn your television on!" He said, spinning around towards the drawing room. "Turn your television on."

Tilly hesitated, and slowly walked backwards through the drawing room's glass doors. "Any channel, Mark. You're scaring me a little. Has there been another explosion or something in town?"

He shook his head violently, "No, no! Any channel. It's happening everywhere."

Tilly looked around confused

Nathan at a potted plant, food filling his jowls. "The remote in over in that plant, baby," he said, returning to his plate.

Mark then whispered something, as he watched Tilly examine the potted palm in the corner of the room.

"What did you say, Mark?" Jenna turned towards her cabinets, and opened them up, "I'll get you a small plate, okay? I know you young people are immune to breakfast these days."

His mumbling became louder. "The delivery truck didn't make it to town," he seemed to be saying to himself.

Tilly shook off the dirt from the remote, and aimed it at the television, "The delivery truck? You mean for the grocery store?"

Mark nodded, his eyes fixed on the television screen. "No deliveries appear to have come in this morning: the grocery store, the newspaper trucks, gasoline trucks…"

This last one startled everyone. "What do you mean the gas trucks have not come into town?" Jenna finally said.

"I stopped by Bobby's gas station this morning, and he had closed four of the tanks waiting for the fuel trucks to arrive from outside of town. Nothing."

"The television was on, and Tilly stared at it baffled. "Is the satellite down again, Granddaddy?"

He didn't respond, only leaned forward a bit, to take a better look at the monitor. Tilly quickly changed the channel, stared at it, and Nathan stood up. Something was wrong.

"Wow, it's happening everywhere," Mark said, crossing over into the drawing room.

"What's going on here?" Tilly asked, her arm dropping, still holding the remote.

Jenna stepped across the kitchen, a spatula still gripped in her hand. "There is a fog rolling up outside the town. Maybe that's why the trucks haven't come in," she said, only glancing at the back of his head, as she squinted at the television.

Tilly flipped the channel again.

Mark stared, "Maybe, Mrs. Reed. Bobby was trying to get some update on the news this morning and saw this."

Three channels Mark turned to, and still the same odd picture reflected on them all; nothing moved. On all three news channels, nothing, no one…moved.

Faces frozen in time, their looks crooked, eyes shifted, bodies petrified during a mid-laugh, or speaking with their eyes closed. Each channel offered two news anchors sitting at a desk (all of them broadcasting out of town), not moving, not talking, not gesturing; as if something had cast a spell on them.

"What the hell…is going on?" Jenna said, the only question to break the stillness in a room that remained silent for some time.

Part II

Mildred thought she might have had a hangover. It had been so long since she had one, that it could have been that, or her monthly cycle. Of course, the latter had occurred during the last ice age, so she opted for the hangover.

The car was a bit bumpy, and even though it took only 30 minutes to reach Erica's home, Mildred felt as if she had traveled a lifetime.

"Are you feeling okay, Mildred?" Luther asked, as he pulled into the dirt road that led up to Erica's mobile home.

Mildred stared at her lap where her hands were clasped together in a sweaty heap, surrounding a watch she was beginning to believe was somehow mystical – yea, she said, she had to be hungover to be thinking up something like that. "I'm fine, Luther. Maybe we should be concerned about Erica, calling us over here with this kind of news."

Luther looked over at her, looking at the watch she clenched in her hands. She managed to tell him her tale of last night, about Carl handing her this watch as she sat in the cemetery; of how she had been thinking about her missing brother that same evening.

Mildred refused to let Luther see her rattled. She quickly stepped from the car, ready to be done with this whole ordeal. She couldn't believe any of it was happening, but she was not going to allow one frantic woman to take up any more of her time.

Luther stepped out of the car, looking at the house, with its elevated foundation, ready to be hitched up and rolled away at a moment's notice. It was a small 3-bedroom mobile home, with a quaint window canopy shading her flower garden below. The front porch was wide, barring an old wicker chair. The property was surrounded by a large picket fence that ran around towards an even larger backyard. Luther looked closely at the wicker chair. He could make out a thick bundle there, heaving, emitting short, quick sighs.

"Is that Erica?" Mildred questioned, raising her hands across her forehead to block off the morning sun's glare. *She looked exhausted*, Mildred thought. "This doesn't seem good at all, Luther," she said.

"No Mildred, it doesn't," he said, as he bounded for the steps leading to the stoop.

Mildred clutched the watch tighter, her legs refusing to move. Erica called last night to say that Eric, her husband, who disappeared three years ago, was suddenly back home, saying things she could not, would not believe.

Luther bounded all four stairs to instantly reach Erica. He noticed she was wearing a simple pair of sweat pants and a large t-shirt. She was sitting with her back to the wall, legs spread out. She was sipping from a water bottle she held. Luther stooped down towards her. "How are you feeling, Erica?"

She pushed back a sweaty thatch of loose hair from her forehead. "I don't know, Luther," she said, as she looked around at him, to see Mildred coming up behind.

Mildred glared at Erica. "Have we suddenly come to a first name basis, Erica?" she questioned.

"Not now, Mildred," Luther said, his voice low, chastising.

Mildred produced a too-wide of grin. "Why hello, Erica, it has been so long since I have seen my sister-in-law."

Erica began to stand, "I'm doing okay, First Lady. I believe it-"

She motioned forward, placing a foot on the first step, "What's going on, Erica? Where is my brother?"

Erica was still chewing on the texture of her last words, having been cut off by Mildred so bluntly. "He's in the living room, watching the television with Timmy."

"Watching television?" Luther questioned

"You called us over here frantic about Eric returning, wanting to speak with us all, and they are in there watching television?" Mildred said, stuffing the watch in her pocket.

Erica addressed Luther. "Have you two seen the news this morning? I know I was frantic, and I still am, but I screamed and cursed all night. I cried 'till I couldn't speak. Then I turned on the television. It was just too much for me…all this oddness. I had to get out of that house. I had to get out, Luther."

"That's Pastor Reynolds," Mildred corrected.

"What?" Erica said, as if just realizing Mildred was addressing her. "Oh, sorry…so much is going on, I can't think straight."

Mildred covered the last few steps leading to the house, anger still displayed on her face. "Yes, I'll say you are not thinking straight. Are you telling me you talked to Eric all last night, and got distracted by a television? Where the hell was the man for the last three-years? What are you doing sitting out here, and letting him sit comfy-cozy in your house watching television with a son he has not laid eyes upon in ages? Why isn't he out here in this heat trying to catch *his* breath?"

Erica held the knob of her screen door as she slowly opened it. "For some reason, he wants to wait for a First Lady to arrive, who isn't much of a lady at all if you ask me. I would have rather he showed up at your door, but he didn't. I would have rather he waited out on the road for you, instead of having to guide you into my home, but he wouldn't move. I'm angry too First Lady, but maybe we should save some of that anger for the one that deserves it," and with that, she turned, opened the door, and held it at arm's length, "*After you,* First Lady."

Mildred stepped over the threshold as if the floor would suddenly liquefy, sucking her in. "At least now we'll finally get some answers," she said, as she walked past Erica, heading for the sound of Timothy's voice.

Erica stifled her reply, and quickly reached out to grab her wrist. "Wait. You can't just go in there and start hitting him with questions. Something is not right. He's different somehow, quieter, slower. Something happened to him when he left I think."

"Erica!" Mildred said at a low grunt and twisted her arm away. "I want to see my brother. He abandoned you, not me, so if I want to talk with him, then that's what I plan to do."

Luther moved in front of Mildred, halting her advance. "Erica. Have you told him about, Eric Jr.?"

Mildred thought for a moment, looked at Luther, then back at Erica. "That happened right after he left you. Eric Jr. was just turning seven when his father left, a year before that accident you had with him in the car, a year before he died. You must have told him his son died, blamed him for not being there. What did he have to say about that?"

"He didn't." Erica said.

The statement was too direct to be correct. "He didn't? What do you mean, Erica? Have you told him that his son is dead?"

She took a sip from the water bottle she carried. "Before I began, he told me that he already knew."

"Excuse me," Mildred managed.

Erica moved aside, pushed closed the door, and spoke directly to Mildred. "I said Eric already knew his son was dead the moment I began to bring up his name." Her eyes were starting to wet. She didn't want to have to think about her son right now.

Mildred's head dropped, her eyes searched the floor for an answer. "But how? Was he living in Crest Hill County all this time? That's not possible. Did someone here have contact with him, tell him what happened?"

Erica found it hard to speak. "I don't know, but he knew it all. He knew the date of the funeral, how he died, everything."

"Then where the hell was he!"

"Stop this," Luther intervened. He moved his large face between the two women. "We need to talk to Eric, ladies." He addressed Erica now, "How is he right now, Erica? What can we expect?"

"He's, he's…calm. Not saying much at all. He's just waiting patiently for your two."

"His youngest son dies in a tragic car accident, and he is calm? He hears the news, and he doesn't even talk to you about it, other than *he knows*? And now you have him sitting in your living room simply watching television as if he didn't leave, as if he had been sitting there all this time and you just missed him somehow?"

"Mildred, please be quiet." Luther said. "I think we need to go talk to this man right now. Maybe Erica's right, and he's experienced something that caused him to leave for so long, and he's in some state of shock. Maybe he just wants to talk with his family, to discuss a personal emergency. Maybe he's sick, we don't know. Perhaps it's a good thing for him to be watching television with Timothy, it may put him at ease, more willing to give us straight answers without accusations," he moved his face back a little more, straightened the lapels of his sports coat.

"There is something about the television too Luther…I mean, Pastor Reynolds. It's not really playing anything, but he's staring into it, smiling, nodding."

Mildred began to move ahead, "I don't have time to hear how shoddy your television reception is, Erica. Maybe the boy has gone bonkers…staring into the television. What does that have to do with anything?"

Luther and Erica watched as Mildred headed towards the living room, and beyond to a smaller room that was home to a small entertainment center. Erica pulled gently at Luther, gathering his attention.

"He's talking to the television too, Luther, not normal at all. I know you're not a psychiatrist but be careful in there."

"Why, what is he saying, Erica?"

"He says something about the time has come for Crest Hill County…the time for the end."

Part III

Benny was afraid.

Mr. Death himself, wearing a pendant across his neck with his picture in it, singing, "Somewhere Over The Rainbow," in a Darth Vader costume (from the first 3 installments, not the last 3, which was somehow the first…), holding the tail of his deceased childhood parakeet in one hand, and a basket filled with fire & brimstone in the other…was not vaguely as frightening, odd, or unexpected, as what he was about to experience today.

The afternoon was humid, and Benny could feel his legs starting to sweat beneath his khaki cargo pants, and cotton tee shirt. The pants had many pockets lining the sides, and as Benny began to brush his fingers over the material, he could feel the slight bulge of the knife he carried, albeit, it was a butter knife.

He could see the bench. It stood beyond the jogging trail a few yards away, to the left of the monkey bars. Baxter Park was one of the largest in Crest Hill County, with a fountain and basketball court at one end, and a picnic area and tennis court at the other. It was near the center of town and was a great refuge for the young and old alike. City Hall was only a mile from it, and Benny could see the red steeple that topped the great building.

The dome-shaped building was quite impressive, but as it peaked to a pinnacle resembling a triangle, there, at the very tip, sat an actual barn. The story went that a hundred years ago, there was a so powerful, that it took a whole barn, along with the animals, into the air. The barn landed on the triangle atop City Hall, and amazingly enough, there were 2 goats and a pig still inside.

The goat and pig were rescued, but the barn remained. It was repainted and has become an iconic symbol for the city flag, standing for survival.

Now Benny looked at that barn and recalled when he saw it from Jason's hospital window, and how it had brought him hope that Jason would survive this. But that didn't happen. The world moved on. It survived, leaving Benny to always wonder, why Jason did not. It seemed unfair.

Now, to get this phone call, this cruel joke, from someone obviously pretending to be Jason, was insulting. Yet, something made him listen, made him believe the voice he heard, made him question his better judgment, caused his feet to move to meet this person.

"Hello Benny," said a voice behind him, as he sat on the bench. He was afraid to turn around.

There were footsteps, trailing around him.

A shadow.

A scent.

A familiar pair of shoes.

Benny remembered that Jason was buried in those shoes. His head and eyes dropped, afraid to look up, and eventually, as he did, he saw a man who seemed so familiar that he didn't seem real at all. Strong jaw, cleft, blue eyes, sandy brown eyebrows, lean, five-o'clock shadow, blue shirt, pin stripped two-piece suit; the only outfit he swore he would take to his grave.

Benny was speechless. If this was a hoax, then it was a damned good one. "What is this all about?" he said, half not knowing what to say, half knowing the answer.

"Should I have brought some wheat toast?" Jason said; his hands casually in his pockets.

"Excuse me?"

Jason ran a palm across his jaws; smiling. "For the butter knife you have in your pocket."

Benny looked down at his hands, seeing that he was unconsciously patting the pocket where the knife was stored. The heaviness of it was hitting against his thigh. "Who are you?" He said slowly, his eyes continuing to examine this illusion.

Jason locked his hands behind him, his tone serious. "It's me Benny," he stepped closer, "It's me, Jason."

And while Benny was still there, standing utterly in shock, Jason took another step forward, and leaned slightly down to hug Benny.

That's when Benny knew it was real. The smell, the gentle but firm touch, the way his chest stammered when he breathed, the smell of his breath, the way he stood so close with legs spread out. This was Jason. This was a vision, and not illusion.

This was also when Benny passed out.

How much time had passed, he was not sure, but the shadows of the trees had shifted slightly. He slowly opened his eyes and found that he had been leaning against Jason's shoulder.

"How long was I out?" Benny asked, surprisingly calm he realized, as he stared out at the rather empty park.

"Two hours."

The voice was the same, Benny thought. "And you've been sitting here all this time with my head on your shoulder."

"It seemed more natural to choose this pose, especially when I was suddenly appointed with your unconscious body. It made for a very compromising scene, Benny."

"True," he simply offered, as he sat up, with his mind continuing to race. Was this some sort of punishment? To be taunted by the man he cheated on? "Are you a ghost?"

A chuckle. "No, I'm not a ghost, Benny."

"Then who are you, some actor with a damned good make-up artist?"

"You don't believe that, Benny, I know you don't."

"Then what is this? Am I dreaming? I can't believe this is happening?"

Jason glanced at him for only a moment, and then turned away. "I miss seeing you like this, with these eyes, in these colors. I have been dead so long it seems, and yet I can remember you being in that hospital with me, staring out the window, as if it were only yesterday."

So, there it was, Benny thought, the truth slapped down for him, on a cold platter of his denial.

Benny turned in his seat, facing Jason, facing a certain reality. "What are you doing here, Jason? Do you know how much your funeral cost? You can't be coming back from the dead. I won't get my money back you know."

They restrained for a moment, but the laughter broke free.

Laughter...*and not a damned thing was funny*, Benny thought. "I was thinking about you yesterday. Is that what brought you back?

"No, Benny, your mere thoughts cannot raise the dead."

No laughter this time, and Benny stood up. He'd had enough of this insanity. He would walk back across the park and go home. He tried almost running, but strangely enough, his legs would not move.

Jason continued to speak, "I am here because something is going on in this town that I cannot explain. There is something unsettled here, something that you're connected to. Yes, I came back, and I don't know why exactly, but right now, I am glad I did."

"Dammit, I've missed you Jason," Benny blurted like a popped bubble.

"I know you have. I can sense that in my afterlife. I sense that you are also very happy too."

"Really?" Benny asked, as he turned around to face Jason.

Jason stood. His height was a bit taller than Benny's.

"Yes really. You've handled my death very well."

"Thanks, I guess."

A short silence.

"You have no idea how scared I am right now Jason, do you?"

"I do. I'm also scared."

"Then maybe we should go do something a little more relaxing."

"What's that?"

"Let's go see where we can dine on Turtles Candy."

"Yes, I would like that," Jason said, "I would like that very much."

And so Benny led the way, and oddly, he was tranquil with this whole affair, because it wasn't often he got to dine with his dead boyfriends.

Chapter 5

Part I

Pastor Luther Reynolds reached out to touch the surface of the television. His thick fingers pressed into the liquid screen. "I don't understand what is happening." He said, "And you say the same thing is occurring on Timothy's television too?"

Erica was sitting in a recliner, while Eric and Mildred sat together on the sofa, all watching the Pastor staring at the television. It had been one-hour, and still the image on the screen had not moved! Eric had also attempted to explain where he had been. He said he'd been out of town, and then Mildred shouted at him so long, that Luther thought Jesus Christ would have to come back before she stopped chastising him. Meanwhile Erica, the host that she is, decided to bring in some finger-foods to quiet everyone's tongues, engage in conversation, and slowly attempt to help Eric bring out a truth that everyone in that house knew had not been uttered yet.

Eric was donned in a plaid short-sleeved shirt and brown jeans. His curly black hair was hugged closely to his light brown scalp, as if he had just taken off a cap. He had a smooth mannerism about him, very give-and-take, as if he were listening intently, not wanting to say too much too fast. Everyone was suddenly afraid for him.

"Well, maybe there's something wrong with the television signal in

Springfield. I'm not an expert in these matters," Pastor Reynolds said, as he backed away from the unit, and pushed it back against the wall.

It appeared no one in town was an expert in this matter either. Pastor Reynolds had called the hardware store, which also does a little television repair, and the place had been inundated with calls regarding this, and the hardware store was clueless on the matter. This was something that went beyond a mere burned out tube, or Station Identification Signal, because it was happening with every television in Crest Hill County: local, cable, or satellite. On the screen at Erica's house, were the news casters: Brian Sanders and Avery Lorde. Avery was caught in an eerie half-laugh; a frozen image capturing her forever it seems. Her long brown hair was flipping off her shoulder in a kind of time lapse. Brian's large black face was caught in an even more disturbing half-blink, as a stack of papers lay vertical in his hands.

Well, I'm tired of looking at it, "Erica said, as she held the remote steady and turned the television off. "It's creeping me out. I wish they would fix the picture or put some 'Technical Difficulties' warning out there."

Pastor Reynolds shook his head, "But I don't understand. The news is broadcast live. How can you stop a live signal?"

Eric sat with legs crossed. His hands occupied by the watch Mildred gave him. He fondled it between his fingers. He was pleased with the gift, but he didn't yet give them a reason why it was found at the cemetery where Mildred had retrieved it.

This really upset Mildred, for she and Eric had a bond. Something was lost now. She would not judge him for leaving his wife; the truth was she never liked the woman; too mousy. But if he wanted to leave, he could have done it without hurting so many other people; Mildred being one of them. She would have understood his need to get away, to escape, to be out there living life – and not saddled up with a spouse whose only ambition was to stay rooted in the realm of status-quo. Now, after one of the largest funerals in Crest Hill County, he shows up. There had to be more to his arrival than a mere yearning for family bonding.

Pastor Reynolds sat in a chair, rocking back on it, arms folded. He was not about wasting time like this. This man comes back to a family he walked out on; a family he was very close to, to sit there offering up half-truths and cloaked conversation. It just had to end.

"What's going on Eric," Pastor Reynolds said, his gaze pressed into Eric's own. "Are you in trouble? On drugs? Mentally ill? Physically Ill?

Another woman? Another man? This family is worried about you, and you had to know by coming here, that there would be questions. You had to."

Without a word, Mildred and Erica stilled their tongues, and pulled themselves closer into the group. Either truth would flow, or a damned good sermon was about to begin.

"I am not in any of those situations, Pastor Reynolds. I do thank you for being concerned however it shows a lot of love." He had placed his hands in his lap and pivoted his body in the direction of the Pastor.

"Then why did you leave Timothy, your oldest son? You also did not bother to return when you discovered your youngest son had died? I would have truly needed your backbone at that time of sorrow. To bury a child so young is devastating for a family, your family, but you were nowhere to help deal with this," Pastor Reynolds said, as he stopped rocking.

"What do you feel about all of this, Timothy? You have a right to say how you feel about not having your father here," Mildred said, addressing the young man, who had opted to sit quietly at the far end of the kitchen.

Timothy looked up from the computer gaming magazine he was holding; hazel eyes just like his father's. A stack of half-eaten pancakes sat before him at the table, along with a partial glass of orange juice. He had lost his appetite while sitting with a father who acted as if everything was back to normal. But Timothy knew he and his father were alike in so many ways, and one of those ways was to be cautious when attacked. That is what Timothy felt was happening to his father. He was being ambushed by questions from people that seemed to now want to hear the answers. He got the feeling that his father was hiding something, and the only reason he was not saying anything, was that no one in this room was asking the *right* questions.

His father winked at him as if he had just read his mind.

So, Timothy responded. "I think dad has a lot more to say, a lot more you guys don't want to hear, but he is waiting for the right moment, and I am going to be silent until then." He then went back to his magazine.

Erica nodded, and leaned back face Eric. "Maybe we should give you a moment to say something; the chance to finish your thoughts."

"Just explain what happened to you," Mildred blurted.

He cleared his throat. "If you're sure, I will. But I need you to be strong, and to not become scared. What I have to say may bring more questions. Okay?"

"Sure..." everyone agreed.

"I also need you not to run."

A pause commanded the room, but the room still agreed.

"I need you not to question me and take what I say for truth."

Timothy placed his magazine on the table. He could see all the adults stare at each other, before agreeing to this last one. Timothy felt something was about to be said that he should really listen to.

Eric closed his eyes and took a deep breath. "I had no intention of leaving Erica. I loved her, and still do."

"Now that is hard to believe," Mildred said, jokingly.

Eric opened his eyes, and without looking at Mildred, spoke. "I'll also ask you not to interrupt me."

Silence.

"Unfortunately, everyone, I haven't come back to stay. I will have to leave again."

Erica sat up, stiffened, and thrust her hand over her open mouth.

He looked at her, "I'm sorry, but in a minute, you'll understand why." He turned back to face everyone, his head down.

Erica scooted from the sofa. "I need to get a little water," she said, her voice a bit choked.

He began to look at the watch again, twirling it around his finger as Mildred had seen him do countless of times. He must have been doing this at the cemetery – maybe visiting his son's grave.

"A few years ago, there was an explosion that killed many school children. Everyone in this room is aware of that great tragedy. Yes, along with my son's death, I heard about that incident too, even though I had left a full year and some months before. On that afternoon, when my only goal for the day was to bring back some groceries from the store for my wonderful wife and children, I suddenly thought about what I was returning to: My family, my wife, and my two boys. I thought about my sister Mildred, and the situation she was in. On that afternoon, although I had no intentions of leaving Erica...I did."

A low rumble within the kitchen, and a sigh from Erica could be heard.

He continued, "I suddenly got scared of being married, of responsibility to others, and foregoing responsibility to myself. I stayed at a motel that night, and that night turned into weeks, and that week turned into holidays, and before I knew it I had walked out of Crest Hill County and into a world of cross-country hikes, white water rafting, swimming with dolphins, and trying to be good to myself. I got new ID, used cash, and became someone else."

"But your family-" Pastor Reynolds began.

Eric closed his eyes once more. "But what had become easy, now became frightening. I loved my wife, my children, my sister, my brother-in-law, my neighbors, Maya, Lisa, The Reeds, and so many more people. I didn't need to leave. I just needed to experience these adventures with them. But it had been a year, and that can be a lifetime for those waiting, wondering, and worried about you. But I decided to take a chance. So on a certain morning, when I stopped by Delany's Floral Shop, to buy one rose, not for Erica, but as a promise to myself to never do this again, I heard a noise like tires exploding, and from the back of Crest Hill, a huge oil tanker broke through a road barrier, tumbled above me, just as a school bus passed near me. The impact nearly ripped the school bus in two, and then the explosion was deafening."

A collective sigh.

"You saw the explosion, Eric? My god, it's a wonder you didn't become deaf. How close were you?"

He cleared his throat and looked at everyone slowly. "Two-feet away."

Mildred shook her head, "What? You're saying you were just two feet from the explosion?"

"Yes," Eric assured.

"But my Son, that can't be right. That fire, along with the gas, burned for almost a day, destroyed over half a mile of land, killing everyone within an eighty-yard radius. A lot of the bodies were never really identified."

"Pastor Reynolds...I never said I actually *survived* the explosion."

Part II

The house was in chaos.

I don't give a fuck who is requesting who," Jenna said, while washing dishes at her sink. She splashed her hand in the water for effect. "You are not going over to that cemetery. The man is crazy, and I see the way he looks at you, Tilly."

"I'm going over there with her, Mrs. Reed," Mark said, standing beside Tilly.

"Jenna took one look at this thin child, with the Creole complexion, and was too angry to laugh. "And who will be going with you? Mark, this is no weak man, he still works out, and he'll smother your little wiry frame."

"It's only Carl, Mrs. Reed. He's an old man," Mark said.

"You watch that Old Man stuff," Nathan said, as he lay on the sofa, amusingly flipping channels on the flat-screen. "I thought they would have fixed this stuff by now. Even the local access channel is broadcasting."

"Quiet, Old Man, can't you see we have better things to discuss," Jenna said, and she turned back to Tilly, "And you can't go running up to that Cemetery every time that man need something. You don't work there anymore, and he needs to know how to handle his own crisis."

"I don't see what the big deal is, Grandma. It's only the cemetery, and you know I can handle myself there. I'm just helping a friend. I don't understand what you have against him."

"We are not going to get into that discussion, Tilly. You know that man wants you, and although Carl is a nice guy, even nice guys, especially old single guys, get ideas in their heads."

"Oh, let the girl go, Jenna, and be grateful she at least tells you where she going to be. You know the girl can take care of herself," Nathan said, as he hit the remote control into the palm of his hand. "I'm gonna miss my Celebrity Poker!"

Jenna turned towards her sink and began to resume her dishes. "I'm only looking out for you, Tilly. You are a grown woman, and we know your mother is too busy to be here to look after you, as she scouts the world for a new man. I'm just trying to give you a little guidance is all, but maybe you don't trust your Grandmother, and I understand if you don't."

"Oh, here we go with *Grandma Guilt*," Nathan said.

Jenna twisted her neck and went back to her dishes.

"Oh, why don't we all just go down there together," Mark said suddenly.

"That sounds like a good idea, Mark," Jenna said, nodding approvingly. "Maybe it will give me a chance to talk with Carl. Doesn't he know you're trying to get through college, and can't take these endless calls for help?"

Tilly threw her hands up, "Now look what you've done, Mark. We might as well put the steering wheels in the back seat," she said, defeated, and went into the drawing room to sit beside her Grandpa."

"What…what did I do?" Mark said.

+++++

The drive seemed long, and despite his youth, Mark was a rather slow driver; but lucky for him, there were three people driving the car this afternoon.

"Can you punch it a little harder? This does happen to be a Bentley," Nathan said, from the backseat.

"He's a cautious driver, Grandpa," Tilly said, also in the backseat.

"Cautious my ass. This car costs too much for it to be going the speed limit. They put those extra numbers on there for a reason."

"Quiet back there, old man. This boy is doing just fine. I'm not trying to send us to the grave."

"Well, as slow as he's driving, you might as well pull up to my plot, and let me slide on in, since I'll be long dead when I reach the cemetery."

Tilly rested her head in the palms of her hands.

As Mark went around the back of the Morning Glory Cemetery, Jenna looked at the grounds, and as she did, something caught her eye; a woman sat on one of the many benches on the property. A white girl, who appeared to have an infant in her arms, wrapped in a beige blanket. She wasn't close enough to recognize.

"Hey Mark, do you see what I see out there?" Tilly said.

Everyone turned, while Mark commented, "I thought I was seeing things."

"What happened here last night?" Jenna said, placing a palm across her chest. She then glanced back at the bench. The woman was gone.

"I don't know if I like this, Mark," Nathan said. He rolled down his window.

What they saw were graves that appeared to have been dug up. Piled up earth, concave in shape, were stacked atop many of them. To Tilly, this was beyond bizarre.

"Grave robbers?" Mark said, almost at a whisper.

"No," Tilly began to answer. "Carl would have been able to handle something like that. This is different somehow. The ground isn't crumbled, nor is it scattered. I'm not sure what could have done this."

"Or who," Mark said.

"Reminds me a little of a gopher hole that has been filled in," Nathan said.

"I don't like this Tilly," Jenna voiced, "And I don't know if any of us should be here."

"Well, Grandma, we are here, and Carl needs our help somehow. I think he wants me to see if I can guess what has happened here."

"And what do you think has, happened here?" Mark asked.

"I think something much larger than a gopher may have dug these holes, but I can't say what. A dog perhaps, I'm not sure, but the way the hole is pushing up, it looks as if something was trying to get out."

Part III

"…yes, I'm just taking a little time away from the office to do some thinking," Benny said on the phone, as he and Jason sat at an outside café. "With Maya gone…well so many people I have loved gone, I just don't feel like dealing with any clients today…okay, I'll call you later…have a good day at work."

Jason took a bite of the warm Turtles candy that lay on his plate. "Trouble at work?" he asked, licking caramel from his fingertips.

"Not anything Harold can't handle. He says that more than half the beauticians have called in sick, and many of the customers are calling in canceling their appointments; even the receptionist has called in sick today."

"Interesting," Jason said, as he looked off in the distance.

Benny took a bite from his dessert, "What's going on? Does this have anything to do with you being able to come back?"

"I can't say. Information comes to me a little at a time."

Benny could not believe this day. He was at a café eating a warmed turtle dessert with a cold dead lover; what are the odds?

"So…is Harold the new man in your life?"

That statement broke him out of his melancholy. "I'm not really sure if I am comfortable talking about him to you," Benny confessed.

Jason shrugged, "I can understand that, I suppose. There is no reason for me to be jealous at this point in my death, and I want you to continue to be happy."

Benny stuffed another piece of food in his mouth, if only to stop him from replying right away. He was finding it hard to look at Jason and was finding it even harder to get over a sudden feeling of guilt. Jason never knew that he was unfaithful, and when he had planned on telling him, Jason went and got himself killed by a hit-and-run driver; and that made it impossible to tell him anything. He'd only pretended to care for those first few weeks in the hospital...until those weeks turned into months, and old feelings renewed themselves again. Then Jason died.

"There is something that I would like to know, Benny," Jason suddenly began to ask, "And that is, why are you not frightened at this? I know you never expected to be talking to me again, at least not on this level. Most people would be running to their nearest Physic Friend, and yet here you are taking this all in as if I have never left."

Benny nodded. "Good question, and I have a good answer," He reached across the table to grab Jason's hand; the feeling of it was very neutral, like the air around them. "Because this is what I have been wanting, Jason. There were times I have thought of you as if you were right here. There were times that I carried on conversations as if you were in the same room. I have never stopped wishing, hoping, and praying to have another chance to talk with you, eat with you - to say goodbye. You died on the operating table. I thought I would see you later, that you would be fine."

"I know, I heard you," Jason interrupted.

"You did?"

"Yes, but I knew I was slipping away from you at that time. There is a moment in death when you realize you are about to crossover but are unable to speak it. There was no floating above the room like you see in the movies; I was still attached to my body, but I could feel my flesh slipping away from it like loose clothing. I could turn my hands, my head within my own self; feel my own skin start to give way. I hadn't understood it then, but I knew something was happening. When the flesh begins its journey of death, your spirit begins its journey of life. So yes, I heard your well wishes for me, and was unable to tell you that it was not to be."

Benny was not sure what to say about this. "Why do people put themselves through that, Jason? Why do we hold out such hope in a hopeless situation? I could have shared so much, said goodbye, made some sort of peace. We can never accept that the end is near, so close, so real. We never get to say what we really want."

Jason cupped his hand over Benny's this time. "Hope is a selfish thing. We don't hope for the dying to survive, any more then we hope that we won't have to be alone without them. Hope calms us and allows us to deny what is real. Resting in peace is not always reserved to the dead."

Chapter 6

Part I

Mildred rushed into the house, forgetting to close the door behind her. Her hair was like uncut grass pulled atop her head, and she found that all the energy she had moments ago, propelled from her body like a popped balloon. She collapsed on the sofa covered in a fear that wrapped around her, smothering her thoughts.

Luther Reynolds remained in the car. His head still beat at a rapid pace. His hands still shook. His mind still raced. What he had witnessed just a few moments ago, was not possible, and yet he was still holding onto the steering wheel of the car as if to let it go was to let go of the little sanity he once had. In one day, his whole life had been tossed in a blender and turned into puree.

From the car he could hear his phone ringing. It was not a simple ring, but one where his private and personal lines were blaring like a symphony throughout the house. His spirit shook. Was this the end of the world? He had studied, preached, examined the Bible for ages about the End Times, and this was not going according to that plan, and yet here he was, in the center of something that was more spiritual than he had every wanted to be witnessed to. He would have remained in that car, been very happy to sit there until the sun had finished its revolutions…

…and would have if Mildred had not screamed.

He rushed into the house to see his wife lying back on the sofa, the handle of a phone in her limp hands. "No, my God, this can't be happening!" she shouted towards the ceiling.

"What is it?" Luther questioned, looking around quickly, but seeing no danger.

Mildred lowered her head, gazed at him as if she were not sure who he was, "We have to get out of here! I tried calling the police, the ones in the next town, and there is no answer. I tried calling Pastor Oncard Williams, but there is nothing but silence. There is static on the lines, Luther! Pastor Oncard lives in Stationville, a little roadside shopping village kind of town. Not far."

"What are you saying, Mildred," he said, closing the door.

"The phones are ringing here Luther! What has happened outside of town? Where is the rest of the world? What just happened at Erica's house! We must get out of here! I'm scared for god's sake, very scared. We can't stay here…"

And Luther watched her go on, and on, and on. He could not answer. He was still in as much shock as his wife; without the useless ramblings. The phones continued to ring, and he continued to stand there with his back against the door as if it held him, refused to release him.

His mind was beginning to experience guilt. They ran from Erica's home, while her husband was still there; a husband who had given them the scare of their lives. Luther began to recall what transpired after Eric told them he had been in the middle of an accident that had killed many in this town.

…only a few hours ago…when their lives collapsed.

"…what do you mean, you didn't survive the explosion, Eric?" Pastor Reynolds asked; not even sure if his lips had moved.

Eric didn't answer right away. He had a faraway look, his eyes wet, and his mind elsewhere. He grabbed at his jaws as if what he had said was a surprise to him; as if he could not believe it, and spoke again, as if the whole scene were playing right in front of him. "The truck fell from an embankment I believe. I heard a loud crash, and there was a smell, like gas coming from someplace, I can't quite remember," he took a deep breath, "But maybe it didn't quite fall, this gas truck, but it did come barreling down the hill, as if out of control, as if it had broken past the guard rail and managed to stay on its wheels somehow, and before I knew it, there was the school bus, there were other people, there was a mail truck, there was so much going on…and then it happened. The explosion. I could see it for a moment; the brightness of it, the sound deafening, my skin getting hotter, tighter and I was somehow flying. I hit something, maybe the corner of a building, but something stopped me, and I continued to burn."

"Wow!" Timothy said suddenly from the kitchen.

"Shut up, Timmy!" Erica said, sitting near him at the table. She gave him a disapproving look. She looked back at her husband, "Maybe your dad was just in shock, and doesn't remember what really happened to him."

Eric turned to look at Erica, "No, I do remember, or at least I am starting to remember more. I was in shock, very much, at what was happening to me. I couldn't breathe I remember, and my eyesight was hurting, getting brighter, and yet growing dimmer. I think I was starting to die then, because the noises stopped, and became a constant chime, and then-"

"What the hell is this?" Mildred interrupted, slowly rising from the sofa. "What are you talking about, Eric?"

He turned in her direction, still not appearing to see her at all, just following the direction of her voice, "I died, Mildred."

"Enough Eric," Pastor Reynolds said, waving his hands, "Enough of these lies! How dare you blaspheme here, in front of me, in front of your family."

"What sort of cult has gotten a hold of you, Eric? Talk to me," Mildred pleaded, as she stood back, between her brother and her husband.

"This is no cult, Mildred. I have come back from the dead. I have risen from…"

"Go to your room, Timothy!" Erica blared hysterically.

"He's my dad, mom. Why can't I know what's going on?" Timothy pleaded.

Erica turned towards him, and slammed her palm on the table, "I said take your ass to your room, young man!"

"Let him stay," Eric said, his voice rather calm despite the hostility in the air.

She spun in his directions. "I will do no such thing, Eric. I will do no such thing," and she began to walk in Eric's direction, but directed her voice at her son. "Get-in-your-room-Timothy!"

The boy, sullenly and slowly, backed away into the small hallway that led to his room.

Erica continued to advance, "Who are you to tell this boy what to do? You run away from this family to live some carefree life, only to come back with this crazy story. You didn't have to come back, Eric. Do you know that? I was handling your little disappearing act. I was handling being without you."

"Were you, Erica?"

"Excuse me?"

"Did you stop loving me so quickly? Did you stop crying for me at nights when Timothy was asleep? Did you stop smelling the scent of my clothes that you still have in that closet? Did you stop picking up items at the store that you knew I would need, but I was not here to receive? Did you stop crying on Maya's shoulder about not being able to get me out of your mind?"

"Shut up, Eric! How could you know that?"

"Yes, enough of this, Eric. You are going too far," Pastor Reynolds said.

"Is he, Luther?" Mildred interjected. "Are you the expert on going too far?"

Pastor Reynolds looked at his wife suddenly, "This isn't about us, Mildred." He turned back to look at Eric, ignoring the sour look Mildred continued to cast upon him, "And I am very ashamed at you Eric. I think you need to leave this house."

"I would only come back, Pastor Reynolds," he replied, the voice very bold, very sure.

Pastor Reynolds was taken aback by the tone and began to rise out of his seat; his immense form causing a shadow to fall across Eric. "You need to get out of here, Eric."

"I was brought back here for a reason, Pastor Reynolds, and if anyone should know about spiritual purposes, then you should know that my reason has only just begun. It is about to happen everywhere, Pastor Reynolds. Talk to Carl at the graveyard. I am not the only dead man to walk these streets tonight."

"Shut the hell up, you bastard!" came a shout.

Before anyone could react to the sound of Erica's voice, something flew past them all, and a crash of water and glass erupted. Flowers from a broken vase lay at Eric's feet. Mildred screamed. Pastor Reynolds stood back. Tiny glass shards from the vase that Erica threw caused some to turn away, but for Eric, a large gash had been cut into his forehead.

He stood suddenly, grabbing his head, closing his eyes, remaining silent.

The cut was deep, but from it, there was something other than blood. Something flowed, almost clear in color.

The wound pumped, seemed to want to suck the clear liquid back in, but didn't, and Eric reached up to touch it. As he pulled his fingers back, it looked sticky, clinging to his hand like egg yolk; the wound it came from was already growing smaller.

Pastor Reynolds jumped back, hitting the chair behind him.

Mildred placed both hands over her mouth, her body trembling.

Erica screamed.

"Holy Shit!" Timothy said, from the back of the room, his head peering from behind his door.

"In the name of God, who are you!" Pastor Reynolds said, as sweat beaded on his forehead.

Mildred ran behind Pastor Reynolds, pulling at him from the back, "We need to get out of here, Luther!"

Erica looked at him oddly, stepped up to him, "What are you? What have you done to my husband?"

Pastor Reynolds looked at her. She was not as afraid as she seemed. He looked back at Eric, and reached out towards him, grabbing his arm. "Get out of here, Satan! Get out of this house!"

He looked at the Pastor. "I am hardly Satan, Pastor Reynolds," Eric said, unmoved.

Pastor Reynolds looked at the grip he had on this man, and could feel his fingers slip from him. He quickly twisted his hands, trying to get a new grip, but it was as if the skin beneath his fingers was melted butter, and he was starting to lose the grip again.

"You'll start to accept the truth very soon," Eric said, "but yes, I believe I should be leaving." He then turned to look back at Erica, who too was shaking, holding herself, sweaty arms wrapped around her. "There is a gift awaiting you too, Erica. I'm sorry for bringing it to you this way."

She said nothing; not knowing what to say, and not knowing exactly what he was talking about.

Eric silently walked past them all and left; heavy breathing the only sound.

Mildred stumbled towards the door, "Jesus! This is not happening. I need to get home Luther. I need to get home!" And without a word she was out the door, running down the stairs and into the car.

Pastor Reynolds looked at Erica, his body tight with tension, his eyes saying more than his lips. He was scared, and she knew it. There were no words for what just happened, nothing he could say, as if suddenly, it did not happen.

He hadn't even the courage to close the door on his way out of her home.

…and that is the last thing Erica remembered, until now.

…until her son called her from his room, only to point outside at his window.

She leaned out of the window, and looked around, and could see in the distance near the back of the house a large tree that was a part of their backyard. There was a man standing there.

She could tell at once that it was Eric.

She looked at Timothy. He looked up, worry in his eyes. "I'm going out there, Timothy. Watch me from the window. Watch mommy."

"Do you believe what this guy says?"

She didn't want to answer that one, but she could tell that Timothy knew the answer.

She walked to the backyard, toward her husband. Eric stood there unmoved, didn't turn around, and didn't face her.

"I know you need proof, Erica."

His voice, once again back in her range, back in her life. She wanted so badly to believe this ghostly visit - if it was indeed that- of this man that vanished from her life. She wanted so badly to believe, that she had no fear.

"Who are you?"

"I'm the father of your two children, Erica."

And that part was right. She remembered him telling her about their son's death before she got a chance to. And here they were, in the backyard where he played the most. She stood just behind this man, who claimed to be her husband, and from this angle, she could see a small cut on the side of his face, where a few hours ago, there was a large wound.

She looked past Eric, out unto the lawn. She saw the sandbox, the slide, a small barbeque area, some bushes, and that big tree, with the chain hanging from it, holding an old tire swing.

A tire swing that was now *swinging*.

"Someone else has come back to say goodbye, Erica."

Her heart stopped. She watched the chain arch, swing, and the end of it moving more and more into view.

Then she saw it; the tiny feet, the small arms, the head of hair; dark brown just like his father's.

Her lips parted, and a whisper glided across her teeth, *"Eric Jr...?"*

Part II

Mark handed Carl a glass of water and everyone watched him drink; tossing his head back as if it were a shot glass; his Adam's apple bouncing like a paddle ball. His hands were shaking when he returned the glass back to his lap.

"Are you certain that these activities aren't because of grave robbers?" Jenna asked. It took two hours, and 3 gallons of water to get this man to talk the least amount of sense.

"No, this is not the work of grave robbers," he said, taking a deep breath. He looked back into the empty glass, as if wanting to make sure it was empty.

"But you said that the dirt was moved."

He looked up at her from the recliner where he was sitting, in the waiting area of Morning Glory Cemetery, and glanced at Tilly, who was beside her. Behind them both, sitting in a love seat, was Audrey Li; she was the daughter of the cemetery owners. Here today to handle some much-needed paperwork.

Audrey spoke, her naturally thin eyes looked away. "It was not moved, Mrs. Reeds. It was sifted."

Jenna turned towards the woman, "Oh, what is the difference? I just want to know, what is the meaning of bringing my granddaughter down here to deal with something of this nature? Do you think she had something to do with this?"

"No, we don't think that. We trust your daughter," Audrey replied.

Carl cleared his throat, reaching forward to place the glass on a coffee table in front of him. "No, we don't think that, Jenna, and I just wanted Tilly to come down here to look at them with me. There is a lot of ground to cover, and the rest of the staff is out at a convention up in Downers Grove."

Both Nathan and Mark were at the far end of the room, near a bookshelf that stood close to a large stain glassed window. Nathan was standing in one of two chairs that bordered that window, and Mark was standing in the center, looking out.

"I find all of this a waste of time, if you ask me," Nathan said.

"Mr. Reed, some of the grave markers have been disturbed, and Tilly used to work here, and was extremely good in helping Carl in the past. We just need her to help his old eyes, that's all," Audrey said, as she began to reach for an empty glass and the pitcher of water left on the coffee table.

"And why can't you go out there and help them?" Nathan charged.

"Grandfather!" Tilly defended.

Nathan brushed a hand in her direction.

"I knew I should have come alone," Tilly said, as she faced Carl.

Carl shrugged his shoulders. "Well, it's much too late now that the circus has arrived. I can only expect a show at this point."

"Well, leave it up to the clown to do all the talking," Jenna said, her hands posthumously on her hips.

"Oh, stop this nonsense," Audrey said, waving her glass in the air. "This is a place of business, and a place of mourning. We can do without all of this bickering." She picked up the pitcher, shook it, and addressed Mark. "Can you get me some more ice, Mark, from the small kitchen in the back, behind the stairs?"

He turned from looking out of the window. "Sure, no problem," he said taking the container.

She then ran a finger through her cropped shoulder-length hair and took a sip from the glass in her other hand. "The dirt was sifted," she then turned to look at Jenna, "and yes, there is a difference. Not only is there a difference, but there is something mysterious happening, that me and Carl at first, refused to believe. Before you both arrived, we managed, with the help of another friend of mine, to dig up the grave of Mrs. Lawdry. Do you remember her, Jenna?"

Jenna did. Mrs. Lawdry was a woman who used to live in a mansion next to her parents when they were alive. A bitter old woman, who placed two picket fences around her home a few distances apart, for fear that a 'Nigger' might jump the first one with ease. There was always one, like them, Jenna thought, yet they managed to hold the contempt of a nation beneath their flesh. "Yes, I can remember," Jenna responded.

"Well, she was buried with a royal set of diamonds, that any grave robber would have been able to claim a sizable fortune from. The pearls that draped her neck were from blue Australian oysters. Priceless."

"So?" Jenna said, obviously perturbed.

"So, nothing," Audrey said, "The jewels were still there when we looked."

"Here you are, Ms. Li," it was Mark returning with a filled pitcher.

"Thank you, Mark," she said, grabbing it from him, and using it to top-off her own glass, before sitting it back on the coffee table. She held the glass in both hands, looking into it as she spoke. "The dirt we removed was packed very light, Jenna; so light that you could run your fingers through it like sifted flour. Mrs. Lawdry's jewels by the way were not moved. They were still there."

"So, you have some stupid pranksters on your hands," Jenna quickly said.

Audrey shook her head and began to pace in front of the love seat, "No. We don't think pranksters would dig a grave up, only to repack it with dirt, and not take anything. We only dug up Mrs. Lawdry's because we thought it were robbers, but there are others that seem disturbed also; less wealthy people."

"How did anyone manage to even dig up the first casket?" Mark asked, standing just behind Tilly. "I mean, I know the equipment you use, and well, it's hard to think with Carl living in a guest house at the end of the property, that he could not hear anything."

"I didn't," Carl said quickly. "I didn't."

"Well, maybe he was in a deep sleep or something. The man is old for God's sake," Jenna said, crossing her arms, and trotting around towards the window where Nathan was sitting.

Carl looked at her, cursing under his breath. "Have you seen it out there? The fog? It would be very hard for anyone to do anything out there with that fog lifting and falling so thick. That and the noise would discourage anyone from creeping in here at night to do anything, 'cause I would hear them."

"And there is more," Audrey said, as she took a seat on the arm of the love seat. "Something that scared us both."

"What," Tilly said, as she moved near Carl, and placed a hand on his shoulder. He still had that faraway look.

"I was up last night, not very late, when I saw shadows. Shadows in the fog."

"Oh boy! The man is crazy," Nathan said, slapping a hand on his forehead. "You gettin' too old to be hanging around this place, Carl."

"This is no joke!" Carl shouted, and then took a deep breath, "This is no joke. They had human shapes, appeared to be floating, but you could see them, the legs and arms swinging, their heads were turning like they were...looking around."

"I don't believe this," Jenna said, stepping up to her grandchild to pull her away from Carl. "I don't believe this, and I certainly don't believe you trying to involve Tilly in this foolishness."

"It's true," Audrey said. "I am not sure if it was real or not, but when I started to leave, I thought I saw someone as I turned the car lights on. I thought it was Carl, but when I turned the lights off the image vanished."

"So, what are you saying, Ms. Li?" Jenna asked, very upset. She wrapped her arm around Tilly. "What are any of you saying?"

Nathan stood. "I think we should get out of here. I have heard enough."

"No," Tilly said. "Carl has seen something, and if it was real or not, we need to hear him out. She pulled away from her grandmother's grip, and once again, went near Carl, placing a hand on his shoulder.

"Thank you, Tilly," Carl said warmly, and slowly told them about the shadows, of how they asked him questions, how they hid their faces from him, and how he was not as frightened as he should have been. Some voices claimed to speak for the dead and asked about the living. There were things they told him, that he should not have been aware of. Secrets. Secrets many in this room knew.

Jenna was fed up with this entire ordeal, and walked up to Tilly and Carl, grabbing Tilly's hand, pulling it away, and leading her to the loveseat.

"Are you saying that this cemetery is haunted or something?" Mark asked, stepping back as Tilly and Jenna moved towards the love seat, and taking the opportunity to take Tilly's hand from her, and place it in his own.

"I can't believe this," she said, rolling her eyes.

"What was that?" Audrey questioned.

"Oh, nothing," Jenna said, as she reclined in the loveseat alone.

"Well, I have to agree with Jenna," Nathan said, "I can't believe this myself. Have you called anyone else about this; the police perhaps?"

"No, I haven't tried doing that yet. I was just trying to sort this out with Audrey this morning. I told her a little about this last night before she left, and she wanted to think more clearly about it in the morning."

"And that's when we saw the graves," Audrey said. "I did try calling the local authorities, but the phones are busy everywhere. You would not believe it. And most of the police seem to be out of town at some national convention. I was then informed that investigating rumored stories about the walking dead were not on their list of priorities, because there are enough things happening with *living* people in this town."

"What things?" Mark asked.

"They would not say."

Carl stood up, "Well, we're getting nowhere with this. I need to go outside and look at the other graves, and I want Tilly there to make sure I am not seeing anything strange."

"The hell you are," Jenna said, standing.

"The hell I am. I am going out there with or without Tilly. Ms. Li can stay here to answer the phones. We had to cut them off a minute ago; they were ringing off the hook."

Jenna turned to the woman, "They were? Why did you do that?"

"I needed a break from what I was hearing. There have never been so many callers wanting to view their loved ones. With graves seeming to be upturned, I could not allow any visitors. I had no choice but to close the cemetery."

"And we are leaving," Nathan said, standing and beginning to walk towards the door.

"I'm going to help Carl," Tilly said.

"What," Jenna protested.

"I don't know what you all have against each other, but I am going to help Carl to see what is going on with these graves. I'm not scared, and he is, and it is not fair to send him out there on his own. He trusts me…it's too bad none of the rest of you can show me the same concern."

Carl grabbed a windbreaker from a nearby coat rack and tossed an additional one towards Tilly.

She grabbed it and handed her empty glass to Mark. "Just stay here or come with me. I know we could use an extra pair of eyes out there. It's getting very foggy it seems.

"I'll go," Mark said.

"Let the young folk go," Jenna said, waving her arm.

The three of them began to leave out of the waiting area, and Audrey reached down to pick up the pitcher again, which now stood nearly empty. "Would you two like some more water?"

"No, just crack the container over my head," Jenna said.

Part III

Are you listening to me, Benny?" Harold said, his arm outstretched towards the television, remote control in hand.

He shook his head, bringing himself back to the present. "Yes, Harold, I hear you. So, the salon was a little slow today."

Harold raked his fingers through his thick black hair. "No, you're not listening." He pulled his feet from the coffee table, stood, tossed the remote on the sofa, and walked towards the television. "What's going on with this plasma screen? Is the satellite frozen, or do you not know how to work the TiVo yet?" He hit the side of the television, but the picture remained unchanged.

"Not sure. It's been like that all day, Harold." Benny said, hopping off the bar stool so fast that his elbow knocked the appointment book to the floor.

"Can you be a little more careful with that," Harold said, looking back at the television, pulling it from the wall to peer behind it.

Benny picked up the book, and placed it back on the counter, then walked over to where Harold was, resting a hand on his back. "I'll call someone about the television later. The cable company's phones are not working."

"Figures," Harold huffed. He stood, and looking over at Benny, who was opening one of the drawers at the bottom of the coffee table. "And what are you doing?"

Benny looked very cross at Harold, "I am getting a new pen to finish this scheduling. It's Monday, and I know this is the one Monday of the month we open the shop, and I am behind on some of the paperwork. And now the cable isn't working? I have plenty of movies on DVD in the cabinet under there."

"I know where the movies are, Benny," Harold said, his tone short.

"I'm sure you do, Mr. Gaines, but you don't have to bite my head off," Benny said, as he walked back towards the counter, pen in hand, boots clacking against the hardwood floors.

"How many have called to reschedule?" he said

"Quite a few cancellations this week, with not many reschedules. It should be an easy week. I may need to call Rowena, to tell her that she can take the week off."

Harold picked up the remote control again, looked at it, and then tossed it to the other end of the sofa. "This has been a bad week for business already."

"I think we'll survive."

Harold said nothing.

"You want a beer, wine, or tequila?"

Harold crossed his arms, and bit at his lower lip. He slowly looked up at Benny. "I want you to tell me where you were this morning. I was at the shop, and yes it was a smooth day. It was smooth, because of canceling clients and the receptionist having called in sick. We had one beautician that was able to handle everyone, but it could have gotten very busy, and still you decided to take the day off."

"I think a tequila will do the trick. I can whip up my Aunt Maria's margarita recipe," Benny said, walking towards the kitchen cabinets.

"No Benny. I need an answer, not a drink."

Benny pulled down a few margarita glasses, "I visited Jason today, if you must know."

He sighed and slammed a fist into the cushions of the sofa. "I figured as much. You went to waste your day like that, your *whole* day? You know how sad that makes you, how guilty that makes you feel, and yet you still go there."

"You want a double-shot of the Patron?" Benny said, as he pulled fruit from the refrigerator.

"You're ignoring me, Benny."

"No, I'm just not listening."

"You have got to stop this obsession, Benny. You can't go on feeling bad about what we did behind Jason's back. You have to stop. I know you loved him, I know you missed him, but to sneak off to visit his grave…" Harold stopped, as Benny turned the blender on.

Benny held back his words, and simply served the drinks to him.

"Here, try this," Benny said, deciding to sit in an adjacent seat closer to the television, opposite Harold.

Harold sipped. "What's going on, Benny?"

Benny gulped. "You mean the recipe? I put just a touch of Tabasco in it, nothing special."

"No. I need to know what is really going on. I called the cemetery, and it's been closed all day. Are you sure you went there to visit Jason?"

Benny gulped again. He looked at Harold over the rim of his glass. "You called the cemetery?"

Harold placed the glass on the counter. "I called. I couldn't sit and hear you lie anymore, Benny. If you are cheating, you need to be man enough to tell me."

"I'm not cheating, Harold," Benny said, his voice stammering, searching for the right words. "I did visit Jason today."

"You mean you visited another man by the name of Jason. Is that what you're trying to tell me?"

Benny didn't know what to say. The truth was hard for even him to believe, but it was the only answer he had at this moment. "Believe me, Harold, I didn't meet another man today, but you're not going to believe what happened, so I don't know if I should even tell you."

"This is a small town, Benny," Harold said, "People will talk."

Benny knew, from the activity, or lack of activity on the street, that no one he knew had seen him walking with Jason. It was only a stroll in the park, and an ice cream parlor visit - nothing romantic about it at all. "Are you saying someone saw me do something that would have you think I was cheating on you, Harold?"

Harold thought, "No, Benny…at least not yet."

Benny took another sip of his drink, running his fingers across the rim to catch the salt, and run it across his tongue. "Then drop it. I took the day off and spent some time with me and my thoughts about Jason."

"Your thoughts…is that it? You didn't answer you phone because of your thoughts?"

"I'm sorry about not answering the phone, Harold."

"I don't want apologies, Benny. I want the truth. I know you. I know how you are when you visit Jason's grave, when you think about things, and when you have cheated. You are acting more like the latter than the former."

Benny stood up. "I'm going to get some more to drink, Harold. I think you should get started on yours, if you don't want me to finish it all."

"I think I am finished," Harold said, standing.

Benny turned, "What are you getting ready to do?"

"I'm tired, and I think I need to see you tomorrow. I can tell when you are hiding something, and for you to not return my calls, not say where you were, not to give me any information on whatever you did yesterday, shows that you do not trust me, for whatever reason. I don't like that."

Benny stood silently and poured his drink. "Harold," he began, nodding his head, "Maybe you are right. I should tell you about my day, as unbelievable as it may seem."

Harold stood, arms folded across his chest. "Yea, why don't you try me?"

As Benny thought about it, he realized he was beginning to smile. "I was visited by Jason's ghost today."

"What?" Harold said in Benny's direction. "What did you say?"

"I said, I was visited with the spirit of Jason today, and that is why I didn't call you or tell you about it."

"Oh my God," were the only words Harold expelled, as he watched Benny walk back towards the chair he had been sitting in. He stood by it, stirring his drink with his finger. "I don't believe you."

"I told you that you wouldn't believe it, and that-"

"No," Harold interrupted. If you are going to be with someone else, the least you can do is want to talk about it. What you don't do, is say you were out on the town with a dean man. Even if I were to believe you saw Jason's spirit, how do you think I feel hearing that? How do you think that I, the man you cheated on him with, feels about that? You are still feeling guilty about the whole affair, and if you feel guilty about that, then where does that leave me? Maybe that's what you want, with all these visits to his grave, to have him back, to have me gone, or just to start all over."

"I think maybe you should be leaving, Harold," Benny said.

"What?"

"I'm not used to being called a liar and a cheat all in one breath. So maybe you need to take your own day off, away from me."

Harold's leather coat was lying on the back of the sofa, and he reached out to grab it. "I can't believe you. Maybe I'll just head to the library to pick a better selection of fiction than the one you're telling."

Benny sipped at his drink and stood unmoved. "Call me tomorrow, when you've cooled down…and enjoy your visit to the library."

Harold slung the jacket across his shoulder, opened the door, and walked out.

And Benny walked over to the coffee table, to finish his drink.

Part IV

Lisa stood behind her office door, frightened. She had not called Pastor Reynolds yet, but it would soon be necessary. She tried calling the local sheriff station, but when she heard a busy signal – can you imagine, a busy signal – she swiftly hung up.

Then she thought she was simply dreaming - or caught in a nightmare that just couldn't make up its mind.

Monday. The church was usually open at this day of the week, and in the mornings, it was mostly dedicated for prayer. So, when Lisa opened the doors, she had expected a few people to come in to pray about situations that were challenging in their lives, for relatives that were in pain, for themselves and their prosperity.

Her small office was adjacent to Pastor Reynolds; separated by a lounge area. She could relax here, and if anyone entered the church, there was a red light above the doors that alerted them; its flash was also accompanied by a "Clicking" sound. She could count on some of the staff to handle a few of the worshipers that came in, and she could handle any vendors or staff concerns.

Click, Click

Two more members had entered.

She thought about the church again, and what she had seen this morning. There were so many people out front that she had to call in two more auxiliary helpers. At least 30 people were milling about with endless questions. 30 wasn't a large number by the end of church day, but to have 30 people waiting *before* she got there was something Lisa had never encountered.

Two people had wanted to speak with the Pastor Reynolds, and they were putting up such a fuss about wanting a Prayer Session with the Pastor, that she felt a need to call one of the police from the local station to send an officer over, just in case they did not take no for an answer. Pastor Reynolds never showed up on a Monday for a simple prayer session. The woman ought to have known that.

Click, Click.

But they were steadily coming in; very odd. And it began to remind her that perhaps this was due to Maya's funeral yesterday. Maybe a few members wanted some solace. Lisa was at odds with this, because she never really knew the woman, never really liked her, but in a sense, respected her.

She could remember when that respect began, because Lisa never liked the sins Maya was obviously caught up in, but one day, on another Monday, Maya taught her that the spiritual nature was not to be judged by her human sins.

...and as Lisa watched the light above the door, she began to think of the time that Maya put a light in her heart.

She was standing behind the curtain that hung at the rear of the stage, where usually, the choir would be on any given Sunday. It was dark behind that curtain and to her left and right were two sets of dressing rooms. There also stood a large tub built upon a wide wooden stand, for the once-a-month baptismal ceremonies. Behind her was a short flight of stairs leading to a set of doors: a large one leading out to the side of the church used as a service entrance, and the other leading to a set of rooms and offices; the Pastor's and hers included.

No doors were opened, no light came through, and she stood there looking out unto the main sanctuary (on a very odd Monday morning, where no one had come in to pray), and saw this solitary white woman stroll in, hair slightly red and sun-bleached, wrapped in a strikingly red trench coat that matched in hue to her red boots, giving her some much needed color against the backdrop of her pale skin.

The coat was buttoned all the way up to her neck, as if she feared her head would float away. Tucked under her arm, was a Bible. Lisa watched as she came closer towards the front of the church, her eyes darting in her head at the emptiness of the place.

Her gaze stopped on a hanging statue of Jesus, where underneath there was erected a small set of stairs and an alter holding a copper bowl, a water goblet, and a few standing candles. The eyes of the statue, as it hung with arms out on the cross, its head tilted slightly downward, was created with eyes that were wider than usual and pushed back slightly within the head, to give it the illusion that it was always looking at you. This is what may have captured Maya's attention at that moment.

Lisa had never seen Maya in here on a Monday and figured with the recent rumors surfacing, that she had just *too many* sins to pray for. Maybe today was the day of her repentance.

Lisa stepped from behind the curtain and unto the darkened stage, "Mrs. Ohlms? Are you looking for something?" She said, and Maya immediately jumped, "I believe our auditions for a piano player were scheduled for next week. The Pastor was only looking over your application just yesterday I believe."

Maya caught her breath as she spun around to see Lisa stepping from the shadows of the stage, "Lisa, you startled me. I know about my audition next week, but I was told that there was Intercessory Prayer on Mondays here."

Lisa walked out near the edge of the stage and placed a hand on the podium there. She looked around, and nodded, "Yes, although for some reason it is a little empty right now, but you are right, this is the place where our Saints come to pray," she said looking up at the statue of Jesus, pausing for a moment, before looking back at Maya, "Oh, and for the Sinner too."

Maya nodded, and then looked around the church, "And is there a certain order to which they pray? Are people allowed to come to the stage, is there a prayer leader for groups, or is it done individually in the pews?"

Lisa looked harder at Maya; the way her shoulders drooped, the nervousness of her eyes. She was here to pray *for* something; something in particular…something she probably deserved in the first place. "I am the prayer leader on occasions when there is one required, as with a group perhaps, or if there is a global need, but not for the individual. How you pray Maya, is up to you. God has no prerequisite on how you may want to pray, just that you do it, and cleanse yourself somehow of your immorality."

She looked at the area under the statue. "Are the stairs, below the alter, used for kneeling? I think I would want to pray there."

Lisa nodded, clasped her hands together, and walked slowly to the edge of the stage, noticing the stairs. "Yes, yes, perhaps that is a good place for you. The closer and nearer to God you are, just might do you the greatest good."

This time Maya's eyes darted upward at Lisa, "I'm sorry? Is there a reason why that would be so good for me?"

She shrugged her shoulders, "Not really I suppose, but some believe that God hears the greatest sinners only if they confess closer to him."

"And I should be right under him if I have anything to confess, I suppose," Maya said, folding her arms.

Lisa looked up at the statue again, as she addressed Maya, "Well truthfully, I would suggest you get a ladder, but we do have safety policies within the church to think about."

Maya's bottom lip began to quiver, her eyes to squint, and she turned away to mumble something under her breath.

"I'm sorry Mrs. Ohlms, was there something you asked?"

"Oh no, Lisa, nothing you would want to hear."

Lisa smiled, and walked back towards the podium to stand behind it, reaching forward to rest her elbows there. "Surely, Mrs. Ohlms, a woman as open in her affairs as you, has very little to hide under her breath. God knows all."

Without turning, Maya replied, "Yes, you're right," and she began to unbutton her coat, draping it across her arm, "And He keeps an especially vigil eye on those that take pride in passing judgment."

Lisa's eyes widened. "You can't really pass judgment on those that are open in their shame."

"I feel no shame, Lisa," Maya said sharply, as she turned and walked towards the alter.

"Well you should," and this stopped Maya. "To bring this type of disgrace to the Pastor is deplorable. To pull him into your maze of mischief, and to know that this whole town is aware of it, is shameful."

"This town knows nothing," and she faced her, "I hear the whispers. Gossip here travels on one side of a two-way street. Sometimes I wish I had never decided to stay in this town, and continued the missionary work I had started in my homeland. But I made a mistake in thinking this place, this backwards town, with its backward people, as any kind of home to me."

"You have no right to speak about this town or its people."

"Then what happened? How do you keep rumors alive in a sea of gossip and sleep at night? You keep talking and spreading lies about me, about the Pastor, about innocent fold who have committed no sin."

"Nonsense!" Lisa said, waving her hand at Maya, "You may need a lot more than those prayer steps if you are going to stand there and believe you have committed no sin. The desire to carry your affair further is in your heart. I can see it there; and if you have thought it, you might as well have done it."

"You are the liar, Lisa, and you know it...God knows it!"

"Be careful, Maya. You are on the verge of blasphemy."

"No, I don't think so. I have cursed no one, nor have I talked about anyone. Desire is not a sin Lisa, but what is a sin is our inability to express our desires. That, you may understand, because I see a woman that desires children, but because of her inability to have them, she has taken this position to oversee the church as if it were an act of adoption. The people of the church have now become the children she has always wanted. And just like a mother, she chastises, she judges, and she ridicules them as if they actually fell from her womb."

Lisa swallowed thickly.

"But she acts this way because she hurts so much inside. The Pastor saw this and thought helping others would be the solution. But she has so much bitterness bottled up in her, that she can only express it in hate; a hate for the families, the children, the mothers and fathers that she is supposed to assist, because she can't help looking at what she will never have."

Lisa stood silent.

Maya turned back towards the prayer steps, and casually placed her coat on the front pew. "So before you judge, remember who the ultimate judge of us all is. You don't have the right to take His job away. So I suggest Lisa, that you stick to your *chosen* job."

Lisa began to crumble from within.

"And now, I need to get to business…if you will excuse me," Maya said, as she knelt at the bottom rung of stairs.

Lisa walked down from the stage; saying nothing, and slowly, knelt beside her.

As she sat in the office now, she continued to think about that moment, as the light above the door continued to blink, and click…

…Click, Click

The stream of people was at least steady. There was no reason for her to go out there now.

…Click, Click, Click, Click

She concentrated on the prayer she was going to have on Thursday; that was the usual day of the week when the church had intercessory prayer, where they prayed for people that could not pray for themselves; or needed extra prayer around the world. She was working on praying for the city of New Jersey, where one of their churches caught fire, as well as some of the businesses in the area.

…Click, Click, Click, Click, Click, Click, Click

Now her attention was pulled back on the light…

…Click, Click, Click, Click, Click, Click, Click, Click, Click, Click

Her heart began to pound.

… Click, Click…

She stood up so fast that her chair toppled backwards. Something was happening in the church, or that light was malfunctioning. She walked briskly out the door and unto the back area behind the stage's curtain. She slowly parted the thick folds of drapery, only to be witnessed to a church overflowing!

What was going on, she thought.

People were walking in, cramming into the pews; already the stairs under the statue of Jesus was filled with members that were beginning to spill into the walkway. The silence was heavy enough to crush bricks, and this frightened Lisa. Such reverence they must have for the House of the Lord. She could feel the heat begin to swell around her as more bodies came in. All of them looked up at the statue, focused on it as if it were the only thing in the room.

Then she saw the faces, and what she saw caused her to come out and step on the stage. Many of the faces she saw she knew, but some, sprinkled amongst the crowd were faces she could not quite remember, or perhaps it was better to say they resembled people that she recalled as having passed away.

That was when she reached up to feel the beat of her own heart…just to make sure it hadn't stopped.

Chapter 7

Part I

Pastor Luther Reynolds sat in the living room. His head ached, his eyes felt pasty, and his body was incredibly fatigued. The phones in his house had been ringing so much, that Luther could no longer hear them and they converted into simple white-noise. He realized he hadn't the stamina to answer them anymore; so many calls, with so many questions, from people who thought the world was vehemently approaching some sort of doomsday. Mildred however, was too afraid to take any calls; she'd answered only one this morning and realized that she was no longer on the side of empathy, and the caller had introduced her to a few new choice words she had never realized could be strung together. And as Luther sat there, his thoughts as useless as burnt ash, he listened calmly to the constant rings of the telephones as their cries did a dance along the walls. For the last hour, he could do nothing but sit in his lounging jacket, the silk growing hot beneath him, as his foot constantly flopped against the floor; the sound of it like raw meat falling from a counter.

He could smell coffee in the air and could hear Mildred shuffling in the kitchen. Last night he'd had a nightmare, apocalyptic in nature; dreams of angels and nightmares of demons. These visions coalesced with the ringing of the phones this morning, tumbling him from a warm bed to a cold floor.

So now he sat, remembering those phone calls. People claiming to see ghosts, the dead walking, stalking shadows of loved ones wandering the streets, voices from the past echoing in their ears, fear, guilt and longing had overwhelmed many.

Today, the phones rang again, but what woke him up this time, were the church bells' frantic chimes.

Mildred appeared in the living room carrying two cups of coffee. She wore a robe with the embroidered image of a kimono dragon inching up along the side of her body, and on her face…she wore a question, "Is Lisa ringing the church bell?"

"I'm sure she is. She is the one I know on the church staff that actually uses it to get my attention, instead of simply picking up a phone."

Mildred turned her lips up at one corner, annoyed. She took a sip from one of the cups and stared at some of the artwork that lined the walls; pieces reflecting her yearning to escape, like that of Van Gough's *Starry Night*, which she was admiring now. "I tried calling her at the church, and on her cell phone, but she wasn't answering." She stepped closer to Luther, handing him the remaining cup.

He took it, sipping on its edge. He paused for a moment, looking intently into the cup, and then up at Mildred.

"Bailey's Irish Crème" she said, taking another measured sip. She then turned around in the direction of the white sectional sofa laced in delicate Persian silk, imported from the country itself. The large oval mirror, its huge intricately carved frame, commanded her attention for a split moment, as she laced her fingers through her unkempt hair. "With that church bell blasting off as much as the telephones, I thought you could use a little *extra* coffee with your coffee."

His next sip quickly drained the cup, and he stretched his arm out in her direction, "Yes, that was an unexpected answer I believe I needed. Do we have more of that in the kitchen?"

She leaned forward to place her cup on the glass coffee table, and with a low grunt, pushed her body from the sofa's enthralling grip. She snatched the cup so fast that he thought his fingers were still attached within the holder. When she returned from the kitchen, she carried a different cup, of noticeably immeasurable size, that it could very well be used as a baseball cap if flipped on its brim. She handed it to him, and the heat from it almost caused him to drop it; and he swiftly held it by its sizable handle – large enough to fit two of his thick digits through. "I think this might be a better size for you," she said, returning to the island of her sofa.

He rolled his eyes at her, but she was unaware, and took a careful taste from the cup. The sigh that followed came satisfyingly of its own accord.

"I'm afraid, Luther," Mildred said, bringing her legs up to rest on the sofa, and looking up at their wide screened television, mounted like a modern-day work of art, inside a custom-made frame above the fireplace. On it were the frozen images of the station's news casters staring at them like voyeurs.

Luther had forgotten Mildred insisted in keeping it on, just in case there was some technical error that would fix itself soon. After the scene at Erica's place, this image began to unnerve him. It reminded him of the Bible tale concerning Lot's Wife, and God having turned her into a pillar of salt for her disobedience.

"What does God have to say about all of *this* Luther?" Mildred said, as if she had read his thoughts.

He looked intently at her. There was a bite to her words, as if this wasn't really the question, and she was attempting to ask another veiled one within. "The Lord hasn't revealed anything to me yet, Mildred. If this is Spiritual, and from His hand, then I am sure he will disclose its meaning."

"Maybe the answer is just too obvious for you to see," she said, her silk robe and dragon shimmered from the light coming in through their large bay windows. The embroidered eyes seemed to direct their attention upon him, warning him perhaps.

Luther chose not to respond, and he watched as Mildred reached towards a glass end table, whose lower half was used as a wine holder, and she picked up one of the many remotes she had stationed there. She aimed it at the fireplace, and it instantly came to life. Mildred always could feel the slightest draft and regulated the heat within the house on a constant basis. This action, as the fire slowly reached towards its ultimate billowing conflagration, translated its many colors along the edges of Mildred's robe. It melded about her as if alive, and made her somehow look less so, somehow alien. What next came out of her mouth went to confirm that suspicion.

"You know, as well as I do, that the wages of sin are always death. I just never thought I, nor this town, would be caught up in another man's sin."

"We are not going to have this conversation, Mildred."

She turned her attention from the fireplace unto Luther, letting the crackle of the flames, and the sporadic peal of the phones command the air. "You sinned, Luther, and you need to realize that God is not only punishing you but is condemning this town for accepting you."

He stilled his tongue by taking another long sip from the mug.

"You've lusted after another woman that was not your wife."

Another sip.

"A woman who had fallen from her faith and her duties with God."

Another sip.

She smiled. "A woman that appears to pick up other people's trash.

God calls that kind of woman a whore, Luther.

He stopped sipping. "Now that will be enough, Mildred!"

"I'm sorry? Were you saying something?"

"I said, that will be enough. You are not going to talk about a woman who cannot be here to defend herself."

"Defend herself?" Mildred said, sitting up, "Defend herself from what? God saw what she was doing and saw where you were headed. He did you a favor by getting her out of your life, Luther."

"Shut your foul mouth, Mildred!" Luther shouted, but quickly recomposed, closing his eyes, and slowly unrolling the fists that suddenly found themselves at the edge of his wrists. "Don't put God in this situation, Mildred. I have enough on my mind right now, without hearing your accusations about anyone. Have you been paying attention to what has been going on around you: your brother claims to be back from the dead, the televisions around town are not broadcasting, no traffic has come into town, Tilly has not come over today to do her duties around this house; and neither has she called, the phones are ringing off the hook with frightened church-goers, Maya died from mysterious circumstances that had nothing to do with God, I have not taken a shower so my ass is dirty, and your mouth continues to be filthy. Enough is enough," then he slammed his empty coffee cup on the marble telephone stand next to his chair, stood up, and began to walk out of the living room.

And then their doorbell rang, and he stared back at the door, reassuring himself of a sound once familiar, yet had become lost in a symphony of clangor. He had walked past the sofa Mildred occupied, and was standing in the small alcove area that occupied the winding staircase leading up to their bedroom. He let out a sigh of exhaustion.

"And could you make yourself useful, and answer the door?" he asked, his back to her, awaiting an answer.

She rose from the sofa, the doorbell ringing a second time, and ambled towards Luther, purposely brushing her dragon against him. She faced him, and stood so close, that he could feel the heated air escape from her nostrils. They looked at each other; a silent exchange that caused Luther to back-peddle his actions. He was too late, and the sudden sting of her hand against his cheek drowned out his hearing, and another bell of sorts filled his world.

"I'm not a dog, Luther, and I am not your bitch! We buried the bitch, remember," she then spun on her heels, "You get the goddamned door! Or have you forgotten that I'm the wife around here, and you are the adulterer."

The doorbell rang again, before he found the strength to move. As he looked in the peep-hole, he could not believe what he was seeing -Tilly standing there, as if he brought her to him by the mere mentioning of her name. He opened the door.

"Pastor Reynolds!" Tilly said rushing past him, "I tried calling you all day, and even used your private number, but no one answered the phone."

"Yes, I'm aware of that, Tilly," he said, rubbing his cheek as he closed the door, "There have been a couple of family issues that I've had to deal with."

Tilly crossed her arms, and pulled at the strap of her purse, which ran across her chest. "I hope everything is going okay," she said, turning back to look at the closed door. "I don't have much time. My boyfriend is out in the car."

"Why didn't you have him come in with you?"

"This was just going to be a quick stop-over, to tell you I won't be able to work this week. Carl needs my help at Morning Glory, and Mark may need me at the grocery store. He was called in because of some rioting going on near there."

He stared at Tilly; most of what she was saying had not fully registered with him. "Carl needs help at the cemetery?" He questioned.

Tilly began to rub the strap of her purse nervously; "Yea. Seems some graves had been disturbed last night. It was really freaking him out."

"Graves? What are you saying? Grave robbers? Whose graves?" he asked, his body almost wanting to shake the information out of Tilly.

Tilly flinched. She could see this sudden movement, but almost immediately, she guessed at its motivation. "Some, yes Pastor, but don't worry; Maya's was not among them."

He drew back, embarrassed.

"I'm sorry," she said, realizing she had spoken prematurely. "I didn't mean to imply-"

He smiled, "No Tilly…it's okay. Your implications were right."

She reached out and he grabbed his hand. "It's okay. If you had *not* been thinking it, I probably would have worried more."

He squeezed her hand. "Thank you. A week will be fine. Keep me posted on what's happening at the cemetery, and if I can be of assistance."

She took her hand back, and began to fiddle with her purse strap again,

"I appreciate that Pastor. We hope it's nothing serious, and maybe some restless kids had a little too much time on their hands, but of the one grave I saw, I am not too sure."

"Why?"

"Well, I am not sure if you know this person, but the grave we recently examined belonged to a Mrs. Lawdry. Do you know her?"

Pastor Reynolds remembered Mrs. Lawdry; a very rich old woman who used to live on the hill of Crest Hill, not far from Jenna Reed in fact. He had been an assistant Pastor at that time, more than 15 years ago, and the family had asked that he direct the eulogy. "Yes, I remember her. I remember she was buried in her jewelry. I was very apprehensive about it then and offered the family to obtain them at the end of the services. Even in a small town like this, the propensity for crime is still a reality."

"No...no...Pastor Reynolds," Tilly seemed to correct him, "Her jewelry was still intact; and although the grave was disturbed, there was no robbery discovered."

Pastor Reynolds looked concerned and confused. Graves could also play victim to foul or sacrilegious rituals too. "This doesn't sound right, Tilly. I'm not sure you guys should be going around digging up family remains without their consent. I'm surprised at Carl for involving you in this, and what does Mr. Hadley say about all of this? He is still the owner I believe."

She shrugged her shoulders, "Not sure. I believe they are at some big seminar in Michigan right now. Most of the staff left last Friday. Audrey Li is in charge right now, and she authorized everything. That grave was the only one we investigated. I think I'm there for moral support more than anything. Carl is a bit spooked by all of this I think."

"Okay," he said with a slight chuckle. "If you can take care of old laundry here, I am sure you can take care of old bones there."

She chuckled at the analogy as well, "Well, about Mrs. Lawdry, when we opened the casket, there was another disturbing fact I noticed. The body was very well preserved. She looked as if she had died only yesterday. No sign of any decay whatsoever."

This caught his attention. "Are you certain, Tilly? This was well over twenty years ago when she was still a senior."

"I know, believe me, I did the calculations in my head. But really, her body had not deteriorated in the least," she said, her voice suddenly trailing off, as if she were still trying to convince herself of the events. "And then I noticed her holding a yellow piece of paper."

"I can't remember if she was holding something when we buried her, Tilly," Pastor Reynolds offered.

"No Pastor, this was a page from the phone book...*this* year's phone book."

"Now that has to be a joke. Some pranksters out to spook you guys," Pastor Reynolds said, half believing himself.

"And you also think they gave her a new face lift? No joke could be that twisted or elaborate. Wasn't there a big controversy about her death?"

Pastor Reynolds thought about it, "Yea, she never liked her only grandson, David Earlington III. She managed to change her will before she died, taking David out, and leaving all her money in a living trust to some big charity, but she never had a chance to change her insurance policy to eliminate David as a beneficiary. He managed to walk away with millions after her heart attack. He owns a few strip clubs in Vegas and comes here a few times out of the year to stay at his grandmother's home, which he purchased soon as it went on the market."

"Is that house on Mannory Lane?"

"Yea, I believe it is."

"Well, that phone book page Mrs. Lawdry was holding, had his name and address on it. Carl recognized the name, but wasn't sure where he lived."

"Really?"

A horn blared.

"That's Mark. I have to go. With no delivery trucks showing up today, I'm sure the inventory is a mess, and they may need him for that."

"No delivery? That usually comes in on a Monday, doesn't it? That was yesterday."

"And nothing today. No newspapers were delivered either, so who knows if something happened to the roads since television reception is gone haywire. I hear the sheriff is going to see what's happening outside of town," Tilly said, walking back towards the door.

Suddenly, a loud chime shook the air.

"Isn't that the church bell?"

Pastor Reynolds looked towards the ceiling, and was about to speak, but another voice interrupted the air.

"Why, hello Tilly," Mildred said, wearing a long black, silk robe that clung off her body like black oil. Underneath the hem, she sported a pair of black open-toed pumps; with toenails donned in a bright orange. "You've finally come to take care of the housekeeping?"

Pastor Reynolds turned, "No. She has a few personal matters that need addressing. I've excused her for the week."

She rolled her eyes at him, "You? The one who spends the least time at home? And Tilly, if you're deserting your responsibilities this week on such short notice, I'm sure you've managed to supply us with at least a replacement."

"I'm sorry, First Lady. I didn't have time to arrange a replacement, but I will let you know if things change," she said hurriedly, opening the door. "Is there a special church service today?" she asked, the church bell growing louder.

"No, my dear," Mildred answered, "It appears there is a situation at the church that Lisa is unable to handle. I'm sure Luther will be over there in no time to see what it's all about and supply our assistant with *assistance*."

Pastor Reynolds spoke to Tilly, while still facing Mildred, "Yes, I'm sure it is a small emergency Tilly, as the First Lady has been very perceptive in determining. I wish you God's speed to your destination, Tilly, and may the situation work itself out for you and Mark."

The bell continued to ring.

Tilly whispered, "Thank you Pastor Reynolds, and let me know what's happening at the church. Looks like you could use a week off yourself."

"We'll see you next week, Tilly," Mildred rushed.

"Yes, First Lady," she said, walking out and closing the door.

"You didn't have to rush the girl out, Mildred," Pastor Reynolds said, hand resting on the door. "She's not your indentured servant, you know."

Mildred huffed, and spun on her heels, "Aren't you tired of being the hero of so many women, *outside* of this house?"

"I'm not getting into another discussion right now, Mildred."

"Of course, you're not…you've got a bell to catch."

Part II

Benny opened the door to his condo for the tenth time this morning, in as just as many minutes. This time he looked into the eyes of Marci, her skin as dark as the braids twisted on her head, swirling around her scalp like a giant cinnamon bun. Her breasts nearly knocked him in the head a full hour before the rest of her did.

"Is it true?" she asked, stopping just beyond the door to take notice of who was inside.

He pulled her in, so he could close the door, and immediately could smell the scent of lavender. "Were you on a date this early? It's still morning."

She lifted her large wrist to her nose, "Is the perfume too strong? I was going to a brunch date later."

Benny looked amazed, "How do you manage to get dates while the sun is still out?"

"It's one more girl-on-girl secret I am not going to share. Besides, it also gives me enough time to make another date for this evening."

"Always the multi-tasker," he said as he turned to face everyone. "Marci, everyone…everyone, Marci."

There were at least fifty to sixty people greeting her in the living room alone. "I take it that the rumors are true."

He stood beside her, arms folded. "Yes, they are. My phone was ringing off the hook yesterday, and today I decided to invite everyone over."

"Did everyone get a visit…from him?"

"Mostly."

"That's a lot of folks. What is everyone saying it was?"

"Depends on what you believe in. Some are saying ghost, some spirit, some apparition, essence, vision, phantom, poltergeist, you name it."

"And no one is freaked out about this?" She asked, scratching at her cinnamon bun.

"That's the funny thing. No one was very shocked, or scared, as if his presence brought a sense of peace," he said, walking Marci into the living room.

Benny led her to one of the chairs scattered about on the floors. A tall Latina walked in their direction, carrying a tray of finger foods. She stopped in front of Marci, bending forward to offer the food.

"I just saw you come in, and wondered if you would something to nibble on? Just a few breakfast snacks I made," said the Latina, her long dark hair tied in a ponytail.

"Thanks Rosa," Benny said, taking a pigs-in-a-blanket from the tray.

Marci took a tuna-on-watercress cracker. "Yea, thanks *Rosa*. My name is Marci. I don't believe I have seen you around town. I would have remembered your beautiful gray eyes, if nothing else," she said, grinning as she chewed.

Rosa also smiled. "I work in the gift shop at the clinic."

"I'll have to get someone…anyone, a gift card there in the next few days then," Marci said, lapping her tongue at the corners of her mouth.

"Yea, do that."

Marci rubbed her hands. "That was quite delicious. Do you mind if I have another," she said, pointing at the tray, but moving her fingers slightly north, so they appeared to be pointing at Marci's breasts.

Benny quickly interjected, "Can you get us something to drink, Rosa? I have some orange juice and champagne in the fridge."

"Sure," Rosa said, grinning at Marci, before she headed back towards the kitchen.

Benny slapped Marci on the shoulder. "I thought you said you had a date later today."

She waved her hand at him dismissively, "I might need a backup plan."

"Shameful," Benny said, and was distracted by a tap on his shoulder. He turned to see a tall black guy standing behind him. It was Antonio, a mutual friend of he and Jason's.

"Hey there, Benny," he said, adjusting his thick-framed Prada glasses on his nose. "Someone just let me in, and I thought I would steal your time."

"Sure, Antonio. It has been forever. Thought you had moved to Los Angeles, to pursue that acting bug."

He smiled, "I did, and I'm visiting my family for a few weeks. I had no idea all of *this* would be going on."

"None of us did," he reached down to touch Marci, just as Rosa returned with their drinks. "Will you excuse me, Marci?"

"Sure. I'm certain Rosa can service my needs."

He rolled his eyes, "You just remember you have someplace to be."

"I'm trying to be someplace I can remember," she said with a wink.

"Oh Brother," he exhaled, and looked up at Rosa. "Be careful with this one."

"He then took Antonio's wrist, "Let's go to my bedroom, Antonio.

++++++

Inside the bedroom, Benny sat on his bed, while Antonio stood. There was a long silence between them, as both men became suddenly flooded with the memories they shared in the life and death of Jason. It was a hard time for them both; for Benny as his lover, and for Antonio as his best friend.

"You never attended the funeral, Antonio," Benny said, almost at a whisper.

Antonio looked at him, his face a mask of guilt. He began to walk in Benny's direction, around his bed, and towards the vanity mirror. "No, I didn't go. I had my clothes all laid out on the bed, still trying to accept that Jason was gone. Seeing him buried would have made it all too real for me."

"I didn't see you at Maya's funeral either, and you say you've been in town for a while?" Benny added.

Antonio turned around, leaned against the vanity, and folded his arms, "Yea, I heard what happened there. Did they say why she died?"

"The sheriff had no idea. The coroner's report was unable to find anything physically wrong with her."

"She was a wonderful woman. I talked to her about wanting to be an actor, and she gave me some names in Los Angeles to call." Antonio then walked to the corner of the bed to sit down, "I'm sorry I haven't called you, Benny. I know you must have been having a difficult time dealing with Jason's passing."

"Not to mention his second birth."

There was subdued laugh from them both.

"So, how has this whole resurrection experience been for everyone…for you in general? At least while I am here, I can give you an ear to bend."

Benny leaned back on the bed, placing his hands behind his head, and looked at Antonio. He thought he would say something very light, but looking at Antonio, was like looking at his past; a past they both shared, with people that were no longer here. "I'm hurting Antonio. I am hurting very much. I thought I was handling this, but between Jason, and Harold, and Maya, I feel like an unraveling piece of yarn."

Antonio reached out to place a hand on Benny's ankle, "I thought I saw your mask slipping out there. I've had a chance to at least escape into a new place, and into new life, and you are here dealing with so much old reality."

Benny closed his eyes and ground his teeth. "I don't know why I haven't fallen apart by now, Antonio. Jason is here, can you believe it. He is here, and his friends are celebrating his appearances as if he had gone on some long vacation. I have yet to tell him that I had cheated on him with Harold."

Antonio nodded. He remembered when Benny told him after Jason's death. He was angry for a long time but forgave him, when he saw his love for Harold was true.

"I was so busy fooling everyone, being in love with two men. Jason's death made it easier to decide which one to be with, but I am back in the same boat."

"And now that boat appears to be sinking, and you still have to make that choice."

He batted tears from his eyes, "Then why couldn't I have what is happening now? Why couldn't Jason have them both in my life?"

"Because Jason was killed, thus making your decision easier. If he had lived, he might have just died inside anyway. So, you have a chance to enjoy him now, while this thing lasts. I am not sure however, what could be going through Harold's mind."

"He's seems to be in denial about the whole thing. We had a huge argument when I tried to tell him about Jason's return."

"I am sure word had gotten back to him about all of these visitations. You guys need to talk."

Benny sat up and brought his feet around to the floor. "I'm sure," he sighed, "And how did Jason come to you?"

Antonio shook his head, and smiled, "He simply knocked at my door at the hotel. I was in shock, but Jason came up and hugged me, then said, 'Don't be scared my best friend...my very best friend. Even in the afterlife, there has been no one that I have missed more.' I continued to stand there trembling, trying to force air into my lungs."

"I think most of us, are still trying to breath."

Just then Marci opened the door, "Okay you two love birds, we need you out here."

"What are you still doing here? I thought you had a breakfast date?" Benny asked.

She shrugged, "Not to worry. I invited her over."

"Well, this is going to be an interesting morning. Now what is happening out there?"

"Well, considering Jason isn't here now, we thought it would be fun to hold a séance for him. Come on, we turned off all the lights, closed the curtains, and got the candles going."

Benny could only shake his head, "I tell you, only gay folks can create a party from any circumstance."

"I think it would be fun," Antonio said, standing. He then cupped a hand to his ear, "Do you hear that?"

Benny listened. "Is that the church bell?"

"I think it is," Marci added. "Why would it be ringing today? Is there a religious holiday of some kind?"

"No, but I don't like the sound of it," Benny said, walking to his open window, and looking out at the dome of the church, and the steeple atop it, watching the large bell rock back and forth. Its sound blaring across town, as he wondered what hope would bring this time.

Part III

Tilly found her nose pressed against the window of the car, the coldness of it sent chills along the bones of her face, past her scalp, along her spine, and down to the back of her legs. "What in God's name is going on here?"

Mark said nothing, but his breathing was so heavy that it seemed to speak languages unheard.

The parking lot of the grocery store was filled. Mark could not remember seeing it packed with so many cars. It made him wonder just how many people lived in this town.

"I'm not sure what's happening," Mark said, as he eased the car along the street and careened to the back of the store. "It looks like people were preparing for the end of the world."

Cars were lined up like scattered toys. People walked over vehicles, yelled at each other, frantic children and parents carried bags of groceries, clerks tried to create some sort of order from the chaos, only to end up being altogether ignored, as customers created their own routes into and out of the store.

Beyond the large building's windows, he could see even more mayhem occurring, with scattered police cars gathering out front (meaning there could only be pandemonium within).

He parked the car a few yards away from the dock, his mind still trying to comprehend what was happening while looking in Tilly's direction. When she turned to look at him, her eyes veered away for a moment, and hung there in confusion; a signal: *someone is coming this way.*

He turned to see a rather large man trotting in their direction. His arms were waving above his head, while his thick round-rimmed glasses bounced upon his nose. His wispy hair draped thinly about his pale sweaty forehead. Sweat also covered the white dress shirt that hung half-tucked on his frame. Mark recognized him as Mr. Nelson Starks, the manager of this Bag-A-Bargain Grocery Store.

"My man Mark," he said, as he ran up to Mark's window, "Don't ask me what happened around here. The two other big stores in town are getting this same craziness. People are on a buying frenzy; short on conversation, and long on grocery spending. The delivery trucks didn't show at all this morning, and no one has been able to get a hold of the distributors…"

There were other words that Mr. Starks spat out, as his breath and verbiage seemed to comingle, and Mark was lost trying to decipher the first few words of this diatribe.

"…I have started to limit the amount of groceries that people can buy, at least until I can figure out what is happening with the deliveries, and the police are trying to make sure no one steals, or abuses the clerks…"

"Is it that bad in there?" Mark said, looking briefly at Tilly.

Mr. Starks eased himself down, if only to get a better look at the passenger, then continued without addressing her, "Yes, but not as bad as it was earlier this morning. I called you because I am going to need some help keeping the inventory we have in the warehouse in check, and for you to let me know when we get below a certain level." He raked his fingers through his thin hair, "And I am paying triple-time for your trouble."

Mark turned to Tilly, as if hoping she would make a decision for him, but instead heard himself ask, "How long do you think this will be, Mr. Starks? You said on the phone, that you only needed me for a few hours."

"I do…for now, but you can decide to come back later if you want."

Mark addressed Tilly, "Do you mind if I go in there for an hour or two?"

"Hell yea! It's looking pretty scary out here," she said, at a rather controlled whisper.

He placed a hand on her shoulder, "I won't be long, and the warehouse is right next to the dock. I'll be able to see you from there, and you can come and get me too," then he lowered his voice a bit more, "and this will give me a chance to get some groceries for our families."

She thought about that, and slowly nodded herself into agreement.

"And I have Nelson coming in to help you. He should be here in about thirty minutes."

Mark turned towards Mr. Starks, "Okay, I get it, Mr. Starks. Don't worry. I'll be back there in a few minutes, okay," he said, his subsequent silence and stare gave Mr. Starks all the answers he needed, and he walked away.

Mark slowly opened his door, and spoke without turning to look at Tilly, "I promise I won't be long. I really want to thank you for driving up here with me."

She leaned back in her seat, taking out her cell phone, "You are very lucky I like you, but hurry, because I'm counting the minutes here."

He closed the door and walked away, and Tilly was grateful for the solitude. It gave herself a chance to process this situation among the honking horns, screeching tires, loud voices, and police bullhorns, along with grave robbers, missing delivery trucks, ghost stories from Carl, and now calamity at the grocery store…what did it all mean?

And as Tilly leaned back in her seat, she considered calling Pastor Reynolds. She looked outside of the driver's side window, to see a white woman; long ebony hair pushed into a bandana on her head – who glanced in her direction. She carried a bundle at her shoulder the shape of a small child. She was craned forward, eyes squinting at Tilly.

Maybe she's trying to figure out what was happening in the store, and not really looking in this direction, Tilly thought, *or maybe she's waiting for someone inside the store.* Tilly looked at her phone but reconsidered; *Carl has been through more than enough*, she thought, and placed her phone in her lap.

She turned to glance back at the woman and nearly screamed; she had was now at her window!

She tapped on the glass, "Excuse me," she said, her voice barely audible past the thick pane.

Tilly rolled the window down scarcely an inch. "Is there something I can help you with?" She asked.

The woman came closer. The movements beyond the cloth were unmistakable. A child was there. "I'm sorry if I startled you, but I was so afraid to come over. I didn't know when the young man would return."

Was she thinking to break into the car? Tilly thought, trying to size up this woman, "You thought the car was empty until you saw me?"

She moved the unseen child to her other shoulder. "No, not exactly. I was hoping someone was here."

"For what?" Tilly questioned, her eyes captivated at the familiarity of this woman. It was as if she remembered her.

"What's happening at the grocery store? I was about to head over there; but with all the police and people rushing in and out, I thought there was an accident. Would you happen to know what's was going on?"

"I'm sorry I don't. I think they're here because there might be a shortage on…groceries, I guess." She thought about that statement, and how it didn't make the situation sound any more hopeful.

"Is that why your friend went in there; to see what was going on?"

"I suppose," she said, hoping this stranger wasn't thinking about waiting with her until Mark returned. "But I'm not sure how long they will be. I plan to leave and come back later."

"I see," she said, moving the child from her shoulder to the next. "Maybe I'll do the same, and perhaps things will have calmed down a bit more."

"Good idea," Tilly remarked, but her eyes became focused on the child. "Is it a boy or girl?"

"A boy," the woman said, offering nothing more. "You know, I have a confession to make, Tilly."

"What?" Tilly said, caught off guard with the mention of her name. "Do I know you?"

"We have seen each other, briefly," she said, as she looked back at the entrance of the store as another police car approached.

Tilly tried to recall but couldn't seem to place her anywhere. "Really? This is a small town for the most part. Are you sure it was me?"

"Back at the cemetery," she said.

And that's when she remembered her, when she saw her grandma staring out the car's window, staring at a woman on a bench holding a child…this child. She closed the window, looked out to see any sign of Mark. "That's nice," Tilly said, looking over to see the car keys left for her in the seat. "I saw you sitting in the cemetery, but I wouldn't call it a meeting."

"I suppose," this woman said, walking around the car, observing Tilly as she maneuvered into the driver's seat. "Don't go, Tilly. There's nothing to fear."

How is it that she could hear this woman so clearly, even with the windows closed? "That's nice…I'm not scared."

"Wait…I just need to quickly speak with you, Tilly."

"Stop saying my name as if you know me. How did you get that information? Why were you just sitting in the cemetery? Did you sneak in the back gate? The front should have still been closed. You homeless and need some money? You will have better luck going to Springfield, or even Chicago."

"God no, I'm not here for any of that. I have all that I could ever need."

The confidence in her voice caused Tilly to pause for a moment. Maybe she had gone to the cemetery before Audrey could close it and discovered the grave of a loved one had been tampered with. "Are you here about the graves?"

"You could say that?" she said.

That would explain why Tilly had seen her at the cemetery. But that still didn't explain why this woman had known her name, so she rolled the window down a bit more. "I really don't care at this point. I'm sorry. I made a resolution not to talk to any crazy folks this year. So, you're going to have to move away from this car, before you or your baby get hurt."

"I just needed to see you up close, to look at you. That's all," the woman said.

"And you've looked," she said, fumbling with the keys to get them in the ignition.

Then something slipped from the blanket; an arm fell out. A most dark, black, arm.

Tilly was frozen, fixed upon this image – maybe even transfixed. She didn't know what came across her breath, but fear caused her to speak; words of concern and confusion. The woman quickly hoisted the arm back into the confines of the blanket.

"Sorry about that. A bit startling, I know. Even in this day and age, seeing a white woman with a black child, can raise a few eyebrows."

What she said may have been true, Tilly thought, but white or not, she was still the shade of crazy – a crazy with a child in her arms…*if* that was her child at all. "No need to be sorry," Tilly said, regaining her movement, "I am still on a non-crazy goal for the year."

The engine started, and this woman slapped her hand on the roof of the car, "I need to talk to someone in your family. That's all. I need you to let them know I am here. I thought she may have passed on, but she was not there at the cemetery. I was told she lived here."

Tilly reached for the drive stick, "I don't have time to listen to you lady."

"But it's a message for Jenna: your grandmother."

Tilly rolled her window down a little more. "What do you know about my grandmother? You don't know anything about her, and if you try to harm her…"

"I do know her, Tilly, just as she knows me. She will tell you. Just say that Ella was asking for her."

Tilly could remember her grandma looking at this woman when they drove through the cemetery that day; a very intense look. "Okay…who should I say you are? How does my grandma know you, Ms. Ella?"

She didn't crack a smile when she spoke. "Why…I'm her daughter."

Chapter 8

Part I

And so, it begins, Pastor Reynolds thought, as he pulled into the driveway of the church, sweat covering his brow like unwanted dew. Mildred had decided to go with him, and was now sitting next to him, silently - *that in itself was a small miracle.*

"My God, what is happening here? Look at all of the cars in the lot,"

Mildred said, rubbing her neck nervously. "How many people could be in the church?"

Luther could barely hear his wife, with so many internal conversations vying for his attention. He didn't quite know how to prepare himself for an ordeal of this nature. He could not remember dealing with the possibility of renewed spirits, disrupted television signals, endless mayhem, and a more-than-maniacal wife, as being a part of his ministerial studies. He was also finding it hard to deal with the resurfaced memories of only a few days ago, when he presided over Maya's funeral.

As these thoughts distracted him, Mildred had already stepped out of the car, and was tapping on his windshield. "No time to sit there and keep the seat warm, Luther. The sooner we get in there, the sooner we can find out what preventable drama Lisa must be going through."

He looked up at the large bell tower above the church. Mildred was right, and despite what drama had already happened, this may be just another twist in the yarn. So, he gathered his composure, reached for the handle of his door, and slowly stepped out of the car to join his wife. He stood there for a moment, preparing himself internally. "Okay, let's go."

"Wait," Mildred said, pointing towards the church.

From the rear of the church, he could see Lisa running in their direction. Her shoes were off, and her hair looked like pulled grass. Her eyes were wide, frightened, and he could hear her breathing long before she had reached them.

"Thank God you're here," she said, her words battling with her breath for space. "This is too much for me to handle. I tried calling some of the staff, tried calling you on the phone, but had to just ring the bell and hope someone would come."

At this point, Lisa's focus was mainly on the Pastor - she had not addressed the First Lady. "Lisa, what is going on here?" Mildred asked.

She looked at Mildred, her eyes vacant, as if she were slowly realizing that Mildred was present. "First Lady!" she said, with more emphasis than needed. "It's so unreal in there. I had been waiting back there, hoping to see your car pull up. Some of the ushers came in to help with the crowd. I was trying to call the police, but by then the fighting had stopped outside. It's a little calmer now than it was…"

Mildred grabbed the woman's arm in such a grip, that it began to turn red around Mildred's fingers. "Calm down, Lisa. You're rambling. Take some time to collect yourself." Mildred then released her.

Lisa watched Mildred's hand, as if it were something foreign to her. Her breathing slowed, and she unclenched her balled up fingers. "The church; it has more people in there than I have ever seen. A few came in yesterday to pray; and more this morning, and then before I knew it, we were running out of space. Etta James came in with her son and said nothing. Murray Lipton from the hardware store came in wearing pajamas. Chrissie Ashton came in with her twin girls, eyes red as a cherry, as if they had been crying for hours."

"But Lisa, that's a bell, not a telephone. Do you know how much attention that could bring, only because people want to have some prayer time?" Mildred said, her tone very condescending.

"Mildred, give Lisa some room here. Can't you see that she's very upset," Luther said.

She looked at him harshly. "We've all been a little on upset, and on edge lately, Luther. I'm just trying to get to the point here."

"And I am sure Lisa is getting there," he said turning to address Lisa. "Now, take your time and tell us what's happening in there," he said reaching to smooth out her hair.

Mildred reached out to stop him and pulled his arm back down at his side. Luther could only shake his head.

"These people are not just praying. They are in some deep reverence. They came into church as if they *had* to pray, as if their life depended on it. I have never seen this before, such blind subjection to prayer. They asked me nothing, however they did inquire if you were going to be here. That's it. I thought to say no but realized that this wasn't actually a question at all, but a statement, a request, a desire."

"Yes, there have been some things I have seen that I had not been familiar with too, Lisa. Maybe we will get a better idea once we go inside," Mildred said.

Lisa looked from the Pastor to his wife, "Yes, I think that would be better," and as they headed for the church, she continued to describe the people she had seen, and what they were doing.

Luther tried to listen to every word as Lisa frantically explained the situation; but in truth, he was having the hardest time concentrating at all, as his mind attempted to prepare for the unknown. When he reached the church, traveling through its small array of offices and hallways leading to the back of the stage, he was met with such heat, that he knew the place had to be filled to capacity.

From the back of the choir stand; where the curtain separated the main sanctuary from the back offices of the church, Luther looked out unto the crowd. So many people, so many nationalities, so many ages, so many expressions of worship; hands clasped together in prayer, raised in praise, palms pressed against the floor in abdication. The low rumble of the voices had such a tone of desperation, as if a common sorrow had shrouded the place.

"It has been like this all morning," Lisa said over his shoulder. "It's as if they are all seeking the same answer. Answers I could not give them."

"And some of them were asking for me?" Luther asked.

"Yes…many of them," she replied.

"I hope I can give them some solace, but at this time I'm not sure if even I have the answers they are looking for," he said, stepping from behind the curtain and unto the stage. His shoes could be heard clacking against the wood. The deep, steady sound caused one head to look up…

…then another,

…then another,

…then another.

"Pastor Reynolds?" came a whisper from within the crowd, and then an arm slowly raised, attached to a small old woman with white hair and bleached features.

"Mrs. Bailey?" Luther whispered, as he neared the edge of the stage where she was standing. "Yes, it's me."

There were tears in her eyes, and they followed the same dried course that previous tears had left. "What's going on, Pastor? Why did Henry visit me? What have I done?"

He thought for a moment. Henry was her husband, dead almost two years now. He reached out to grab Mrs. Bailey's hand. Her grip was very strong. "It's what I'm going to try and find out. I do hope that you're okay."

She nodded and produced a tiny smile.

"I suppose I am, Pastor. I suppose I should have been scared, but I wasn't. I'd been missing him so much lately, so you think, maybe that's why I'm having these visions?"

"Pastor?"

Luther looked up, and behind Mrs. Bailey stood another man, his thin brown hair falling across his forehead, large bags hugged his tired eyes. It was Aaron Stanley; he owned a small hot dog stand near the center of town. His tiny Asian wife stood beside him, holding his arm. "Yes, Aaron," the Pastor replied.

Aaron walked up beside Mrs. Bailey, and turned to look at her, "Hello, Mrs. Bailey."

She nodded, "Aaron, it's good to see you again." She let go of the Pastor's hand and reached out to touch her fingers lightly upon the shoulder of Aaron's wife, "Good to see you also, my dear."

Aaron's wife gave a simple nod.

"Do you know what's happening, Pastor? My wife and I saw Lindsey yesterday. My wife went to the garage to clean out a few things, and there Lindsey was, playing paddle ball like she used to."

Luther glanced over at his wife, and she caught his glimpse for only a second before diverting her attention to the floor. Lindsey, age seven, was one of the school children to die in the school bus accident those few years ago. "What did your wife end up doing, Aaron?"

He looked in her direction for a split moment. Her eyes remained downcast, her mouth pursed inward. He hugged her closer while he spoke, "Mia simply brought her into the house, fed her a sandwich, and then made her some chocolate chip cookies. I came home and stood at the doorway. I could not move past the smell of those cookies. She hasn't cooked something like that since Lindsey passed. I went up to her room, and opened the door, and there she was, sleeping, with an empty plate covered with cookie crumbs sitting on the nightstand near her bed. I'm not sure how long I stood there, just looking at her, wanted this...this dream, to continue forever. When I went to her room the next morning, she was gone."

Luther was unable to speak for a moment. He looked at Mrs. Bailey and saw that her lips were moving in silent prayer. "I'm really trying to understand all of this myself, Aaron. I'm sure God has a plan, however He has yet to reveal it to me." Someone touched his shoulder suddenly, and he looked back to see Lisa and Mildred standing there.

"What can we do, Pastor," Lisa whispered, "There are so many people here."

He looked back at Aaron and his wife, to notice that beyond them, the congregation was slowly beginning to form a line. The line was threatening to not only lead out of the church doors, but it could very well wrap around the building a few times. He then responded to Lisa, "Me and the First Lady are just going to have to remain here and talk to as many people as we can. All we can do now is listen and attempt to console them. In doing that, I hope that an answer will come. I think most of these people are confused and want a small assurance that what they have seen has been real."

"And is it?" Lisa asked.

"I'm afraid so, Lisa. I'm afraid so.

Part II

Jenna slowly hung up the phone; Tilly's voice could still be heard on the other end just before she rested it on its cradle. She tried to hear everything the girl had to say, but the strength it took to even hold the phone any longer was impossible after hearing what she said. She stood there, immobile, trying to rewind the conversation in her mind, just to validate its reality.

"So, what did the girl have to talk about this time?" Nathan asked, as he sat on the sofa in the family room, which was just a short hallway and a sliding glass door away from the kitchen, where Jenna was standing. He was flipping through a magazine.

Jenna continued to say nothing, her fingers twirling around the cord of the phone, her eyes staring into space.

Nathan looked up at her, "What's going on old woman? We need to go out and shop for a hearing aid for you, or do you just need a swab to grind out that ear wax?"

Jenna looked around the room, as if going over a conversation in her own head, and then she looked at her husband, "Tilly said there was a mad rush of people at the grocery store where Mark works. When Mark went inside, she said some crazy woman came up to her while she was still in the car."

He dropped the magazine in his lap, "You mean to tell me that Mark left Tilly in the car by herself? I knew that boy was no good and irresponsible. Do we have to go out there to get her? I tell you, the lighter the skin, the crazier they are."

Jenna walked over to the sofa and sat beside Nathan. "The girl is okay. The woman left, but as they were talking, she said something very strange."

Nathan went back to reading his magazine, "What did she say, Jenna? Did she use one of those young folk words that you can't figure out? Run it by me, maybe I can figure it out for you."

"It's not what she said, but what this lady told her."

"Crazy old women can say just about anything," he then looked at Jenna, "And you better than anyone should know that." There was a grin on his face.

"This isn't funny Nathan!"

Nathan looked at her wide-eyed. His wife was nervously rubbing her thigh, she maintained no eye contact, her breathing was very uneven, and he could hear it through her nose. No, this was no laughing matter, and further from a joke than he realized.

So, he waited.

He had been married to Jenna long enough, to realize that some conversations needed time to be discussed, and Jenna's silence, this deep silence, caused Nathan to be concerned at what she was about to reveal.

Finally, she spoke. "Tilly said the woman she spoke to was a relative of mine. Her name was, Ella."

Nathan looked in Jenna's direction, staring at her lips, as if to make sure what she had said had really come from her. "What did you say?"

"She said that her name was Ella. Do you know what this means Nathan?"

It was a rhetorical question, and although there was a reply sitting on Nathan's lips, he swallowed it back. "That can't be right. You must have misunderstood the child."

She leaned over to grab his arm, "No, no, she sounded too confident. This was a white woman, Nathan. Ella was a white woman, in this town, and I am sure she was the right age. Can you imagine what this means?"

Nathan stood up, forcing Jenna to break the grip. "I'm not listening to another word Jenna. Tilly is going to have to explain this to us when she gets home. I need to hear the full story."

Jenna looked at her husband curiously, "But Nathan…"

"Jenna, I'm tired. I am going to lie down. I really don't have time to discuss the conversations of you and a young woman that must clearly be confused, or in shock. We'll talk more about this when Tilly gets home, okay."

Jenna felt as if she had been struck. "Sure Nathan," and once she said that, she watched him storm past her, and into his bedroom; the closing of the door shook the rafters. She looked at that closed door as if it were a time machine revealing her past. He was angry, and she understood why; just as she understood her joy. There was pain in their past; pain they both thought would not come back to haunt them, but suddenly it had…

…and Jenna, looking into that time machine, could see that past one again, as well as the story that went along with it…

…she remembered a time when there was less sorrow in this town, although danger still sprouted up at times like untamed weeds. She remembered a time when she was much younger, when she lived her life in rebellion. Rebellion of what was expected of her.

It cost her dearly to live so.

Her family was very wealthy, because the land surrounding Crest Hill County was rich in oil. Her family had land there, and the mansion in which she lived offered Jenna many opportunities other blacks in Crest Hill County could only deposit in their pillows as hopeful dreams.

Jenna, being only 14, was really quite unaware of her opportunities; and her choices in life reflected this. She was a tomboy of sorts, besting most boys her age in sports one would consider unbecoming a girl of her upbringing. Because of this, and the many men that appeared to always be in her company, she was thought of as a loose woman. There were even rumors that she may have been a lesbian; but that was quickly dispelled when a group of such girls tried to force her into joining their ranks, and the doctor had told these girls, that because of the beating that they took from Jenna, their stitches would take weeks to heal.

As a young teenager, she had a male friend that she liked very much; Nathan Ross Reed was his name, and while she was very rich, Nathan was very poor. He was sweet, trustworthy, and honest with her, which was something that she found rare of anyone she had known. She worried about this friendship, because while Jenna was content with their associations with each other, she could tell that Nathan wanted more. She was content to call him boyfriend. Her family, to say the least, was appalled; as well as ashamed, and in their efforts to reform Jenna, they sent her to Springfield for private schooling. They also hoped that while attending high school in a more distinguished establishment, miles away from her own home town, she would also find a more proper suitor to call, her boyfriend.

Each summer she would come home, and each summer she would see Nathan. Her attending a private school so far out of the area made her more hated and envied in the community, and to make matters worse, her tomboy ways never seemed to leave her. When she was only 17 years old, a group of boys attempted to accost her after what seemed a friendly game of basketball. It had been quite late, and the park they played in wasn't lit very well. It was rumored later that there had been talk about town by the local white boys that they wanted to see just how loose Jenna could be. On that night, they had intended to find out.

So on that night, five boys attempted to rape Jenna; two of them succeeded. She could only remember leaving the court after playing a game of free-throw with a group of local boys. She walked away; the sound of the basketball was replaced with the sound of steady whispers. She looked back once to see those five guys standing in the middle of the court, huddled under a single floodlight (one of only a few that were working in the park that night). Soon those whispers were replaced by footsteps, and before she could react, there was a blow to her back that sent her to her knees, and another one pushing her to the ground.

Her ears burned with words that scared her, of things they wanted to do to her, of how uppity she acted for a *Negro*, and how she tried to show off all the time. She tried to scream, but someone turned her around, and tossed a coat on her eyes. She could feel hands pressed against her face, the rough denim of the jacket that was thrown on her, had pressed heavily against her lips, muffling her, suffocating her. She could feel hands all over her; sweaty, cold hands, with calloused palms and chipped nails. She tried to swing, but her hands were held down. She tried to kick, but her ankles were pulled apart. She could feel those cold hands on her breasts, pulling at her panties, forcing their way into her warmth.

She could feel consciousness slipping away from her, as darkness and heat enveloped her. She could feel her womanhood being probed, pushed inward, a sharp, twisting pain took hold of her like never before, sliding roughly against her skin, losing itself deep within her, and when she thought it had ended, it was replaced by another.

Then suddenly - she could not remember when - the coat slid from her face, and cool air rushed into her heaving lungs. Tears blurred her vision, but she could see shadows moving before her, amidst shouts and curses. There was fighting around her. Someone was swinging a baseball bat…someone she knew! The light flickered above for just a moment, but it was enough for her to catch a glimpse of this – batman – and she saw that it was Nathan.

She blacked out at that point.

She awoke listening to Nathan's heartbeat as she rested on his chest. She could feel him rubbing her shoulder, and she remained still, the reality of that night being recalled back to her in what felt like an instant. He must have realized she was awake, because she remembered his hands ceased rubbing her, and he began to talk; telling her about the fight, about taking off his shirt and running it under the water fountain to clean her off, about dragging her to a safe part of the park, a dark secluded section, in case they returned. What he didn't tell her was how they attacked him, took that bat from him for a moment and cracked it across his legs.

He must have suffered the pain as he walked her home to a pair of very angry parents, who charged him with blatant accusations of neglect for bringing their daughter home at such an hour, claiming to have called the police (but those were times where such a call would not have been heeded for a rich little black girl who had a reputation for getting into trouble). Nathan apologized and took the abuse as if he'd deserved it.

It was at that moment that Jenna secretly fell in love with Nathan.

That love blossomed, and luckily it did, because not long after, Jenna visited an out of town clinic, and received the news that she was pregnant. This incident propelled into a series of incidents that would forever change Jenna's life. She first talked this over with Nathan; whom everyone in town assumed Jenna was going steady with, and reassured her that he would always stand by any decision she made.

Her decision had become simple: she would tell her parents, and just as she predicted, they suggested she get an immediate abortion. They were sure that Nathan was the father, and with his lack of adequate education and dark skin tone, would only be a burden as anyone's father or caregiver. Jenna thought differently however, and told her parents there was no way she was going through something as horrid as an abortion; there were very few doctors that would admit a colored girl for a procedure like that, no matter what amount of money was offered. They insisted she take the risk, rather than put the family through the shame of a pregnant, unwed daughter.

Her parents were a proud pair: Matilda & Verdel Jenkins. They were like a pair of stone monoliths whose money made them more than what they actually were; a Negro couple that got very lucky, and who tried to raise their only daughter as if she were of another race besides their own. This became the irony of why she never told them of the way she found herself with child. As white as they tried to make her, it would have been an utter shock to realize that in truth, her child could come out in that most cherished hue.

Jenna decided that the best thing to do was to leave town, take a train up to Springfield, finish her schooling there, have the baby, and make a decision then: if the child was white, she would give it away – there would be trouble to boot if she was to think of raising such a child at those times. If the child were black, she would keep it, and talk to her parents into accepting their grandchild before returning home.

So, one night, she left with Nathan, who'd insisted on being with her (his own parents, consisting of a drunk mother, and an invisible father, barely noticed him at home most of the time), so she could have someone she could trust watching over her. She wrote letters to her parents about her decision to have the child out of the city to relieve them of any shame and give the child away when time came fit to do so (even though she had already decided to keep it).

When the time came for her to deliver, she hired a local midwife to deliver the child, and to the astonishment of the four souls present (her, Nathan, The Midwife, and the Witness – a colored waitress from the diner they frequented), Jenna had twins; fraternal - both girls - one black, and the other white. Her decision became simple, and she would keep the black girl, and have Nathan send the white one to the orphanage on the north side of town.

When Jenna informed her parents that she was not only keeping the child, but she had also decided to marry Nathan to keep the child legitimate, her parents took it upon themselves to pay for both of their educations in Chicago – Jenna wanted to study to be a teacher, and Nathan a builder. In fact, it was he that had directed the construction of the New Sheldon Hills Grammar School Jenna was to soon teach at in Crest Hill.

When her daughters had been born, she looked at the one she would give away, and scrawled on a piece of chewing gum wrapper, the child's name, rolled it up, and tied it with a few slick strands of the child's hair. The name was Ella.

She had not heard that name mentioned again in all her years of living...

...that is until now.

She sat there on the sofa; Nathan's snores were already making their mark on the silent, stilled air. She eased back upon the down filled cushions, her hand absentmindedly turning the pages of the magazine Nathan had left behind. It was a sports magazine, displaying a basketball player on the cover; body cascaded in an aura of stadium lights. She glanced back at her husband's bedroom and thought perhaps he still dreamed of himself as a star basketball player – dreams that were dashed on that night he saved her, and suffered a broken leg he would never recover completely from. It was a basketball court where they had first met, she was using his bicycle pump to fill her basketball. She thought he was sweet, and on that afternoon, she played him in a game of free throw, and he became the only man she ever let beat her.

Ella was coming back, and that thought gave her the hope that even tragedy can lead to moments of inexplicable joy.

Part III

Too many Eric's is all that Erica could think about as she felt a cool breeze flutter through her hair.

Her name was Erica.

Her son's name was Eric Jr.

Her husband's name was Eric Sr. (she was every so grateful that he too wasn't a Junior).

This union in names, was cute when they were at the height of their honeymoon years, and the thought of their like names seemed gooey sweet like pulled taffy. Now, the novelty of those names, left her feeling bitter and vacant, considering that both the Eric's who shared her life, had left her to deal with a life, without them.

And now that was all changing.

She stood silently, the solace of her thoughts were becoming her only reference of reality. Eric was at her side, holding her hand; the feel of his fingers was slightly cool, almost clammy, like meat accidentally left on the counter.

"Are you scared?" he asked, as they stood silently in the backyard, the sun glistened atop the moist grass.

"Yes," she replied without thinking.

"Don't be. He's expecting you."

"That's what I'm afraid of," Erica said, his words holding little consolation for her. She could feel the coolness squeeze her hand tighter, pulling slightly on her arm and shoulder. She regarded the action with a simple glance in her husband's direction, and then she continued to look around, to see Timothy sitting on the back steps of the house, bare feet tapping the worn wood, as he raised his hands just above his eyebrows, and slowly shook his head.

"The boy will come around soon," Eric said, as if reading Timothy's disapproval.

"He hates you, you know," Erica said, glancing at him again, before looking back upon the horizon.

"He only hates me for leaving you."

"I hate you for that too, you know."

He turned to look at her, his eyes darting over her face for a moment, as if he were admiring a work of art. Then he turned to look straight ahead again, "And I see you were able to come around quickly. I trust Timothy will too." He then took a small step forward.

Erica remained grounded, her arm carried forward within Eric's grip. She didn't know if she were as ready for this as she'd thought.

"You have to be brave," her husband said, looking back at her with those inquisitive hazel eyes. "We don't have the luxury of wasting time, Erica. I don't know how long we have to be here…with you. What is happening in Crest Hill, is not supposed to happen, and eventually it won't."

She swallowed dryly, working her jaws to well up more moisture in her suddenly desert-like jowls. "It's just that I have been dealing with this in my dreams for so long, Eric."

"Dreams are a bit more pleasant than what you were having."

She didn't respond. He was right. She had begun to regard the backs of her eyelids as something evil, only projecting visions she thoroughly disliked. Sleep had not been the solitude it had once served when she would lay awake crying for her husband to return. Sleep had betrayed her lately.

She stared out at her spacious backyard, with its lush greenery spitting up a colony of free-flying insects that distracted her focus. In the distance she could see a wide wooden tool shed where Eric had spent a lot of his time fixing up and rearranging. This lay to the right, along her iron fence, and behind it was a small pear tree preparing to give its shade once the sun reached its crest. She turned her vision a few paces to the left, where the barbecue deck stood, two tiers high, with two benches, and a huge brick oven that spanned out to either side at a concave shape dipping at its ends to form two more sitting areas. Further to the left there was a small play area: sandbox, slide, and inflatable pool sitting there empty and riddled with debris. Back to the right, beyond the barbecue deck, was a large oak tree, its thick branches like mangled fingers reaching out towards the sky. Along its trunk were a series of horizontal planks that trailed up to is knotted hands, revealing the entryway to a large tree house, the purple curtains she made still hung out over the sill like a lazy tongue. It housed little more than a small cedar trunk, two stump chairs, a plastic Playschool Activity Desk, a mirror and a shoebox filled with miniature toys, and an assortment of coloring books.

Timothy never enjoyed that tree house as much as Eric Jr. but then it stood to reason, considering Timothy had never really asked Santa Clause for it. Timothy had also never asked for the tire swing, whose thick chains still rested across the one sturdy branch that projected oddly from the tree itself. Erica followed the chain down, but it became lost in the hill that pushed up slightly in her backyard where the barbecue stand was, and beyond it a small picnic area; both of which had actually stood unfinished since Eric's departure. She looked back at the chain hanging from the tree; the thick fused metal appeared to sparkle a bit as the sun reflected upon its interlocking loops. Since the death of her son, she had come out here on many windy nights, watching as the chain danced in the moonlight, as if it were once again alive with the delight of her son's actions. But it had never been him.

Now…as she sat motionless, limply holding unto Eric's hands, she closed her eyes, testing the air, sensing its stillness, and when she opened her eyes, it continued just as it had before. The chain was swinging, with a slow, steady rhythm…yet there was no wind.

"Promise me that everything is going to be okay, Eric," she asked, her dry throat straining to push the words forward. She then took a tentative step in his direction, as if Lego blocks loosely held her ankles together.

"I can't promise you that, but I can promise you that I will be right by your side…this time."

She smiled, pulling on his hand, as she leaned in closer to him, their shoulders resting against one another. "Guess that will have to do."

They both stood at the edge of the gravel walkway that surrounded the house, they were but one step away from the grass, and a tiny rock walkway, whose edges were crowded by overgrowth. Eric started the trek, and when his wife followed, he could hear her breath suddenly rush into her lungs as if she were taking an ocean plunge. He slowed his pace.

Erica felt as if she had stepped from her backyard into a grassy marshland that would suddenly pull her down into its murkiness. She took another step into the unknown; an unknown she was still not believing but was accepting without question. She began accepting what Eric had told her, shortly after he arrived, when she accused him of not being there. Then she told him about their son's death and he stood there quietly…too quiet.

He then said that, *he knew*. He said he knew about his son's death, and she felt as if she had been slapped with the side of an office building. That was when she called Pastor Reynolds to come over, but later realized she should have called an exorcist. Later that evening, she talked with Eric about their son, and what he claimed to know. He began to tell her about her son, not as she knew him on Earth, but as he had met him, in the afterlife. Son talked with dad and was able to tell him about mom, about her pain; about his brother Timothy, who cried all the time, and he began to tell his father how he too had died. How his mother talked with him, how tired she looked, how they shared the last stick of bubble gum she had in her purse…and about the crash.

She listened to him and said nothing.

She listened to him and accepted.

Now, as they walked in a backyard, overgrown with the grass a certain teenager forgot to include in his daily chores, she realized once again, she was heading towards acceptance. She was heading out to meet with her son, Eric Jr., at his favorite place on earth: a tire swing which swung right near his very own tree house.

Erica stopped. His laughter. She could hear his laughter, giddy and fast. She could hear the snap of the chain as it arched through the air. But it was that laughter that made her stop.

"Be strong Erica," came her husband's voice, direct and commanding.

"I'm trying, Eric, truly I am."

"Remember, he wants to see you too. He wants to see you again, just like you want to see him."

She lowered her head, making sure she was still on solid ground. "Yea, I understand that, but I never thought that day would come in *this* life."

"Then consider yourself to be a very lucky woman. You can enjoy this moment, and use it as a replacement for all those horrid memories of the accident, of the guilt, of the pain you've been putting on yourself. He's returned back here to life, so you can start living with his death."

Eric's words rolled from her memory as letters strung together in an attempt to comfort her; it did little to achieve that. She didn't know why this was happening, or whether it was supposed to. What she did know however, was that sometimes your only comfort is grief, which you wear like a collar, as it guides and controls you, and keeps you trapped, instead of allowing you to take responsibility in the mourning process – where the freedom of grief lies.

So Erica stood there, hugging herself, her once broad even steps, becoming tinier and unsure.

Then she saw the top of his head swing across her view, and nearly screamed. She covered her eyes, letting go of Eric's hand, and retreated into the darkened familiarity of her shadowed palms. Her hyperventilating lungs cut off her sobs.

She could feel Eric's fingers pull at hers, one by one, very gently; reclaiming the grip she had before. She could feel the heartbeat of the veins in his hand; it was slowing…or was that hers? She lowered her other hand to her side, and looked back at the head, which became a face, that swung to her left, only to fall back out of view again. It was a face with a smile, tiny teeth brimming behind pulled lips. He had not seen her yet; his eyebrows were pushed forward, contorted by his effort at concentration.

Head became shoulders, and that became waist, became knees, became feet. He was wearing the same stripped red shirt and khaki pants he had at the moment he died. This caused Erica to shed more tears than she realized could come out of her face. "My Baby," her lips mumbled, "God, I'm so sorry." She stepped past Eric this time, letting go of his hand. She was close enough to reach out and touch him.

He turned to see her, "Mommy! I didn't see you there. I was trying to go higher this time. Did you see me?"

She nodded as if her neck was constructed by Slinky wire, "Yes, honey, I saw you. You were really going high that time. You must be getting stronger."

He let his legs hang, letting his momentum ebb, "I know. I was really *consecrating* this time," and then he held out an arm to curl it, as he made a fist. "See, my muscles are getting stroooooonger!"

She smiled, reaching out to press her fingers on his tiny muscle, "Yea, it must be because of all of that *consecrating,* you're doing." Then, before she knew it, she stepped around the swing to face him, and instinctively hugged him. She exhaled. "And how are you doing, baby. Is everything okay?"

He waited until she released him, his mannerism very nonchalant. "I'm doing okay, mommy," he then turned to notice Eric, and waved slightly. "Hi

Daddy. Look, Mommy is here. Did you see her?"

He crossed his arms across his chest, and nodded with a slight grin, "I sure did. She still looks beautiful, don't she? I know you mentioned how you missed seeing mommy, because she was the best-looking mommy of all time."

Eric Jr. brought his arms up to crisscross atop his head, and he closed his eyes, "Noooooo...I didn't say that, Daddy. You said you weren't gonna tell her I said that," he said, lowering his arms, his lips poked out.

"You know I didn't say that, Eric Jr. 'cause it is sooooooo true. Mommy likes to know you think she is beautiful."

His features seemed to smooth back into it childlike innocence, his wide eyes sweeping in the direction of his mother in an overly exaggerated motion. "Is that true mommy?"

"It sure is, honey," she said, unable to speak for a moment, as if she were watching a stage play acted out for her enjoyment. "It sure is."

He nodded as if he understood this, and began to swing his legs again a little, "Are we gonna have lunch in the tree house today, Mommy? Are we?"

"Of course, we are. Peanut Butter and Bologna?"

"Yes Mommy, Peanut Butter and Bologna."

Part IV

Benny walked into the salon and could have sworn a tumbleweed had crossed his path. It had been that way on the streets as he drove here; an emptiness both barren and silent.

Even the smell of the Clips n' Snips salon was void of the relaxer, shampoo, and iron scents he was used to.

He looked around and notice that the receptionist was absent again, while two customers sat on the bench near the window, another was in a chair getting a color treatment, and one stylist; Judy (no last name please), was speaking to a new customer Benny hadn't seen before.

Judy (no last name) was a rather lean, very tall white girl from Alabama. She had striking red hair, and an army of freckles that started at one cheek, bridged her nose, and ended at the other cheek. She was a very beautiful woman, whose thin, light blue, cat-like eyes made even a gay man's rainbow flag wave.

She was one of their best hair stylists, who was always long on anecdotes, but quick with her honesty. If a black customer came in with a magazine wanting the latest Halle Berry style and look, you better believe Judy would tell you truthfully if it were at all possible. She once told a customer, "Doll...even Halle Berry couldn't come up in here requesting to look like herself, so you would be better off pasting the magazine cover to your face."

She hadn't seen Benny walk in, as she concentrated on brushing auburn highlights into this new customer's hair. "Hey Judy, I see you're holding down the fort once again," he addressed, walking in her direction, while at the same time slipping off his suede Armani blazer.

She turned one cat-eye in his direction, and smiled, "Bennnnny! Doll, where have you been? As you see *Receptionist* Angela is off again today, but she called saying there was a death in her family or something, so Harold let her have a few more days off."

He draped his blazer across his arm, "Well, that was nice of him. I can handle the front for a few days I suppose, and how are things here? Not much buzzing."

She looked down at her customer, "Can you tilt your head forward a little for me, Veronica? Thank you," she said, as she rolled another piece of aluminum around a section of Veronica's hair.

"Good to see we are at least bringing in some new subjects for you to work on," Benny said.

"Yea, it's seasonal, but at least it's steady. Veronica here just got divorced, and was driving through town, on her way to a new life. She saw your dedication to Michelangelo out there, and decided to drop in."

"Well, it's good to have you here, Veronica," Benny greeted, with a slight nod of his head.

Veronica, with her brown skin and thick lips, returned the nod with a wink and a smile. "Thank You," she said. "It's always good to realize when you've made a mistake, and have the time to fix it, I always say."

"I have been living by that motto as much as I can. I'm sure Judy will take really good care of you, and let her know what city you might be heading to. We have many salon friends abroad that we might be able to recommend you to."

"Thank you again," Veronica said.

Benny returned to Judy, who had somehow found a lollipop to occupy her orifice. "What's up, Judy?"

Judy's eyes went skyward, and she directed a pair of curling tongs behind her in the same direction. Benny looked to the back, where a set of stairs rounded from the right and left of the walls, and led to the second level of the salon, where a few offices were housed. The second level jutted out slightly to form a balcony, which had a huge city map painted on it. It helped with the tourists, as it highlighted a few good spots.

In a window (between the Querly's Aquarium and Gales Bakery) stood Harold, overlooking the salon, his eyes trained on Benny. Before Benny had a chance to acknowledge, Harold broke the glare, and spun on his heels; his shoes tick-tacking on the hollowed wood – towards his office - where he slammed the door so hard the windows rattled.

"I believe that's your cue, Doll," Judy said, the lollipop clacking against her teeth.

"Yea, I gathered," Benny said, slinging his blazer across his other arm, as he headed for the stairway, which was by no means the ones to Heaven.

Harold was deep into paperwork when he entered the tiny office, crammed to the gills with two sets of filing cabinets whose drawers appeared to be knocked from their hinges, a used salon chair in one corner and a computer desk littered with books, used pens, and a mini-coffee maker in another.

Although Harold tried to keep things tidy and neat, there was always the smell of dust and wood that permeated the air. As for the other two offices on this level: one stood vacant, and the other was used as a sort of conference room; which became more of a boxing ring where arrogant stylists were eventually fired in a battle of words.

"Good morning, Harold," Benny said, placing his blazer on a wall-mounted coat rack bolted into the wall above the salon chair. "I love what you've done with the place."

Harold glanced at him, showing his malcontent, then returned his attention back on the assortment of papers he held in his hand. "I assume you've been enjoying your sudden vacation from this place these last few days. I checked my messages and didn't hear anything from you."

Benny looked at the top of Harold's black curly mane. Harold's desk was littered with pens, a desk calendar, a beauty supply catalog, and a few Post Notes tacked at one corner. "I have spoken to you since then, Harold, and I see you are still mad because I didn't get back to you right away on yesterday."

"I'm glad to see you treat your business responsibilities with the same disregard as your personal relationships, Benny," Harold accused, placing the papers he was holding flat on the desk. He brushed his open palms across them, an obvious distraction that proved futile. "Yes, I am still angry at that, and I have a right to be, and I wouldn't have made anything of it, but you are really being evasive, and it burns me up, Benny."

"Are you thinking that because our relationship was built on a foundation of evasiveness?" Benny said, his back to Benny, as he looked out of the plate glass window that overlooked the salon. He could see there was a large discussion going on with everyone, and Judy was laughing at something Veronica had said. Times like this, he wished he had a few distractions to divert his thinking. He turned to face Harold, "I'm not getting into a battle of words with you Harold. I'll just take calls at the reception desk, while you sit up here in your Office of Anger, and we'll talk again later."

"You needn't bother, since I've forwarded the phone up here, and the schedule is pretty much clear this afternoon," Harold said, propping his elbows on the table, and resting his chin on his locked fingers. "I just want to know if it's true."

Benny's eyes widened for a moment. "You mean about Jason?"

Harold rolled his eyes, "Of course I mean about Jason. Talk travels fast around here, and drama even faster. But when people are mumbling about having seen your dead ex-lover enjoying the sights and sounds of Crest Hill County, I have to wonder what the hell everyone is talking about."

Benny's eyes became sidetracked as he looked at the appointment booklet under Harold's elbows. "You say that we are short on appointments?"

Harold spoke through clenched teeth. "Stop Benny, this is serious."

"I'd decided to stay home yesterday. I really don't know if I can talk about this right now."

"So, it is true, isn't it? I'd heard you had some sort of raise-the-dead party at your place yesterday," he quickly shook his head, "I can't believe I'm having this conversation."

"A raise-the-dead-party? Who told you something like that? It must've been Antonio…where did you meet him?"

Harold slapped his hands on the desk, blew out a winded breath, and leaned back in his seat. "Who cares where I heard it from, Benny? Who cares? I'm just wondering about my lover, who gets a visit from his dead ex-lover; who coincidentally you cheated on with me, who not only hides the details of their little meeting, he also arranges a party to bring his spirit or whatever it is, back from the dead and into his home."

Benny flayed his hand through the air, and collapsed in the salon chair, "That little séance was a total flop; some people had watched just too many episodes of Murder She Wrote, I guess."

"Forget the party Benny," Harold said, followed by a deep growl, as he raised his fists in the air, and spun a 360 in the swivel chair. "You don't get it do you? You really don't."

Benny crossed his legs, and leaned back a bit, sucking at his teeth, "No, maybe I don't *Get It*, Harold. I visit the grave of Jason, as I always have, and you are unnerved as you always are. You forget that I loved him first?"

Harold's eyes widened. "You know Benny it's possible your friends are grieved to the point that their private conversations have led to some unbelievable dreams. I don't really care."

And Benny could see that he didn't. There was something more on Harold's mind, and this conversation about Jason was only a ruse to get him to confess something else. "He hasn't visited you, has he?"

"No, and I don't believe he will."

There was such finality to that statement, and Benny found it hard to understand what this discussion could really be about. "What are you getting at, Harold? I hear you talking, but the meaning is getting lost in this jumble of words you're using. Spit it out, why don't you."

"I want to know if you were visiting more than graves two days ago, Benny."

"How many graves do you think I can visit on a given day, Harold? The truth is I didn't visit his grave, because Jason phoned me before I'd decided to go."

"Oh really? And, where was I?" Harold said, folding his arms.

"In the bathroom, getting ready for dinner. He wanted to meet me the next day, and I did."

"Just like that? A stranger calls you, and you decide to meet them, just like that?"

Now he was getting it! "I know what you're thinking, Harold, and I'm not sure I like it. Do you think I was cheating on you, and making up this visit to see Jason?"

He didn't answer.

Benny raked his fingers through his brown hair, and took a moment to think. "I know we cheated on Jason, and I know that puts to question if both of us can do that again to each other. The lines of trust get twisted with such thinking, but even if that were true, I think I could come up with a better story than a visit from a ghost."

Harold's eyes went soft, as if that was not the answer he'd been expecting. Benny tried reading him, evaluating his emotions, determining just where he was coming from, but he was dealing with a level of Harold he was not familiar with. There was something he wanted to say, but was afraid to, and it wasn't being revealed to him in this little interchange they were having.

Benny leaned forward, and lowered his tone a notch, keeping his eyes locked upon Harold's. "Harold, what's going on with you? I know this is hard to believe, and I'm sorry about not telling you, but I am still trying to sort it out myself. But you're not telling me everything. We have been a pair surrounded by our own secrets, so I know when you are not being up front with me. Are you angry because you think I lied about seeing Jason?"

Harold looked down at his paper and guided a finger across his forehead to wipe away a line of sweat. "No, I'm afraid you could be telling the truth, Benny," he said, his voice wounded. He looked up at Benny, "If you had not called me back one day, I might not begin to believe this. I was hoping you were cheating, but even if you were, it may have been something I could handle.

"But the next day, when a few clients called to ask me if *you* were all right, I inquired as to what all the concern was about? They said the spirit of Jason was back from the grave; that perhaps he looked for his killer, perhaps he came to say good bye to those he left so suddenly," he swallowed, reaching down towards the floor where he kept his gym bag, and brought out a sports bottle filled with water. He drank, then resumed, "But I was thinking, maybe he came back for you, Benny. You never really broke up with him, and who knows, maybe his wanting to be with you has caused him to return. But I wonder; if someone calls you claiming to be Jason, and you take little hesitation to meet with them, and you don't take the time to discuss it with me; it just makes me wonder, who really wanted who back."

Deep. That was the only word Benny felt that statement had been. Deep. Harold went through a lot to be with him, and now that he had, he feared that even the dead could rise up and steal the man he loved away. It was at once, both tragic and amazing.

"Maybe you should meet with him, Harold," Benny said, rising from the chair.

"What?" Harold said, still caught up in his own thinking. "You mean with your ghost?"

"Yes," Benny assured, leaning over Harold's desk, pressing his knuckles into the leather cushioned top. "He's not sure why he's been called back, and maybe we can both find out why."

Harold waved his hand through the air, "No, no I can't see you there, trying to help him again. I'm still trying to figure out what caused him to come back, in whatever form he's come back in. This is some scary shit, Benny, very scary. Haven't you even thought that?"

"I don't have this great fear of death like most people do, Harold. I felt relieved for both Jason and Maya; because they were able to escape the lies and deceit that would have eventually destroyed them," he stood straight, and put a hand in his pocket. "We can talk about this later. There should be at least one of the bosses down there, and since I have been playing hooky the most, I'll go."

"Yea, you do that. I need to order more supplies and call the accountant about next week's paychecks," Harold said, reaching for the supply catalog and thumbing through its pages. "But tell me, Benny..."

He was already at the door, when he stopped to look back at his lover, worry pasted on his face, as if those eyes were borrowed from someone else. "Yea, shoot."

"Are you glad he's back? Are you glad that Jason has been given the chance to live again, to see you?"

He shrugged his shoulders, "I really hadn't thought about it, Harold," and then he left, closing the door behind him. And as he walked down the stairs leading to the main level of the salon, he said to himself, "...but I am sure glad it happened, Harold. It's what I've dreamed about for a very long time."

Chapter 9

Part I

Luther was exhausted, his hands were sore, his head ached, his thoughts disorganized, his sense of reality shattered. His foot was heavy, as it bore down on the car's accelerator, the road leading up towards Erica's home blurred as it crossed into his vision. He had had enough mystery to last him though many sermons, but this morning he was in the mood for something a little more palatable.

This morning, he needed answers.

Being in church yesterday, had turned into the most horrid experience in his life.

It was so real, as to be unreal. It had become much too *surreal* to intelligently comprehend. He wasn't exactly sure what he was dealing with; whether it was of a spiritual nature, or an unnatural one. He talked with the members of his church, and what appeared the community at large; reaching out to hold hands, to offer a shoulder, and allow the sweat to continue to drain from his face – no time for wiping. He listened to what people were commonly encountering; deceased loved ones visiting them, whose flesh was real, their touch certain, and while he was consoling them, he felt no one to console him.

Driving through town he observed how vacant the streets seemed. The local coffee shop had a sprinkling of customers inside, but their sidewalk tables stood empty, the park had a few wayward joggers trotting through its trails, the Sheldon Hills Grammar School playground was void of children milling about, but the building's doors were open, signifying no holiday of any sort was being honored.

As he headed towards the outskirts of town in the directions of Erica's home, he could see what looked like cloud cover along the distant horizon. The Morning Glory Cemetery was on the north side of town, and Erica lived on the south; Luther hadn't expected that a *fog* could have gotten so far. *It was as if it were surrounding the town instead of passing through*, he thought. It loomed slightly above, the clearness of the skies almost caused it look invisible, but there it was, as immobile as a brick wall. It became even more astonishing when he drove out from the center of town, where the homes were scattered, and the acreage large. The scent of nature was crisper, the air dry, with horse stables and feed mills coming up in the distance, hidden among the corn fields and apple groves.

This is where Erica lived; in a sparse region occupied by fabricated mobile homes, a senior center, a tackle & bait shop, and the homes of those who preferred a more modest living. It had been out here that Maya lived (not too far from Erica), preferring the open spaces. Remembering those drives to her place, where they would discuss a new song, or chat about her life in South Africa, made Luther feel as if he had gone to some far-a-way land. He missed those times.

But now, as he pulled into Erica's gravel driveway; the motion of his tires caused small dust eddies to creep up the sides of his car, he found fear trying to revisit him, and held his breath to keep from suddenly hyperventilating. He could not believe he was actually doing this, and the more ironic thing was, if he was doing this, did that mean he believed it was happening as well?

Before the dust settled about his car, Luther looked up at Erica's tiny house just in time to see Timothy bounding down the stairs, wearing a torn t-shirt and jeans. He stopped in front of the car, breathing heavily, his hand lifted to conceal his eyes from the glare that was obviously coming off the windshield. "Pastor Reynolds, is that you?"

Luther leaned his head out the window, "Yea, it's me. Is your mother home today?"

He looked back at the house, then walked around to the driver's side of the car, "Yea, she's in there all right, having breakfast with them."

He looked up at the boy, noticing a grimace on his face, "Do you mean, your mother and father?"

"No, I mean with my *zombie* father and...."

"Timothy..." Pastor Reynolds interrupted, "I know you're angry, but don't let me hear you disrespect your dad so." Pastor Reynolds chastised, as he waved his hand at the youth to move back while he stepped out of the car.

"I can't take it in there, Pastor Reynolds," Timothy said. He scratched nervously at his thick plumes of curly brown hair, which looked like banded confetti. "I can't be in there with them, it's creepy. And mom's acting giddy all the time, like we're the damned Adam's Family or something."

"Your mouth, young man!" Luther said, reaching out to squeeze Timothy's shoulder.

He looked to his feet, embarrassed. "I'm sorry, Pastor. I'm just scared being in there, and mom is acting as if everything is normal. Before you know it she'll be off buying a station wagon, and we'll be doing road trips n'shit."

Pastor Reynolds let that last one slide. The boy was obviously troubled, and who could blame him. *I'm sure Erica didn't act this motherly when everyone was ALIVE!*

"Timothy!" said a voice with such sharpness, that it startled them both. "You don't just run out of this house in the middle of breakfast without first excusing yourself, young man." And with that, the screen door burst open, and out stepped Erica, a sky blue robe delicately trimmed in white lace, hugged her waist. Billowing curls framed a face absent of any makeup. The rest of her hair was pushed into blue netting that hung from the back, and was only seen for a moment as she scanned the perimeter of her driveway, before settling her eyes on the pair.

Timothy hugged himself closer to the Pastor.

"Hey there, Pastor Reynolds," she said, lowering her head for a moment, and shaking it slowly from side to side while she grinned. "I mean, Luther," and brought her head back up, the grin still very pleasant, belying her earlier disposition. "What brings you out here so early in the morning?"

Luther could feel Timothy's heavy breathing fall against his body, and reached an arm out to him, placing it gently across his shoulders. He needed to address Timothy verbally later, but for now, his arm would serve to pacify the young lad. "Can Timothy sit in my car for a moment, while I come up there to talk with you?"

She appeared perplexed at the sudden request, her body halfway out the door, hand resting on her hip. She sighed, then went back into the house; the door rested slowly back upon its frame.

Pastor Reynolds looked down at Timothy, "I don't think your mother is very pleased with you."

"I don't see what I could have done. I'm the only one acting normal around here," he said, his eyes forlorn, almost saddened; a soul in utter confusion.

Just then, Erica reappeared in the doorway, and stepped out unto the stairway, something slim and white lay in her upturned palm; a plate. "Well, if he wants to sit out here, then he will also be finishing this breakfast I've cooked for him." She said, standing at the foot of the stairs, the tail of her robe snapping in the soft morning breeze.

Timothy looked up at the Pastor, then at his mother, and without much contemplation he broke loose from his stance and dashed in his mother's direction. He reached out to grab the plate, and then returned back to the Pastor, moving towards the car's open door, and sat himself in the driver's seat.

Pastor Reynolds closed the door. "Don't get any food on my leather, you hear, Timothy." The child only nodded his compliance. "Great. I shouldn't be long."

As Luther approached the house, Erica stood there gazing at her son. He noticed how calm she looked; a very different contrast from the woman he had seen yesterday who was huddled up near the door afraid, worn and fatigued. Her eyes shone bright, her light sandy skin glowed. She reached out to grab Luther's hands in her own.

This was not the actions of a woman who was recovering from the death of a best friend, and the realization of a lover – once thought absconded, now confirmed deceased, now having reemerged. He continued to mull over this, as she backed up the stairs, pulling him after her, like a school girl giddily leading her blindfolded father up to a well-orchestrated surprise; except in this case, Luther was going in with his eyes wide open.

"I have more than enough breakfast left, if you're hungry," her smile beaming all the way to the door.

He stopped there, gently reclaiming his hands, "Sure Erica…perhaps another time," he could see some of the gleam leave her eyes, as if she were guessing at what he was about to say, "But this isn't a social visit."

Her mouth dropped, and she probed it with a finger, "Okay, I suppose," she replied wistfully, "Is there something going on at home?"

"No Erica. I've really come to talk with your husband. I need to ask him a few things."

The smile returned, and she shrugged her shoulders, "Oh, is that all? I guess you've accepted this like I have," she said, pushing back the main door, and stepping into the house; her arm holding onto the screen as an invitation to Luther.

He grabbed the door and stepped inside. He faced the hallway that lead to the back of the house where the bedroom, sitting room, bathroom, and indoor patio lay. The corner of the washer and dryer could be seen, as well as the pulled back curtains of the row-windows that gave a view of Erica's backyard with its large oak tree in the distance.

He looked to his left for a split second, as the television came into view; it was off, but it reminded him of yesterday, and all the ciaos that had transpired. Then he looked to his right, at Erica's kitchen…and immediately had the shock of his life.

"Are you sure you wouldn't want something to eat?" Erica said walking into the kitchen area, where on the eating table, was a collection of two plates, half-eaten.

He couldn't answer.

"Hey there, Pastor," came a familiar voice, in a most unfamiliar setting. Eric was leaning back in one of the chairs at the table, wearing an unbuttoned plaid shirt, a black tank top underneath, with black denim slacks hanging past his bare feet.

He still couldn't answer.

Because when he looked past Eric, at the far end of the table, he saw a sight he was not sure he could believe.

"And what do you say to the Pastor? You remember him, don't you?" Erica said, taking a glass off the tray of a high-chair, he had forgotten even existed, and refilling it with orange juice.

It was Eric Jr.! Luther could not believe what he was seeing, until the small child in his newly pressed pullover Sponge Bob shirt and shorts set, waved at him, and said, "Hey there Passst'r," the words coming out as if he were testing their letters, "I'm eating with mommy." He smiled.

Infectiously, Pastor Reynolds smiled also. "Yes, I see you eating there."

Erica pushed the filled glass in his direction and ran her fingers through the child's dark brown hair. "He was the one who said such nice things at your funeral, Eric Jr.," she said, looking down at the child, "Now say, thank you."

"Thank you, Passst'r," Eric Jr. obeyed, picking up the juice glass, and bringing it slowly to his lips, his attention suddenly on the task at hand.

"Now, I have some oatmeal, eggs, and bacon already done. I can make some toast if you want, because I have some really good preserves that I got from…"

"Erica," Luther swiftly cut off, "Can I see you outside for a moment," his voice stern. "Eric, I apologize. I need to steal her for a moment, okay?"

"Sure Pastor, I know this must be tough on you."

Luther stepped towards the door, but something in Eric's statement jarred him. It had not seemed a reply for what he had asked, but more for what he may have been thinking. He continued out the door, and down the stairs, where his legs continued to pace until Erica came out to meet him.

"My God, Erica. What is happening in that house? What are you doing?" Luther said, the words spilling out without any forethought.

She looked back at her home, her gaze returning to him while her eyed danced in her head. "What are you talking about, Luther?"

"Do you have any idea who you are entertaining? Why are these people up there eating at your table?" He said, pointing his hand out towards the house, and having it slap back against his side. "I don't understand this."

She stabbed her hands into her hips, "I'm having breakfast. I don't know what you're getting at. I always cook breakfast."

He leaned into her; his body shook from the nerves he tried to bridle. "These people, your family…my God, Eric Jr." He took a deep breath, licking at his dried lips, "We are dealing with spirits here, Erica. I know these people look like your family, but how can we be sure they don't just wear the flesh of your family? How can you know what you have let into your house? You are feeding them, as if…as if…nothing has ever happened to them. You are feeding the dead breakfast?"

She took a step back, arms crossed. "I don't think I am going to like where this talk is going, Luther. I don't think I like you telling me that I don't know my own family. Do you think I am so easily fooled?"

He looked at her wide-eyed and gaped mouth. He waited for words to climb from his belly to rest on his tongue. Nothing came. He paced, and that seemed to bring up something, "No, of course you know you family, Erica. I just know this is not normal. I believe something has happened, but I don't know what. Death has been somehow cast aside for a moment, its pull on man lifted, the great gulf separating man from the afterlife merged somehow," he stopped to look at her, "We can't accept this so readily, can we?"

"And what are you suggesting I do, Luther – Pastor Reynolds, toss them to the streets? You want me to throw my child out in the dirt? Is that what you're asking me?"

He swallowed thick air. "No…" he replied, the word barely audible, as if it were less a response to her question, and more a rejection of the interpretation she made of his. "No, that is not what I meant, Erica. I am only thinking about your well-being."

"And this had nothing to do with Maya?"

That question sideswiped him. He looked at her closely, a tinge of anger in her eyes, crossed arms, a wide-legged stance. No, she was speaking of something else, something more personal in her inquiry about Maya; because in reality, that is *exactly* why he was here.

She continued, "Do you think I am so grieved by my best friend's death, that I need to carry that grief in the presence of my son and husband, both of whom I have also lost? Do you think my accepting of my husband and son's life, is so I don't have to think about Maya's death?"

He hadn't thought about that, but it was very possible. She could be so straddled with accepting death, that it has made her almost hungry to welcome some life back into her existence. "I don't know Erica. I suppose that may be what I was thinking. You, more than anyone in this town, have dealt with a lot of loss. It only makes sense that you would use these odd circumstances to fool yourself into forgetting that loss, and the pain associated with it."

"I've thought about that Luther, and I will have to deal with it in the way that God sees fit that I should. But until he intervenes, Erica is going to do what Erica thinks she should do."

Luther could see at this point, that there was no sense in talking further. He was frightened for her, because she was acting like a sheep, and the foxes had been invited over for dinner – or in this case breakfast. He then thought about Timothy, peeked over his shoulder, to see him looking quite disturbed at the pair of them. He had almost forgotten he was there. He could understand now the child's fear.

"Fine," he said finally, "But if something out of the ordinary happens, I want you to try and call me at once."

This caused her to drop her hands, and a tiny grin appeared. "Who else would I call silly?" Then she turned around to head back to the house.

"So, am I interrupting a family moment," Luther said, not believing the words that just fell past his lips, "Or is Eric available for me to have a few words with?"

She paused for a moment at the top of the stairs, holding the screen door open. "Sure, he is. Just head around to the back, and I will send him to meet you," she said, her voice as light as a song, and then she was gone.

Luther rounded the house, unhinging the iron gate that was positioned next to the tool shed. He continued to stroll to the picnic deck at the top of the tiny crest in the center of the yard. The scent of burnt ash and cedar chips surrounded the air around him. He remembered this grill as being only half finished, but the look of it now was pretty well complete, and with the scent in the air, he could tell that it had been recently used, perhaps as early as last night. A chill went through him just thinking about the idea that Eric may have been the one to complete this grill, and that a celebration of sorts ensued. He feared for Erica, who must have accepted this without any qualms, and for that to happen, she may have suffered more emotionally than he had at first thought.

He really worried about her.

"So, what can I help you with?" he heard a voice say behind him. He turned to see Eric there.

Pastor Reynolds sat down at one of the benches, as he watched Eric, who had changed his clothes, to something a little more pressed; garments that made him wonder just how many of these clothes Erica held unto. He got the feeling that Erica may have never really understood that her husband had no intentions in life to really come back to her.

"I just have a few concerns, Eric," Pastor Reynolds said, his body stiff with tension. "I am worried about your wife, and whatever is going on here. There are some things that I had not really thought about until seeing Erica here today."

"I understand," Eric said, easing closer to the Pastor.

Pastor Reynolds looked up at Eric, and leaned back upon the bench. His approach was very non-threatening, but all the same cocky. "Do you, Eric? Do you really know what I am so concerned about?"

Eric smiled, and looked casually around the backyard. "Yes I do, Pastor. But you have to understand that there are going to be some things that are going to be beyond your comprehension."

"Perhaps," Pastor Reynolds said, crossing his legs, "Should I not be concerned about my friend?"

Eric stood quietly for a moment; the only sound was that of a few cars along the main street, gravel being crunched under tires. "Yes, I know you have an underlying concern about Erica…and you should. But aren't you really here for something else?"

Now it was Pastor Reynolds who took a moment to think. "Are you saying that you are able to read minds?"

"No, no...nothing like that," Eric said amusingly. "Your thoughts are safe, but you better than anyone, should know of the great rift that has been fixed between the living and the dead."

"Yes, I am aware."

"Then Pastor, you must understand that the constrains of the flesh are something that I am not a prisoner of. Your nature, your emotions, your sense of being are something I can see as if it were a mural painted on the side of a building. I can read this whole town if I choose to, and it has been going through a grief that has been insurmountable. Just recently, there has been a grief caused by the death of a woman who meant a lot to this town...a lot to *you*."

Pastor Reynolds sat up. "Yes, there has been, Eric," he swallowed dryly before continuing, "So what does Maya have to do with any of this?"

"Why, Pastor Reynolds...isn't that why you have come here to see me? You are not as concerned by the fact that I have come back to Erica. Your real concern, is when will Maya return to you."

Suddenly Eric became invisible to Pastor Reynolds, and his thoughts went blank. And all he could think was, *yes...yes, he **could** actually read minds!*

Part II

Lisa contemplated.

She sat on the sofa in the side chambers of Pastor Reynolds office, doing more thinking than she thought she could muster.

She was frightened.

She was sad.

She was dealing with *many* thoughts.

There was a knock at the door. She'd gotten up early this morning to open the church doors. Yesterday had been a day she would never quite forget. So many people experiencing so many spiritual visits, that she believed she would have lost her mind if she had not been so very busy consoling everyone.

When she opened the door, a short plump man dashed by her and into the office. His wispy hair and dark features became an instant blur, but even at a glance it was hard to mistake Earl Sanders; one of the many ushers of the church. He was the and thick like a polish bratwurst, and he reached his thick fingers to the back of his head where he re-tied his ponytail. He turned to face Lisa, with one of the prettiest faces she could remember ever encountering; long lashes, and rounded lips that sat cushioned between his bubble-like cheeks. With features like that, she could forgive him the outdated ponytail.

"What's happening Earl?" she asked, the words dragging from her tired throat.

Earl looked lost for a moment, as if gathering his thoughts. "What is going on here, Lisa. I could not believe what I had been hearing. But now that I am here, and listening to these people, I don't mind saying that this is really scaring me. Do you believe any of this?"

Lisa watched him pace the floor – something she'd found herself doing only a few hours ago. "I have to believe it, Earl, but I have no explanation for it. I'm not even sure what is behind all of this; whether it is from Heaven or Hell."

Earl dropped his gaze, and adjusted his tie. His white dress shirt was soaked under the arms, as well as partly tucked in. Lisa remembered telling him that this was one time that he could leave the three-piece suite at home; it was obvious that he didn't believe her.

"I'm trying to help as best as I can Lisa, but I am not sure what to tell these people."

Lisa reached out to grab his arm. "I know Earl, and I thank you for coming. A lot of the other deacons were out of town at that church revival in Washington, and those of the staff who are in town, didn't return my calls. From what I experienced last night, I think everyone out there just wants to be heard and put at ease that this is actually happening."

"Well you know I would do anything for you and the Pastor. I'm just not experienced in any of this, and I am not sure what's going on. How are you holding out this morning?"

Lisa pulled back. She had to think about that for a moment. Yes, she was tired from a night of encouraging, but there was a truth she could not tell Earl; and that was the fact that a lot of envy had surfaced in her last night. Children. There were so many children: the one thing she could never really have. She had met so many men, loved so many, but when they realized she could not bare children a rumor began that Lisa was better for recreation, not procreation. For so long she had been used, and with that use, came years of hate. She cared for the church now as if it had become the child she would never have.

Earl reached out to offer his hand, and she reached out to take it.

"I guess I am holding up pretty well," Lisa said in answer to his question.

He grinned at her, squeezing her hand just a bit. "I know that's a lie, but you hold on to it. I have known you far too long to not know when something is not really bothering you."

She allowed him this...truth. They were both very similar in their yearnings for families, and their shortcomings in having them. Earl was stout and shorter than what most women would find comfort in when choosing a husband, and so if she were the mistress of the church, then Earl had become its man-servant. "Thanks Earl," Lisa said, their hands unclasping.

"We have to remind ourselves once in a while, that we are still human, Lisa."

She looked up at the ceiling. "You seem to almost read my thoughts, Earl. Have I told you that?"

"Constantly."

"And here I was thinking about all those people out there, whose loved ones have come back. It seems that everyone in town has had someone they love return to them...then what does it mean that no one has come back to me. Was I not loved by anyone?"

He stepped closer to her, her leg brushing against his cheek, and he laid a hand along it – nothing sexual, but very apathetically. "No...it just means all those that love you are still alive. I love you."

She looked down at him, and brushed her fingers through his jet-black hair, the look of it like ebony dental floss. "Yes, I know that. I love you too, Earl."

He slowly backed away, patting down his tussled hair, and walked towards the door, "Good. Now I can only give you about ten more minutes to sit here and feel sorry about yourself, but after that time, I do expect to see you back out there on stage, taking care of the *people* you love most."

She knew he meant the *congregation*. "Of course you do, and I will. Thanks again Earl."

He nodded, and then headed out the door.

Before she could settle herself, she could hear a small, almost silent knocking at the back door. She lazily walked through the tiny corridor of rooms until she was able to get to the back door; ushered within what had become a storage room, where stacked boxes of old church bulletins and mailers were. She stepped around some discarded office furniture, kicking dust along the way, and reached out to open the door.

To her surprise she was met with a rather tall gentleman, handsome features, deep brown hair, and tanned skin. When he smiled, with wide thick lips, Lisa could feel a rush of unwanted memories trail along her insides, like fallen rubble.

"Andre Kincaid?" she questioned aloud. She had not seen him since his mother had died almost two years ago. Their history of course, went a little longer than that.

"It's been a long time Lisa," he said, with a most reminiscent baritone voice.

"Yes, it has been quite a long time since I have seen you, even in a town this small. I suppose you are here because of your mother?" Lisa said, as she continued to stand at the door's threshold. Even under these odd circumstances, it was better to get right to the point than to belabor it in the presence of an unwanted ex-lover.

His nod was very slow, as if she had come to a point he had not wanted. "Yes, I suppose," he replied, brushing at the lapels of his tweed jacket, the silk shirt underneath was open slightly at the neck, revealing just a hint of chest hair.

She had always been attracted to his manner of dress; neat and modern. She stepped back a bit, her feet brushing against the corner of a tattered podium that Pastor Reynolds wanted repaired; the hammer atop it slid to the floor. Lisa ignored it. "You want to step in for a moment?"

"Thank you," he said; his steps ginger as he maneuvered past planks of wood and a few empty suitcases. "I suppose you have heard what's been happening around town?"

She watched him slowly, his words like an echo to her ears, as she closed the door behind him. She had loved this man. She had loved him so much, until he realized she could not give him children, and that their maiden of honor could.

"How is Maria?" she asked faster than her tongue could be caught.

He looked at her dumbstruck, his eyes searching in his head as if it were a projector to their past. "She left me soon after I broke up with you, Lisa."

More like 'broke off' with me, she thought, considering it was only weeks before their engagement was to turn into their wedding. This news however, did not make her feel any more vindicated; perhaps because she had begun to change her life after her time with Andre, to a more Christian lifestyle; using it as a patch to erase her former life.

She walked past him, leading him into the central lounge area that connected most of the offices. "What can I do for you, Andre? I have heard what was going on in town, and I have to assume that you are here because of your mother. Is that right?"

"Yes. You were not at the funeral."

She turned to face him as she reached the marble coffee table in the center of the room. He had almost stumbled into her. She looked up at his deep blue eyes, the eyes and lashes that she had pictured their children would someday have…have if they had just tried hard enough. She still loved him. "I am sorry for your loss, Andre. I know this comes at a late date, but I am. I liked your mother. I am sure you know why I could not be at her funeral," she said, swinging out her hand to offer him a seat on the wide sofa that swung around the coffee table in a 'U' shape.

He leaned back upon the sofa, eyes downcast, "I suppose I do know the answer to that."

She continued to stand, her eyes not yet able to focus upon him; there were too many bad memories that appeared to be written upon his face. She looked around the lounge area: the tiny dorm refrigerator, the pair of crystal lamps and stands at each corner, a wall mounted stereo system lightly playing some operatic music, a ceiling mounted television screen with the purpose of giving a view of what was going on in the main sanctuary, and on each wall was a depiction of Jesus Christ in the nationalities of Black, Caucasian, and Chinese. She looked everywhere but upon Andre.

"Would you like some water?" she finally said, her body already heading in the direction of the refrigerator.

"No, not right now. I think maybe I should speak my peace, and then be on my way. I can tell that I am making you a little uncomfortable," he said, wringing his hands.

She looked at him, and slowly backed up towards the sofa, and eased herself down upon it. "Maybe, but that is not solely because of you, nor really should it concern you. There have been a lot more things happening in this town than your sudden appearance to this church," she said, and was a bit startled at her own frankness. She took in a slow breath. "Maybe you're right. Tell me what brings you here today, and how I can help."

There was a moment of silence before Andre spoke…silence that stood for such a length of time that it had begun to feel awkward. "I did have a word with my mother, and she told me something that I had known for quite some time, but was unable to do until now…and that was to apologize to you. You have been very angry with me, and I know it has made you bitter for many of the men you've encountered thereafter."

She could not deny such a blatant truth. "Yes, I must say that your mother has brought much wisdom to your ears."

Silence again.

"Perhaps I *will* have some of that water you offered earlier," he said, "Suddenly my throat feels too dry to work properly."

She stood up quickly, almost too quickly, as if her body was pressing to do something to break the uneasiness that had suddenly been let into the room. "I suppose your mother told you this, because on some level you had been thinking about that time or was it that she wanted a chance to make me her daughter-in-law," Lisa said, trying her best to make light of a most heavy subject, as she reached into the fridge for the drink.

"Both. She could always read things in people even when there were no words spoken."

She returned with two bottles of cold water, "And what did you manage to do after you called off our wedding, Andre? You had only quit your job at the trucking company a month before, wanting to get something local to make married life a little easier," she said, reaching her hand out for his bottle, and dropping hers on the coffee table.

He grabbed the bottle, his thick fingers not bothered by the icy coldness of the plastic. "I found a job at the postal office, driving the mail truck. It was a good job, until that school bus rammed into us."

His words caught her at mid-sitting position. "What did you say?"

He twisted the cap on the bottle with ease. "The oil truck must have pushed that school bus mighty hard before exploding, because I was right alongside it on the same street."

She began to shake.

He cocked his shoulder, as if a split second thought distracted him, and then he brought the bottle to his lips. When he pulled away, he spoke as if to himself, "Cool…I forgot how wonderful cool water is to the taste buds."

She sat looking at her own bottle; afraid to reach for it. "You said something about an explosion. Would this be the explosion that happened two years ago involving those two school buses? You were near it?"

He wiped his lips with the back of his hand. "No, I wasn't just near it…I died in it, Lisa. My mother asked me to come talk to you while we were both in the afterlife. I was sent back to relieve some of your grief."

She stared in horror, and when the phone rang in the office, she could feel her skin rattle. She was unable to move, her mind immediately shutting off, trying to understand what had just been said. She listened to the answering machine come on. It was Carl's voice. He was saying something about being at the cemetery, and about graves opening up, and then he started to ramble frantically.

"Are you okay, Lisa?" Andre said, as he reached out to her trembling hands, "You're shaking," he paused. "I guess it is normal, considering we have quite a lot of catching up to do."

Part III

"You want to do what!" Jenna said, nearly dropping the partially dried dish into the sink.

Nathan placed his head in his palms as he sat at the table. "I knew that boy was nothing but a well full of bad ideas when I first saw him. What did you say he was? Some Creole French Mix? Mixed up in the head, if you ask me," he mumbled aloud.

Tilly moved in closer to her grandpa. "Creole *is* a mix of French and Canadian, Grandpa. He is right in the other room and can hear you for god's sake."

He slapped his hand on the table, shaking the tiny glass salt and pepper holders there. "Then let him hear me! Tilly, you're not going anywhere with him, do you hear me? This whole thing will fix itself sooner or later."

Jenna continued to shake her head as she vigorously continued to clean the same plate, over and over again. "I can't understand you Tilly. How can you even consider something like this?" She pointed a clean plate in Mark's direction as he sat in the entertainment room on the sofa, frozen in an expression of feigned ignorance. "I'm very disappointed in you young man."

He tried not to glance her way.

"I know you can hear us," she said, spinning back in the direction of the sink.

He began to slither down in his seat, as if the cushions were made of warm gelatin.

Tilly folded her arms. "This is my decision Grandma. We have to find out what's going on outside of this town. Everybody is so wrapped up in ghost stories, that no one is doing anything about it. We have relatives out of town, what are they thinking? Springfield is less than a-hundred miles away. Something must have happened. Isn't anyone scared?"

"The young are always scared about nothing," Jenna said, dishes rattling like loose change. "That does not mean that you have to go anywhere."

"Damned right," Nathan said, slapping his hands again, "If that young boyfriend of yours wants to kill himself doing something as foolish as heading out of town with a caravan of ruffians, than let him. You will not have anything to do with it."

"Kill himself?" she asked. "I can't believe this. I really can't believe this." She walked towards the table where her grandfather was sitting. "We have to do something Grandpa, we just have to. We just want to find out what is happening outside of town, ask some questions, and see if there is something we should be worrying about."

"We have Sheriff's in this town that can handle that sort of thing. We have a Mayor, sitting up in that big building in the center of town to do stuff like that, Tilly. Besides, I hear that a few of the police that went out of town, have not even come back," Jenna said over her shoulder, as she continued to dry her dishes.

Tilly leaned on the back of a chair, her fingers gripping around its frame. "That Sheriff Department is only half-staffed this week, and those rookies in there couldn't find the yellow on an ear of corn," Tilly sighed, and pulled the seat she was holding out, and flopped down into it. "Besides, the Sheriff, the Mayor, and his staff, are all out of town at some political convention I hear."

"Well, we are just going to have to wait and see what they have to say, Tilly. I know you like this boy, but you can't jump up and go somewhere with him just because he says so," Nathan said, glancing at Mark. "Can you talk some sense into this young lady, Jenna?"

"Well, Tilly. You do seem to be a little love-struck," Jenna agreed.

Tilly looked at them both, as if they had been replaced by aliens. "This has nothing to do with me liking Mark. People are saying that there are ghosts walking around this town. What about that woman I talked to that said she was your daughter Grandma. What about that?"

The tea kettle went off; its chime suddenly silencing everyone.

Nathan reached out to the empty cup in front of him, "We aren't talking about that right now, Tilly. That little news really upset your Grandma, and we don't know who this woman really is."

Jenna walked over to lower the flame under the kettle, while grabbing Nathan's cup. "We are only thinking about you, Tilly. Remember how you thought you were so in love with someone else, that you were filled with images of getting married and having babies?"

Tilly crossed her arms across the table, lowering her head. She closed her eyes and let loose a long-winded huff through her nostrils. "I can't believe how you two always have to make everything I do, about the man I am seeing. I care about this town, and I want to know what is going on. We have family outside this town that may be worried about us, my mom is out there, your friends are out there, and no one seems to care about it," she said, swinging her hands out across the table, as if wiping her mind of images, "And who cares who I like? You two better than anyone, should know how hard it is trying to like someone that no one else approves of."

Jenna said nothing, but she and Nathan locked looks and a flash of memories were shared between them. Jenna filled his cup with slices of lemon, followed by the tea, "We are not trying to judge you, Tilly," Jenna finally said.

Nathan reached towards the cup as Jenna passed it to him, and said, "No, don't think that. I know you are trying very hard *not* to be like your mother; running from one man to the next. And yes, we did try to tell her that your father wasn't the best man for her, and we were right, but that's not what we are trying to tell you." He cut his eyes at Mark again.

Jenna filled another cup with tea, and joined the table, where there sat a small container of sugar cubes in the center, and with the included tongs, she fished out some cubes to place in both her and Nathan's cup. "Did you want some tea, Tilly?" Jenna said, trying to sooth the wounds her grandchild was intent on licking.

"No, I…" she began to say, but was interrupted by the ringing of her cell.

"Hello, Carl? You want what? Is everything okay there? Sure, that should be no problem. Yes…yes…I know. Okay, see you soon."

"What does he want," Nathan said, blowing at his tea.

"I need to head over to the cemetery Grandma. Carl is a little shorthanded this week and wants me to help with some lost records he's trying to locate," she said, sliding her chair back.

"You be careful over there, young lady. That man can be a little crazy," Nathan said.

"Oh, Grandpa," Tilly exhaled, as she stood and waved at Mark. "I'm going to have Mark drive me over there," she said. "And tell your friends I said hello, Grandma."

"I will, baby," Jenna replied.

"What friends?" Nathan asked, as he reached out to grab a few more sugar cubes to put into his tea.

Jenna quickly rapped his knuckles with the end of her spoon, "You put those down. That tea is plenty sweet for you and besides, you know it's for my little gathering today, and the girls like their tea."

"You still having that little senior gossip fest of yours today, with the state of emergency in this town?" Nathan asked, nursing his knuckles.

"Sure I am," Jenna said, just as Mark came into the kitchen. "You make sure you drive carefully, Mark."

"I sure will Mrs. Reed," Mark replied, as he followed Tilly outside.

Tilly slowly closed the door, and they both headed towards Mark's car. "Sorry about all of the dramatics back there. They can both be a little too much."

"I suppose you aren't going with us to find out what's happening with that mist, or what's going on outside of town."

She waved her hand at him, "The hell I'm not. I live in this town too, and have a right to find out what's going on. We'll talk about that later. I'm still a little spooked about how scared Carl sounded over the phone."

"All about some lost records, right?" Mark asked, as he opened the car door for Tilly, and began to walk around towards the driver's side.

She replied when Mark lowered himself in his seat, "No. I just said that to get out of the house. What Carl told me, you are just not going to believe, but if it's true, God help us."

Part IV

Pastor Reynolds didn't know what to say, and even if he did, he believed he was still in too much shock to be able to form complete sentences.

Eric stood by silently, allowing Pastor Reynolds the time he needed to address the many questions that were on his mind.

Pastor Reynolds ran his tongue around in his mouth, just to make sure it could move. He watched as Eric stared at the horizon, and was baffled as where to begin – for if a man had the ability to read your thoughts, are you able to ask a question that they would not have already known?

After much hesitation, Pastor Reynolds spoke, "I want to know why this is happening to Crest Hill County, Eric?"

Eric pushed himself away from the grill he'd been leaning against, and dropped his arms. "Is that really the question you'd like to ask, Pastor? I would have thought you were curious about-"

"No!" Pastor Reynolds bellowed, his tense fingers curling up. He could tell Eric was about to reveal a truth he was not ready to investigate. He had to proceed on a calmer note, so he took a deep breath, and slowly began to unfurl his fingers. "Eric. I only want to know what is affecting this town, and how to stop it."

He bobbed his head, swinging his arms towards his back, where he kept them, fingers laced. "Okay…I see that you are choosing to discuss matters on a more social scale than emotional. Admirable."

Pastor Reynolds kept his mouth stilled, and stared into Eric's eyes, while his ears listened to the sharp hollowed sound of shoes that once belonged to a dead man, as they made their way across the wooden planks that floored this deck, to stand closer to him.

"What I know today, Pastor Reynolds, will change as the days go by, because the veil of this mystery has yet to be pulled. What is happening is lesser of a query than why it is happening. I cannot answer the whole of the question, for many answers are going to come when the finale has been reached."

Pastor Reynolds looked at Eric dumbfounded. He tried to remember the man he knew a few years ago, the one that didn't speak in such philosophical undertones, but that memory was quickly starting to fade the more this reborn Eric spoke. Pastor Reynolds leaned forward, "Well, maybe I should be more specific, considering that I am working with a Higher Power – but am still unsure which one that could be. Why are you here? What has brought you back to the living? If it is God that has renewed your flesh, then He must have given you a reason."

Eric stood in front of Pastor Reynolds, and looked above him, out into the distance horizon. "Yes…there is a reason, or at least a link, that had brought me back. I can't say that God gave me a set of instructions on why this is happening."

Pastor Reynolds raised his eyebrows, and Eric lowered his gaze to look at him.

"No, Pastor, I know what you are thinking, but there is no evil work happening here. This is not a work controlled by evil spirits, raising the dead to wreak havoc upon the living. God does have a hand in this, but I can't be sure. That memory was taken away from me. I just know there is a spiritual gateway, a holding area, where we all came to, and in that area, we realized that we were dead, and were being pulled back into the living. We know of the afterlife, there are memories of it, but they are cloudy now as our bodies, as are minds, can only be allowed gradual snippets of information," he stopped and turned around, his back to the Pastor. "I'm sorry Pastor, this may be confusing you."

"Take your time, Eric," Pastor Reynolds said. He began to realize that this may be hard on him as well; to be wretched back into the limitations of the human body against his will, trapped within the confines of his own skin.

Eric turned back to face Pastor Reynolds, his expression almost featureless as it had been before. "I am not sure of my purpose for being here, but I do know it is linked to my son Timothy and my sister, Mildred. Erica fits in there somewhere, but I'm not sure. But when I left, something in them changed, and when I died, even though they hadn't known, their minds had already treated me as if I were dead. They hated me, they grieved me, and they generated a pain so deep that it began to disrupt their core being. This whole town had been experiencing this, from others that have died in their lives, and there are so many souls crying out at such depth, that even the Heavens can feel their sting."

"I haven't noticed any change," Pastor Reynolds said, "I haven't noticed a change that deep in Mildred, or even in Erica or Timothy for that matter. They seem to have moved on, despite your disappearance."

"No, you wouldn't notice the difference, because it resides too deep within the spirit for you to see it clearly. But the residue of it, the proof of its existence, has already been revealed to you Pastor, only you didn't realize it."

"It has?" Pastor Reynolds asked, staring blankly at Eric.

"Yes, in Erica. I am sure you have observed how easily she is accepting me and her son's return. She has suppressed her anger, her grief, and her dismay to such a degree that it's almost as if it had not happened. It is a very dangerous sort of denial, one that will keep her from moving ahead in her own life. How can you continue to wrap your life around a past that no longer exists? In some small part, it will become a reality you can never escape from."

"But she loves you, Eric. Is it wrong to continue loving you? Are we all being punished for loving too hard?"

"I think this town is being punished for not letting love run its course, and letting go."

Pastor Reynolds thought on this. This town would have a tough time letting go of grief, considering all of the grief it has been through. He has overseen a lot of funeral services in the past two years; and many times, before one had a chance to grieve, another tragedy would befall them or someone they knew. This was a small town, and what affected one was bound to affect all. This was almost in line with what he taught about Christ in his church, because although He died, his Spirit lived on in the people that believed in Him; so in fact He never really died at all. The dead now, although dead, were now known to the living- as living. Can a town exist on the premise that death has been defeated? It was scary.

"How does this all end Eric? How can we undo what had been done?"

Eric took a seat next to the Pastor, his voice began at a very low timbre, "I don't know Pastor. I really don't. How do you make a whole town forget their past pains? And it gets even deeper than that, because there are some deaths that have not caused pain, but pleasure. If you wanted someone dead, took pleasure in their demise, what can you now feel to discover their return to life? There are many skeletons, good and bad, that are about to be unearthed in Crest Hill County, Pastor. How they all will be handled is anybody's guess."

"Then if you don't know, what is it that we can do? Are we to just wait until this town falls apart at the seams?"

"I don't know that either, Pastor. It is too soon to see where this is going, but there is one thing that is a definite, and that is the sorrow in this town must stop. People must learn to accept what life and death has to offer. Even you have to deal with some things too…especially the final question that you are afraid to ask."

"Are you a mind reader, Eric?"

Eric smiled. "No, but you have to remember that I am no longer a part of this world, although I live in my old flesh. I have seen its limitations, and I can now read your human nature, your flesh, as if it were a chalkboard etched with your feelings, your thoughts. It may seem like mind reading, but to see what is on your mind, is as easy as watching a dog's tail to understand if he is happy. You, Pastor Reynolds, are sad."

"You can see that can you?" Pastor Reynolds questioned.

"Well," Eric began to say, reaching out to place a hand on the Pastors shoulder, "The art of letting go has to start with you."

Without Eric stating exactly what he was referring to, Pastor Reynolds picked up on it. He tried glancing at Eric, but found it hard to hold eye contact. He tapped the back of his heel against the wooden platforms, and interlocked his fingers. "But I don't know if I can Eric. I don't know if I want to."

"Then you understand what may be this town's greatest downfall. I may not know why I am here, I may not know how to save this town, but if you realize how hard it is for you, than it is going to be twice as hard for others who have suffered much longer."

Pastor Reynolds wasn't sure what was happening here, but he did feel the truth in Eric's statement, and he also had another question that sat at the tip of his taste buds, drowning in his saliva.

Eric could not wait for the question any longer, and decided to just give the answer, "I'm sorry Pastor, but I don't know why Maya has not come back to you."

The quickness of an answer where there was no previous question caught Pastor Reynolds completely off guard. It was not only the answer that he didn't want to hear, it was also an answer that made him want her back even more…and deep within his spirit, he could feel a tear slide off the edges of his heart.

Part V

Benny needed to get away. He needed to escape his reality. He needed to be with the one man he thought he would have spent the rest of his life together with. Jason Colby.

So he invited Jason to walk with him near the bottom of the Crest Hill's hill: Crest Hill, where there stood an array of highly priced homes that traveled up and around the hill through a maze of roads and trails leading to the uppermost (which included the one owned by Jenna Reed). He wanted to talk with Jason because, even though he had cheated on him, he had never wished him dead, and he had never stopped regarding him as friend.

"I don't know how to deal with this, Jason. This whole situation has become very difficult for me," Benny said, looking out at the many homes they passed, the streets were very quiet.

"Are you speaking about the situation of me being here, the matter with the salon, or the matter with your boyfriend? Perhaps you are speaking of all three."

Benny looked up at Jason. He was always the blunt one, he thought. "Maybe it is all three. I want to enjoy the time that you are here, but I also need to remember that I have another life too."

Jason was silent for a moment. "I am glad to be back, Benny, believe me, but the question remains to be, why am I back here. It certainly isn't because of you."

"And what about our friends…do you think you came back for one of them?"

Jason kicked his heels along the pavement. "I don't know. Someone is grieved about me being here, someone I can't put a finger on. I still have to talk to Anthony more, because I am thinking it may be him. As for everyone else, well during my visitations, they all acted as if I had gone on some spiritual retreat or day spa for a year; everyone was just happy to see me, but their lives went on as usual. Some said they wanted to throw a going away party for me before I head back to the hereafter."

Benny smiled at this. "The gay community and their excuse to throw a party."

"I suppose…it's just very interesting that everyone appears to have come to terms with my death."

Benny stopped; grabbing a hold of Jason's wrist. "We seem that way, because it took a while for you to die, Jason. You were unconscious most of the time, drugged up the other, and even when you could speak in complete sentences, they were tiny words you seemed to just string together. It was hard on all of us, but it also gave us a chance to accept what was happening to you."

Jason pulled Benny closer. "You were so very good to me then. It all came back when I died, when I was able to piece my life back together at those last moments." He broke the grip and could see Benny's eyes streaming with tears. How he wished he were able to shed tears again, but the dead do not know such small miracles. "My mind could not tell me what my eyes were seeing, until I was lifted into a higher form, a spiritual form, without limits."

"I try to forget those moments, in that hospital…"

"I know you do. I felt your sorrow. You somehow felt useless after I passed. I was not there for you to take care of anymore."

Benny looked up at Jason. "I didn't tell you that," he said. "What else have you seen?"

Jason slung an arm around Benny's shoulder, just as a young group of girls came along the street to glare at them. He smiled at them, as they passed by giggling. "No Benny, I didn't see anything from where I was. The dead can't view the living, and why would we? There is no real time in the afterlife. Watching humans would be like watching dust gather." He leaned his head closer to Benny and could sense that this calmed him. "What I understood were the feelings you had; small moments of happiness, sadness, melancholy, anger. They came to me in an array of colors and sensations that I really can't explain. Feelings of our loved ones are the pleasures of the afterlife. Heaven or Hell; It is the one real thing you miss when you die."

"And where were you, Jason," Benny turned to ask, but looked shocked, as if it was something he had not intended to inquiry about.

Jason gave Benny a slight pat on the back, and resumed their walk side by side, "That is a fair question, Benny. But I can't say. Heaven or Hell, I am not sure if many of us are allowed to remember much of our afterlife. I am not even sure if they can be explained in the human sense. There is an incubation period between life, death, and life again – it is akin to an infant going from sperm, to fetus, to child. You don't remember the transition, but you know it happened. I do get bits and pieces of information, but never the whole." He stopped. "Does that make any sense?"

"No," Benny quickly said smiling, "But you were always a smart ass."

Jason smiled at this too, and the feeling of bliss both surprised and thrilled him. "And that is how I knew you had met someone, that you had a boyfriend, because your emotions told me so."

"And you were okay with that?"

"Of course. We all die Benny, but some of us sooner than others. Understanding that you will die, makes you cherish life a little more; but once you die, you can no longer relish in your past life. So yes, it would have been great if we had experienced this side of existence together, but you are here. Take advantage of it…with whomever you wish.

"Then I am really glad to be sharing some of my living now with you," Benny said.

"I suppose this is our second chance to do so, even though it is not the reason for me being here, at least it allows even me a final chance at existence."

"And if you can enjoy this, are there any other things that you can enjoy again," Benny asked, as he sized up Jason with the strangest look.

Jason smacked Benny along the back of his head, "Now get your mind out of the gutter. There are some things that are not going to be possible."

Benny rubbed the back of his head and managed to retain his laughter behind a most stretched grin, "Well…I did have to ask."

CHAPTER 10

Part I

"Closed!" Tilly looked at the sign on the door as if just by staring at it long and hard enough, the words themselves would suddenly change. "How in the world do you just up and close a cemetery?"

Mark stepped beside her to also take a look at the sign. He ran his finger across the metal plaque and pushed away a line of dust, revealing a crisp whiteness beneath. "They obviously haven't used this sign since the beginning of time. What do you think would make them dig it out now?"

Tilly shook her head, and walked over a short hedge beside the walkway, towards the side windows along the building. "I can't see much happening inside. Try the bell again, Mark," she said, using the hem of her shirt to clean the window.

The sound of the doorbell echoed within the Morning Glory Cemetery, but no one came.

"Try knocking on the window," Mark suggested.

She did, and still there was no response. "I don't get it," Tilly said, walking back to the entrance. "Carl called me to come over, and now it seems that the place is locked."

Mark scratched at his curly hair, and turned away from the door. "Maybe he left a note around here or something, and that…" he paused suddenly, bringing a hand to rest above his eyebrows. "Is that somebody coming this way?"

Tilly looked in the direction he was speaking of. She took a few steps nearer to Mark. Along the street leading up to the mortuary, there was someone skipping along the pavement. "It's someone's little girl."

The girl was moving at a smooth but hurried pace in their direction. She wore a bright floral dress that spanned from her knees, white gloves, and bouncing pigtails. She wiped at her dark brow, before finally reaching the end of the walkway.

"I don't see anyone behind her," Mark said, stepping closer to the girl, as he continued to look along the street.

The girl looked down the street too, as if to see who Mark was looking for. She grinned; the edges of her mouth gleamed with hints of pink lip gloss. "No one is following me. I came up here by myself."

Before Mark could respond, Tilly brushed past him, and stared at the young girl.

"Hey, are you Tilly?" the young girl quickly said, swinging her arm out to point. Tilly moved closer, her steps cautious.

"Yea, it's me. Do I know you? Should you be out here without your parents?" Tilly asked, lowering herself on one knee. The girl was slightly taller than her, and Tilly thought she had to be at least about eleven-years old.

"I'm on my way home now I believe," the girl said, sounding unsure. She scratched at her head, "Yea, of course I am. Carl just gave me the directions."

"Carl…the caretaker?" Tilly asked, looking around at Mark; who appeared more baffled than her.

"Yea, he wants you to go around to the back entrance, near the south gate. It will be unlocked for you," the little girl said, folding her arms and bobbing her head, as if she were proud of herself for remembering such a long message.

Tilly stood, stepping closer to Mark. "What do you think this could mean?"

Mark looked down at the young girl. "I say, with all that is happening we better listen to her."

And that is when Tilly remembered. She turned to face the girl again, and fell once more on her knees to speak more personable. "What is your name, young lady?" Tilly asked in her softest voice.

"Natalie," she said, her hands linked behind her back.

"And when did you *die*?"

She shrugged her shoulders. "Not sure. All I remember is talking to Renee; she is my best friend, and then a loud noise on the school bus. I can't remember when that was right now."

Tilly rested her hand on the girl's shoulder, "It's okay."

The girl receded a few steps, then glanced back at the sidewalk. "Okay. I have to go now."

"Of course," Tilly said, giving the girl a reassuring smile. "Thank you for the message, Natalie."

The girl smiled back. "You're welcome," she said, and without another word was on her heels, heading back down the street.

Tilly watched the girl skip away. "I take it we need to go to that back entrance. Are you coming with me Mark?"

"Something tells me I should."

When they went around to the south wall, there was the gate, neatly hidden behind some untrimmed shrubs, and nestled between two brick walls. It was unlocked, just as the girl said. The mist was still hovering about, blurring their vision, and as they walked through the gate, they had to pause for a minute just to get their bearings – even the high pointed structure atop the mortuaries roof, was difficult to pinpoint.

As they began to travel along a familiar path that lead through the cemetery, Mark noticed something else very odd. "Look over there, Tilly. What is going on today?" Mark asked, as he pointed to Tilly's right.

She looked beyond the mist, and the dips and curves of the landscape, she could see small pockets of people strolling about. "What are so many people doing here?" she mumbled to herself. It was as if a large family reunion was happening, with people chatting, walking, laughing, and embracing shoulder to shoulder.

"This is starting to get very freaky," Mark said.

She had to agree, and the faster they found Carl, the clearer this whole incident would be for them. Or at least that is what she hoped would transpire.

But when they navigated through the grounds, they noticed a line of people, all waiting to get to a large folding table that was stationed near the rear of the building.

At the table, Tilly noticed Carl there, hunched over the table, in what appeared to be a deep discussion with a rather large man that happened to be at the head of the line.

Someone else was beside Carl at the table; it was Audrey Monroe, the daughter of the owner of the Morning Glory Cemetery. She was in a seat, pouring over a barrage of papers and open books. It took a while before Carl broke eye contact with the person in front of him, to see Tilly and Mark heading in his direction. He waved at them.

Carl was looking haggard, wearing striped overalls with one strap loosened, and a cotton brown shirt that was opened at the neck revealing his gray, stringy chest hairs. There was a streak of dirt on his sweat riddled face that ran the length of his cheek. Audrey was no better, with hair pulled back across her yellow skin, frayed at the ends – uncombed and dry – she wore a dark blue blouse with the sleeves rolled up, and next to her was a steaming coffee cup.

"Carl, what is this?" Tilly asked as she got closer, dragging Mark behind.

"One second Tilly," Carl said, holding up a single finger. He turned to the man in front of him, who was much taller, at least six-feet six, and his wide form seemed to cast Carl in shadow. He was white, with a shaved head and golden beard. He glanced at Tilly with the most aqua eyes she had ever seen. Tilly could tell he was at least Carl's age, from the amount of crow's feet at his eyes and the way his chin doubled up, but she could also tell that he was stunning in his youth. "Just take a left at what used to be the old firehouse. I'm sure you remember where that is. They haven't moved very far from when you were alive, Alex."

The man leaned back and offered his hand towards Carl. "Thank you, Carl. You would be amazed at how much you forget."

Carl shook the man's hand. "I am sure. Forgetting is a continual process I suppose, whether in this lifetime or beyond."

Alex placed a hand on Carl's and smiled. "Yes, I would have to agree with you there," he said, and moved unceremoniously out of the line.

"Did you hear what that man said?" Mark whispered to Tilly.

She didn't reply, and while still processing what had happened, she released Mark's fingers, and stepped closer towards Carl. It was then that Audrey looked up to notice them.

"Tilly…Mark. It's so good to see you both," she addressed casually, and then returned her attention back to the well-dressed assembly of individuals she'd been assisting; which consisted of about ten people – a number that was slowly mounting.

"Are these who I think they are?" Tilly finally asked; an assumption disguised as a question.

"They are," Carl replied. "Some of them seem to need a little direction." He explained, his eyes, puffy and bloodshot.

Tilly looked through the line. There were people of all ages and races, with listless expressions that appeared plastered on like stucco. "Directions you say?" she repeated.

Tilly could see Carl nodding his head as the mist muddled his image. "These people want to go back to the loved ones they left behind," at this he scratched his scalp, as if taking a moment to arrange his own thoughts. "From what I can gather, they are here for a purpose, but what that purpose is they can't rightly remember."

"What is Thomas Hadley saying about all of this, Carl? Isn't he still the mayor around here?" She wasn't sure why she asked such a question, but this sudden air of irresponsibility was stifling; as if this town were not a town at all, and there was no duty to its protection.

Carl smiled again, and turned to look over at Mark, who had gone to talk with Audrey. "I hear he is out of town on some sort of convention," and then he turned to look at Tilly again, and there was the strangest look on his face. "You are feeling it too, aren't you?"

She was a bit confused by his statement, but his determined look made it seem that she was supposed to know what he was talking about. "…feeling it?"

He leaned in closer to the table, brandishing a stiff finger towards the next person in line, while he steadied his voice to speak words that would unravel her every nerve, "The feeling of fear, Tilly. Don't you feel that it has somehow *left* you?"

She thought about this. She thought about this very hard. She was standing in a cemetery, amongst the walking dead, in the middle of the strangest mist she had ever encountered, talking to a groundskeeper who had turned the grounds into some sort of Informational Booth for the Deceased…and she felt as calm as if this was an everyday occurrence. This realization alone is what actually scared the hell out of her. "What's happening Carl?" she said, stepping back from the table. She glanced in Mark's direction, as Audrey whispered to him; and she could see the same realization creep up on his face like ivy.

"I realized that there is a Comic Book convention in Chicago, a Mortuary Convention in Gary, Indiana; an Electronics Convention in Schaumburg; a Police Convention happening someplace in Springfield. The list is endless."

"What has that got to do with anything, Carl?" Tilly asked, the fear in her voice escalating her tone.

Carl reached out to hold her hand. "It means that someone…or something, wanted certain people to stay in town, and certain people to stay out. I also found it odd by the ones I have talked to, at how calm we all seem to be. There should be mayhem in the streets at the dead coming back to life…but there isn't."

She pulled her hand back and held her arms; rubbing them nervously. She looked deeply at this mist now, trying to see something that was not there – hoping to see something that was not there. And found it suddenly hard to breath. "But isn't this growing? It looks somehow thicker."

"It is growing, and from what I hear, it may soon threaten to cover the whole town."

She reached out to it. There was a slick yet gritty feel to it; barely noticeable - but it seemed to leave little moisture. "If this has the power to raise the dead Carl, what will it do to the living?"

Fear was still in him, Tilly noted. "I don't know...but I'm afraid it's something we won't find calming at all."

Part II

Mildred continued to look out her bedroom window. The horizon was hazy, and she strained her eyes against it. She was watching a certain car stream along the road, the dust eddies it produced from its churning tires seemed a distant relative of the haze she was now staring at.

She was also busy shoveling spoonfuls of Crispy Wafer-Chocolate Chip-Swirl Fudge-Natural Ice Cream into her mouth; and it would only take a few more mouthfuls to empty the one-gallon container. As she continued to watch the car advance, she recognized that it was Luther, but there was something different, something else she saw, that sent a shiver through her bones with a lightening swiftness. There was a shadow in the passenger's seat – a very human form.

Something snapped inside of her like a bended twig forced beyond its measure. For an instant she pictured Maya sitting there, her form somehow as much alive as her memory had been...*has* been! If the dead were truly beginning to rise, then why hadn't she? Mildred shoveled another creamy spoonful into her mouth, swallowing too quickly, and her throat seemed to lock from the coldness.

The car stopped, and Luther stepped out, walking slowly towards the passenger side, where he opened the door for its occupant...relief! It turned out to be her nephew Timothy. He bounded from the car as if made of springs, and hopped towards the front door of her home, with Luther trailing behind – and just before he went out of view, she could see his eyes glance up at her.

She closed the curtains, brought another measure of ice cream into her mouth, listened as her husband's footsteps bounded the stairs, and continued to wait in silence.

Luther rounded the spiral staircase and eased in to see his wife standing at the window, her back to him. She was wearing a long black robe, but was fully clothed beneath, except for her bare feet one of which was tapping slowly upon the wooden floors. He could see she was dressed in black cotton pants and a white pullover blouse, and even through the sheer robe; he could tell she had just pulled her garments right out of the dryer without investigation. "You been in that window all day?"

She turned around, with the handle of a spoon still stuck from her maw. "I see you've brought a guest with you," she mumbled, taking the spoon from her lips.

He took off his blazer and tossed it on the bed, then headed towards his unkempt credenza at the far end of the room. The chill from the opened balcony doors fluttered a few papers about. "With the way you have your nose plastered to the window glass; it would be surprising if anything missed your watchful eyes."

She scowled at him, watching as he sat at his desk. "I wouldn't have to look for things, if some people weren't hiding so much."

He ignored her comment and reached into a drawer to pull out a large Bible; its pages were stabbed with notes and torn edges. He could hear Mildred sitting on the bed, her eyes burning into his back. He glanced back at her. "Has that been your only lunch today?"

"It's better than being forced to eat all the excuses you've been feeding me," she said, spinning the large spoon around the container that sat pressed between her thighs.

"You're upset. There's no talking to you when you're like this. Have you also drained the liquor cabinet to wash down your meal? You left the door open again."

"Would it really matter to you what I did, or what I left open?"

He slid his seat around in her direction, looking steadily at her, unblinking. Their marriage was so filled with pain that communication had somehow become a lethal weapon. "Your nephew is downstairs, Mildred. I have him sitting in the entertainment room seeing what he can find on cable to watch. He is not doing well with his mother and father acting so…I don't know; I guess the word would be *strange*."

"Strangeness is happening all around us, Luther. That is nothing new, my very inquisitive and watchful husband."

Her words were losing their edge, Luther thought. She was exhausted from the effort of verbal daggers too. "Why don't you just clean yourself up a little, and visit the poor boy. I have a little work to do concerning the spiritual things that have been happening lately."

"Do you really think working on finding a solution to this whole mess, is going to be some kind of penance for you?"

He slid his chair back in the direction of his desk. "I don't know what you're talking about, Mildred."

"You seem to be keeping yourself busy, because you no longer have a mistress to occupy your time. Is that what all this sudden investigative work is about? Your sins have not vanished just because she's gotten what she's deserved."

"Enough, Mildred!" He said, his shoulders suddenly shaking.

"Enough of what? Are you still thinking about her? You know that whatsoever a man thinketh, he so also does."

He stood, pushing his seat away with the backs of his legs, and raised his arms, the ends displaying the curl of his tightened fingers. "Don't start quoting Bible verses to me. I'm not in the mood for this. I have had enough to deal with trying to communicate to a back-to-life-brother in law, to have to deal with a larger-than-life-wife."

She watched him come closer to her and stilled her tongue. There was a certain satisfaction that she could still generate such emotions in him...even if they were of the negative kind. Luther's shoulders were hunched forward, drooped, heavy looking, but his walk was steady and determined, as if his mind was on a journey his legs were pursuing. He sat beside her, leaning forward. His silence made Mildred very nervous.

"I saw your brother," he began, his breaths were drawn out, "...and have come to realize that this is becoming more real than any of us could have imagined." With that, he turned to look at his wife, studying her reaction. He couldn't readily see any. "The big question is, why have you not gone to see him? You seem to be angry at him too, Mildred."

She wasn't prepared for this sort of exchange, and it jarred her a bit. She lapped at her tongue; the remains of ice cream along her lips fell easily into her mouth. Yes...she was angry at him, she thought, for leaving her here with an invisible husband. Yes, she was very angry at that. But she wasn't about to give Luther the satisfaction of knowing it.

"I am angry, Luther. Don't I have every right to be angry? I am your wife, and you made the decision to forget that," she said, turning to look at the window again and away from him. "I didn't deserve what you put me through. I didn't"

He pursed his lips. "Maybe you didn't, and maybe you did, Mildred."

She looked at him puzzled. "What did you say to me?"

He slowly stood up without a glance in her direction. "Mildred, I never said that I wasn't in love with you. Perhaps I did stray in my mind, I'll admit that, but you strayed long before I did. You strayed with each piece of jewelry you bought, with each drive you took out to the city, with each second you spent with your brother instead of with me. I strayed because in this marriage, I realized I had been the only one in love."

And suddenly her ice cream began to taste a little different, a little bitter, a bit more like crow perhaps, but it would take more than a jolt of reality to bring her down. "I am still your wife Luther, and it is only respectful for you to discuss something like that with me first."

"Maybe," he said sullenly, and walked past his desk to close the glass patio doors before taking his seat again. "But when you're in a loveless marriage, your mind gets a little preoccupied."

She let this also sink in, and realized at that moment, that her ice cream was now gone. There was so much more she wanted to say, wanted to yell at him about, but he craned over his desk like an unconscious Griffin, and she realized he was as tired of the battles as she was.

"You have a nephew downstairs that would like to see his aunt. I think you may want to pay him at least a social visit, before he raids the refrigerator of the rest of your ice cream reserve. He too has a certain amount of hate welled up in him, and I figure you two will be good for each other," he stood at his desk for a moment, his head held down, slapped his palm atop it in an act of frustration. "I'm going to spend some time in the backyard. I think I need a moment for myself right now; a quiet place."

She watched him walk out the door, saying nothing. She was very angry at him, that part was true, and perhaps the part about her not really loving him was another truism. But one thing she was most assured of, and that was, if she found out that that teenager had exhausted her supply of Crispy Wafer-Chocolate Chip-Swirl Fudge-Natural Ice Cream, she would ring his neck.

Part III

Jenna looked at the group sitting in her living room, and was quite frankly tired of the mundane chatter they had embarked upon. They all knew why they were here, so she thought it was time to get things started.

"So, what do you think about all the rumors of dead folks walkin' the streets," Jenna said, her eyes glaring over the rim of her tea cup. The sudden silence from everyone present frightened her for a moment.

Five of them were sitting around the wide coffee table in Jenna's living room, which looked less like a living room and more like an antique showroom. There was enough porcelain and drapery hanging about and inlaid with smooth finishes and intricate cuts, that with adequate sunlight the area seemed to come alive all on its own. This illusion was never more present as the sudden silence mounted.

Across from Jenna was Ruth, a fellow retired schoolteacher near to her own age. She appeared mild and meek, with her tiny face and thin frame. She caught many new students unawares at her knowledge of youth and attitude; a powerful woman who spent the last few years of her tenure substituting. Something she continued to do till this day.

She reached out to grab a shortbread cookie when Jenna made her statement, her beautiful eyes bucked like a newborn doe. "Well Jenna, I thought you knew that this whole ordeal was no longer a rumor," she announced, cookie crumbs darting from her wide mouth.

Jenna reached across the table, trying to grab the tea kettle. It was just beyond her fingertips. "Phillip, can you pass Ruth some tea, so she can wash down all my good homemade cookies, instead of propelling them across the table."

Phillip, a retired fireman, who had a broad build, and stone features, also owned one of the tiniest voices anyone had ever heard come out of a man. He became a part of this small band of friends when his lover, Jerry Obeck, died in an office fire that Phillip was dispatched to. They had been together for almost 20 years. Maya was known to bring him dinners twice a week to keep in his freezer while he grieved. It was one of the many acts of kindness she had bestowed on this town. Soon after, Jenna asked that he join their small gathering. Of all the lives he had saved, it was Maya and Jenna's acts of kindness that had finally saved his sanity.

Phillip was dark as coal, with a crescent of gray surrounding the back of his head like a glued-on boomerang. He was very beautiful, with a full set of his original teeth, and a distinguishing dimple pressed into the center of his chin. At nearly 65, he was still quite attractive to very young men, and this had become the topic of many interesting stories within the group.

"Here Ruth, try sucking on this for a moment," Phillip joked, as he began to pour fresh tea into her cup.

Ruth gave him a wily smirk, as she steadied her cup, "Very funny, Phillip. I see both you and Jenna are both making light of this situation since we got here." She tilted her head to stop Phillips pouring, and sat back in her seat. "Jenna just hasn't had the dead come back to visit her just yet. So I can understand the doubt in her voice."

Jenna was at one end of the oblong coffee table, and Phillip was at the other. At the opposite ends was a sofa, which was shared by Ruth and Alice Hornsby, and opposite them was Dorcas Haans, and her big hair, resembling a settled cloud. Her and Jenna could be sisters with their similar features; lean and long. Their style was very opposite, where Jenna chose to wear clothes with small prints, Dorcas chose the biggest and loudest she could find. Even now, her hair was wound in such wide curls; it was as if she used logs to roll them.

"Your time is coming soon, Jenna. I can feel it," Dorcas said.

Jenna shook her head. "Of all the days to hear you sprout your hocus-pocus, this is not the time."

Dorcas leaned forward a bit to reach for the sugar bowl on the table, taking up the tongs slowly in her slender fingers, and plucked out a sugar cube. "You know I'm gifted, Jenna. I would keep my wits about me if I were you. Death is going to be paying you a visit, mark my words."

Jenna rolled her eyes. "I realize that there is something going on in this town, but before Dorcas decides to read our charts, can we ladies get back to the subject?" She waved a hand in Phillips direction, "No offense Phillip."

"Not to worry, I was about to take it as a compliment. This is a hard group to be in, you know."

Everyone chuckled, and the mood was soothed.

"How are you dealing with Conner, Ruth?"

This was Alice speaking. She was soft spoken, and the only one at the group that had not fully retired. She was a nurse's aide, having spent many years as a nurse herself at the local clinic in town. She was very reserved, which everyone thought belied her Latin heritage; but in this group many stereotypes had been reevaluated. She persisted in plastering on a canvas full of makeup, and highlighting her hair in abundant hues - but the cracks in her foundation and the contrast between her dark hair and aged features, made it more than obvious that she mourned her youth, and was not at all ready to accept its passing; at almost 70, the whole group could not wait for that funeral to be over.

Conner was Ruth's deceased husband come back from the grave. He died of a heart attack four-years ago; in the middle of a park, pushing the swing of a little girl; a stranger to him. "He is sitting back in his favorite chair, asking me for another beer as always," Ruth said, looking away from the group and down the hallway that lead to the Jenna's kitchen.

"Even the dead don't have the decency to quench their own palettes. Laziness in the hereafter…who'da thought?" Alice said, lightheartedly.

Phillip shook his head. "Why hadn't you thrown that old chair away, Ruth? I can still remember how tattered it was when he was alive.

She let out an unintentional giggle. "You guys don't know this, but I bought that chair soon after our honeymoon, because," her pale cheeks suddenly flushed. "We had worn out all the other pieces of furniture, and well…"

"Ewww!" Jenna protested. "I am never sitting in your house again."

Ruth shrugged her shoulders, "Well, I still get kinda hot just sitting in it, and…"

"Whoa!" Phillip said, raising his hand, "No details, please."

"Yea Ruth," Alice said, reaching out her empty cup in Phillips direction, as he graciously refilled it. "I must get you some of my toys!"

"If you don't have enough, she can borrow some of mine," Phillip interjected.

This brought on laughter from everyone.

Jenna rocked a bit in her seat, not wanting to ask anything more, but she had to know what was really happening in a town where her friends were experiencing something she had not encountered. It was as if Crest Hill County was becoming a ghost town in the real sense of the word. "And for you Alice, how are you dealing with your nephew?"

Her smile was strained. Her nephew Miguel had come to Crest Hill County to gain more experience in being a construction worker. He helped fix a lot of the issues that dealt with the school. One day, more than 5 years ago, the school was building an addition to the gym, and while he was working on the roof, a wooden beam buckled and fell 20 feet, taking Miguel with it. He died 6 hours later. "I am glad he is here," Alice said, her eyes unsure. "I know this is a most strange thing, and I am not sure if it is from Heaven or Hell, but I am glad he is home."

Jenna could feel her pain. She turned to look at Dorcas, whose hands were shaking, "And what about you Dorcas? What about your boy."

Dorcas jumped slightly. Her mind had already traveled to that moment, when the Sheriffs came to her door, saying her son had died driving one of the school busses caught in the explosion that leveled this town. "He's at home watching videos in his room as if he'd never left. Sometimes I just stand at his door, peeping in, and stare at him. I want this to be real so bad, and yet it is scary, Jenna. It is scary, because I was beginning to accept his death, and now, now I don't know if I have the will to lose him again."

"Are they leaving? Is that what they say?"

"We really don't know," Phillip said, standing up. "Jerry tells me that he is here for a purpose, but he is not sure what. He says he can't stay, but he is not sure when or how he is supposed to leave…" and Phillip's words cut off, as his already tiny voice began to choke. "You're out of tea. I'll make a little more."

"There's more hot water on the stove," Jenna said, as Phillip eased down the hallway, his shoulders almost wide enough to scrape the pictures that hung on the walls. "I'm not sure if I should be happy or sad for everyone."

"You'll know soon enough," Dorcas said, placing her empty cup on the coffee table. She brushed at the bright butterflies colored on her dress.

Jenna wanted to protest Dorcas' comment, but leaned forward, and glanced at her, and Ruth, and Alice. This was real. This was real, and ghosts, or the living-dead, were walking around Crest Hill County as if all the laws of nature had gone asunder. "But who would come back to me," Jenna said aloud, although not wanting to. "I have seen so many deaths, have known so many people, have had so many experiences. I am one of the oldest living citizens in this town."

"On that I am not sure," Dorcas said bluntly, not looking at anyone in particular. "I know you don't want to consider it Jenna, but there is a messenger I believe, that is going to tell you more than you may want to hear. I believe, and I could be wrong, but I believe that through this messenger, you are going to get your answer."

"But what if it is the kids?" Jenna found herself saying.

"What was that?" Ruth questioned.

She could now feel her body begin to tremble, and Jenna gripped the sides of her chair. "What if all those kids, the ones from the bus, the ones that all knew my name, or that I helped to teach during the summer, or tutor in the winters, all came back to me…" she put her head in her hands, and the tears came immediately. There was a hand at her back. She looked up to see Phillip there.

"We're all scared, Jenna," he said.

The statement was so simple, delivered so easily, that for some reason, it calmed her. "Yes, I am Phillip." She noticed he hadn't brought the tea pot back. "Wasn't there any hot water left?"

He walked over to stand behind the chair he had originally sat at. "There was plenty…but Nathan…your husband, wants to talk with you."

She looked up at him in confusion. "Nathan?"

Phillip looked at the others seated, "And I think we need to be leaving. They are going to need a minute or two to talk."

Jenna then looked at Dorcas, who was already beginning to stand. And suddenly the whole room was bathed in a silence that was foreboding and intense. She walked to the kitchen to where Nathan was sitting…waiting.

The only thing was that he was not alone.

There was a young woman sitting with him, holding a baby in her arms. A white woman and a most black child. Her eyes were having the most difficult time comprehending what she was seeing. "Who is this, Nathan?"

Nathan looked weary, sitting in nothing more than a t-shirt and khaki pants, in his bare feet. "You tell her," Nathan said, addressing the young lady.

She looked up at Jenna, glanced at Nathan, and then returned her attention to the old woman who was now staring at her with a mixture of fright and wonderment. "I'm Ella…your daughter."

That's when she heard the front door close shut.

Chapter 11

Part I

There was a change in the air, Eric thought. He could feel it as if it were hands embracing his cheeks. He continued to ponder this as the sun began its dip behind the city, sitting on the horizon giving it one last gaze. The air was becoming cooler, and he leaned back on the wooden bench, pulling the collar of his plaid cotton shirt closed a little, which was more out of a forgotten habit than necessity. He wanted to fear tomorrow, considering the circumstances of what he was feeling; fear would be the closest emotion that his human flesh should be feeling. But he was not.

The town was beginning to settle into the idea of acceptance. The haze that was now motioning towards Crest Hill, had a most numbing effect on everyone, and it needed to, otherwise there would be havoc in the streets. But this mist produced a calm that the human psyche was not used to; almost like a drug, that would eventually make them want to embrace the dead, their loved ones, and their departed, as never before. It would almost strip away any previous mourning they may have experienced or gotten over.

That would only be half the fear, and the least dangerous, because this mist-type fog, not only affected the living, it would also affect the dead. It is one thing to realize you are dead…it is quite another to realize you have been resurrected.

"What are you doing out here?" Erica said, as she began to walk unto the tiny stairs that led to the barbecue deck.

Her sudden appearance did startle him a bit, and he could feel his body shake slightly and unexpectedly. He should have been able to sense her approach. This only went to prove that the strength behind the mist was getting stronger; it could also mean that the gap between the living and the dead was slowly beginning to close.

"I was just doing some thinking," he said, noticing the thick blue robe, and pearl silk pajamas she was wearing. "It's getting cold out here, and a little late. It will be pretty dark soon."

She slid beside him on the bench, reaching out to move his hand away from his collar, so that she could button it for him. "I know that," she said, her voice low and steady, "But I was just wondering if you were going to stay out here all night, or would you just humor me and pretend to sleep inside…in our bedroom."

She eased closer, and a breeze caught at her robe, the softness of it brushed across Eric's face, catching him off guard for a moment. "No, I don't think that would be a good idea. Aren't you going to work in the morning?"

She didn't like the aggressive and off-putting tone he used, and leaned back a bit to make sure he saw how inappropriate that question was. "You mean at the library?" she said, moving her hands away from him, and turned to glance back at the house. "I called them up already, and told them I was taking a week of my vacation."

"Now why would you do that? Is it because I'm here?" When he said that, she spun back to face him at such a speed, he wondered why her neck didn't snap in two.

"What a question, Eric Colefield Ross. Of course I did it because of you. Do you expect any of us in this town to act like things are normal? Half the staff at the library has called in sick, and the place is going to be open for only half a day." She shook her head, "What a question."

He had to admit that the question did sound a bit odd. Of course the town could not pretend that it was business as usual. "I guess that's why Timothy went over to Uncle Reynolds'."

"He just needs some time to adjust to this, I think. To have his little brother and father return must be very hard on him. He's young, but I'm sure he will take no time to warm up to the idea."

"The idea of what?" Eric found himself asking.

She leaned back in his direction, their shoulders touching. "The idea of us being a family again, of course."

It was going to be hard, he thought. He could see it in her eyes that it was going to be hard for her to let go. He allowed her the serenity of her thoughts for the moment. As the sun began to fade, his senses became more aware. He became aware of others who had been resurrected, and the living they had come to visit. Moments, memories, actions, all came to him like a rush of rain upon his skin.

What he could see…feel: The Andersons were talking to their three-year old son, and he was telling them that the dog mauling that killed him, was not a random act, but it was from the neighbor's pit bull when his chain broke. They went out to buy a new dog the next morning, knowing precisely what had happened to him, but acted as if it were some other look-a-like animal.

The Kirk family was about to discover that their daughter fell from the fifth-floor condo balcony at a friend's homecoming party, not because she had been drinking, but because her jealous boyfriend pushed her over the edge.

The Donner family will discover in about an hour, that grandpa was killed when grandma cut his heart medication pills in half, letting him think he was getting a full dose. She confessed this to him as he was having his heart attack, unwilling to live with him any longer in poverty, and needing the insurance money to finally live her life without the burden of children, being a wife, or having a husband.

…there were others, so many others.

There would be rage, anger, confusion, but no mourning. The mist will have brought a peace to their mourning that they would not be aware of. No matter how their loved ones died, no matter how they would have missed them, no matter what they had done…they would be forgiven. They would be welcomed. The living will not want them to die again. But in order for Crest Hill County to move on…they would have to let the dead go in peace...something the living may not be ready to do.

"So what do you plan on doing Eric, staying up all night? That can't be healthy," Erica said, reaching out to grab his arm.

Her actions were harmless enough, Eric thought, but he wanted to laugh at her question. He could not be in any better health. "Erica," he began, his words forming slowing in his head as they unraveled past his lips. "I know you want to have our family back very much. I know it was difficult for you to deal with the loss of me, but more greatly, Eric Jr. But you do understand that we both have to leave again sometime?"

She smiled at him; or was it *through* him? "I'm sorry, what were you talking about?"

"Me and your son are going to eventually have to go back to the afterlife, where he came from. Do you understand that?" He tried to be as gentle as he could.

She leaned into him, resting her head against his shoulder as the sun finally dipped its hat to the night. "What a lovely sunset. Now, if you're going to be staying out here for the rest of the night, at least you can tell me what you would like to have for breakfast in the morning."

He sighed. This was going to be much harder than he thought.

Part II

Lisa could smell the pot roast cooking, and she'd changed the sheets on the bed at least twice. The apartment was bathed in candlelight, and a soft jazzy tune was playing on the radio. Earl said he and a few other ushers were going to stay at the church, and they all thought it best she remain home and try to relax. Pastor Reynolds even called her to say that while his wife and nephew were at home, he was going to take a moment to go to the church and talk with some of the congregation; ease as many grief-stricken minds as he spiritually could. He too had suggested that she take the night off.

What they all didn't know, was that she had already planned to do just that.

The doorbell rang, and she rushed to it, the heels of her new black lace slip-ons catching in the fray of her rug. A full-length mirror hung against a partition of wall that jutted out next to the door; an odd piece of architecture she thought was originally created as a place for coat hanging. She looked at herself in the reflection and was pleased with the way her golden hair lay shimmering against her shoulders, the silkiness of her silver lip gloss, the hint of cheek color softened the paleness of her face, and the cream two-piece outfit with hints of yellow really made this look more like a business meeting than what she was proposing.

The doorbell rang again just as she began to open it, and she was at once baffled at the sudden alarmed look upon Andre's face.

"Hello Lisa. I've come as you've asked me to."

He was dressed the same as this morning, but somehow looking much more refreshed. His skin all but glowed, as did his wavy mane of hair, which always managed to put a smile on her face. Maybe that is why he was looking at her so strangely; she just realized her stretched lips had not relaxed. How could they, with him still able to stir up feelings unwanted inside her.

"Hello Andre. I'm glad you could make it. Your news at the church became just a little too much for me to bear, considering all that was happening at the time. I was really not expecting to see you back in town," she said, finally stepping aside, as to let him enter. "I was actually cooking a little dinner, which I need to check on really quickly," she said, as she swiftly ran towards the back of the house into the kitchen.

He stood there, watching as she walked away. *She didn't believe him*, he thought. After all that conversation back at the church, she still didn't believe that he had died.

"Just have a seat on the sofa," she yelled from the kitchen.

"Lisa, I think we are going to have to go over the conversation we had at the church...again."

"Sure Andre. Are you hungry?"

He slowly closed and locked the door, and reluctantly walked towards the sofa. It was then that he noticed the music, candlelight, and could catch the scent of one well-seasoned meal on the horizon.

"I have a glass of wine on the table for you, just in case you felt a need to relax," her voice came echoing back, followed by her, as she re-entered the living room, carrying a wine glass of her own.

"I'm sorry, Lisa. Were you expecting company? The ambiance isn't exactly what I was expecting."

She took a glance around, "Why thank you, I think. I'm glad you noticed. I thought it would be nice, considering how long it has been since we have seen each other," she said, taking a seat at the other end of the sofa.

"You mean since the time I destroyed our engagement," he corrected.

She looked intently at him, took a loud final sip of her wine, and slammed the glass back unto the coffee table. "We're not talking about that just yet, Andre!"

He was taken aback. "We're not?"

"Did you want your wine or some juice with your dinner? I do remember you being a pretty strict health nut back then and wasn't sure. Although they do say there are some great antioxidants in wine, you know."

He said nothing.

"Don't worry about it. You can decide at dinner. I'm just letting it simmer a little longer," she said, taking a bold move to slide a bit closer to him.

He could smell the tart-sweetness of her perfume. The scent caused him to jolt for a moment; it had been a long time since such an aroma made his flesh react so…considering he had been without flesh, *per say*, for a long time. He had to shake his head to bolster himself back into reality.

"Lisa. Why did you invite me over here?"

She appeared puzzled, and attempted to reach for her wine glass, but pulled back, as if unable to continue with such an obvious distraction – or detraction – of the question. She continued to stare at it however, as if it were some sort of crystal ball guiding her in her answer, "So we can…talk. So, we can understand what happened to us those years back. So, we can talk about where that leaves us now."

"Where that…" he found he couldn't finish the statement. "Didn't you understand anything that I said back at the church? Did you even believe it?"

She tried looking up at him, her eyes trailing along his black leather shoes, seeing the gray of his socks, the hem in his wool pants, his knees; where his hands rested, embraced by the white cuffs of his shirt, the gold circled links with an onyx center. She could still not find it within herself to look directly at him, into his eyes, where truth may lay. "Do you have any idea what happened in this town after that accident Andre, after you died?"

The question stumped him. "No," was all he could manage to say.

This time she did look up at him, her lips cocked into a smirk. "I see," she responded, and reached for her half-drained glass of wine, and finished it. "You died two years ago, and your mother died just last year. That could explain why she came into so much money, but it doesn't explain why you came back…" she said, as if to herself, and stood, wineglass in hand. "I'm going to refresh my drink, and check on the roast, it should be done. I suggest you have a sip or two of yours, before the chill wears off."

He watched her go off into the kitchen, not sure what she was just rambling about, or how his mother ended up in the conversation. But there was something he was beginning to understand, and it had to do with Lisa's soul, her inner spirit. The haze that crept around town a few nights ago was doing something to her, he just knew it, but he didn't know what. It was like she was developing a shell, one he could almost see masking her, one of total denial. Something was also happening to him, and from the signs his old flesh was giving him, he could swear it was dread.

Lisa returned with a set of napkins in her hands. She placed them on the dinner table, "I know I wasn't too good a cook a few years back, but I have gotten better, believe me," she said, pulling the chairs out, "I think you will be impressed. Did you want to go wash your hands before we sit down to eat?"

Andre waved his hands through the air as if he were trying to get the attention of a car that was threatening to run him down. "No Lisa. No, I am not going to wash my hands, or join you to eat, or believe that you are standing there ignoring what I have been telling you."

She dismissed him with a wave of her hand, and began to head back into the kitchen, "Andre, stop with the theatrics. I don't see why we can't start off at least as friends. You are going to have to let go of your anger. You were always quick tempered."

He exhaled so loudly, one would have thought he had just come in from a marathon. What was happening here? He could hear the clattering of silverware in the kitchen, the scent of the meat was thick in the air, heat swelled about his head. Frustration! My god, he'd forgotten what that felt like. He waited until she appeared, this time carrying a small plate with rolls atop them. "What did you mean about my mother, Lisa? I am no longer playing this game. What happened in this town after the explosion? Tell me!"

She jumped at his voice, the plate nearly falling from her hands. "You really don't know?"

"No more games. This is nothing like you. Why are you acting like this?"

"How would you know anything about me, Andre," she said, her voice rising. "If you knew anything about me, you wouldn't have left me weeks before our marriage, you wouldn't have fucked my bridesmaid, and you wouldn't have come back here to this town with all these lies! There are real people in this town who are having real problems, and you come here and expect me to…" she could go on no more. She was frozen, looking at him, seeing him in a past he no longer was, a menagerie of images pelted her mind like tiny assaults to her conscience.

Andre stood, wanting to run to her, to hold her, to squeeze out all of this hurt that was bottled up in her. But he couldn't. Now was not the time. "I'm sorry about that, Lisa. I am sorry I hurt you."

As the tears began to stream, she wiped them away, refusing to have them expose her. "After that accident, this town went into a frenzy. There was horror, grief, fear, and evil. There was an evil that came out of that accident that I still cannot believe is a part of human nature. Insurance claims were filed by the hundreds. Homes, people, cars, it crippled our way of life here. It made world news for the moment and made a lot of people rich. People, who were thought dead, had left town while their spouse collected the insurance money. So many bodies, so many of children, who could not be identified – parts torn asunder, singed to ash. The heat from the oil tanker was immense. "The Ghosts of Crest Hill County" is what one paper called it when the conspiracy came out of adults and their false claims. The government support nearly stopped. Families that deserved that money to rebuild could not get it."

Andre didn't know what to say. No wonder there was a feeling of denial in this town; it had started long before the dead began to walk this earth again. "And you think my mother cashed in on my death? You think I worked for the post office, and when the accident happened, that I just suddenly disappeared?"

She stood there, arms locked across her chest, her features icy. "I don't claim anything, Andre. I wasn't here when the accident happened, but I knew while I was gone, your mother had financial problems, many families did, and suddenly, months later, you are gone along with her family issues. I hadn't put the pieces together, because I thought you had already left town, but you just disappeared in it by the time I returned, and the town never spoke of you to me again."

"The reason you didn't know where I was working, where your friends were, what my mother was really going through, was because you buried yourself into that church, and pushed the rest of the world away. You only know what you know, because you know how to listen to walls and hearsay, Lisa." He turned from her. That *anger* came out so suddenly that he had to turn away from her, just so he could turn it off. "I can't do this Lisa. You are making me say things I should not be. We can't be what we once were, because I am no longer who I once was. I can't make you believe it," he said, his tone washed out. He lowered himself on the arm of the sofa.

"But you are here," she said, her timber slowly coming under control. "I see you. You are flesh and blood, I know. I can smell you. I can touch you. Spirits don't come this real, Andre. Spirits don't make me feel this…this…lustful."

The last word made him look up at her. That was the shell he was sensing about her. She was yearning for him to such a degree, that she was willing to believe anything he told her, except any indication that he was leaving again. He had come to her, and she believed it was not by way of death, but by way of desire. He began to feel very sorry for this woman, and even sorrier for what he had done to her.

He then realized that with the advent of his body having been burned beyond recognition, and the charred remains of his uniform, and identification, along with the fact that his mother only had a memorial service for him; that even if Lisa had been here when he died, that she would have still been hard pressed into believing it. "You're not ready for this conversation," he finally said, rising from the arm of the sofa. "But before this night is over, I think you will soon be more inclined."

She stepped quickly in his direction, noticing that he was motioning towards the door. "Does that mean you're leaving? Don't leave Andre, please don't. I'm sorry I couldn't give you children. I really am. But don't leave me again…"

Her agony sent chills through him. "Children have nothing to do with this now, Lisa. But I can see why your case has become one of the special ones."

"The special ones? What are you talking about?"

Andre let his arms hang at his sides, swinging them like a child. He was not really sure he should be saying what he was about to reveal. "Lisa. In your talks with the people at the church, did you notice how many of them had seen loved ones that had died in Crest Hill – how that most of the people that have not left town, are the same ones that have had loved ones pass here?"

She covered her forehead with her palm; her eyes were wild, wet with moisture that would not fall. "What are you talking about?"

"But there are a special few, who are linked to others that did not die in Crest Hill County. Did you know that Marc Biance died of an aneurysm at a Chicago airport?"

Her heart thumped. "How did you know that? Marc never lived here. He didn't know anyone from Crest Hill County."

"I know he didn't. You met him in Waukegan, I believe. It was one of the reasons you were out there during the accident. You made a visit to his mother. You had grown fond of her, even though Marc was growing apart from you."

She replaced the hand that was on her forehead to now embrace her mouth. "Oh my god! What kinda evil have you brought to my house, to be sprouting this voodoo stuff?"

"Lisa," Andre continued quickly, seeing that her mind was opening up, but it was also becoming extremely frazzled. "Some grief is so strong, that from this town, there are others who are also connected to it that may not have died here. Perhaps I should have expected you not to believe, with your religious beliefs so enmeshed to you, but perhaps through me, you will be prepared to meet others."

Just then the doorbell rang.

Lisa barely heard it, while she tried to ascertain what was happening at this very moment. She was even more startled when Andre moved towards the door, his hands reaching for the doorknob. "What are you doing?" she questioned, just as the doorbell rang out again.

"I think there is someone else that would be glad to share a fine dinner such as this with you…but it will not be me," Andre said, as he opened the door. "Because some of us have traveled a lot further than most, and would be better deserving of your company."

In her doorway stood a man, slightly shorter than Andre, with thick curly black hair, and a slight olive tone to his skin.

"Hello Lisa," said the man with a distinct Latin American accent.

For a moment, a slim instant in time, the name Marc Biance slipped from her throat.

Part II

Midnight.

Benny pressed the fast forward on the remote control, as he and Jason watched a DVD belonging to them both: "Interview with a Vampire". Jason leaned over to try and grab the remote from Benny's hand, but Benny wrenched it even more out of his way.

"Stop it Jason. I'm trying to get to the good part."

Jason shoved him in the shoulder, "You're just trying to get to the part where Brad Pitt burns up the theatre, and he meets up with Antonio Banderas."

Benny gave him a sly look, "And what is wrong with that?"

"I can't believe that you are still turned on by that."

"But it is so hot! When Brad and Antonio; Louis and Armand respectively, were arguing about the aftermath of the fire, and they got so close together that you swear in their heated debate, they were going to just lock lips right there! Whoa!" He shouted, raising his hands in the air.

Jason shook his head solemnly. "You could use some serious counseling, you know that Benny."

"I might really need some, once this raising-of-the-dead trauma is over."

"And is this how you and your new boyfriend would spend your time?"

Benny reached forward, to place his hand in a bowl of popcorn that sat on the coffee table, while his eyes continued to stay glued upon the television. "No... this was something that *we* did. My boyfriend and I spent most of our time doing something you can no longer engage in," Benny said, sticking his tongue out in Jason's direction.

"Please, spare me the details," he responded, but slowly found himself smiling. He was glad that Benny was able to continue his life with someone new. Life was too valuable a thing to waste in complete solitude, without the companionship of this type of love; at least it would have been for Benny. He thrived on loving and being loved. "But I was wondering, just how long had you two been dating?"

"Oh…here is the part, when they are just about to kiss," he said, distracted for a moment by the television. "We've been together for about three and-a-half years I suppose."

Jason's eyes furrowed.

Benny stopped chewing.

And suddenly the most minutiae sound of a dripping faucet could be heard in the kitchen, despite the noise from the television.

Jason continued to look ahead, in the direction of the kitchen. "Am I missing the math here, Benny?"

Benny found it difficult to swallow the last bits of popcorn in his mouth. He was unable to speak, and there was a much pregnant pause hanging between them, that was well beyond its labor.

"No…your math isn't wrong, Jason," Benny said, the words rolling off his tongue like spittle. What else was he to have said? How could it benefit him, to lie to a lover that had already died?

And still, Jason could not look at him. "Perhaps you should take some time to explain this, Benny," and slowly he found the strength to look at his former partner. "I could have sworn it was you at the hospital each and every day looking over me. I could have sworn that not long before that we were here in this place huddled together nibbling each other's ears. I only died two years ago, Benny, and yet you have been in a relationship with someone for three and-a-half?

Benny put the television on mute, and this time, he was the one who found it hard to look at this man in the face. "I'm sorry, Jason. I don't know what to say. I really don't know what to say."

Jason stood, raking his fingers through his thick blonde hair. "You were cheating on me right before the accident, and all through it? Did you even hope that I would survive?"

"Of course, I did," Benny said, placing the remote on the table. He was not sure how to handle this right now, and as he thought about what to say, an internal thought came softly out from his lips, "…this was all much easier when you were dead," and then he looked up startled at Jason, with a most fake smile on his face.

"This is not at all funny, Benny. Had I done something wrong to you in my life? Did you come to that hospital out of love for me, or out of guilt? Did you even love me at the end of my own life, or at just the beginning of my life with you?" Jason said. He was amazed at how calm his voice was sounding.

Benny noted a calmness too, and it rather unnerved him; he thought there were more volatile emotions that Jason must have bottled up. "I loved you at the beginning and at the end."

"And what about the middle?"

"It was a bit shaky in the middle, Jason," Benny admitted.

The pregnant pause returned.

"Why? Hadn't I done enough for you?"

Benny stood, and spun in a slow circle, while holding the back of his neck. "Yes, yes, yes. You were amazing Jason…but amazing I was not prepared for. "I pushed myself away from you, because I didn't think I deserved you. I didn't think I could be the same for you, as you were for me."

Jason took a deep breath. He could feel the truth in that statement as if Benny had waved a banner above his head. "What could make you think something like that?"

"You did Jason. You did," he raised his head for a second, lips moving in tune to what he was thinking, but he didn't let his words go so freely this time. "Sometimes I felt devalued being with you. In a relationship, your value is sometimes determined by the contribution level you can put into it."

"Oh, and you are saying I treated you too good? You are saying that maybe I should have been abusive to you, maybe neglected you, perhaps even have cheated on you..." he tried to stop those last words from coming out, but it was too late.

Benny felt those words as if a whip had lashed his skin. "This has nothing to do with you, Jason; or how you treated me. This has to do with the fact that I didn't need a man that was 100-percent perfect. I didn't realize it, but I needed to feel as if I were needed by you, and I didn't. It scared me. So I searched for someone that I could feel needed me, and able to use what I had to offer."

"But I was there-"

"No, let me talk. This has been in me ever since you died, because when you were dying; I had never felt more needed. I was scared for you, but I was also useful. I began to love you again, but it was all wrapped around the fact that you were helpless. You have always helped yourself, and I couldn't have very well asked you to be a little needier for me. So you being in that coma was sadly, the best moments I had with you." He covered his face with his hands, and fell back unto the sofa. "I've hated myself for thinking that way, for wanting you to suffer a little more, to give me the chance to use up all this giving, this love I wanted to express to you."

"And then I went and put a wrench in it by dying," Jason said, with a slight laugh.

Benny found himself humored by the statement as well, "Well, at least it stopped you from protesting, and trying to redo things your way. But by that time, I was falling in love with two men. I was afraid of you living again, because that would mean I would have had to make a choice, and I think I would have chosen to leave you both, if I had to make a choice at all."

Jason walked in Benny direction, standing over him. He placed a hand on his trembling shoulders. "I guess my death did make things a little easier for you," he said.

Benny took hold of Jason's wrist. "But I never wanted it to end like it did, Jason. I would have rather lived away from you, than to live without you...than to wish you dead."

"I know Benny, I know," he replied, reaching his other hand out, the palm exposed.

Benny stood, and moved himself into Jason's open embrace. "I've missed you so much, Jason."

Jason hugged him harder. "I know you have. I don't know why I even asked you so many questions. I'm dead. What do I know now? I never expected that walking across a street would start me on the road to walking out of your life. But I am beginning to feel that one of us had to walk away."

"But to be hit by a car, and have your life cut short. That was not deserving of you Jason," Benny said, his head touching Jason's tall shoulders. He pulled back to look into Jason's eyes.

Jason stared back into Benny's brown pupils, his breath filled with the butter from the popcorn he'd consumed. They were as close as Brad Pitt had been to Antonio Banderas…so close, so very close…

Then suddenly there was a noise behind them – a thrashing sound so loud, that it startled them both. As they turned around, they could see the condo's door was opened, *pushed*, by what stood in the threshold. Harold was there, keys in lock, and a mixed look on his face of both shock and horror.

No words were exchanged as they all stared at each other, until Benny shouted, "Harold!"

But Harold didn't reply, and as his shoulders dropped, he spun on his heels, and was out the door; his keys still hanging limply from the lock of the opened door.

Benny pulled his discarded keys from the lock, and ran down the hall after him. He didn't have to go far, because at the end of the hall was Harold, crouched down near the floor, with his back against the wall. He sounded nearly out of breath. "I'm sorry you saw that, Harold," Benny said, bending down towards him, "Nothing was going on, I swear." He held out his fingers, the loop of the keys swinging from them.

"What was that Benny? Are you fucking the dead now?"

"Don't be silly, Harold."

Harold looked at Benny hard, his eyes unblinking. He reached out to snatch the keys from Benny's finger. "I'm not joking Benny. What has gotten into you?" He began to stand up, looking back along the hallway at Benny's door. "I'm not sure if I can handle any of this Benny."

Benny raised himself up, to look Harold directly in the eyes. "We were only watching television, Harold. You know there was nothing that could be going on."

Harold pressed a stiff finger into Benny's chest. "I wasn't worried about what was going on out there, Benny. I was worried about what may have been going on in there.

Benny looked down at the finger that was pressed very close to his heart. He had no words.

"I'm leaving. I need some time to think."

"But you are here," Benny began anxiously, "You can talk with Jason yourself."

"No Benny. I can't. I love you too much to go through this again," and with his finger still pressed into the Benny chest, he began to push him back, until he was at arm's length.

"I'm sorry about this, Harold," Benny said, not really sure what he was meant to say. "Don't be angry at this. There was nothing happening."

Harold gave a half-grin, as he headed towards the elevators. "There is nothing to be sorry about, Benny, nothing at all. Call me when you are done with your bewitching ceremony." He pressed the button on the elevator, it opened, and he stepped in. He turned to face Benny. "And Benny...*I'm sorry too.*"

The doors closed.

When Benny returned to his place, he saw Jason still standing in the center of the room, with the strangest look on his face. "I'm sorry about that Jason," he said, his voice frustrated. "I feel as though I am always apologizing."

Jason said nothing and continued to look at Benny. Finally, he uttered, "Benny, I think you should sit down."

Benny closed the door and looked curiously at Jason. "Was that scene too emotional for you? I know how you are able to feel certain things now."

"It has nothing to do with that, but I must urge you to have a seat."

There was a certain challenge in his voice, that Benny thought it better to be ready. "I think I will stand. Do you have something to tell me? You're acting odd."

"I do have something to tell you, but I am not sure if you are quite ready to hear it."

Benny crossed his arms. "Try me. Are you going to tell me that I behaved wrongly, in what had happened in the past, when you were in the hospital?"

Jason shook his head. "That matter is over. There is something else I have to talk to you about," and he took a deep breath before continuing. "I thought I was here for you, but I was wrong. When I saw your boyfriend, I realized that I may have come back here for him."

Benny looked back at the door as if Harold was still standing in its threshold. "But you've never met Harold."

"No…I believe that may not be true."

"I don't understand, Jason. What are you talking about?"

"Benny…" another breath, "Harold was the driver of the car that struck me two years ago. Harold was the one that killed me. I remember his face in the windshield with that look on his face. The same look he had at that door."

"What! Are you saying Harold killed you?" Benny repeated nervously.

"Yes."

There was sort silence. "I think I will have that seat."

Part IV

Nathan felt as if he'd just come in from a morning's rain, with the amount of sweat that lay riddled on his forehead.

"What was the big idea?" Jenna stammered, as she closed the door, and looked out at the arched window, watching her daughter and her grandchild walk away from view. "You had no right to usher her out here like that."

Nathan closed his eyes, as if that act alone would shut his wife's mouth from the accusations that she was flailing at him. Ella had been here, at this table, and she was talking to them both, without really having said anything. She knew what was rumored to be going on in town and was not sure if this was the right time for a visit, but she had been searching for Jenna, searching hard from the likes of it, and wanted to just see her, wanted to see the mother that wanted to give her away.

Jenna stood at the door, seeing Nathan with his eyes closed, acting like some damned child. For years she had wondered what had happened to her daughter, how the orphanage had treated her, how she grew up…if she had had any children. But Ella had not wanted to talk about that just yet; she wanted to find out about their lives, her parents (or in a sense her parents, because with her white-as-ivory complexion, she knew that Nathan was not her real father.

"Sit down, Jenna. I need to talk to you."

"I don't know if I want to be in the same room as you, old man. I really don't," she said, looking back out of the window, but seeing the emptiness of the street – it matched the emptiness she was feeling inside.

"Really Jenna, I need for you to sit."

She snapped her neck in his direction. "What was wrong with you, Nathan? Our daughter didn't want to speak about her life with us, and you sat there agreeing with her, acting as if you were somehow scared of her," She could feel herself getting emotional, her hands still clutched to the doorknob. "How could you let her get out of this house like that? Do you know how long I have wanted this moment?"

"I know," he responded blandly, finally opening his eyes. "I know."

She walked in his direction, each step punctuated with a word, "Then-how-could-you-allow-her-to-go? We may never see her again."

"She said she would be back."

"I don't give a damned what she said. She was here now," and then she lowered her head, her tone becoming stammered. She was holding back the sobs she could feel rising in her chest. "She was here now!"

"I need you to sit-"

"No! You sit," she said, knowing her words made no sense, "Or just spit out what you want to talk about. Just spit it out Nathan Reed."

"Jenna," he began, trying to look into her eyes, but couldn't, and glanced about, his eyes like loose marbles, "I never took our daughter to the orphanage when she was an infant, like you thought."

When she'd asked him to spit it out, she didn't expect such regurgitation. "What do you mean, you never took her? How is that possible? What did you do with her?"

"I killed her."

She thought her legs had fallen from beneath her.

"*What*, did you say?" Jenna said, backing away from the table.

"This is a little difficult to say, Jenna."

"Nathan, I'm thinking this is going to be impossible to say." That was when her vision became cloudy, and her throat tight. "To sit here and tell me something like that, especially with all that is going on in this town. I don't want to believe you, to know how it was done, to know what was going through your mind when I trusted you with my baby those many years ago…but I have to believe you. I felt something was going on with you at the table; the way you were staring at Ella, the way she was looking at you. I thought, '*she's dead. Something is telling me that she died as a young girl, a woman, and somehow Nathan knows about it.*' I may have even knew it way back then, when you came to the hotel, looking very strange, out of breath, dirty, not wanting to tell me what had happened, but that you made it to the orphanage in Springfield, and how difficult it was for you to get there; so many white folks wondering what a black man was carrying under those sheets, asking you questions, why were you in their neighborhood. I had been so proud you were able to do it, but you didn't seem to feel the pain I felt, as if you knew it was over." She took a bold step forward, striking her hand on the back of one of the chairs at the table. It startled Nathan. "What did you do, Nathan? Did you kill our child so that you would not have to take her into a white neighborhood? Were you upset because this white child was not yours, and that I had been raped, and you took your anger out on it, thinking it was okay? I know you hated white folks Nathan, but I didn't want to believe you would hate my own child so."

Nathan let her go on. He was not ready to interrupt her yet. His own mind was racing with the real story, the actual events, and he felt as wound up about it on the inside, as Jenna was displaying on the outside. But she was a twister now, in full spin, and there would be no lull in the storm. He had to stop her.

"Quiet Jenna!" He said, holding his head, and standing. With his bad knee, he stumbled a bit from the sudden motion, and braced a hand on the table. "Just shut up! This isn't easy for me either. I've been holding this inside most of my life – our lives. How do you think I felt to see that woman walk through this door, and know it was Ella? How do you think I felt to know that I had killed her? How do you think it was for me to have that kind of pain to resurface?

Jenna was too weak inside to speak any more. Her mind could barely catch up to what Nathan was trying to say. She pulled out a chair to finally sit down. "Can you just tell me what happened, Nathan," she said. Her voice was barely audible.

He took a deep breath before he began.

He began to explain that day, the one a long time ago, when they were sitting in a hotel room holding the two children Jenna had just given birth to: one black, the other white. They'd decided that the white child would be better off left at an orphanage near the center of town. He never made it. As he started off, the child wrapped tightly in a bundle of rags, he realized that it was a monumental task for a black man, carrying a white child, to get to an all-white orphanage, without too much attention. It would be nearly impossible.

As he was walking through town, he came upon the boys that had raped Jenna; three of them. He had hardly remembered their faces from that night – but they remembered him. They noticed him from across the street as he rounded a corner and surrounded him. One of the boys noticed the arm of the white child and wanted to take a closer look. He refused, bundling the infant closer to his body. They pushed him, reaching out to take the child, and while he was being taunted, they tossed pebbles at his head – obviously looking for larger objects.

'Whose baby is that you got there nigger!' one of them yelled, and such accusations were beginning to get the attention of the few people that were milling about on the streets. He became scared...very scared.

He ran.

The woods were not far, and that was where he went – or where he was chased.

"Come back here darky, and get your ass kicked!"

The shouts were upon him; sweat and dirt covered his skin. He knew they would kill him when they caught him. It would be simple sport for them to do so. He had lasted this long because he had remained hidden among his own people, in his own neighborhood, and Jenna's family had a strong, if not small influence in the town of Crest Hill; dating her had been his godsend.

But amidst the shrubs, the rocks, the wet mud of the thickets, he could hear the voices fade; confused in the thickened brush, and he thought he might be spared; the small whimpers of the child falling to his ears. But something unexpected happened: something so utterly out of the ordinary, that he continued to replay the incident over in his mind endlessly for the next 40 years.

He tripped.

The child flew from his arms.

There was a loud cracking noise.

Then silence.

Ella had died.

Nathan was frantic. A black man. A white child. Dead. There was no way he could tell anyone - no way would anyone believe him. With tears in his eyes, he prayed over this child; this stranger he would never get to know, an infant that was not even his, and used a flint stone near the river's edge to dig a hole – a grave; the tinniest grave he would ever see – and buried this child.

He then fabricated the lie about leaving the child at the orphanage, so that he could relay it to Jenna – all the while it began to eat away at his insides.

He could not tell her what had happened, because there was a lot more to think about with just the one child that was left – Ella's sister. He decided that he would have to carry the burden of this truth alone.

"*My God*!" was all Jenna could say, as she stared at Nathan as if a stranger were sitting directly across from her. "This would explain why Tilly's mother is going from man to man. She is missing a connection with someone she doesn't even know was alive."

"I'm sorry I was not able to tell you Jenna. I am so sorry," Nathan said, wringing his hands.

Jenna clenched her fists and pressed them into the sides of her skull. She didn't know how to be mad at him, but she was. "My baby is dead, Nathan! My baby is dead," she said, and began to weep. It all just suddenly came out of her as if her whole body was trying to project through her mouth.

"I'm so sorry…"

Nathan's words came to her ears as an inaudible echo. She closed her eyes and let her grief flow. Even when she could hear Nathan scoot his chair back along the floor, and his footsteps track away from her, and the lock on their guest room open then close, she could not move, she could not respond, she could not concentrate…

…all she could seem to do was weep.

CHAPTER 12

Part 1

Friday Morning: 6am

Hate was in the air…keeping company with fear.

The Monroe Family was dealing with the fact that their eldest son died in what was thought a drowning accident, when in fact it was from a push from his youngest brother, which caused him to die at Crystal Lake.

Lisette was just finding out that the old woman who came to visit her a few days ago, was the same woman in the car she had sideswiped. Lisette had sped off, not realizing that the impact of the accident had frightened this old woman into having an immediate heart attack.

Mrs. Hillsdale was leaving her husband, because their dead son shot himself to escape the sexual abuse of the father.

The Barns Family was now discovering that their daughter didn't die from a head injury caused by gang members trying to rob her; it was from her drunken boyfriend beating her because he thought she may have been seeing another man.

This morning, the dead and the living were finding the reasons they were now coexisting – secretes were now being revealed, their truths come to surface.

Mark could feel the sense of hate and fear in Crest Hill County; as he drove in a town that was way too silent, on a street that was way too bare, in the direction of Tilly's home. The sun was barely creeping above the horizon, and yet the lights were on in almost all the homes on the block. He could see shadows moving beyond the curtains and separated blinds. There was a feeling of dread in this town the likes he had never felt. Most of the younger kids his age felt the same way; every morning becoming as unsure as the next; but this morning, Mark was hoping to put an end to that.

Behind Mark was a small caravan of cars, and as he pulled up to Tilly's home, they did also. He unlatched his passenger side door, and watched it swing out. He could see Tilly slipping from around the back of her home, and unto the street, a backpack hunched over her shoulder.

"This haze is looking thicker, don't you think?" she asked, as she slid inside the car, and closed the door.

Mark kept his eyes on the road, "Yea it does. I don't like it at all."

"Neither do I," Tilly responded.

"Well, turn around and wave at the rest of the crew," Mark said, and he glanced up and adjusted his mirror, "There will be nine of us on this little adventure, and we don't have much time."

Tilly leaned her head out of the window, to observe the three vehicles behind her. She waved, and in response, each car flashed their headlights. As she looked out at the car, flatbed truck, and minivan, she realized that this was real, what they were doing was real, and they were about to head out beyond town…beyond the edges of this most odd haze, this most unnatural mist.

"My Grandparents were acting real strange last night," Tilly unveiled to Mark, as she settled back into her seat. "There was a lot of soft arguing last night, and when I got up this morning, the guest room door was closed tight. They must have eventually slept in separate rooms."

Mark nodded. "I'm not surprised. I was talking with most of the gang last night, and their folks were also acting weird. My Grandma had come back to life, but my mother called to tell me not to come over yet. She sounded really angry. I could hear Grandma in the background yelling at my mother, and wanting to talk to me. I tried sleeping last night, but could feel her reaching out to me in my sleep."

"And you say this was happening to other people?"

"As far as I can tell," Mark responded. "People seem to be going from scared to angry. I just don't know how to explain it better than that. I know it has to do with this mist out here. It has been so hard to get any of the older folks to listen to us, and to do something about all of this."

Tilly had to agree. There were no police knocking doors down, there were no fire trucks, there were no protests or gatherings in the streets. It was as if everyone was confined into their own little world, dealing with their on individual dilemmas. "Then I am glad we are at least trying to do something," she finally said.

"I am too."

They rode in silence as early morning bands of sunlight began to stream out along the streets. The folds of white mist could be seen easing through the town like loose filters of smoke; barely noticed when moving in a car, but visible if you fixated your attention to one point in the horizon. The grayness of the morning sky was not giving way to the brightness of the sun, as it almost vanished behind the haze caught at the horizon.

Tilly pulled down her sun visor, and glance in the attached mirror at the procession behind her. Directly to their rear was an orange Mustang convertible; where sitting in the front seats were Beth Cedar and John Barns, both laughing and enjoying the wind in their hair. They had been dating for about as long as she and Mark had: about 2 years, but there was still no real sign that any of it was getting serious. John was driving, and his dark brown hair was falling about his head like untamed fingers slapping at his face. Beth wore dark shades on her sunburned features. Behind them Tilly could also see a pair of snakeskin boots hiked up against the back seat.

"I see that Derrick has come along too. Is he already drunk?"

"Already? It's morning isn't it? Of course, he's hammered."

"Why did you have him come along? I know he's Brian's best friend, but they do have operations for folk conjoined at the hip."

Mark looked at them in his rear-view. "Well, we wouldn't have asked him, but he works at the strip mall, at that cell phone place, and he was able to get us the phones we're going to be communicating with today. He thinks we're on some kinda redneck adventure."

She could find no response to that answer, considering that Derrick was always on some adventure or another – the drunker he appeared, the more adventurous he became. She continued to look past the Mustang at the pickup truck that rode behind it; with a body that was covered in dirt and rust, and a bumper braced with rope. Ashley and Arnold Tryst were in the front seats, looking like two mirrored images of each other within the opposite sex. Their pale skin was sorely in need of some sun, and with their fiery red hair, they resembled two wooden matchsticks propped up against the front windshield. And like the fire it produced, these two were not to be played with.

Tilly could look through their back window at the barrage of equipment they were hauling. "What do we expect to discover, Mark? They have enough stuff back there to construct a battleship."

"They just brought whatever we may need to get in and out of this mist, in case something happened to the cars, like if they stalled or fell into some ditch."

She didn't like the sound of that. Once again, this mission was beginning to get a little too real for her.

Bringing up the rear, Tilly could see the SUV belonging to Kwon and Nina Nguyen – a rather conservative pair, still in their honeymoon, who teetered between intellectual and party animal. Tilly was unable to see them past the sun's reflection on their windshield, but she could hear the classical music they played on their stereo, as loudly as some kids played rap music.

They rode in silence for a few minutes; it would take less than an hour until they actually reached the edge of town from the direction they were headed – when Mark suddenly snapped his fingers and pointed to the glove compartment, "Quick! Open that up."

With a swift flick of her index finger, she undid the tiny latch, and inside were a few objects that had been tossed about.

"Grab those," he said, offering her a quick glance, "I thought it may have been a little tough getting out of the house, and I didn't know if you would have had time to fix yourself anything."

She pulled out a muffin, apple, yogurt, and juice. She was and reached over to give Mark a kiss on the cheek. "You are just too much sometimes, you know that."

He was about to reply, when there suddenly came a crackling noise on the phone strapped around his hip. He quickly picked it up, and through it, Tilly could hear the stammered voices of Beth and John from the Mustang behind them. From what she could gather, they were talking about what their next move might be.

"Just wait until we get to where this fog is thicker, John. We don't have time for you to be… I know…well it's not just you and Beth that are involved in this…what? I can't…" Mark went on, his ear pressed to the tiny silver phone, as he continued to focus his eyes on the road.

"What are they talking about?" Tilly whispered, as she began to eat.

Mark leaned his body in her direction, but kept his eyes ahead, and whispered in response, "He wants to go ahead and check out what's in the mist."

"What!" Tilly was stunned at the idea. The voices on the phone became clearer, and Tilly could hear Nina cutting into the conversation saying, "I have to agree with Mark. I think we need to wait until we get a little closer to the edge of town, and then from there we can look around, and figure out what we all need to do."

John's voice came back, "But we already agree that we have to go in there at intervals, and someone has to at least get in there to figure out what is going on without all of us taking that risk."

"This is no time to play hero, John," Mark said, his voice becoming more animated.

"Beth and I agree that this would be the best thing. We are tired of all this waiting, and if we are going to be out here, then we need to get right to the problem."

Tilly could only shake her head. John and Beth were the adventurous type: exploits of rock climbing, hang gliding, volcano exploring, or going off the beaten path in the rainforests of Puerto Rico and South America, were always a topic of conversation with them. Both their families had large companies, and constantly lived abroad. John and Beth chose to remain in the *quaint* town of Crest Hill County; the town their parents too grew up in.

"And what if you don't return," came a new voice over the phone. Tilly recognized it as Ashley *and* Arnold; they had the uncanny habit of occasionally talking at the same time.

"Don't return?" John said, his tone indicating annoyance. "I have been watching this fog for a few days, and I mentioned this to Mark, but it is moving *into* the town. The danger is not going *into* it, but it *coming* to us."

"Maybe he's right," Tilly whispered to Mark. Mark quickly looked in her direction. "We don't have time for being too cautious, with the way this mist seems to be moving. John wants some immediate answers, and to tell you the truth, so do I."

Mark lowered the phone into his lap; the crackling voices of the others could still be heard. "Tilly, we are talking about John and Beth here. We don't know what is out there. I don't want anyone to get killed because they want to rush out into danger. You and I both know that it wouldn't take much for John to just up and leave our group and head into town on his own - just to satisfy his own ego. I am trying to prevent that."

Just as Mark said that, Tilly saw something jump out of the corner of her eye, distracted her in the side-view mirror. "Mark…?"

Mark leaned over to look in her rear-view mirror in time to see John attempting what he had feared; quickly pulling out of line and into the thick of the mist, and its hoary strands of smoke seemed to reach slowly out towards them. Mark grappled with his phone, swerving a bit as he plucked it from between his legs. "What do you think you're doing, John!"

"Too much babbling for me and Beth's liking. I have the newest and fastest car here, and these phones that Derrick got are working great if we get into any trouble, but it's time we started this little investigation to rolling."

Mark was about to speak, but Nina's voice rang back through the phone, "You never listen, do you? We need to all go into this together."

John gunned his motor, and Mark could hear it both on the phone, and at his window, as the Mustang began to pass by. Mark looked over at John and could see him on the phone directing his conversation towards Nina, but his and Beth's eyes were on him. They both shrugged their shoulders, and John said, "That makes no sense, Nina. We have no choice to all be in this together – the mist is calling the shots, not us."

"I think John should go ahead," said the voice of Ashley; a single voice ringing out. "He could go ahead and keep us posted on what is happening. At least we will know what to expect, and if he gets into any danger, he can stop, and we will be right there behind him."

"My God, People! It's only a little fog. This is not a horror movie, or some scary novel," John said, as he drove past Mark. "As long as you guys are watching my tail, I think we will all find out what is going on soon enough."

"Are we there yet?" Came Derrick's faintly groggy voice in the background of the phone.

Tilly could see Mark's leg easing down a bit more, and the engine of the car revving up. She reached out a hand to place on his shoulder, "I think you better let him go, Mark. We don't need you getting hot-headed too."

He sighed, shoulders dropping. "I think you're right."

John kept a steady pace in front of the group, but eventually, as the whiteness of the mist became slightly thicker, he sped up a little more. "Can you guys hear me?" he said over the phones. "I'm going to drive ahead and let you know what we see."

Everyone acknowledged this through the phones.

Mark was finding it hard to see very well, as the fog grew denser. He was eventually forced to slow his car down, and just as he did, John's voice rang out over their phones.

"…seems to be empty, and there is no one on the road. I can barely see out across the fields beyond the shoulder…"

"I can hear Beth's voice in the background," Tilly said, looking across at Mark, as she pressed her phone closer to her ear. "Can't you hear it?"

Mark picked up his phone, and too pressed it against his ear, "I think so."

"John, what is Beth trying to say? Beth, can you hear me?" Tilly said.

"…I see them, Beth!" John said suddenly. "Sorry guys. Beth is trying to grab my wheel. She was noticing some *dead* birds along the road."

Just then, Beth cut in on the conversation, "No…not dead. Look at them, John!"

"Let me get the wheel back first," John said, the noise of their tires screeching along the road squealed over the phones. "Hold up!"

"What's going on your two?" Mark asked.

There was a short silence before John replied, "Well, that is a little freaky…" he said, his voice trailing off before he resumed, "There are a ton of birds on the road, but they don't look to be dead at all. They seem frozen somehow, because we are driving right up to them and they are not moving. Freakiest thing I have ever seen."

"Look, up there!" came the shrill of Beth's voice.

"I'll be damned!" John said.

"What happening?" said the voice of the twins Ashley and Arnold, "What is going on up there? How far ahead are you guys?"

"Calm down, Tweedle Dee," John joked. "There are some birds overhead too, and…well…I don't know what to say."

"…and look at those animals over there," Beth's voice interrupted. Her voice suddenly blared over the phones, as if she had the device right up against her mouth, "You guys should be seeing this very soon. Maybe we should turn the car back around, John."

Just then, John's horn could be heard blaring. "Wow. Nothing is moving. This is too weird…I wonder what's going on up ahead. That might explain why no one has returned to town."

"Slow down a little!" Beth shouted.

"I think you should stop the car until we catch up with you, John," Mark instructed, suddenly finding himself slowing down even more as the plumes of mist buffeted off his windshield. He tried looking at his rearview mirror at those behind him, but was only able to see the truck that held Ashley and Arnold. He was unable to see beyond them. "Nina? Kwon? You guys still with us?"

"Still here," Kwon said, "I've been trying to see if we can get anything on the radio, and still nothing. We have satellite radio, and still nothing is coming through. Maybe the mist is blocking the reception here and all through town."

"Maybe," Mark said weakly. "John...what's going on now?"

Nothing.

"John?" Mark repeated. He shook the phone, and there was a crackling sound.

"Can...hear..." said a voice that could have been either Beth's or John's.

"What? I can't hear you guys..."

"Mark, look!" said Tilly suddenly, pointing ahead at the road.

Mark placed his phone at his side and leaned a bit forward to take a better look in the direction that Tilly was indicating. The road spilled out in large patches before him, slightly hidden by the dissipating mist around them. Suddenly something caught his eye, and he lurched the steering wheel to avoid it. "What was that?" he bellowed, as he regained his handling of the car.

"What happened up there you two," said Ashley's tiny voice.

"Look at the road," Tilly responded.

Mark took another look, and this time he was aware of something moving past him on the bank of the road. It looked like... "Are those birds...in the road?" he questioned aloud. Birds, sitting on the road, some looked to be pecking at the shoulder; some had their little heads turned up looking in his direction. "Are they dead?" he whispered to himself.

"...clearing up a little more..." burst John over the phones.

Mark quickly shouted into his unit, "Hey there guys! You're breaking up! Is everything okay?"

"Hey everyone," came Kwon's voice from the rear of the caravan, "We need to pull over. I can't see you anymore!"

Mark had to agree. The mist was becoming impossible to see at this point. "John, you have to turn back around. It's getting too thick for us to drive in any further...Kwon I am going to pull over at the shoulder, you guys do the same...John? Are you there?"

No answer.

"I don't like this, Mark. What if they don't come back?" Tilly said, nervously running her fingers through her hair. "I think we need to go back to town and talk with the police."

Mark didn't respond, and slowly began to pull his car toward the shoulder.

There were other voices coming in over the phones, and they began to overlap so much that it was hard to tell who was talking to whom, "...what are we going to do...John, why aren't you answering...I can't see the road anymore...Mark, what's happening up there with you guys..." It became so much that Mark just simply reached down to turn his phone off. "Tell everyone to just pull in behind me," he said to Tilly.

She looked at him strangely, staring at his phone, then him, then back at his phone. Slowly she began to follow his direction and raised the phone up and closer to her lips, "Hey guys, just pull in behind us. We're going to have to figure this out together."

They all gathered in around Ashley and Arnold's truck, as it sat in the center of the three vehicles and stared at each other in silence for what seemed like a very long time.

"Something must have happened," Nina said, her thin arms wrapped around her mid- section, eyes looking around frantically at the closing mist. "I don't think they're coming back."

"I don't think the problem is with them," her husband, Kwon broke in, as he leaned over towards his wife, embracing her.

"What do you mean?" questioned Ashley, who was sitting cross-legged on the ground, her brother Arnold standing behind her. "It's going to be hard going into that mist without knowing what's in there. Their phones are silent. I don't even hear static from the line."

"I think Kwon is right," Mark said. "The danger isn't what is in the mist, or beyond it. I believe that it is the town that is in danger. It is surrounding us from all sides, and not just rolling in from one direction. Can't you somehow feel that?"

Nina nodded, and looked at her husband, "I do. Somehow I do."

"But something is happening outside of Crest Hill too, but I just can't imagine what. It isn't hurting us now, but it's managing to keep those inside in, while keeping out those who are out," Kwon said.

"So, what are we going to do? John is gone out there, and we don't know what has happened. Shouldn't we be telling someone?"

"Like who…the police?" Ashley said, reaching up to grab her brother's hand.

He looked down at her, his hair of the same red hue, but cut shout about his shoulders. "I don't know if that can work, Ashley. The police have gone out there too I hear, but no one has come back either. They can't possibly spare any more men just to go out into this fog for John and Beth. It's enough for them to stop the panic in town and keep people from killing each other."

"Especially with all this other odd stuff happening," Nina said, shaking her head. "You have been hearing about it haven't you."

"About the ghosts?' Mark said, looking over at Tilly, as they both stood between the groups, "As matter of fact we have."

"It's no wonder the police are helpless," Nina said. "I'm sure their phones are ringing off the hooks."

Tilly had to agree. The police would be useless. She stared at Mark again, who would only glance at her. She knew he was thinking about the incident at the Morning Glory Cemetery. That scene had been so unbelievable, that they'd decided not to speak on it for the moment, but now, the reality of it was sinking in for them…sinking into this whole town it seemed.

"One of us is going to have to go into the mist to see what's going on. It's what we have all this equipment for," Arnold said, pointing back at the cab of his truck filled with all manner of heavy rope, wire, clamps, locks, chains, hammers, and the like.

"I don't know if it will be worth it," Nina said, saddling in closer to her husband. There was fear lacing her words.

"I know, but something has to be done," Arnold continued, as billows of mist swam across the paleness of his features. "We have to tether someone up and have them see what may be going on."

"Maybe I will go. It is my scooter we have attached at the back of our minivan," Kwon said.

Nina pulled at him. "You haven't ridden that thing in forever, Kwon," Nina pleaded.

"No, maybe I can do it," Ashley interrupted.

Arnold held her hand, "That can be a little dangerous, if you remember Ashley."

"Oh…I'll go!" Tilly shouted to her surprise and dismay. Mark was about to say something, but she held up her hand. "No Mark. We have wasted enough time. Our friends are in there, and our town could be next. We can't stand around here *thinking* about what to do…we just have to *do*."

Mark could see there was no point in pushing her on this subject. Someone had to go, so with a bit of dismay crawling past his lips, he said, "Okay…then let's do it."

Part II

Benny felt sick.

He had been unable to sleep and continued to stare at the stucco ceiling above his head. He hadn't even realized that morning had come; until he saw the shadows around him begin to shift in time with the moving sun.

Harold had killed Jason.

He mulled this statement over in his head like a cow chewing on its cud. He wished he could simply spit it out of his thoughts but couldn't. His thoughts were filled with questions and bombarded with regrets. Could his act of infidelity have led somehow to his undoing? He accused Jason of lying, but he knew in his heart that Jason was right. Benny then went to his room, slamming the door.

As he lay on his bed there was a knock on his door.

"Are you okay in there?"

"No." Benny said.

"Are you in need of a little morning breakfast? I may have died, but I can still remember how to cook up a little something."

Benny laughed in spite of himself. "Whatever you feel best Jason, is fine with me."

The door creaked ajar; "I think it best you not spend all day in here thinking about this situation."

Benny slightly turned to stare at a section of Jason's head as he peered in; blond hair falling across one strikingly blue eye. "Doesn't any of this disturb you, Jason? Has the afterlife taken most of what we call emotion here on earth, away from you?"

The blond section of head became lips, a cleft chin, and then eventually a whole neck. "Yes Benny, this does disturb me, and no, my emotions are still intact."

He turned back to the ceiling, "Good to hear it. I assume that means you feel as fucked up on the inside as I do?"

"What I feel right now is your obvious need for a full breakfast with all the fixings."

Benny huffed. "You can tell that can you?"

Jason timidly stepped into the room and stood just beyond the threshold of the door. "Yes, you need a little something more to put on your stomach, than all the hate and confusion you are digesting right now."

"Maybe you're right," Benny said, "I'll come out there in a minute to at least show you where things are…"

Jason held his hand up, "Don't bother with that. If I know you, then I am sure I can figure out your kitchen."

Benny could only smile.

It wasn't long before a cavalcade of odors came to vanquish his senses, literally lifting him from the bed and carrying him into the kitchen. There, he saw his small dinette table overrun at its edges with an array of dishes.

"I thought you would like some time away from your thoughts," Jason said, as he stood, leaning on the back of a chair that sat at the table.

What Benny saw were a battalion of small plates, filled with scrambled eggs, pigs-in-a-blanket, mini flap jacks, fruit kabobs, country fries, cream cereal, a selection of juices, crab cakes, and used as a centerpiece were an assortment of turtle's candies on a glass tray. He was flabbergasted.

And then something else hit him, as he looked up at Jason.

"I see you still remember," Jason said.

Benny was not sure how to react. What Jason had created was an exact display of the buffet table they'd experienced many years ago, when they first met on that cruise. Unhinged tears streamed past his lashes. "Why are you doing this, Jason? Eventually you'll have to go back to where you came from, and here you stand, creating more memories I'll have to be saddled with."

Jason walked past the table to reach out towards Benny, who willingly took the hand. "I'm just trying to make sure the memories you're left with are good ones, Benny. Please, let's sit down and enjoy."

And slowly, that is what they began to do.

"I'm sorry, Jason," Benny confessed, as the meal satisfied them both.

Jason shook his head and leaned back in his seat. "Let's not dwell in sorrow, Benny. This town has seen enough.

"I can't help it. I also can't help thinking about you. What exactly is on your mind?

"What do you mean?" Jason said, folding his arms.

"Are you angry at me? Are you upset with Harold? Are you angry at being dead?"

"I am feeling hate."

Benny lowered his head and cupped his forehead within his palm. "You feel hate because of me, I am sure. You are mad and angry for what has happened to you...and my part in it..."

"No, Benny. That's not it at all," he replied, slowly standing up, to gather some of the empty dishes from the table. "I am feeling hate at the idea that I am going to have to speak with Harold. I must confront him. I have to meet him."

That was not the answer Benny expected. "You have to do what? I say we just call the police on him."

"We can't really do that, Benny. What would be the charge?"

Benny rammed a fist in the palm of his hand, "Murder of course!"

Jason draped his arms out, "Do I look dead to you, Benny? With no witnesses having been around, we can't even get him on attempted murder. It would be my word against his."

"But there has to be something that can be done," Benny said, standing up, and stomping his foot in aggravation. "This is criminal."

"Yes, it is. But how can the dead possibly defend themselves? If I were some sort of ghost, then maybe the police could believe that, believe what I say when I identify my killer, but it changes when I look this...well, this...alive, Benny."

And at that, Benny could say nothing. He could only stare at Jason and marvel at the truth of that statement. He was alive...deliciously alive. He turned himself away, folding his arms, folding his feelings. "I still don't see why you have to see Harold."

"You don't do you," Jason said, with a sense of pity in his voice. "You really don't, with all your human emotions bottled up in you. I forgot just how blind that can make you in light of the bigger picture, Benny."

"And what would that big picture be?" Benny asked.

Jason took some of the dishes he had gathered and began to walk into the kitchen towards the sink. "That you are still in love with a dead man."

There was a quick, much unexpected intake of breath from Benny. The statement was so quick, so final, that to him it felt as if Jason had slapped an opened palm into his chest.

Jason looked at him from the kitchen, as he carefully placed the dishes into the sink. "It's true I see."

Benny turned around purposely, his body tense, stiff with embarrassment it seemed. There was a sigh that escaped his lips, and then he moved himself away from the eating table and headed towards the sofa. "Yes…I suppose it is true. Dead or alive, it seems I will always love you."

Jason took a quick step forward, his body wanting to run over to Benny, and squeeze out all the sadness from his skin but thought better of it.

Instead he pulled out a chair at the table and sat down. "I love you too Benny. This is a most odd triangle because love is coming from everyone involved. Harold didn't do what he did because he hated me - he did it because he loved you to such an extreme that even he was unable to deal with it."

Benny sat on the arm of the sofa, his gaze directed at the floor, his head shaking uncontrollably, "Nothing good could come from seeing Harold. He could try to kill you a second time, now that you know what he has done." He looked up at Jason, eyes unblinking, "I could kill him myself."

Jason slowly rose from his seat; his eyes registered concern. "No, you couldn't Benny," he said walking in Benny's direction, hands held out. "You don't understand what is going on, but realize, I have died. I have died, Benny, and it doesn't matter now how I got there, it can't be reversed."

Benny reached up to take hold of Jason's hands. "This can't be right, Jason."

"No, it isn't, but the truth is, I have to go back. This town is going to be filled with the dead come-alive, and they have to eventually go back too. They no longer belong here. The afterlife is a *new* life, and we don't belong here, just as a grown man no longer belongs to his mother's womb." He pulled Benny up to his feet, just to look at him, to stare into his eyes and see him, to feel his pain, his confusion, and try to select the right words that would console a soul so racked in grief. "Crest Hill County is feeling the pain you are feeling for me. They need to somehow release their pain, and they have to do this by talking with those that are most affected by it. If they, if Harold, does not release his anger, then he like this whole town, are going to be trapped in it…forever. With so much sorrow, pain, regret, and anger swallowing this town whole, there really will no longer be a need for Crest Hill County to exist – it would just cease to be."

Benny could feel his hands shaking. "You mean that God, Buddha, Allah, or whoever brought you back from the dead is going to eventually destroy this town because we can't stop being sad?'

"Yes."

"That is crazy, Jason. When do you think the town will start to, I don't know…disappear from the rest of the world? 	"

"Benny," Jason said, squeezing his hands a little tighter, "It has already begun."

Part III

Cool.

Like liquid sunshine hitting her face.

Smooth.

Like heavy silk sliding along her neck.

Softly, she hears her name.

Like the sound of an echo that was pulled back from her memory.

"…Lisa?"

Yes…that was her name. The voice was so sullen, that it made her want to swoon…and in some parts of her brain, she had.

"Lisa? Are you okay?"

Slowly, she began to open her eyes.

An angel; that is what she thought she was seeing. Beautiful features, with smooth light-brown skin, strong teeth and thick neck. The wavy hair that fell across his forehead like thin black strips of holiday ribbon, made her almost giddy inside. Handsome…and yet so familiar that she began to wonder if she could go to Hell just from what she was now thinking.

"No Lisa, you won't. Now tell me, are you okay?"

Good Lord, she thought, it was reading her mind! "Yes, I'm starting to feel fine," she found herself mumbling, as she brushed at her eyes…and something wet slid across her fingers. She lay on her back, looking up at this angel, and while her sense of sight was trying to work, her other senses were tuning in too. She could hear another person breathing in the room, she could smell something in the air…food of some sort, and her pallet had become dry enough to her tongue that it began to feel as if it were stuck to the roof of her mouth.

"Lisa, get up. This is Marc. Do you remember me?"

His eyes were so clear, like drops of dark caramel. Marc? She knew that name. Marc. Marc. Marc. She knew a Marc once. He died in Chicago from some ailment she couldn't quite remember. Marc. His mother had called to tell her the news, and yet here he was…here he was!

She bolted upright on her elbows. Her vision became crystal clear. Something fell from her forehead and into her lap. She looked down to see a washcloth. She wiped her forehead and could feel the cool wetness that the cloth had left behind. Then she looked up at Marc, and behind him, she could see Andrea standing there, starting at her.

"What's going on!" she demanded, easing back upon the sofa, her body locked in an unknown fear, as she stared wide-eyed at two men that should not possibly be here, both staring at her, both as real as that moist washcloth in her lap.

"You fainted, Lisa. We thought we should be here when you came to," Marc said, as he moved from the sofa to the coffee table, avoiding Lisa's kicking feet, as they dug into the cushions. "How are you feeling?"

Her lips; they tried to speak, but she could only hear her words in her head. Not words…but screams.

Marc looked back at Andrea. "I think she's in some sort of shock," he said, as he looked back at Lisa, who was now slowly raising her hand in their direction.

"I rebuke you evil spirits, IN THE NAME OF JESUS!"

"What?" Marc said, standing up, and placing his hands on his hips. "I don't believe…"

"Get out," Lisa continued, her eyes closing, and her voice falling into a ramble of inaudible prayers.

Marc began to walk towards her, "Are you in a trance or something?" he asked, reaching out to touch her shoulder.

Andrea pulled him back, "Don't touch her, Marc. She's speaking in *tongues*. Let her finish."

Marc adjusted his clothes where Andrea had tussled them. "*Tongues*? What is that? We need her to snap out of this craziness."

"GET THEE BEHIND ME SATAN!" Lisa shouted, her outstretched hand forming into a fist.

"This isn't Satan!" Marc yelled, his hands also rolling into fists.

"Quiet! I'm not listening to you!" Lisa pronounced, opening her eyes to glare at Marc. The stare was piercing, and when enough silence had passed, she began to close them again, her litany never wavering.

Marc looked back at Andrea, who had a single finger pressed against his lips. Exhausted, Marc moved back to the coffee table, where he sat. Andrea continued to stand, arms folded, breathing even, as he waited patiently upon Lisa. Lisa began to sweat as she prayed, and after about twenty-minutes her energy could be seen as waning, and she slowly began to open her eyes again. When she saw that they were still there, she quickly closed her eyes again, and continued her prayer in full force.

"Lisa!" Marc shouted, stomping his foot.

"Marc!" Andrea countered.

He turned to face Andrea. "She needs to snap out of this. We don't have this kind of time."

"Time? Where do you have to be Marc?"

"You know what I mean. We are here because of her, and you know it."

"Well we don't want to scare her out of her senses."

"I doubt that very much, with all this mumbo jumbo she's speaking. I don't want to sit here listening to all her religious trappings."

Andrea looked at the ceiling, exasperated. "I can certainly see which direction you were heading to in the afterlife."

"What's that supposed to mean? You know a lot of those religious rituals are not really applicable once you get beyond this world. Why am I even bothering to tell you this? It is obvious that being a hard head is what broke you and Lisa up in the first place."

"And you can tell that from only a few hours of meeting me. I very much doubt you were that bright even when you were alive."

"You are not the one to speak on brightness, Andrea."

"Boys!"

They both turned to look at Lisa, who was now sitting comfortably on the sofa, her eyes fully opened, and her head shaking. She could see that even in heaven, the male species remained stuck in the evolution process.

"How long was I out?" she asked, as she began to stand, looking beyond her guests at the window behind them, noticing the haze in the air, and the brightness of the day. Not only had she fainted, she must have slept a good while too.

"A few hours actually," Marc replied.

She looked at them both for a few moments. "And you both watched over me until I awoke?"

"Yea," Marc said.

"You two truly must have come from the dead, because I know for a fact that you both never would have cared that much if you were still alive."

Marc took a tentative step forward. "We need to talk Lisa."

She stood, remembering last night's dinner, and looked around at the discarded dishes on the table, the candles that had long since died out leaving their waxy scent in the air which mingled with the thick dissipating aroma of the roast beef, the flowers that sat in tiny shot glasses that she had stationed around the house, the blinking light on her CD player indicating that it was filled with - yet to be played - romantic music. She began to pity herself at her futile attempts to capture something from someone that had long since left her. Suddenly she felt an urge to clear this room of everything last night recalled…of the loves she lost but could not let go.

So, without another word, she spun around and began to clear the table. "I don't think I want to talk to any of you any longer."

"You have to speak to us, Lisa," Marc said, stepping in her direction, and stopping short of her. "You can't just wish us away, you know. You can't just pretend that we aren't here."

She looked into Marc's eyes, and her mouth stood pursed, until she turned away, carrying her trays of food into the kitchen. She returned and began to gather a tray filled with dinner rolls, her movements stiff, her eyes diverting.

Andrea nudged past Marc and walked up to Lisa. He tried to reach out to her; place a hand on her shoulder – but she jerked her body away so fast, that she dropped the dinner rolls from the tray she was carrying. She ignored them, and continued to stare at Andrea, her breathing suddenly rapid and uneven.

"You have to get over this…get over us," he said.

She closed her eyes, brows pressed, before turning on her heel to take the food into the kitchen.

"She's in some serious denial, Andrea," Marc whispered.

"She's in some serious pain, Marc, that's what's going on," Andrea said, looking angrily at Marc. "Can't you understand what we did to her was horrible. Why do you think we're here in the first place? It's for the amount of pain she's feeling?"

From the kitchen Lisa listened to the two men, and absently began to nibble on one of the rolls in the tray. She found her thoughts going back to when she was with these two, and she could once again feel the knot pressing in her stomach. The truth was as hard to swallow as the bread in her hands.

"Then she needs to try and get over this grief. I came a long way to get here, and my journey wasn't as instantaneous as yours may have been, Andrea," Marc said, as he walked around to the back of the sofa, bracing it. It feels too strange for me to be back in this town, to be alive again."

"It's supposed to feel like that. It's as if we're being born again. You should remember this Marc. You have been dead a lot longer than I have."

Marc waved his hands through the air, "Who cares what I remember. I remember what I am supposed to remember, Andrea. But if we have to wait on Lisa to get her mind together, and she isn't, what is she going to do when the others come?"

Andrea looked towards the kitchen at Lisa, their eyes locked. She didn't know about the others yet, and he could see that this statement had jolted her senses. "I would say that she knows now, Marc."

"Others?" Lisa said at a timid whisper, as if the words were pushing their way past her closed lips. "What others are you talking about?"

Andrea reached out to tug at Marc's shoulder. "I think it's time we left."

Marc shrugged his shoulder away, and raked his hands through his hair, "Left? What are you talking about? Where are we to go? My grave is miles from here, and we both know we are not allowed to walk past the boundary of the mist. We both know what is causing it, and we have to…."

"Quiet!" Andrea shouted. "You know we are not supposed to speak on that, especially here on earth. You must have died with the least amount of scruples. You can't be so casual in your conversations."

Marc had a look of worry on his face, and sullenly walked to the front of the sofa, to quietly sit. "You're right. I've forgotten. I've gotten a little too comfortable in my skin on my travels here."

"You can't get that way. Your flesh and your spirit are at war. Each is pulling at you to survive. That's why being here does not exactly feel right."

Lisa continued to listen in silence. She eased into the living room with the men and pulled out a chair at her small eating table to sit.

"But what's wrong with wanting to live again?" Marc said. "Maybe this is our second chance at something."

"You're right. It's our second chance to give those we left behind a new life, not for us to gain another one."

"Maybe leaving now isn't a bad idea," he said looking up at Lisa. "Maybe we need to resume this another time. I don't feel like dealing with a lot of disbelief right now."

There was a sting to Marc's word which Lisa could feel in her skin. He was unhappy with her, unhappy with her making this hard on him. Marc was always selfish. "Andrea," she finally said, her eyes still looking in Marc's direction.

"Yes Lisa."

"Could you stay," she said, then turned her eyes towards this tall, handsome man, "I will at least try and listen to you right now."

He smiled at her. "Yes Lisa. I can stay."

Part IV

United in pain.

That is what Mildred thought as she watched Timothy finish the last remnants of his breakfast. She could feel the unity they shared. There was an awkward silence between them, like an invisible balloon keeping them apart.

She could guess what may have been on his mind; hell – she could practically see it past the light skin of his forehead, just under the tight curled strands of his brown hair. They were both sick to death of the dead.

"Can I have some more juice, Aunt Mildred?" Timothy asked, as he rested a chin in the cup of his hand.

"Sure," Mildred replied, as she scooted her stool back from the kitchen island. She almost didn't respond, since the moniker of AUNT, was something she had not gotten used to. "What kind do you want?"

He shrugged, "Maybe the red one you're having," he said, looking back at the counter, where there stood a tall glass.

She looked back at it, not sure if she should tell him that what she had wasn't juice at all, but a nice glass of Chablis. "I'll see if I have any more of that," she said, as she opened the refrigerator, glad to see a container of cranberry-lemonade on the top shelf. "Did you manage to sleep well in our guest room?"

He looked back at her oddly. "Yea! That is like the biggest room I have ever seen. I want to ask mommy if it would be okay if I spend the night again when she is feeling a little better."

She handed him the glass of juice and sat back at the counter. "Do you mean, when mommy is acting a little more normal?"

He slowly sipped, as if he were avoiding the question, but finally said, "Yea, I guess, when she is being a little more normal."

Mildred stared silently at Timothy, draped in one of Luther's shirts and a pair of sweatpants. She could feel herself smiling at him; the Pastor and her never had the desire for children, but there was a soothing effect that Timothy had upon her, and for the first time she wondered what being a mother would have been like.

"I'm sure your mother wouldn't mind you coming over here every once in a while," she said, going back to her wine, "You know, just to get away from home sometimes when you think things are getting a little rough for you. You're not scared, are you?"

He looked away from her, and down the hall leading to a few more rooms, "Can we watch TV, Aunt Mildred?"

Yea, he was a little scared, she thought. "The television still isn't working, Timothy, but we do have some games stored on there that you can play, and uncle Luther has a PlayStation back there I believe, when he would hold Bible Study here for some of the troubled boys at school."

"Wow!"

"Now tell me," Mildred began, as she eased her stool closer to him, "What are you afraid of? I thought it would be pretty cool to have your dad and brother back. I know it's kinda weird, but isn't it kinda cool too?" She could see that this caused him to look coldly at her, and she could see that this child-rearing thing takes a lot more practice than she realized.

He began to swing nervously in his stool as he answered, "Mom's acting all weird, that's all. She runs around the house like she's everybody's maid. So, who has time to talk to dad much, or even get used to my little brother being here. I just don't like being around any of it."

She could understand. Seeing people you once thought were dead, only to wish they had stayed that way. "I'm a little scared too, Timothy," she decided to admit.

"You are?"

"Sure I am. Eric is, after all, my brother – my only brother, just like Eric. Jr. is yours. You spend all this time missing someone, and then when they come back, you just don't know what you're supposed to feel. But your mother is just hogging everyone's time so much that I haven't even had a chance to talk with my brother," Mildred said, poking her finger in Timothy's chest, and making snorting-pig noises.

Timothy's spirits lifted as he pushed away Mildred's fingers, and laughed lightly, "Stop!" Timothy said mirthfully between guffaws.

She playfully eased up a bit. "Do you think you will want to go back, Timothy? You know we can't be sure how long our departed family will be here."

"I don't know, Aunt Mildred. I don't know," he pondered, then took a moment to finish his drink. "I can't really even remember my brother. I hope Uncle Luther can figure something out about this. This seems like his department."

She had to agree, it did. "I am sure Luther is going to try to do the best he can. This isn't like the movies, where he has the power to send them back where they came from."

"Well he sure spoke well at Maya's funeral. If anyone can do it, I am sure he can. Wasn't he great at her funeral, Aunt Mildred?"

This stunned her into an unexpected silence.

"Wasn't he?" he repeated.

She grabbed his empty glass and went back to the refrigerator to refill it. "Timothy, we try not to mention that woman's name in this house." She returned to him, glass filled. "Do you understand that," she said, trying to take the edge off her voice.

"But don't you like Aunt Maya?" he said, timidly.

She reached out a comforting hand on his shoulder. "You know Timothy, there are many who like Maya, and the very thought of her makes a lot of folks miss her even more. So much missing can hurt an awful lot, that's all. I'm sure your mother was very hurt when she died, wasn't she?"

He nodded, "Yea."

"Yea, I'm sure you all were," she said. "Is she acting sad now?"

"No. She's just acting…"

"Weird. I know. It's tough when adults start acting weird, especially when one of them is your mother. But she has a lot on her mind," Mildred said, glad to have finally shifted the conversation from Maya. "And we're not sure when she may stop acting weird, but I want you to make me a promise."

"What's that?"

She began to lower her voice a bit, as if disclosing a secret, "Well, your old uncle upstairs seems to be acting a little weird too, and I don't see him nearly as much as I used to with all this stuff happening in town. So let's make a promise to call each other and talk whenever we find something weird happening with the people around us."

He smiled, and then jumped off the stool, to stretch out his open palm. "Okay, that's a deal!"

Mildred reached out to grasp his hand. "And there is one more thing we should do."

"Okay," Timothy agreed, while vigorously shaking Mildred's hand.

"We have to promise not to say anything to each other that will make us sad. And for me…that would be the name Maya."

"It really makes you sad, huh?"

"Yes it does."

And with that, Timothy broke the handshake, and reached out to give Mildred a hug. "Then I promise not to mention her."

"Thanks Timothy."

Outside the kitchen entryway, Luther stood near the wall, listening to them. What Mildred said, almost broke his heart…not because she didn't want to mention Maya's name in his house, nor even the way she manipulated Timothy into doing the same. But he listened to how they described their loved ones, who had died, and how they on some level still wanted to connect with them, and how he so, so very much, missed Maya. He ached, because in these many days, and these many dead that have risen, he wondered why she had not yet come to visit him.

At least one more time.

Chapter 13

Part I

Jenna had been furious this morning…still furious at what Nathan had revealed to her. She didn't want to be angry with him, but she was, and when night had turned into morning, she thought her volatile disposition would have ebbed, but it had not. So when Ella called to tell Jenna that she would be over to answer her questions, she could not think of carrying on such a meeting in Nathan's presence.

So, she asked him to get out of her sight, take a walk, leave.

He did.

Then moments later, the doorbell rang.

The house was very quiet, and Jenna could hear each timid footfall as she walked towards the door. She wished Tilly had been home, but she had left very early in the morning, and Jenna was in no mood to confront the child as to what had gotten her up so.

Jenna had heard her, but let it go. She still had this thought on her mind as she opened the door, seeing a sight she thought was still hard to believe, standing at her threshold.

"Hello Mother," Ella said, taking a firm grip on the child in her arms.

Her voice was soft, almost southern, and it amused Jenna. It was the accent of one of her father's for sure. She was a tiny woman, fragile looking, with lean limbs that made her appear taller than what she actually was. Her hands and fingers were thick upon her slender arms, and this was a trait that Jenna recognized as coming from her family line. Her eyes were clear and dark, and her skin smooth and white. The black features that stood out in her were definitely her lips, eyebrows, and nose; all resembling Jenna. She had dark hair that curled at the edges; very becoming. The glow of it made her look very angelic. It was a tragedy that she never got to grow up in such a body while alive.

Jenna stepped back to allow Ella into the foyer. "Hello Ella…my daughter," Jenna said, almost as if she were trying out the name for the feel of it against her mouth. "Would you like to have a seat? I can get you some tea to drink."

"That would be nice," Ella said, walking towards the sofa. She cradled her infant in her arms.

Jenna took note of this. "Can I get something for the baby?"

Ella smiled. "No. All of his needs are well taken care of for the moment."

Jenna nodded, went off into the kitchen, and returned with a silver tea tray with all the accents. She gently placed the items on her coffee table, and began to pour Ella a cup of tea, adding a small amount of honey and lemon, before serving it to her. "I'm not sure how you like your tea, so I hope it tastes okay."

Ella took a sip. "It tastes delicious."

Jenna could only stare at her, caught in a collision of joy and grief. There were so many questions she wanted to ask, so much fear of the unknown, and her nerves overtook her, and she could feel herself coming undone.

"It's going to be okay, Mother," Ella said, as she moved to a spot on the sofa next to her.

Jenna watched this dark child, its face so round, its eyes so big, its bulbous fingers reaching up as if he were trying to pluck sunshine from the air. Its laugh was infectious. She wondered whose child this was. It could not have been Ella's, despite the difference in skin color, Jenna was sure there was no intercourse going on in Heaven.

"Your tea is getting cold, Mother. Why don't you sit back and have some yourself?" Ella said.

She did just that, reveling in the fact that although she had not placed anything else in the tea, it tasted remarkable.

"You would agree that it tasted delicious, wouldn't you?" Ella remarked.

Jenna investigated her cup, and peered at Ella across its rim, before taking another sip. *Could Ella's presence have made this tea taste amazing,* she wondered. "Yes, it tastes very good."

"Good. You need something to relax you Mother," Ella said, as she leaned back upon the sofa to cross her legs. "There is much going on in this town, Mother. Much that has to be told. Much you want to ask, I'm sure. Unfortunately, we don't have the time to answer all of your inquiries. There is much danger in Crest Hill County. At this very moment, your granddaughter – my niece Tilly, is on the verge of making a very startling discovery about this town, and what is happening here."

"Tilly?" Jenna said, her desire to drink suddenly diminished. "You know where Tilly is?"

"Yes," Ella replied, adjusting herself on the sofa, taking her time to elaborate. "She is fine, but she has traveled to the outskirts of town. She, like so many others in the days to come, are about to realize the real and true danger that we, and this town are about to be in."

This was not the kind of conversation Jenna was intending on having. She was only getting used to the news that Nathan had killed Ella, and here she was meeting with her dead daughter, only to now get the news that her granddaughter was trying to leave town. She felt overwhelmingly numb.

"She will be okay, Mother. Tilly is in no real danger, just a dangerous discovery. But I say that, because she will discover that this town has very little time, and that also means that we may have very little time. I know there has been a lot on your mind about me, about what happened to me, and even now there is a lot on your mind on other circumstances. There is one in particular that you want to ask…and I want you to ask it."

Jenna realized that she still held her teacup in her hand, the drink long since cooled. She placed it on the tray, hindered about refilling it. She knew it was only an act of stalling, because she did have a question that had been nagging at her – so she asked, "Is what Nathan told me true? Did he kill you by accident? Did you suffer because of it? Are you even able to remember any of it?"

Ella reached forward to grab herself more tea, "Remembering it, I can't really say that I did, at least not in the sense of how you remember things. I did, however, recall what had happened in that time. I remembered my flesh-born self, and I don't remember my death having been painful at all. But I have been told what had happened through the spirit realm, others that saw what had happened, and protected me as I made my journey through transition. Also, Nathan did speak the truth. His only fault was his fear."

"And have you always known about us, about me and Nathan?"

"Yes I have," she paused to test the tea, and nodded her approval. "I have also known about my father as well."

"What?" Jenna said, stunned. That incident had been left so far behind her, but it had always been laced at the back of her head like a ponytail to her scalp. "You know which boy conceived you? You actually know this?" Her lips were quivering too much to say anything else. Suddenly their faces all came back to her. Those young, grimacing, angry, menacing, faces! She had to know who it was that…

"I cannot tell you that, Mother," Ella said swiftly.

"But don't you think that is something I should know? Isn't it my right to know something like that, daughter? Isn't it my right to know who raped me?" she swallowed back her rising anger.

Ella appeared to ignore her, as the child next to her cooed, and she adjusted its blanket. "Perhaps Mother, but that sort of information cannot come through me. I am not permitted to give you that, because in truth I should not be here. The fact that you were raped is enough. The knowledge of knowing who fathered me doesn't matter."

"Of course, it matters, Ella. It all matters."

"Why?" Jenna didn't know how to respond to that, and in that minute silence, Ella continued, "It is in a past we cannot change. You have done very well with my twin sister, and you have a beautiful grandchild because of it. Nathan has proven himself a very good husband and father. The only problem has been the regret and hatred you've had for yourselves at what happened to me. Even my real father has been tortured by what he had done to you. I am here so that we can find a healing factor in all of this. You learning about who fathered me will only add to a pain that has been festering in this town for years."

Jenna thought on these words. She could tell that a lot was not being said. She didn't care about the pain that Nathan was going through; because she believed he caused it himself. She didn't care about the pain that the town had gone through, because that is what life was about – working through your own personal pain. "I don't get it Ella. What are you really here for? What is going on?"

Ella had hoped to avoid this, but she could see that it was needed. "I can't give you all the information, because I really don't know it all, but Crest Hill County is suffering from so much grief, so much death, that in some ways, the mist out there that is surrounding it, is representative of that pain. If it is not corrected, the mist will swallow this town whole – and Crest Hill County will be a victim of its own grief."

"And if we don't learn how to let go of our pain, are you saying that this mist is going to kill us all? That hardly seems fair."

"It's not, and yes, in a sense, it will."

She was so blunt with the answer that it caused Jenna to pause for a moment. She couldn't think. She was so close to the end of her life anyway, and then to hear that it may end for a reason she could not understand, was dumfounding. She looked away from Ella, towards the child next to her. "And this little one…how does he figure in all of this? Are they conceiving children in the afterlife too?"

Ella smiled, and reached for the child, bracing it in her arms. "No. This is not my child. This is your great-grandchild, Jenna."

She felt faint. "What!"

Ella looked up at Jenna, her expression pallid. "This is Tilly's child."

Jenna shook her head. "That boyfriend of hers. I knew that boy was no good. And the child…what happened to it? When was she pregnant? Pregnant! And to think she hid such a thing from me? Mark has a lot of explaining to…"

"Mark isn't the father of this child, Jenna."

This time she did feel a rush of blood to her head. "He isn't…but who? Was she raped as well?" she asked, her voice trembling.

"No. This child was conceived by her other longstanding love interest."

"You mean…Carl?"

"Yes, Carl."

Part II

Tilly stood beside a scooter, in the middle of the road, in the middle of the mist: its smoky fingers reaching out to caress her face.

She was beyond scared now.

She adjusted the rubber harness around her waist, reaching towards the back of it to feel the steel loop with the tips of her fingers, and fastened to that a thick strand of telephone cable.

"Is everything okay, Tilly?" said a voice over her phone. It was Mark.

She unhooked the device near her waist, and answered, "So far so good. I'm at the thick of it now, and I still don't see a sign of John's car."

"You ready to drive a little further. We have miles of telephone wire, and can pull you back if there is trouble, or when we haven't heard from you."

"Give me a minute to catch my breath. This fog is kind of strange out here; I can feel it brushing past me. Let me get my barring's first, I'm a little freaked out here."

"Whatever you need to do is fine. Take your time."

How about I take until tomorrow, she thought. She stood there as the coolness of the mist slid across her cheeks. It was impossible to see past a few feet in from of her, and she was afraid that at any moment something would seize out from within the cloudy whiteness and head into her full force. She brought her phone to her lips, "Okay, I'm ready."

The phone crackled, and Mark's voice said, "Okay. Good luck, babe."

She didn't respond, and quickly hopped back on the scooter before she lost her nerve. She tugged at the cable line tied around her, and could feel the slack of its steel line behind her, its shape resembling a long sleek tail disappearing into the fog. She then took a much needed deep-breath, and started the engine of the scooter, its sound like a chain saw cutting through the air. Then she rode.

The fluctuation of the mist is what amazed her the most as she set off along the road, observing the way that the cloud formations were much thinner in the center of the road than at its edges. It was very hard to see what was beyond the shoulder, even though she could see the shadows of fences, trees, and what may have been the occasional barn animal. She realized then that while they were driving in search for John's Mustang, that they had not bothered to investigate the animals along the road, or to look for any at the shoulder of the road. But now, as she took a closer look at the side draining ditches, and patches of long grass, she could see the small heads of squirrels and bodies of birds.

Odd

"How are things going Tilly?"

She grappled for the phone strapped to her hip, "Everything seems okay right now Mark, although I am not finding a sign of anyone on this road, coming or going."

"Well, you got a little quite for a moment there," Mark said, "and your voice was staggering, but it's okay now."

The communication through the phone was starting to fluctuate a bit. "I'm seeing some shadows along the road. I think it's some of those petrified animals we saw earlier. Do you think something in this mist has caused this?"

"We were thinking that here. Do you have the gas mask with you? Maybe you should start wearing it."

"If this mist could affect humans, I think we would have been goners back at the cemetery. I do wonder if it is affecting animals in some way."

"Maybe," Mark agreed. "And have you seen anything of John's car?"

"No," Tilly replied. She could remember them talking about how no cars had been coming into Crest Hill County, and that maybe this fog was interfering with the engines, electrical systems, and radio waves. That would mean there would be stalled cars all along the road, but she could see nothing. She also had a skateboard strapped to her scooter, in the event they were right and he engine quit.

And then she saw something.

There was a figure, shadowy and opaque, stationed at the side of the road. She looked down at the speedometer of her scooter, and could see that thus far, she had traveled about 1 mile. The rope tied to her would only cover about 3 more. She slowed the scooter down a bit.

"I'm going to pull over for a minute," she said.

"What was that? Your voice is dragging in pretty slow."

"I think I see someone at the side of the road."

"Can you tell if it's moving in your direction, away from you, anything like that?"

"No, nothing yet, but I am going to try to get as close as I can."

"Can'thearyouTilly…saythatagain…"

She looked down at the phone. Not understanding why his voice was coming in so fast. "What was that, Mark? Slow down…can't understand a word you just said," she replied, then she saw something hanging oddly in the air.

"Did…you…say…some…" Mark said, before his voice trailed into silence.

Tilly thought at that very moment that she should just turn back around and forget this whole escapade, but that object that was just above her head, clouded by thick strings of mist, is what suddenly pulled at her. When she was directly below it, and the mist thinned out, she was startled at what she was looking at.

A small group of birds.

They had been flying from within the grove, but for some reason had stopped in midflight: trailing against the sky like a taxidermist's display.

Without even realizing it, she had walked toward the shoulder of the road, where she bumped into the object she had seen earlier. A shoulder met her at her lips, and she stood back, regaining her composure.

"Excuse me," she quickly said, then looked up at the unmoving man, the shine of his badge lit up her eyes.

A policeman, sitting on his motorcycle, did not reply to her act of courtesy. He remained on his bike looking ahead at the road before him. She just noticed that his hazard lights were on, blinking steadily with a slight clicking-noise; she found it odd that they seemed fade in-and-out than to actually 'click'.

"I see a policeman," she said into her phone.

It was still dead.

She walked back to pull her scooter from the center of the road, finding it eerie that this policeman had not moved, much like the birds had not. Maybe this mist was affecting them. She grappled in the storage unit attached to the back of the scooter and pulled out a small gas mask; her hands trembling as she strapped it on. She then walked closer towards the policeman.

"Hello," she said timidly, then once again a bit louder, "Hello!"

He gave no response. She began to walk around him, the silence about her was deafening. Her feet moved as if magnets were holding them down. She wished she were somewhere else right now. When she reached the front of the officer, she was in awe at his frozen mannerism. His features were piercing; eyes squinted on his dark skin, hands near his mouth as he spoke into his radio.

Odd, she thought.

He was peering ahead, so she looked in that direction, but didn't see anything at first because of the thickness of the mist; but there was a flash ahead, a shadowy object sitting at the edge of the road, a few yards away. She decided to investigate.

She hopped back on her bike, now more curious than scared. It was the oddest feeling, and she was reminded about something Carl had said when she and Mark were at the cemetery looking at that line of dead folk asking directions; he mentioned that something in the mist had a calming effect on people – and that is what she had suddenly felt – a pure soothing of her nerves. What if the mask wasn't working and the mist could be absorbed through the skin?

She neared the shadowy figure and decided not to become any more paranoid by asking herself a barrage of questions. As she got closer she could she could see it was a car, but it was angled oddly on the road. She eased up on this large convertible, until she was able to see the passengers – at first she thought she had found John, but this was a Mercedes, and not the Mustang that John had been driving. There was a family of four in it, with a woman, perhaps the mother, driving.

Tilly then paused, as she could see a little clearer, and the woman driving was looking into her side mirror, with a boy and girl in the back; pre-teens. What caused Tilly to pause, was that the woman apparently was driving off the road, but had never quite made it; for her hair was caught mid sweep in the acceleration of the car, and there was a sheet of paper in the young girl's hand, that had just gotten beyond her reach...a piece of paper that hung in the air where Tilly could easily walk up and pluck it from the air.

And then she thought long and hard and came to a most terrifying realization - a realization that was interrupted by the pull of the rope around her waist, leading her back to the group. The gang was worried so soon; and she had only been out of their reach just a little under an hour. She spun the scooter around and allowed them to tug her while she drove carefully back. There was a safety latch on the rope in case they began to pull too hard or fast, and it would snap loose – she was glad they had kept the speed slow and consistent.

"Are you okay?" Mark asked when he could finally see her through the mist.

"Yes," Tilly said, unlatching the rope from around her waist, allowing Arthur to spool it back on the wheel attached to the back of his truck. "I thought you guys were going to give me a little more time. Less than an hour wasn't much time to see what was going on there, and let me tell you, there is indeed something going on within this mist."

Mark remained silent, looking at the others around him. "Less than an hour?"

"Yea," Tilly said, walking the scooter back towards the truck. "Why? Wasn't it about that time?"

Mark stepped closer to her, reaching out a hand towards her shoulder as she balanced the scooter. "Tilly. You were in there at least four-hours. We wanted to make sure you had enough time to look around, and when you didn't come back on your own, and we couldn't communicate to you, we decided to reel you in."

"What? But that's impossible. I was certain I was in there less than an hour," she said, looking down at her watch. She grabbed Mark's wrist – his watch had a time that had elapsed by at least four-hours! She showed him her watch.

He looked confused. "Your watch is a little slow that's all."

Kwon then stepped up to the two, grabbing their wrists again, and looking at Tilly. "Were you thinking what I am thinking now, Tilly?"

She looked at him, his thin eyes casting a quick glance at everyone around him. Yes, she could tell he was very sharp, and they were instantly on the same wavelength.

"What is this supposed to mean?" Ashley said, pulling at the red strands of her hair.

Tilly looked at her watch as she spoke, "It means Crest Hill County may have literally run out of time...we *all* may have."

Part III

It has been years since Lisa sat on the swing bench that hung over her back porch. In the past it held slowly fading dreams of her swinging. Amused as her future children played with their future father...her future husband, in some distant future where motherhood came easy. All fantasy All pain.

She considered deserting the bench all together, or having it torn from its brackets; as if that would kill her desire to be a mother.

But now, at this very moment, as the world around her seemed to become swallowed in some colossal vacuum. She thought about maybe a part of that dream could still come true. A husband.

"Okay Andrea," she began, smiling, "I am ready to listen to what you have to say."

He too smiled. "Really? I get the feeling that you are a little nervous about hearing anything I have to say," he said, swinging his feet. The swing began to sway a little.

She began to follow his lead and swing her feet also, "I guess I was...I have spent so long having conversations with you, without you actually being here." She stared out at her neglected backyard, observing her forlorn flower garden and cracked and peeling bird fountain, surrounded by a cobblestone walkway that lead to a tiny sitting area; she had lost the pleasure of relaxing out there a long time ago, and it showed. "But you have come a long way, and it was not to sit here and admire my property, Andrea."

"No. No, you're right. There has been much pain in you Lisa and a lot of that pain had to do with me. I guess I was sent here in part, to tell you that you had been one of the most amazing partners that I have ever had in my life. I'd loved you very much, there was no doubt in that, but I had been under so much pressure from my family to give them grandchildren, and to stop playing the playboy, that it all became a little overwhelming."

"You...never told me that. I had no idea you were under any pressure to marry me."

"I know. I wanted to talk to you about it, about my families need to see me settle down, and my unwillingness to do so, even in the light of a wonderful woman whom I could have spent my life with. But the discovery of knowing you would not be able to conceive made me both angry and resentful of you."

"And so, you though the best solution was to run away?"

"Not exactly the best, but the easiest."

She sat silent for a while, not knowing how to respond to this. In a sudden revelation, she realized that by his running away, he'd created the situations that eventually led to his death. But what about here and how the whole town was talking about how she was jilted at the alter; that she wished *she* had truly died. Even now, she pondered who had really gotten the better of the deal.

Andrea could sense her inquisitiveness. He could sense the questions within her, and the one that eventually came out of her mouth...

"What was it like, Andrea," Lisa said, the tips of her feet dragging along the wooden planks of the patio floor. "What was it like when you died?"

He glanced at her, and saw that she kept her gaze forward, her eyes trying to look in his direction, but he could feel her desire to do so, to want to, but nevertheless she kept her attention at a constant, away from him. She knew this was a question he was not supposed to answer, but she must have asked it because the need to know was burning inside her. So he answered her.

"At the moment of my death, I hadn't really known I had died. It is that way for everyone, this uncertainty in believing that you have crossed over.

Her eyes bucked a little, as if she were imaging this image of life-after-death; as if she could make herself feel and understand the unknown. "But I thought there was an instant arrival at the Throne of God. I thought you were quickly brought to Judgment, and your life was spoken, and your eternity determined at that moment. You either go to Heaven or Hell."

He grinned. It was amazing to him now at what was believed, and what was reality. "Perhaps there is eventually, but the twinkling of an eye is not always as fast as you may think."

"And you can't elaborate more than that?" Lisa said, her voice edged with a tinge of urgency.

Andrea could feel the excitement coming off of her. "We'll all get there soon enough Lisa, and believe me, once it is over you will begin to question yourself as to why you were always so curious about it all to begin with."

"I suppose," she replied disappointingly.

Andrea edged closer to her on the bench, his legs having stopped swinging, and their own momentum arched the bench slightly. "When my mail truck tumbled right after the explosion, and there was only an immense heat, and the sound of screaming, I found myself lying on the ground for a very long time. I could feel nothing after a moment, and thought I was just in shock as I watched events unfold around me...horrible things."

"I can only imagine the mayhem that was happening at that time," she said, her tone drifting.

Andrea gave her a moment, for he knew that when the explosion happened, she was in Illinois seeing Marc. "Yes...it was quite a disturbing sight. I was watching it all, hours maybe, and could not move a bone in my body. I thought I may have been paralyzed. Then a paramedic spotted me. I was able to maneuver my neck and saw that I was pinned underneath the mail truck, its hull burned and blackened. The paramedic looked at me for a moment, grimaced, and then turned to call others to help. They managed to lift the truck, and then came to hoist me up, and that was when something strange happened."

"Is that when you realized that you were dead?"

"Not quite, but very close. The paramedic bent towards me as if to pick me up, and his hands seemed to go into my body as if I weren't there, and as he brought himself erect, he pulled out another man from within me. He brought out a man that was caked in blood, his skin dark and charred, hanging on in fatty strips that barely hung to the bone. The face was all but blown away, and the midsection was littered with shards of glass and rubble that stuck in him as if he were made of nothing more than clay. It took me a moment to realize that this person was me!"

Lisa covered her hands to her mouth, "My God Andrea!"

He inhaled deeply, almost as if his lungs were actually taking in breath, and said, "That is when I realized I had died. I lay there on the ground for five-days, coming to that realization."

"Five days? How can that be? You were laying there for five days, and no one saw you?"

He reached out to touch her hand and squeezed it, "It takes some people much longer than that, to realize that they are dead. This is what crossing over, making the transition, is really about. You are like a child being born into a new world, and before you are born, you realize that you are no longer a fetus, that you have another journey to go, and you must leave behind the womb you once called home. And even though you are not ready, you realize there is no turning back, and so you wait...you wait to be born again."

"And then you are transported to the Kingdom of God?"

There was an excitement in her voice, and he hated to dismay her. "No. It was then that you realized you are spirit. I lay there getting used to the idea that my lungs were not breathing air, my limbs were not controlled by muscle, my heart had stopped beating, my eyelids did not blink, and yet somehow, I was living...and doing it without any real sense of pain."

"At least I am glad for that," she said, looking down at his hands touching hers. "I am glad you were not in pain."

He followed her gaze and saw her relaxed hand under his. He's always liked her long slender fingers; smooth and delicate as marble. "Thank you for that. I have always marveled at the pain I missed in death, and the pain I left behind in others. I'm sorry about that Lisa."

She turned her hand slightly until her palm faced upward, cradling his, and she flexed her fingers a bit to squeeze his back. "I got used to it, Andrea. I'm glad you came back to finally put it to rest."

They looked at each other, and there was a shift in the air that they both felt; one they could sense in each other as if it were a language only they shared. He slowly lifted his hand, feeling hers slide away. "Can you get me some water, Lisa? I am getting a bit thirsty out here with this dry air."

She stood slowly, hesitation in every move she now made, as if all this would unravel at any moment. "Sure. I have a few cold bottles in the fridge."

"Great," Andrea said, his eyes never peeling away from hers, "There is something else I need to tell you."

She paused; eyebrows flickered in a line of confusion. "What is it? Is there more to your story?"

He shook his head slowly, studying her. "No...but I have to tell you that there could be others coming to see you. Other men who may have caused you pain in your past that also need to talk to you."

She raked her fingers through her golden hair. "You mean other dead lovers that have broken my heart? You mean someone else besides Marc?" When he said nothing, she knew she had gotten her answer. "What am I, the black widow in white?"

"No. You're just unfortunate to have bad circumstances in the form of men who did not understand their nature."

She turned her lips up. "Andrea, you were always bad at double talk."

He smiled. "I guess I still am."

She shook her shoulders and headed back towards the patio door. "Well, I don't want to talk about that right now. I will get your water, and we'll just sit here and pretend that those sorry cases do not exist, at least for now."

"Alright. We won't talk about it anymore, Lisa."

She was quick with her steps as she entered the house, and reached into the fridge to get two bottles of water. But her throat was knotted suddenly, and she stumbled when she reached the door again, but was not surprised at what she saw.

"No! Andrea, No!"

But he was gone.

She felt her body was too tight to cry, to get angry, and to do anything except to fall back down on the swing bench, open up one of the bottles, take a sip, and wait on her ghosts.

Part IV

Benny slammed the phone on its cradle. "Where the fuck is that man!" He shouted and began to pace the floor. "He knows he's guilty! He's gotten away with murder!"

Jason stood aback. This was going terribly wrong. There was more anger and hatred in Benny than he had ever seen or felt before.

"Why would he do such a thing? Was he trying to impress me?"

Jason watched him. "He needs time to think about the consequences that have happened, Benny. When he has thought about it long enough, he will come back.

"What are you talking about, Jason? Are you really listening to what you are saying? Are you telling me that we should just sit by and wait until he comes back to us…and we sit around holding hands?"

Jason looked puzzled. "Of course not Benny. It's not as if he can leave town. He has nowhere to go but back here eventually, no matter how far he runs."

"Can't leave town? Why not? What is going on Jason that you are not telling me? Why can't he…or for that fact, anyone been able to just leave town and come back?"

"I can't tell you that."

"Of course you can't," Benny replied. "You can't tell me anything. How would you know how this feels, to love someone that has betrayed you in this way?"

"I know a little something about betrayal Benny, if you remember."

Benny was stunned by the statement for a moment as his eyes flickered to that distant past. "That was different, Jason. You didn't know I was cheating, and in the end, you were about to die…and had you lived, you may not have ever known about Harold, and our lives would have been different."

"If not for the betrayal in the first place, I would have been alive."

Benny turned his body away. "This conversation is unfair, Jason."

And it is hurting you too, Jason thought. "You're right Benny. I hold no regrets as to what happened before my death, nor to what caused it; because I am literally beyond it now. You have to still deal with it, and yet it is consuming you beyond any rationale."

"Death has made you soft," Benny said finally, turning abruptly. "If I need to comb this city for that killer, then that's what I'll have to do." He then pounded his heels in the direction of the bedroom.

"What are you thinking of doing, Benny?" Jason asked, feeling the floor tremble with Benny's departure.

"I'm going to do what I think I have to, Jason," Benny said, returning to the living room with a leather coat draped across his shoulder. "I'll stop by the salon first, and then his apartment, then the local bar, and…"

"And what Benny? What do you think you are actually going to do to him when you find him? You can't change his actions any more than you can change my death."

"Maybe I'll just find pleasure in kicking his ass!"

"Well, if you are in such a hurry to kick someone's ass, then I would always suggest that you start with your own.

Benny shook his shoulders as if his body was slowly unraveling. He knew what Jason was getting at and didn't like the boomerang this conversation was taking. "I thought you didn't mind being dead. I thought this life was behind you."

"It is, but you are acting as if your lies were not the real cause of all this. You need to admit that by keeping your affair from me you caused Harold to become more jealous, and by not confiding in me about our relationship troubles, you caused yourself to look for another man, and by not being honest with yourself you wasted a lot of your time being in something that you could have moved beyond. Nothing is fair in this situation, Benny"

Benny stumbled towards the sofa, where with one hand outstretched, he fell against it, and eventually collapsed upon it. "What was I do to, Jason? It was hard for me too. It was hard for me to be in love with two men at the same time. I'd wanted to just run away. These things aren't planned, they creep up on you like a bad cold, and before you know it, you're trying to find a cure – you're trying to love two people but realizing you can only have one. You can't know that agony."

Jason stepped in his direction, "No, no I don't, because I had been adult enough to make my choice and stick with it."

"I'm so sorry," Benny said as more of an exhale than choice words.

Jason decided it was time to stop dealing in niceties. "It's too late for your sorrow to mean anything Benny, because in this whole scenario it has been you who has gained the most." He could see that these words hurt Benny, and he was about to continue along these lines, when something else caught his attention.

"I don't know what you expect me to..."

"Quiet," Jason said softly but sternly. Something was being disturbed...he could feel it.

Benny held his tongue, angry at how abruptly he had been cut off. After a short moment, as Jason looked aloof, as if listening to something that could not be heard, Benny charged again, "What is it?"

"It's Harold."

"What?"

"We haven't much time," Jason said, closing his eyes, his golden brows pressed towards the center of his forehead. "Harold has gone beyond the borders of the town. He tried to run away, but the..."

"I knew it! He's trying to skip town because of his guilt at killing you. I knew I should have..."

"Shut up Benny!" Jason said, opening his eyes to stare directly in Benny's direction. "Shut up and stay seated! I have to get a fix on his location. This is not good news."

"You can sense his location?" Benny said. "You didn't tell me you could track where he was in town."

Jason walked over to Benny, his steps hard on the wooden floors, his fingers pointed in Benny's direction in a manner of accusation, his mouth mumbling inaudible words. He was angry. He had not felt this emotion in a long time. He allowed it to take over his flesh, this renewed flesh, which hungered for the days of old; when it was in control. "Harold is caught by the mist out there. It is much more than you think it is. Despite your feelings about him now, he has a link to you and me, and that link is needed in order to banish this mist that will soon be taking over this town. This is bigger than the both of us, and right now I have no need for these feelings of anger, jealousy, and revenge you insist upon holding onto. I have to go and save him...for all of our sakes."

He was right, Benny thought. He was filled with anger and jealousy, and he was not willing to give them up right now. So he brushed Jason aside, and stood in front of the door. "I want to go with you, or you are not going to go anywhere."

Jason shook his head, and as he did, a swell of smoke seeped from the floor surrounding his feet. "I don't have time for this Benny, and when I return, perhaps you will be in more of a mood for understanding." And as the mist quickly overtook him, it just as swiftly vanished...and Jason was gone with it.

"Damned," was the only words Benny could utter.

CHAPTER 14

Part I

Something had changed.

Luther could almost smell it, like a freshly peeled orange; something had been removed from this town, and the sweet, juicy, underbelly had been exposed.

He was becoming very frightened of it.

As he walked up to the church, he could see the fight, and the unbelievability of such a sight caused him to take a second look at the building to be sure he was nearing an actual House of God, and not a common roadside tavern.

Where was Lisa, he wondered, as he observed the growing crowd? He could also see Earl Sanders rushing from the church, arms spread out, heading towards the center of the fray. Luther was able to reach him before either of them caused too much attention to themselves.

"Earl," he whispered strongly, "What is going on?"

Earl turned quickly. "Pastor Reynolds?"

Luther ran a hand across his chin and looked down at his attire. He hadn't shaved, and his clothes consisted of black khaki's and a simple blue dress shirt; sleeves rolled up. He had been involved with so much lately that he forgot to look like the well-dressed pastor people were used to seeing.

"Yes, it's me," he said, pulling at the edge of his shirt, as if that simple action would smooth out the wrinkles, "Am I looking so bad, that you can't recognize me?"

"Worse," Earl said, reaching for Luther's arm, and dragging him away from the ensuing crowd, whose verbiage came clearly across the air.

Luther could hear shouts of: "Get away from me you bastard!", "How dare you come back to this house, this town!", "What are you talking about...I don't believe it!", "I'll kill you for sure if you talk to me again!" It went on almost endlessly, the sounds melding into one loud mix of accusations and blame.

"What's going on here, Earl? Why is there so much fighting in front of the House of the Lord?" Luther asked, his body almost defying the pull of Earl.

Earl latched his remaining hand across Luther's arm, pulling him with more force. "No, come this way. You need to get away from that crowd. Let's get around the back so we can talk."

He allowed Earl to take him to the back of the church. "What's going on inside the church, Earl? Is there something I should be preparing myself for?" Earl didn't answer, and continued to lead him, and as an afterthought, Pastor Reynolds said, "And where is Lisa?"

"Not sure. She didn't call this morning. I tried reaching her at home and only got the machine. It's very unlike her."

"Has anyone been sent to her home?"

Earl shook his head. "Have you seen the mess that is happening in town? No one has the time to check in on Lisa right now, especially with her living so far out."

They stopped at the back stairs of the church. He knew Earl was right, there was too much happening in town, and his duties lay with the church. "Okay," Pastor Reynolds said, with a sigh. "What happened out front?"

"The parents of Bryce Hobbs and Melissa Roach are out there, and there is a lot of screaming and blame on who caused the death of those two young kids."

Pastor Reynolds remembered. Bryce and Melissa were a young black and white interracial couple, whose parents were from a dying breed; who thought such a union as sinful. The two kids decided to run off together on a day of torrential rains, leaving both sets of parents a note, and in their effort to flee, they ended up speeding headlong into the front end of an oncoming semi."

"The kids are among them now, and years of hate and blame are beginning to boil up all over again," Earl added.

Pastor Reynolds could only imagine, "...and inside?"

"More revelations in need of a calm wind to sooth them."

Pastor attempted a smile, but it was more like pressed pasta strings pushed into his face. "Am I supposed to be the wind?"

"I was hoping more of a cyclone."

With those words, Pastor Reynolds moved beyond the grip of Earl, and swiftly went up the stairs and opened the back door of the church.

He could hear the verbal noise as he entered the storage area and made it past the boxes and used furniture littering the area. He stumbled past the lounge area, and past the two offices stationed there, and into the rear dressing areas that lay behind the stage. The sounds of shouting got even louder until it caused his mind to thud as if a hundred anvils were falling on his head at once. He was not used to such sounds of hatred, such words of degradation, such a calamity of chaos that it caused tears to steam his eyes. His flock, his children, were suffering, and it wasn't their mouths that were crying out, it were the pain of their souls that Pastor Reynolds could feel.

As he moved beyond the curtain and onto the stage, he was forced back immediately by a flail of arms and legs that pushed and smacked his flesh with such force he was almost on his knees from the impact. He was stunned a bit, for a man of his build was not used to being pushed around very often, and when he looked up again, this time slowly, more carefully, he saw that the stage was filled with people, all yelling, arms raised with fists as their ballast, teeth and spit among angry scowls and flapping tongues, sweat riddled brows that beaded upon creased and angry ripples of flesh.

He didn't know what had happened. Many did not recognize him in his scuffed look, but they were all too weak from what had happened to them individually to put up much resistance. Death had visited them all, Pastor Reynolds could see, and it had taken the very life away from them.

And then someone said... "Pastor Reynolds?"

The stage was nearly empty when this was spoken.

And then it happened again... "Pastor Reynolds...where?"

"Pastor Reynolds?" it was a female voice, very distinctive – scratchy. It was a determined voice, and it caught his attention. He looked at the bottom of the stage to see an old woman, swinging a cane along the floor with hands that looked very red, sun-whipped with age, with fingers that were adorned with nails that looked like painted mirrors.

Sharon Richards, he murmured when he saw the nails; flashy and gaudy all at the same time. There were few seniors that dressed as ornately as Sharon.

"Anne is back, and Tessie has gotten out of hand too," Sharon said, tapping her cane on the floor for dramatic effect.

Pastor Reynolds noticed that she looked rather frail, as she tried to make her way around the stage towards the stairs. He decided to meet her at the stairs; Earl in tow.

"I think it would be better if you stayed up here on stage, Pastor Reynolds. I don't think it's very safe down there."

"Nonsense Earl," Pastor Reynolds said, as he headed down the stairs to meet with Sharon. "What is going-" his voice stopped short, as Sharon reached out to clasp his forearm in a grip of razor sharp nails that dug into his flesh.

"That old woman has lost her mind, Pastor. I don't know what she's capable of doing to me now," Sharon said, her eyes looking smartly behind her.

Pastor Reynolds followed her gaze. In the crowd, he could see another woman coming in their direction, who was just as old as Sharon.

"How could you tell Annie that, you old bitch!" said the high and tiny voice that came from the senior.

Pastor Reynolds knew this had to be Tessie; Sharon's lover. He could tell Tessie's voice anywhere by its high-pitched timbre, which was quite the opposite of Sharon's raspy smoke-damaged tone. He could see the woman storming in their direction, her large frame knocking people aside. Her face appeared dry and pale and was so sagged with age it looked as if she had been dipped in flour. Pastor Reynolds could feel Sharon's hands shaking, and wondered what fear this 92-year-old woman had from another old woman who was at least in her 80's.

"Get away from that whore Pastor, before she poisons you too!" Tessie said, reaching out to grab Sharon by the wrist, but failed.

"Ladies!" Pastor Reynolds shouted, and suddenly wondered if that was the correct term to use for two women who indulged in the act that *dare-not-speak-its-name* (they both acted like drunken male sailors). This was one of the reasons why he'd decided not to preside over their friend's funeral – one of only a few he'd ever refused. He was not as opposed to the union of Sharon and Tessie, but it was their boldness to include a *third* party in their union that disturbed him. Straight or Gay, that was something he would never ordain.

"She's just a heathen, Pastor," Sharon said.

"Pastor, I think you should get back on the stage," Earl suggested from the top tier of the stairs.

Pastor Reynolds was thinking the same thing, but he was afraid that if he attempted to take his arm back from Tessie, a large amount of flesh would come with it. He turned his head slightly to address Tessie at a whisper, "My arm, Tessie - if you don't mind."

Tessie looked at him, her eyes the tiniest of black pearls that glanced down at her hand. "I'm sorry," she said releasing her grip. "But she needs to stay away from me."

"Fuck that," Tessie mouthed; the looseness of her dentures clacked in her mouth.

"Tessie, your language!"

She looked crossly in Pastor Reynolds direction, and then turned her venom back upon Sharon, and without apologizing, "Well, it is her fault that Annie died! The whole truth comes out now. Annie told us the whole thing."

Sharon reached up to grab Pastor Reynolds' shoulders to turn him around and continue speaking, "How was I to know the woman was going to run off and fall down the stairs."

"You had no business telling her to leave. We were all supposed to be together, the three of us, and..."

"Pastor Reynolds?" Another voice called out.

"Come on Pastor," Earl said, reaching his hand out, "You need to get out of there before you are swallowed up."

Pastor Reynolds' attention was now drawn to the new voice, and as he looked up, he saw Isaac Yoland walking towards him; his thin frame barely keeping up the striped overalls he wore.

"Believe me, Pastor, I was really going to tell them what had happened. It was an accident," Henry said.

"I knew something was wrong that night. You were always hitting her. Always. And you told the police you pushed her away from you."

Pastor Reynolds could see Isaac's son, Henry following close behind, with his spiked hair and loose handmade beads across his neck. "Mother said you beat her cause you thought she was cheating, and it was never her. You were cheating with this new mom we have."

"God will forgive me," Henry said, brushing past Sharon, "Won't he?"

Sharon grabbed Henry's shoulder with her feeble hands, "Who do you think you're pushing asshole! Can't you see me standing here?"

"Yea, we already have the floor," Tessie said, moving from behind Pastor Reynolds.

Isaac looked around at the two women who were at least twice his age, and brushed his hands at them, and looked up at Pastor Reynolds, "Will the Lord forgive me? I didn't mean to hit her so hard."

"Mom said you did!" Henry said. I can tell her to come here..."

"Quiet boy! Grown folks are talking!"

"Isaac, that is no way to talk to your son," Pastor Reynolds said sternly.

"So, you a wife beater, is that it," Sharon said, her hand still on Isaac's shoulder.

He looked over his shoulder at her, and then at the placement of her hand, which was so light despite her girth, that he hadn't even felt it was there. He grabbed it and threw if from him. "Don't touch me, you old pussy eater!"

"Isaac, I will have none of that talk in this church! What is wrong with you?!"

Sharon nursed her hand, "He's a wife beater, that's what's wrong, and if I were just twenty-years younger, I would make it a fair fight."

Pastor Reynolds took a slight step back, in the direction of the stairs, and glanced up at Earl, whose mouth was forming the words *Come-Now*, and as he looked back at the group, he could also see that others were realizing he was there, other eyes that were downcast or looking elsewhere, suddenly glanced up at him. It was as if the whole room was suddenly bathed in the whites of staring eyes. He backed up into the bottom step, and continued to back himself up towards the top, unable to believe what he was seeing and hearing.

On the stage itself, were a scattering of people, and upon closer examination, he noticed that they were a part of his ministerial staff, dressed so casually that he had not recognized them. At the moment he lost track of their names, and before he could even address them, they were leading their way off the stage as well, trying their best to hold back the crowd. And then his attention turned back upon the congregation, and he was in horror at the mayhem he was witnessing; with people climbing over the pews, which also were pushed haphazardly about the church floor. There was yelling, cursing, pushing, and stomping – and so many people crammed together that the church felt hot, and Pastor Reynolds could feel a thin trail of sweat steal across his forehead.

This must be how Moses must have felt on Mount Sinai when he delivered the Ten Commandments to the sinners of his day, Pastor Reynolds thought. He looked back to see that Earl was still there, standing silently waiting. "Bring me a mic," Pastor Reynolds requested of him. He was livid at what was going on here, and it had to stop. When Eric brought him the mic, Pastor Reynolds reached for it before Earl was even ready to hand it to him.

"What are you people doing?!" He shouted into the device, the feedback pierced though the air in a long drawn out squeal. In response, the rumble of the crown lessened. He continued, his voice still retaining a slight edge to it. "I am ashamed of all of you. How dare you act this way in the house of our Lord and Savior? You should be ashamed of yourselves."

The sound of chatter slipped into muffled sighs, followed by stillness. Pastor Reynolds looked out at the crowd, and everyone appeared afraid to move.

"What now," Earl whispered behind him as the silence mounted.

"You will see," Pastor Reynolds said, taking a momentary glance in Earl's direction. "I am sick of looking at all of you," he said, returning towards the crowd, "And I want you all out of my church...now!"

The murmur reverberated off the walls; shaking them.

"I need you to leave here and remember what place this is, and what it represents, because this is not to be a place of confusion, nor a place for a foul tongue, nor a place filled with anger and accusations. It is to be a place of refuge, a place of peace, a place of understanding and compromising conversations. I don't care if you are alive or dead, or what secrets and indiscretions have been exposed of you. Just get out, and remember that you are adults, and once you have left, maybe I will let you back in."

"Pastor Reynolds you can't..." Earl was about to speak, but Pastor Reynolds held his hand up to stop him.

"Earl, can you gather the other ushers together, and lead these people out. Don't let anyone back in until you have heard from me. I need to go to my chambers for a moment and do some thinking. Give me about ten minutes."

Earl looked out at the church, at the scared faces, at the guilt etched into everyone's features, and although there was protest seeping into each fiber of his muscles, he could feel his will conceding. "You can count on me Pastor Reynolds. Did you say ten minutes?"

Pastor Reynolds looked out at the church as well, and what he saw were children, caught up in their sins. They needed to grow up. "Make it thirty, Earl. Make it thirty." And with that said, he brushed past Earl before the tears could be seen streaming across his cheeks. There was more on his mind at this moment than he was capable of sharing with his longtime friend – more than he was willing to admit to himself.

Part II

Pastor Reynolds stumbled into his office and quickly closed the door. He could not make it to his desk fast enough, before he nearly collapsed. He had been trying to push a floodgate of memories from his mind for days, but as he looked out at the congregation, as he looked out at the gathering, he was reminded of another gathering with just as strong of emotions. He remembered Maya's funeral.

There was so much death around him that it was choking the very air he breathed. He was remembering Maya, and found himself looking at the doors in the front of the church, looking to see if at any moment she would come walking in. It caused him to think what may have been. Yes, he was married, and yes, he did the right thing by keeping Maya at arm's length; but there was a moment when he had not been as careful, and it was that moment that pushed at his mind to such a degree, that it was all he could think about.

And it was that moment which now caused his heart to beat, and his lungs to feel as if they'd suddenly popped…remembering a moment from his past…it was as if he could hear the piano playing now, with Maya just finishing a song which she'd created for his choir. Then he heard her footsteps, and the sound of her high heels clacking against the stairs leading into the area where he was. Even in rehearsal she dressed as if it were Sunday. On that day, he had chosen to do some work on his sermon at the church; instead of at home, where he had engaged in just one too many verbal-matches with Mildred.

The door had opened.

"I'm sorry to bother you Pastor Reynolds, but I can't seem to find the music sheet I did my rewrites on," Maya said, standing in the doorway. She wore her red hair in a ponytail, the end draped lightly on her shoulder. She adjusted her black jacket, as her pleated skirt flowed in undulating waves. Her red blouse and red shoes caused Luther's eyes to elevator along her figure. "Did you see me leave something in here?"

"You know I prefer that you call me Luther when we are alone," he reminded her.

She smiled. "Okay, *Luther*...have you?"

He smiled back, their pleasant exchange a sign of their having worked many long months together. "I think I may have seen something you had been working on under those boxes of donuts over there," he said, directing his attention to the other end of the room where a small bookshelf sat, its surface riddled with papers, books, a radio, and a large box of pastries.

Maya could see the corners of the music sheets creeping from beneath the box. "I guess my love of pastries was distracting me from seeing it," she said, heading towards the bookshelf, which rose to the height of her waist.

"Blame it on me," Luther said, pushing some of the many sheets of paper on his desk aside to rest his elbows, "I bought them to bring to rehearsal, but you see where they stayed. Those are the last things I should be buying, as big as I am."

She picked up the box and pulled out her music sheets. At the same time, she reached in to grab a lemon cream donut, biting it slowly. "I am more to blame than you are, considering I have eaten more of these than you have."

"Yea, you should be ashamed of yourself," Luther jested.

Maya purposefully chewed slower, "You're lucky I am here to save your life, by throwing myself between you and these deadly sugars."

"And I am ever so grateful to you for the sacrifice."

"And what are you working on so diligently here?" She said, taking notice of the many papers strewn across Luther's desk.

He leaned back in his seat, and exhaled, "It's the finale for the series I started two weeks ago: Being a Better Man Financially. I can't find a way to tie in financial responsibility to what was prevalent in the days of the Bible. Just can't seem to concentrate today."

"Well, I sort of thought you might be having a little trouble with something," she said, her eyes veering innocently towards the tiny trash bin near his desk, filled with a scattering of rumpled papers – discarded sermons."

He followed her gaze, and a slight laugh pulled his lips.

She walked in his direction, wiping the corners of her lips of derelict crumbs. "I may have a few simple verses that you can use, just to get you started."

He watched as she sauntered closer, perching gently on the corner if his desk. She leaned fluidly towards the opened Bible on his desk and grabbed it along with an accompanying highlighter. "Do you always keep just the right verses continually locked in your head – ready to be unleashed for just such a sermon?"

She winked at him. "Let's just blame the rush of inspiration on the sweets shall we, this way you are free to keep them coming," she replied, and then went to work flipping and highlighting Bible pages. "Maybe the sweets can be my muse in these situations."

Luther watched, but suddenly did not hear Maya. He silently noticed the swing in her head as she mumbled a few of the passages she encountered. Her crimson hair seemed to dapple in the overhead lights, and her ruby lips pursed forward with each concentrated effort. He could smell the perfume she wore, as it cascaded mildly in his direction, and also heeded the lilt of her breath as it escaped her lungs. He was not sure where his mind had been when what happened next, happened. All he knew was that somehow the rest of the world had vanished, and for one moment, they existed on their own plane of reality. He could sense his own inhale; slow and long, as if he stood on the edge of a diving board ready to plunge into the coldest of oceans, and then on his exhale, his lips and tongue moved together, forming words that he had not realized had been expelled...

"...I love you Maya."

He could almost hear the highlighter come to a screeching halt.

"What did you say?" Maya questioned, her eyes continuing to look at the book in her hand.

A trickle of sweat steeled down the nape of his neck. "I'm sorry," he said, his eyes moving from her to a point at the center of his paper-riddled desk. "I know we promised to not say such things to each other and keep this as friendly as possible." He stopped, although his lips appeared to want to say more, and he found himself nervously clasping his hands and pin-wheeling his thumbs.

She reached out to cup his hands in her own. "Don't be sorry Luther. Don't be sorry at all...*because*...I was thinking the same thing," and she squeezed his hands.

Without looking up, he said, "And were you also thinking about how *hard* this whole thing is?"

"Yes. Yes, I was," she said, lifting her hand, and placing it back in the opened Bible that now sat in her lap. "It has been hard not to speak a truth we have been both holding inside."

He slowly looked up to meet with her maple eyes, "I am really trying to deal with this, Maya. I try to think if things were different, if I were not a pastor of a church, if I were not married to Mildred, if I..."

"...if nothing, Luther. You are a pastor, and Mildred is your wife. I know, she is not a good one to you, and I have thoughts also, about the kind of wife I would be in her place, and it exhausts me. It exhausts me because it is not real. God is just going to have to work this one out, for the good of us all."

"I believe He will too, Maya, yet my heart remains steadfast," he said, and was compelled to stand, and suddenly the air around them became warmer.

Maya could feel the quick rise in the temperature too; it snatched at her lungs, hindering her breath.

And before either of them knew what happened, Luther came across the desk, and she was weak. The Bible and highlighter slowly slid from her grasp and past the nave in her skirt, to fall gradually towards the floor. Then they were able to smell the sweet scent of each other's breath, right before the kiss sealed them together as one.

It lasted for a full two minutes.

Two minutes that lasted a lifetime.

When it broke, the revolutions of his world began to spin anew again.

There was nothing but silence from that point. Maya picked up the Bible and highlighter and placed it carefully back on Luther's desk. Luther sat back at his desk, and gathered his loose papers together, his breathing still rapid. Everything was unexpectedly bathed in slow motion, as Luther watched Maya grab her music sheets and head out the door.

Before the door closed, Luther asked, "Is this going to change things between us, Maya?"

She wiped the tears away from her cheeks. "I certainly hope not."

The door then closed the wall between them.

The door to his office opened again, and instead of Maya returning, it was Earl who peered in. "We have about seven minutes left before we reopen the doors again, Pastor. Is everything okay?"

It took him a moment to realize that he was back in the present again. "Yes. Yes, of course Earl, that will be fine."

"Fine then," Earl repeated his roaming eyes very uncertain, "If all is well, and then we will see you out there momentarily?"

"Yes, you will, Earl. Thank you."

"No problem, Pastor Reynolds," he said, as he slipped back out the door, leaving Pastor Reynolds to his own thoughts.

God really did work things out, he thought, allowing Maya to escape him in death. *It wasn't fair at all.*

Part III

Lisa was outraged.

There were two men in her backyard, and on any other day, this would have been a dream come true, but today it was nightmare – and with the knowledge that another man was on his way, Lisa was now sanctioned to her own private Hell.

"Get out, both of you!" Lisa shouted, as she stood on her back porch, leaning against the railing.

Marc was there, telling her more truth than she actually wanted to hear. He said, she'd been too religious for him, and later, when she'd finally consented to sex, he realized it wasn't good enough.

She'd been stumped for words, and the expletives she wanted to dispel had clung to the roof of her mouth like tree moss.

Then Rikki Milner arrived; a person she had not seen since her youth, at least seven-years ago, when she was barely a woman! She dated him for a year before losing him to a dance floor, a good girlfriend, three martinis', and a tequila shot. While she was recovering on a plastic seat in a booth under a disco ball, Rikki was discovering her friend on a porcelain stool in an unkempt bathroom under a flickering florescent light.

He had been the reason she embraced the church so desperately, thinking God had given her a sign because of the bad luck that she was having with men. Eventually He became the only man she would continue to cling to time and time again.

"I think we should leave," Rikki said, backing up a step, "She's in no condition to listen to reason."

She looked at him again – staring at this young boy, with the ivory skin, red lips, and Irish heritage, remembering about that twenty-two-year-old, who just told her about his death; that he was playing a game of stick ball in the street, and fell to his death inside an opened manhole.

It had been a very painful death.

Lisa was surprised at how little sympathy she had at the news.

"Yea. Maybe you both should be leaving."

"No Lisa," Marc said, taking a bold step forward. "You have to listen to us. You have to listen to us for your own good."

"So, I am to listen to the dead…when I already feel dead inside."

"This isn't working," Rikki said, turning to Marc for guidance. "She isn't listening. She's too stuck in her anger to hear a word of what we're saying. We're running out of time!"

Then there followed a silence. Marc just stared at Lisa. He could see that she really didn't care about what happened to this town. She had given up a long time before the mist had arrived. She didn't care to know how her and this town, and their combined anger and grief were inexplicably linked. She needed to release that anger more than she needed to know what caused it. She needed to know that it could change – but at this moment, there was no evidence in her life that it would.

"You were both assholes to me! All you men were assholes! All you men ARE assholes! Dead or alive. Andrea…Andrea…" and this is when she could feel her throat tighten up, "…I loved him, and only when he died, did he want my forgiveness."

Rikki stepped up behind Marc, and leaned in closer to his ear, and whispered, "What are we going to do? I want my afterlife back. I have a feeling that I liked it. Her colors are changing. She is becoming darker, and soon she won't want to hear us at all. If that happens, these feelings will increase – these human feelings that I would rather do without."

"I know that Rikki," Marc whispered back without turning to face him. He feared for Lisa, whose chest was now heaving, her eyes shallow, her blonde hair frazzled. He could see the weakness in her body, its lack of sustenance, its lack of will.

Suddenly Lisa lowered her head, looked directly at her feet, as she shook her head and mumbled words too low to be heard beyond the railing of the porch. "You know, I am tired of talking. I am done with my past, and done with your deaths. None of it was my fault. I really don't care how you two care to spend this *vacation* time here in Crest Hill County, but you can take this *Christmas Carol* someplace else."

She was right, Marc thought. She has done such a good job at hiding her emotions, her sadness, her anger from herself, which she never really considered if she deserved any of it…and she hadn't. She was becoming very melancholy, very distant, and Marc realized, as he watched her saunter back into her home, gently letting the door click in place, that this may be their last chance at reasoning with her.

"Did you see the colors surrounding her?" Rikki said, almost as if to himself.

He'd stepped up next to Marc, this boy who died a boy; who was now wringing his hands and chewing his bottom lip. "I have an idea, Rikki. It's risky, with Lisa being such a devout Follower. But we need to make her understand that the rules to this little game cannot be ignored, and that its consequences are greater than us all."

Rikki's eyebrows meshed mid-center as he glared at Marc. "Wha...what do you have in mind?"

He reached out to lay a hand on Rikki's shoulder. It seemed the common response to someone who appeared so young. "I need you to go back into the *Gulf* – and in a few moments, when you can feel that Lisa's spirit has calmed, I need you to appear near her."

"What!" Rikki said, taking such an unexpected leap back, that Marc's unsupported hand fell to his side. "We are not allowed to do something like that yet. We are to reason with words while here on Earth, and not create grand theatrics to persuade. We still have to let all the living exercise their free will, Marc."

"She will, Rikki. Grand theatrics indeed. She's a believer. Acts of miracles are not strange to her?"

"I can still hear you two out there..."

"I don't like this Marc, but we'll play this card, and see what Lisa reveals.

"We just need her to act like her old self, Rikki. I can see that she is too willing to give that up in order to have peace of mind."

Rikki noticed as Lisa edged open her door so that her sunshine crested head could ease out and see what was happening in her backyard. She glared at Rikki in surprise for a short moment, as fumes surrounded his feet, wrapped around his ankles, coalesced through his thighs, and slithered up his torso. He was caught up with the smoke, and he was gone to that place between life and death; *The Great Fixed Gulf.*

"Demons!" Lisa exclaimed, her eyes wide with terror as she glanced at Marc, right before she took a swift step back to briskly shut *and* bolt her door.

Marc could hear her grapple with the locks.

+++++

She pulled at the door handle just to make sure it was securely shut, and then took a moment to swallow back her heart.

She spun around and ran to her bedroom. The Bible was sitting on the pillow nearest the window as it always does after her morning devotional. She would grab it, and let the Lord lead her to a spot within where there would be words to battle such...such...creatures. But it was silent in her home, and she took a moment to sit upon her bed as she gripped the Good Book in her palm. Her eyes peered at the back door, and she could see no shadows breaking the light from beneath. There was stillness.

"Praise God," she whispered. She guessed she was right in assessing that the dead had to obey the living. She stood, her throat suddenly dry, and walked out of her bedroom and into the kitchen.

That was the plan, but she stopped at the threshold of her bedroom door.

She smelled something.

It was as if someone was burning...a candle perhaps; a scent most unfamiliar. It was as if she had suddenly been bathed in it.

And then she saw a plume of smoke erupt from behind her sofa, right in the middle of her floor. And before she could decipher how to put it out – or for that matter, how it had begun - and the thin plume expanded to a column, and a shadow emerged from its center...

...and Marc stepped out.

Lisa dropped to her knees, closed her eyes, and began speaking in tongues, with arms stretched before her, with palms facing up towards the heavens.

Marc calmly walked in her direction, "Get up Lisa. Andrea had a lot more patients for those showcases, than I do."

"Get thee behind me Satan. You have no place nor authority here!" she exclaimed, her voice caught in a dry spell at the last word, and she ran her tongue past her lips as if she had more to say.

First, she popped open one eye, saw that Marc was still there, then quickly closed her eye again, and began to spew out an epitaph of words strung together so fast, that Marc could only stand there amazed with arms folded.

"Lisa! Get up off that floor. I may be dead, but I still have feelings, and really don't take kindly to being called Satan, if you know what I mean. So Ms. McNally, if you could stop trying to banish me, or exorcise me, or change me into something long enough to realize we just don't have the time for this right now."

There was a short silence.

Lisa opened one eye again.

Still there, she thought.

So, she slowly lowered her arms, and placed them gently on her hips,

"Well with an attitude like that, I can see how I had assumed you had an association with our Fallen Angel."

"Is that supposed to be a joke, or an insult?"

She simply shook her head, stood up, and exhaled. "Get out Marc." Her tone rang with such conviction, such finality, that Marc was taken aback; the human trait of shock revisiting him anew.

"Did you have anything to eat yet, Lisa? I can't communicate with you while you starve your vessel. He glided a bit more in her direction, hoping his concern came across as genuine.

She *looked* past him...then *walked* past him, as if he were nothing more than a ghost. "You used to only be concerned about my hunger, if you were hungry," she took a seat on her sofa. "And if that's the case, you need to head on down the road where Pete still has his Hotdog / Smoothie / Check Cashing Stand."

"Funny. I no longer need food, but you do, and I can tell that your body is weak and tired from your lack of intake."

"And tell me Marc. Why the fuck do you care now?"

Taken aback.

"So, you're talking like a sailor now? Can't you see how all your hate and anger is coming out now? Can't you see how it is changing you? It is happening all over town, Lisa...by saint and sinner alike. We have to do something about this. Right here, me and you, right now."

"I really don't have to do a damned thing, Marc."

He was trying to push this conversation through, to see if bits and pieces of the real information he needed to share came through...but she was throwing up brick walls, from a lifetime of bricks being thrown at her.

He would have to go along another path.

"Yes, you are right. I was an asshole, Lisa; and you are also right about not having to listen to me, or go along with anything I say."

This stunned her. "Yes...yes, you were an asshole."

"I didn't even love you when I was alive. And to tell you the truth, you hadn't even crossed my mind in the afterlife, until I was forced to come back."

Her voice began to stammer, as if she was unsure of how to respond, "Yes...I figured as much."

"So maybe you should tell me how much of an asshole I was. Maybe I deserve to hear it from you."

"What?"

"Tell me how much of an asshole I am, Lisa."

She crossed her arms and leaned back on the sofa. "Do you think we have the time?"

He walked towards the sofa, and leaned on the back of it, just beyond Lisa's shoulder. "Not really, but I want to hear it anyway."

She lowered her head as her face became a twisted rag of memories she couldn't ring out. "Okay, Marc. You were such an asshole to me that you deserve every bit of Hell granted to you – and if Heaven has permitted you entry, then *I* wish not to go there."

Marc held his tongue and could feel his skin shake at the accusations. "What did I do, Lisa? Why have you hated me so much for so long?"

"Are you serious? Are you really serious?"

"Yes, I really am," he said, lowering himself slightly, until he could smell the sweat of Lisa's hair. "Maybe I am like this, maybe I am destined for Heaven or Hell, maybe I deserve to be here suffering your accusations, because no one has had the nerve, the strength, to tell me who I am."

She closed her eyes, fighting back tears, and she could feel her lungs suddenly go tight with tension. She inhaled slowly, "You were a selfish bastard, Marc. You were cruel in the things you said and callous in the way you treated me. You used me. You made me feel dirty, with the things you asked me to do sexually – made me believe you loved me when I would do those things. I thought you loved me. I thought I could trust you, but you were only out for yourself, and you didn't care about how it would affect me. You slept with my friend and destroyed two relationships in the process – mine and yours. I even think you knew how much I loved you, and still you didn't care."

"You believed right, Lisa."

"I hate you, Marc."

"I know you do."

"I wish you would die."

"I have."

"…I know."

And suddenly she began to feel better.

Then out of the corner of her eyes, she could see another plume of smoke, and from it came another body. She didn't move and began somehow to accept all that was happening to her. "Hello Rikki."

Rikki stepped towards the sofa; his steps timid. "Hello Lisa," he replied, then took a quick glance in Marc's direction. "I sensed that her spirit had calmed a bit."

"It has," Lisa replied, her lips barely moving, and her eyes still downcast.

"You might as well let me know too, what kind of man I was. I know it was a time ago, but if you..."

"I won't have any problem remembering it, Rikki."

"Maybe you should eat first, Lisa," said Marc.

She looked over at him, and slowly lifted herself from the sofa, "I think I will. For what I have to say, I need to be on a full stomach."

Part IV

Jason stood on the road leading outside of town. It was a quiet road, nothing stirring, nothing that is except the mist that lay about him, its thickness, its coolness wrapping around him like ice water.

He stood there for a moment, relishing in the sense of feeling that he had suddenly been subjected to. But he could not relish in this too long – he was treading on thin territory already by indulging in these senses.

He had to find Harold.

His presence was near; he just knew it. He could feel the hatred and fear that Harold emitted; his body would simply find Harold on its own.

Knowing what the mist truly was frightened Jason – frightened him more than all the petrified bodies he saw along his journey. Human bodies, animals, insects, birds – they were all trapped in time right now, trapped in another space and moment.

The mist was thick, very hard to see, and navigate through – hence his need to be guided beyond superficial means. There was an incredible feeling of warmth just before he reached Harold's being...

...very warm.

He could see Harold's car against the shoulder of the road, his body standing beside it in a posture of a man who'd decided to step from his car when the fog got heavy in an attempt to see if he could go any further. He must have stood there looking out into this murkiness for a rather long time for the mist to have taken a hold of him.

Jason could feel himself being pulled closer towards Harold's body; their connection to each other was like an invisible tether. He was glad that Harold had not had a chance to get back into his car and drive off, because further into the mist there was a point where the town and the rest of the world separated...and the longer he remained in this mist, the wider that separation became.

Jason had to get Harold back into the center of town, so he acted swiftly. He reached out to touch Harold's shoulder, the soft leather of his jacket was at once warm, but soon it cooled as some sort of slickness began to permeate from beneath Jason's fingers. This sheen reached out to surround them both, and then slowly they began to rise, their bondage from the mist became a short-lived battle, but soon the mist bent inward around them, and propelled them back into the center of town, to a deserted neighborhood park.

Harold was still very stiff as they lowered to the ground. Jason lifted his fingers, and the opaque slickness, like melted sugar, dissipated, and Harold's legs buckled, while he collapsed like a rumpled ragdoll on a small patch of grass.

Harold seemed to cringe, as if tussled from a nightmare, and he jerked a bit as his limbs were renewed, then he opened his eyes, seeing Jason.

"What the hell!" Harold expelled, scrambling backwards, as his shoes slipped on the wet blades of grass.

"Hello Harold. Finally, we meet."

Harold looked around again, frightened, his body crouching defensively. He wiped his wet hands on his jeans before standing. He backed away silently.

"Let's step over here where it's a little dryer," Jason said, his arm directed towards a set of wooden benches surrounding a large marble fountain.

Harold didn't move. Jason allowed him to experience his moment of delirium; how else would one feel to have been driving out of town one moment, only to end up at a park the next? It was enough to drive a sane man...insane. It was not the norm for a fatality victim to meet their killer.

"Am I dead?" Harold asked, still maintaining his crouching stance.

Jason had not expected that response. He understood it – he was looking at one who had been deceased.

"No Harold – you are not dead! I am."

With that statement, something within Harold suddenly clicked. He lifted himself upright and barreled his chest forward – the fear in his eyes however still betrayed him. "What's going on?" Who are you really?"

Jason could feel the confrontation within Harold was rising. He directed once again towards the wooden benches and the fountain. "I think it would be better if we both took a seat, and then we can talk a little more."

"Why? What are you going to do to me?" Harold said, his fingers crimping into fists.

Jason sighed, and boldly stepped in his direction. "Oh, I don't know. What do you think I should do to you Harold?"

Harold fell silent as Jason's words brought back the actions of his sins. Still he tried to appear brave. "I don't regret what I did, you know."

Jason was not moved by such a desperate statement and moved his fingers through his blond locks nonchalantly. "Yes, I know. I'm going to sit over here, Harold. Over here is where you stop running from your lies, your relationship, and yourself. Join me when you're ready."

Harold watched as Jason walked away from him, the rage within him still festering, and he could not help wishing for a chance to kill this man all over again.

Jason kept his pace, even as he read Harold's emotions as if they had been belted aloud. So much love, hate, mixed with an undying coagulation of rage and regret. Jason thought it was any wonder that the man's flesh didn't dissolve into a heap at his ankles.

This was not going to be an easy task.

"Do you expect me to apologize, Jason?"

The statement nearly caused Jason to stumble, but he strolled effortlessly towards the benches to take a seat. He watched as Harold opted to sit on the lower tier of the three-tier fountain. They said nothing, and Jason listened to the water as it cascaded behind Harold, its coolness most welcomed. In the far distance he could hear a group of kids walking home after a game of basketball. It was peaceful enough, but still Harold was unnerved inside. "I don't expect anything from you Harold. You have done *more* than enough thus far."

Harold folded his arms and remained silent. "What happened back there? I was heading out of town, and then suddenly, I'm here."

Jason looked away from Harold. This was rhetoric, and he had grown tired of it – the human trait of restlessness he remembered. "I pulled you back into town, Harold," Jason exhaled.

"Pulled me back?"

"Yes, pulled you back. I know this is confusing for you, but there is a lot going on here."

He stood up. "I don't know what you're talking about, or what you did to me. I don't plan to sit here and be spooked by some ghost."

"I am no ghost, Harold."

"Then why are you here? Are you here for some kind of revenge?"

A suppressed laugh erupted from Jason. "Revenge? No Harold, I am not here for revenge."

"Then I find no reason to talk to you," Harold said, as he pivoted, turned, and began to walk away.

"Don't leave here Harold!" And this time Jason turned to look upon Harold's back, as he began to stride away.

Without turning, Harold said, "And what are you doing to do? Why don't you just leave me and Benny alone?"

"I have left you Harold. I started that when you ran me over in your car and ended my life. You do remember that moment don't you? It was the moment you had Benny all to yourself."

"What's your point, Jason," Harold said, his ears picking up Jason's footfalls tracking behind him, getting closer.

"My point is that you would like more than anything to do it all over again...right now, actually, the urge to kill me again is all you can think about."

Harold's shoulders shook a moment at hearing his own desires unmasked so unabashedly. "And what could stop me, Jason?"

"I would stop you Harold," Jason said, walking closer to Harold, "Dying once is quite enough for me." He reached out to place his hand gently on Harold's shoulder.

Before Jason's fingers could reach him, he spun around to face him, and pulled back his other arm, in a pendulum of knotted fingers casting a fist.

The world suddenly went silent as they stood there staring at each other; Jason looking deeply into Harold's brown eyes.

"Why Harold?"

The pendulum lowered.

"Why don't you go back to where you came from? Benny doesn't need you anymore."

"Is that what this is all about?" Jason said; his voice raising a pitch higher, as an understanding came over him. "Did you kill me, not because you hated me, but because you wanted Benny to love you more?"

The pendulum fell and Harold's head dropped a few inches, his eyes downcast, his breathing suddenly halted. He took a step back.

"You are an evil person, Harold Baines. You can't control who another person loves, and by how much."

"Fuck you Jason! You never deserved the love Benny threw your way. You wasted all that he was – stifled what he had to offer. Benny was better off giving his love to someone that would know how to use it...or at least know it was there."

It started at his feet.

A vibration, as if the ground was about to give way.

It traveled up his body like a thunderbolt; emotions knotting his flesh, twisting his mind, and bridling his intellect. He could not believe how selfish Harold had been...how selfish his own death had become. He was killed for an intangible; killed in an attempt, to stop love. Jason was not sure when the distance between he and Harold closed, but it was pressed in an instant.

Harold had only a moment to throw up his hands before Jason came at him, fists raining upon him. Pain clipped at his chin, his head, his arm, the side of his head, his shoulder...

Jason could feel his body pushing against Harold. He could feel Harold falling backwards, as they both plummeted to the ground, and still Jason continued to assault him.

Jason then pushed down Harold's wrists, and straddled upon his chest. He looked into this frightened man's eyes, and somehow willed himself to stop his flesh from reacting any further. "You don't deserve Benny. You don't deserve me here, doing what I am doing now, you pig. You should be jailed. Do you hear me? You killed a man, Harold. Don't you realize you've committed murder? Do you realize you have caused my family and friends much unneeded grief? This was never about you and Benny, you fool."

Jason waited for Harold to speak, but he continued to display a look of pained discombobulating – and then Jason realized that he had been pressing the man's wrists almost *into* the concentrate. He released him; the feeling of Harold's heartbeat still could be felt beneath his fingers.

Harold panted heavily as feeling came back to his hands. "Get off me!"

"Look at me Harold," Jason said, shamefully covering his face with his hands.

"Get the fuck off me Jason!"

"You look at me Harold," Jason repeated, trashing his hands away, spittle flying from his lips. "You look at the man you killed, Harold Baines. I represent more than the life you see here. Understand that!" And then Jason leaned back, and stood up, his body suddenly deflated.

Harold remained on his back, tears streaming across his eyes. "I hate you so much, Jason. I hate you for making Benny love you more than me."

He's hopeless, Jason thought, as he turned his back on Harold and staggered towards benches along the fountain. "Yes, I understand that Harold. You may always go on hating me, but there are bigger problems here, Harold. Now get up. We must get your car, and we also have to confront Benny. This thing between me and you unfortunately, is not yet over."

Weakly, Harold stood, and walked towards Jason. As a child, Harold never found much interest in church; but suddenly he was beginning to understand the message of reaping what you sew.

CHAPTER 15

Part I

The phone had been ringing at such a steady and unnerving pace, that Mildred decided to listen to what God would want her to do about such a situation.

He told her to unplug all but one of them.

She heard a steady pounding on her door. She did not care about what mayhem may be happening outside. It had to be members of the church, knocking on her door – they must want to see God in person – she thought, to be knocking on *her* door. After another of round of pelts, aggravated, she barreled for the door.

There was a surprise awaiting her when she opened it.

"Mildred!"

It took her a moment to realize that the brother she thought dead was now suddenly standing before her; and speaking in a voice that was way too calm for her understanding. "Eric?" Mildred cleared her throat, "What are you doing here?"

"I am here on urgent matters that Pastor Reynolds needs to be aware of."

"The Police Precinct is only four-miles up the street Eric. I am sure they are more qualified than the local town's clergy," and she started to close the door on him.

There goes the niceties, he thought, and thrust his foot in the doorway. "I said this was an urgent matter, Mildred. You know we're dealing with more than human circumstances. I just need a man who can also relate to the spiritual."

Mildred rolled her eyes to the ceiling. "He's not here, Eric," she said coyly.

He took it upon himself to step inside, "Then I'll need to inform you of this matter, being that you are the First Lady."

There was protest on Mildred's lips, but another voice pierced the air. "Aunt Mildred, where are your DVD's? The satellite is still not working."

"Is that Timothy?" Eric said.

"You know that's Timothy. What do you want with us?" Mildred said, sliding closer towards Eric, daring him to enter further into her home.

"Dad?" said Timothy's unsure voice. He was soon walking up the hallway to stand behind Mildred.

Mildred spoke over her shoulder, "We've got some movies stored on the DVR."

He then whispered, "What's *he* want?"

Eric looked puzzled. "I came to see if everything was alright with you."

"Yea right," he dismissed, turning back down the hallway, "I'll see if I can get them off the DVR Aunt Mildred. I may have some already downloaded on my laptop, I'll check there too."

"Good," she responded, glaring at Eric. "I'll see what your dad wants."

They both hate me, Eric suddenly realized. It was all over them like a shadow. When he was summoned to return to the living, he thought it was to sooth Erica from her grief at having lost both a child and a husband. He may have been wrong.

"So, what do you want to tell me, Eric?" Mildred said, as she headed towards the bar. "What can I fix you?"

Eric looked questioningly at Mildred.

"Don't tell me that the dead can't drink. It's not as if it's bad for your health."

"Do I look like I need a drink, Mildred?"

She examined him. "You look like you could use a double."

He waited quietly for his drink.

When she had finished, she handed it to him without a word, and walked past him to sit in Luther's recliner. He watched her sip, and he did the same. If he had not already been dead, this drink would have surely sent him there.

"Why do you hate me Mildred?" Eric asked; his voice wounded.

"Sit down Eric," Mildred said, directing him to the sofa at his back.

"Timothy hates me too, doesn't he?" he asked, taking another sip from his drink.

She shook her head at him pitifully. "Why hadn't you called me Eric, or come to me? You haven't even called your son."

"I was trying to make sure that Erica was okay. She has been through a lot since losing her son, and then losing our house, and me having disappeared, then Maya having died..."

"So what?"

"What?"

She leaned forward. "I said, so what? You know Erica is a strong woman, and she can handle the shit thrown at her and call it perfume. She was sad about her son, but she went right to making sure Timothy was okay. She lost the house because you left, but she made that trailer home seem like a mansion. She was pissed at you for leaving, but she'd dried those tears a long time ago, and hadn't replaced you because you are, quite frankly, one of a kind. As far as Maya is concerned...we don't mention that name in this house."

"Yes, I know that. So, you're telling me that you hate me for the things I did to her?"

"No. Timothy hates you for spreading his mother thin. She can't be mother and father all the time. She is drained. Timothy hates you for not being there as his father. Even when you were alive, you treated him as your child, but never as your son...you'd reserved that for Eric Jr.

She was right, he thought. "And you? Why do you hate me?"

Mildred shook the ice around in her glass. "You know why, Eric...but I will say it anyway. We were both married Eric, we both were rooted here; and yet you left. I really didn't care that you didn't call Erica. I always thought she was holding you back - but me? You didn't call me."

And then the answer came. "And you wanted to go with me."

She fell back in the seat, and sighed softly, "Bingo."

"I made that decision so last minute. I didn't know if you still wanted to."

"Don't get stupid on me now Eric. Of course, you knew that. We were travelers; it's all we talked about after we married. I am busy dealing with a church that despises me, a husband that desires to cheat on me, and a now dead woman, that was constantly challenging me. I would have left here at your first phone call."

"And now...now what are you plans?"

"You're dead Eric. I would have done this with you. I am trapped in this dirt town by a husband that is duty bound to it. I see you here, my dead beloved brother, and I want to miss you a little, but I can't help but resent you for having lived before you died."

He finished his drink. So, he was not sent back for Erica; to ease her mind. She would adjust. Her world was not altered, because her world was made to shift. Mildred and Timothy relied on him for stability.

He placed the empty glass on the coffee table. "I am sorry about that Mildred. I wish I had called you, and I wish I had loved Timothy more, but I can't undo the past." He stopped there. He didn't have the right words to lead into what he had to say next, and so he stared at his empty glass, watching the ice in it begin to melt, as he formed the words, "Crest Hill County is going to die, Mildred."

She looked at him as if he may have said something else. "What are you talking about Eric?"

He stood, walked around the coffee table, and sat on its opposite edge, his knees just inches from Mildred. "Since Maya's death..."

"I told you about that name."

Eric held up a palm, "I know, I know Mildred, but with her death, came an unbelievable sorrow to this town. It was a grief culminating from the great tragedies this town had to bare. Maya was the last. So many tears have fallen, that they have come back as a mist upon Crest Hill County. This mist has pulled up sorrow from the grave. But it is going to take everyone if this town is to survive."

Mildred was bewildered. "Survive? What is happening to Crest Hill County, Eric? How is this town dying? Instead of telling us about what is happening to this town, shouldn't you be leading us out of here?"

"The mist won't let that happen."

"The who?" Mildred said, tilting back her drink, before she realized it was empty, and the ice cubes clashed against her teeth. She clutched the glass tighter and rested it in her lap. "The mist? You mean the mist that has been lingering around the cemetery? What does that have to do with me and you, and this town? I can't take all this in right now, Eric. I have enough on my mind," she said, staggering to her feet. She headed back towards the min-bar.

She turned to face Eric as soon as she refilled her glass with ice. "Is the mist some kind of poison? Is that why no one has been able to come back into town?"

"No. It is more than that."

"EwwwwWeee!" Mildred exclaimed, placing a hand across her forehead. "This is some not-to-be-believed bullshit! Why don't you get to the point, Eric? What is it exactly am I supposed to do to stop this mist from killing the town?"

"You have to forgive me Mildred. You have to forgive me and stop all this anger you have against me. Then your grieving can start."

She had her back to him when she began to pour her cognac. "You're telling me that in order for Crest Hill County to start its healing process from grief, that I must simply forgive you?"

He was becoming agitated, but let the emotion push through him, "In a sense, yes."

She drank as she walked in his direction – long and slow. "What *is* this mist, Eric?"

For an instant, he marveled at her ability to uncover the bigger truth. "I can't tell you that."

"But it is relying on me to forgive you, in order that this town would be saved."

"Yes."

She flounced back into the recliner. "Then I'm afraid, Eric. That this town is doomed."

Part II

Jenna thought at any moment she would have a heart attack. There was only so much a woman of her stature could shoulder. She could hear the clatter of churned voices and scuffling feet in her living room; she remained in the kitchen, standing in front of the refrigerator, with a glass of cold water in one hand, and her forehead resting against the closed freezer door.

She wanted to catch her breath before going back into a room where her *formerly-dead now-living daughter*, Ella, was on the phone with her *living-granddaughter* Tilly, talking about something that was happening out at the cemetery. Behind her *formerly-dead now-living daughter*, Ella, was an infant, resting on the sofa, who was supposed to be Tilly's *formerly-dead now-living son*, whom she'd aborted. Of course she had thought this to be the child of both Tilly and Mark's, but math was one of Jenna's best subjects; and the math told her that it had to be the child of another man Tilly once loved: Carl – a man three times her age – who was living, but Jenna wished was dead.

Yes, the solace of the kitchen was a hard thing to pull from.

As she slinked back into the living room, she could hear Ella still on the phone, her voice rushed, and the tone urgent... "Yes, Tilly, you already told me about the thickness of the mist...Yes, leave Carl alone there for a moment, we will soon be on our way...It is very scary, but you are in no danger if you stay inside for a while. Yes, I know about that too, and I am glad that they were so helpful, and kept you kids from going back to the outskirts of town. Your friends will be okay once this is over...no...I don't know when that will be..."

Jenna was so preoccupied with eavesdropping on Ella's conversation, that she jumped when Nathan came barreling through the door.

"The car is ready!" He looked up and caught Jenna's surprised gaze, and for a moment a silent conversation passed between them. There was still a lot of anger there.

Ella could sense this, and told Tilly that they were on their way, quickly grabbed the infant from the sofa, and headed out the door, pushing Nathan along with her. "Great Nathan. We have to get to the cemetery, so that I can see what is going on, and so that you two can calm Tilly down."

"Are you sure she is fine, Ella? You said something about her friend disappearing; that she sounded frightened.

We don't have time to talk about that right now, Momma. I have to make sure we can get Tilly out of that mist and back home. It will be very hard for Mark to navigate through it if it is as thick as I predict."

There was no conversation along the way, and the mist *had* become thicker.

Jenna could not believe her eyes as she looked out at the driveway leading into the cemetery; even at the gate the mist had such weight as if to look like a gray wall against the intricate iron fence that surrounded the grounds. It no longer shifted and moved in a hundred directions as it did during the drive up here, for now, it appeared to move in unison, as if it were breathing.

"What is this Ella?" Nathan said, his voice barely heard.

Ella appeared not hear him. "Stay to the right of the driveway, and keep it slow – there are still many dead walking the grounds."

Nathan simply nodded, and veered his car to the right. "The main building shouldn't be that far from this..."

"I see it," Ella cut in. "I can also see Tilly waiting for us at the entrance."

Tilly didn't see them, but she could sense their presence.

The haze surrounding her wasn't as thick as it was on the grounds of the cemetery; as if something, maybe her, maybe the building, was keeping it at bay. She was scared and anxious. The events of a few hours ago had unnerved her....

Only a few hours ago, she was standing outside of town, surrounded by her friends, not sure what to do about John and the way he vanished. However, they did have a theory; that somehow, time itself was askew. The mist seemed to be either slowing things down, or speeding them up, or stopping them all together, or...they just couldn't figure it out. Then Tilly had an answer – she decided to ask the only people in this town that could possibly have the answer.

She would ask the dead.

And so she and Mark came to the cemetery, scared at the amount of mist that had appeared on the grounds. There was no doubt that it not only surrounded Crest Hill County, but is was closing in on it from all direction; smothering it.

Audrey had already been here – as was Carl, but it was Audrey who seemed to be awaiting their arrival. Many of the dead came to Audrey and informed her that Tilly and Mark were coming...and why. So when they arrived, there was a conference room set aside for them, filled with those who had risen, and Tilly could not remember her body haven shaken so much in all her life. Her other friends had returned home – but she and Mark came to get more answers.

And receive them they did.

Ten of the un-living told them that Crest Hill County was speeding up in time. The thicker the mist, the faster the town moved. Those that remained in Crest Hill didn't notice the difference: because as they moved faster in time, it appeared as if the rest of the world was moving much slower. *A week would be as unto a day.* It was the reason the television shows appeared to freeze; when in reality, time had slowed to such a degree, that everything not within

Crest Hill County, appeared to not move at all.

Tilly and her friends had guessed some of this when they noticed the fluctuation in time with their watches, but what they didn't know was that the faster Crest Hill County moved within the fabric of time, the less likely it would be for them to return to their perceived reality. Slowly, the rest of the world would begin to forget them, and at that moment, they would cease to exist. Even those that were heading back on the road that led to this town, would enter its borders at one end, but find themselves leaving it on the opposite end – passing right through it.

So her friend John may have actually gotten frozen in the mist, managed to escape – lost in a time that was slower than their own, or was driving in a loop in an attempt to get back into town. It would remain a mystery, it seemed.

As for them...

She suddenly could see the headlights of Grandpa Nathan's car, and eased out from the doorway to greet them.

When Jenna could see Tilly walking in their direction, she thought she would be glad to see her – but there was so much anger and confusion in her, that she realized she was crushing her grandchild, whom Ella gave her to hold. "I'm sorry," she instinctively whispered to the child. He winked at her, as if to say "It's okay...nothing can hurt me now."

"Hello Ella?" Tilly questioned, trying to remember this white woman. "Have I seen you before?"

"At the grocery store. I told you that Jenna was my mother," Ella explained.

Tilly thought back to that moment. "Yes, of course. I had forgotten about that so quickly. I thought you were some crazy bag-lady."

Ella smiled, and then turned her attention back to the car. "Hurry Momma, I have to see about Carl."

Carl, Jenna thought, as she eased from the back seat, the child braced over her shoulder. Carl, Carl, Carl...the man who fathered this child. "How is Carl, Tilly?"

"He went out on the back patio to take in a smoke. There was a short meeting in one of the conference rooms earlier, and I think it unnerved him?"

"Carl? The man of steel, unnerved?"

Tilly could not reply; her eyes remained fixed on the child in her grandmother's arms; the remarkably dark looking child. "Wasn't that the baby you had with you that day I saw you?" She said to Ella as they moved into the building.

"Yes...yes it is, Tilly."

"He's so beautiful," she said aloud, but not to anyone in particular.

Jenna grinned, and stretched her arms out, "Why don't you hold him for a minute, honey. Your Grandma's arms are tired."

Tilly lifted the child, and felt immediate warmth, as she pulled him closer. "Does this child belong to someone here in town Ella? I can't imagine it being born of you in the afterlife."

Ella said nothing, but watched Nathan and Jenna return indoors. It would be a tough revelation for Tilly when all was revealed. "Yes. Someone lost this child a short time ago."

Tilly pulled the child up on her shoulder, and he began to play with her ear lobes. She smiled. "Friendly too."

Ella walked into a large foyer, where in the back was a spiral staircase, and beyond that a hallway leading to other areas of the building. In the center sat a large crescent desk, its wood surface shone like a mirror, with an Asian woman sitting on its edge. Ella sensed a strong spirit in this woman; one that understood and accepted what was happening all around her. She was talking to Nathan and glanced in Ella's direction for a brief moment; to her right, next to the front door which was surrounded by a wall dedicated to windows and drapes, stood Mark, looking out.

It didn't take her long to realize someone was missing.

She walked towards Nathan, "Where is Jenna, Nathan?"

The Asian woman turned to look in Ella's direction. "I take it you're Ella? Been alive a while I hear."

The response, and the immediate use of her name, took Ella off guard. "Yes, a little over eight-days now. It took me close to a day to understand my body again."

"Yes, yes, I can imagine that would be a challenge," she said, easing herself away from Nathan, "But Jenna came in asking about Carl. I told her he had gone to the smoking patio to partake of a cigarette. I simply pointed in the direction that was, and before I could explain any further, Jenna took off."

"What is your name?" Ella asked.

"Audrey. My family owns Morning Glory, and I come here to make sure the ledgers are in order from time to time."

Ella reached out to gently grasp Audrey's arm, and whispered, "Thank you Audrey. I need you to lead me to this smoking area. Jenna could be in danger."

Audrey leapt from the desk. "Um...sure."

"What's going on, Ella?" Tilly said, easing up to the group.

"Let's hurry, Audrey," Ella said quickly, ignoring Tilly's inquiry.

They were all speeding through the myriad hallways leading through the building until they stopped in a room that had a glass wall to one side. Beyond the glass they saw Carl sitting back in one of the chairs, his eyes closed, legs crossed, with an unlit cigarette in one hand as it lay limp across his knees. On another side of this outdoor patio filled with chairs was the mist, hovering thick, its plumes swimming back and forth as if were being stirred about by some unseen force. And directly in front of Carl, was Jenna, her mouth moving angrily, with her hand raised in the air.

"You bastard! How dare you do that to my granddaughter!"

"Jenna, No!" shouted Ella, as she took a step forward, but it was too late: Jenna's hand came down in a lighting streak and smacked squarely unto Carl's jaw.

Carl didn't move.

But the mist did.

As Jenna looked on perplexed at Carl's non-reaction, she began to raise her hand for another blow, only the mist would not let her.

It reached out like thin white fingers, and took a hold of Jenna's wrist. Jenna glanced back, and a look of horror cloaked her features. She wasn't sure what was happening, and before she could even question it, Ella was on the patio reaching for Jenna.

"You have to get inside, Jenna! Hurry!"

Jenna's mind snapped back to some sense of the present, and she looked down at Ella. "What's going on here? Carl isn't moving."

Ella pulled at her, "You have to get back inside. I'll have to explain all of this to you once we get inside. Now come on!"

She did, and as she did, the mist seemed to recede a little, lessen in its thickness. Everyone saw it, but no one commented on it.

"What is wrong with Carl?" Jenna asked as Ella pushed her back within the building. Mark and Nathan soon caught up to rally behind Jenna; their features were a canvas of fear and curiosity.

"I need everyone to get back into the lobby area," Ella demanded, moving past everyone, and ushering with her hands.

"What the hell is wrong with Carl?" Nathan demanded, but no one replied. With stunned looks, they all walked away.

In the lobby the question still hung in the air – one that Mark now asked, "So why did we leave Carl back there? What was wrong with him? He didn't move at all when Jenna hit him."

Ella spoke, "...he's been out there a very long time, hasn't he?" Her question directed at no one in particular.

"So what? We want to know what is going on here Ella." Nathan impatiently said.

"Don't take your anger out on her, Mr. Reeds." and there was a sting to Jenna's words that had not been heard between them before. "She is just trying to protect her *family*...a thing that does not concern you."

"Grandma didn't mean that, Grandpa," Tilly said. "What is wrong with you two?"

Ella walked towards the large oak desk. Her steps were heavy, and she felt a twinge of nervousness at what she was about to reveal. When she reached the desk, she turned to boost herself upon it, and began to realize the silence in the room. She looked into everyone's eyes. *They are nervous too*, she thought, *for wholly different reasons*. She realized that such nervousness came from a fear of not knowing...and so she now decided to peel the layers of truth back just a little – so that they would finally know what they did not understand.

"This is no ordinary mist" she began, "And the details of it I cannot reveal at this time. Tilly is now aware of just how odd this mist happens to be," and she glanced at the young lady, her arms cradling the infant. "What did the dead say to you Tilly?"

Tilly hesitated; her words desperately clung to her throat. "They said that the mist was somehow causing the town to speed up in time, and the rest of the world to slow down."

You could hear the unclasping of closed mouths.

Ella nodded, keeping her gaze towards the intricate designs etched into the marble floor beneath them. "Time, yes. She is right. They are right. Crest Hill County is moving faster within its borders than the rest of the world without." She lifted her head to look at the hallway that led to the chamber where Carl still remained. "What has happened to Carl – his near petrified condition- is going to happen to this town in a way. The community here is going to slow down, stop, and eventually cease to exist from the rest of the world. One by one, the mist is going to claim the townspeople, going person by person, until the town itself, is the only thing left to claim. It will simply cease to exist."

"What! What are you talking about, Ella?" Jenna said, her tone tasting of restrained anger.

"Why is this happening?" Mark asked.

Ella closed her eyes as she continued, "Death has paid one too many visits to this town, caused too much grief, left many unpleasant tracks."

Jenna raised her hands, and took a glance at everyone around her. "Is this really happening? Are you serious? Does anyone see how crazy this sounds?"

Audrey spoke, "About as crazy as the dead walking, or long-lost relatives suddenly appearing, or an old man sitting on a back patio stiff as a board, or a mist that seems to move on its own, in a town where no one has been able to leave or enter for the last few days." Audrey said, folding her arms, and keeping her eyes stationed in Ella's direction. "I believe what Ella is trying to tell us may only be the beginning of a great many other things that are about to occur."

"That is why I can't explain much more, because the mist has begun to move swiftly beyond the cemetery, and will reach the center of town before nightfall. It, like everyone in this town, has a purpose yet unfulfilled."

"Are you saying this mist is going to kill us all?" Jenna shouted, and turned her back to the group. She was becoming visibly unglued. Audrey concerned, went to embrace her.

"I don't think Ella was saying that. I think she is trying to tell us that there may be a way we can get out of this." Audrey said. Her eyes connecting with Ella's, "But we have to get out of here while it will be safe."

"But I just got my family back, and you're telling me that because of some mist, I have to lose everything I have been wanting all my life?"

"No Mother. That is not what will happen in the end. You will lose nothing, but you will lose everything."

"Stop talking riddles!" Jenna said. Nathan tried to place a comforting hand against her back, but she jerked her shoulders, and could feel his wounded hand fall away. She stared into Ella's eyes. "Then tell us Ella, my daughter…tell us what we must do! I can't lose you again!"

Ella's voice was remarkably even. "But you must Mother – or you will not," she puzzled. "When the town stops living, we all stop living. Our bodies will remain here, this town our limbo, until the outside world has forgotten we ever existed."

She could tell that this truth weighed heavy on them all.

"You can't be serious," Audrey said, and even her solid demeanor crumbled. "Is the town being punished? Have our ancestors sinned, and we are the bearers of some maddening generational curse? Surely Crest Hill isn't a town that owns exclusivity on dead loved ones."

"Your right Audrey," Ella said, "But Crest Hill County is as complex as its occupants. My mother can attest to that – my birth can attest to that. We just haven't the time to discuss it."

"And what of your child," Tilly said, holding out the infant in Ella's direction, "What about your boy? How is he going to grow up without the rest of the world?"

Silence took a seat this time – and stayed for a bit.

"Tilly," Ella said, pushing herself from the desk, "That child is not mine."

"What?" Tilly asked, and instinctively drew the child closer to her. She looked up at her Grandmother, whose eyes had such horror in them for a moment, that Tilly thought she may have imagined it. "Then who's..." she could not finish the words.

Ella finished for her, "Yours. You knew it when I first handed him to you, didn't you?"

She couldn't answer, and barely heard the question, but yes, she did know, and looked down at the young child of mud-like dark skin, and copper-penny reflecting brown eyes. She knew just by looking at the slickness of his hair, and the wideness of his fingers, just who this child belonged to. "Carl?"

"Yes, that is the child father."

"What?" Mark spoke up, taking a defensive step back.

She could not hear Mark now, did not see him. She could only look at the tiny human in the crook of her arm, and remember the time that she and Carl; sweet and loving Carl, sat in the room of the abortion clinic, holding her. He wanted it done in Springfield; a more populated city, where rumors and gossip were less likely to find him. He had been so calm when she told him the news, the moon reflecting off his glasses, as they walked the cemetery grounds. He was calm when he let her decide what to do, and that decision was to abort it. He had been calm when they first made love, their bodies becoming fused with the flesh of experience and the freshness of youth. There was only one condition that had to be met once the abortion was complete. Once its life had ceased to continue, so would their union. There was no protest; for Tilly had realized that they had carried their love as far as they dared.

"We need to go," Ella said, rushing beyond the small group. She looked around quickly. "Where is Nathan?"

Puzzling looks masked everyone. He had gone.

There was a slow-burning creaking sound that slowly melded into the room, and at the far end of it, was an open door leading out unto the courtyard and in its maw stood the thickest, ominous, churning mist that any of them had ever seen; like sand, undulating open and closed like a great organ.

Jenna looked at it as if it stood real, with a name and an address – a being of flesh and blood, and suddenly knew this is where Nathan had gone, into the belly of the beast. "This just can't be happening," she exclaimed.

Ella moved closely behind Jenna. "He's moving fast, into the cemetery somewhere. I can't know exactly," Ella said softly.

"He's mad at the world, and me. I haven't been very nice to him since finding out about his part in your death..."

Ella scanned the others near her. "Mark, stay here with Tilly – your spirit calms her. If you two could also take a walk around the building to make sure Nathan isn't around..."

"Walk around the building? You have got to be kidding. I'm not going out in that," Mark said.

Ella turned back to look into the mist, "I didn't say to linger in it. A quick jog around the property won't affect you. It's not quite that strong. The rest of us need to go out and find Nathan before it's too late."

"This is insane. We don't know what that mist is made of...because I don't think it is normal at all. It may be some government experiment, or a nerve gas, or *something*.

"Quiet, Mark!" Tilly said annoyed. "I don't think our government has the ability to raise people from the dead. How long do you think it will take to find Grandpa, Ella?"

"I really can't say," she stated, stepping beyond the door's threshold, noticing the once sandy texture had shifted to a soupy/milky one. "But we don't have any more time to talk about it. Ladies?"

And with that, Audrey and Jenna joined Ella, as she walked further into the mist.

Part III

The shop was closed today.

No appointments. No follow-ups. No receptionist. No one present, except Benny, sitting in a salon chair, waiting, and attempting very hard to take reign of his emotions.

He was failing at this last thing most miserably.

He saw Jason and Harold walk up the stairs leading to the door. They appeared as lovers, and this irony almost caused him to chortle.

Jason stopped at the door. The hate that surrounded Benny was immense, radiating like an exploding sun.

Jason stepped into the room. "What is going on here? Why are you so angry?"

Benny was astounded at this truth. "What makes you say that?"

"I can see it all over you the moment we came in the door."

Benny smirked, "You walk in here with the man that killed you. How else should I feel?"

Jason wasn't sure how to answer, "I can understand that there has to be an emotional state welling inside you at seeing Harold, but I think you should try listening to him. Nothing can be done about what he did. Too much time has passed, there is no evidence, and although I have not forgiven him, I have not condemned him either."

"Well, good for you," Benny said, flashing a quick sarcastic smile. "Well I'm not there with you." He stood up, "And since you're obviously not interested in your own murder, maybe I should be the one to ask a few questions." He then stood, took a step forward, and pushed Jason aside.

Harold remained by the door.

"Why, Harold? I just need to know why. You were there with me, saw me suffer, saw me in pain each and every day I went to that hospital, saw how much I cared and loved this man, and all the time you were plotting. Did you hate Jason that much that you found it necessary to run him over like a common speed bump?"

Harold could feel the lead pipe of his tongue lay motionless in his mouth.

"Are you at least sorry for any of this? ARE YOU?"

The response was unexpected.

"No."

It was as if he had suddenly been slapped. "What?"

"No, I'm not sorry for what I did?"

"You're not...are you kidding me? You kill a man, and you're proud of yourself?"

He said nothing, and glanced at Jason.

There is remorse in him, Jason thought. Small and red, like a walnut pressed against his throat. .

"I don't know, Benny," Harold said, his gaze cast downward.

"You don't know." Benny said, falling silent. He didn't know how to continue. Who was this stranger that called himself Harold Baines? "Why did you do it, Harold? I don't understand. You run a man down in your car, leave the scene, accompany me to the hospital, watch him slowly succumb to his injuries, then a coma, then death...robbing me the chance to even say goodbye."

Harold looked up. "I did it because I love you...because I still love you."

"And you couldn't love me while Jason was alive? Did you have to put matters into your own hands? Who gave you that right?"

"How was I to know you were going to tell Jason anything about us being together?"

Benny proceeded to answer, but stopped. "Who gives a fuck?! I was the one that was cheating, and I was the one who had to be there for Jason when he died. This was never about you, Harold. You killed a man."

"I didn't know I would kill him!" Harold said, as he turned and walked away from Benny. "I didn't know I would kill him."

"Yes you did," Jason suddenly cut in. "It may not have been your intent, but it was your desire. You have to stop the lies here and now, Harold."

He looked back at Jason, straining to keep his tears at bay. "I don't have to do anything," he quickly said, rushing back towards the open door.

Benny stepped in his path. "No. That is something that you will do, Harold. You will listen. I can't believe how I was such a fool to love you. Were you just going to kill everyone you thought was in your way? How can you stand there and believe what you did was right?"

"But he was making it harder for us. He was in our lives all the time, and you were growing closer to him, not farther. I could see that you missed being with him and that it would have been only a matter of time before you..."

"Shut up, Harold!" Benny said, pushing Harold flush in the chest. "He stole a glance at Jason, "Just shut up."

"No Benny. If we are going to tell the truth here, then let's do it. Let's talk about your boredom with being with Jason: the man that never needs to be taken care of. It was the reason you cheated on him, so you could have a little more to contribute to a relationship besides your name."

"Don't listen to him, Jason. I was never bored with you."

"Yes you were, Benny," Jason said, "We both knew that a very long time ago. You have a great need to be needed, and I have a need not to be catered to."

"What are you saying? Was I too needy for you? Did you not love me?" Benny questioned.

Jason smiled. "My love for you was the one thing about you I continued to carry with me into the afterlife. I loved you very much, Benny."

Benny turned to look at Harold, "And you Harold, did you somehow love me enough to kill on my behalf?"

Harold looked to the ceiling, and took a deep breath. Emotions were wrangling him as well. "I did Benny, although I doubt I would do it again. I didn't want anyone to get between our love, but you were growing closer to Jason and I needed a solution," it was then he looked at Jason, and his eyes lingered there just a bit. "I realized that Jason being in a coma would have been just the thing to bring you even more closely to him, because after years of not being needed, this was when he needed you the most."

"Certainly you didn't expect me to just walk away from him."

"Actually yes. I made you a partner in the salon so you would be helpful to me. But the moment you began to care for Jason, I knew I had lost you forever."

Benny paced for a moment; his footsteps crowded the very air they breathed. His head bobbed with a ricochet of unexposed thoughts. He spoke to the tips of his shoes, "Harold, I don't mean to be abrasive, but get out!"

Harold looked puzzled, "What...I don't understand."

"We've talked, and I am exhausted... I'm also finding it so very hard to stop myself from reaching across this room and beating the shit out of you."

"Benny, what are you saying," Jason said, understanding but not comprehending Benny's tone. "There are more-"

"I will be speaking to you in a minute Jason, but at this time I am speaking with Harold, and right now, I need Harold to leave."

There was little protest from Harold, and although there was a slight hesitation, he headed for the door. "There's still a chance for us Benny. I can feel it," Harold pleaded.

"I can feel something too, but the end result would be a very dirty shoe." Benny quickly said, and walked back to his salon chair.

Harold turned briskly, and left.

"Jason addressed Benny. "What was that all about? I could see in your heart that you were beginning to understand, and maybe forgive Harold. I'm very sure of it."

Calmly, Benny began to take a seat in the chair. "You're right, Jason, I was."

"I don't understand, Benny. We were close to helping Crest Hill County."

Benny grinned slightly, "I knew that was the direction you were leading us in. But strangely enough, Harold was right about something."

"I do not understand. What could Harold have been right about that would cause you not to forgive him for what he had done to me?"

Benny smiled. "He assumed that I would never stop loving you if you had lived," Benny said, looking nonchalant at his nails, "And he was right. I never would have, and at this point I never will."

"What-?" Jason said, but stopped short. HE knew the implications of Benny's actions, but he didn't realize that Benny knew them too."

A short chortle.

"Forgiveness. I knew that was part of this whole thing," Benny said, his eyes lighting up.

Jason moved in closer, and knelt before Benny, placing a hand on his knee. "That's true. That is part of this whole deal, a small part of what it's going to take to save this town. It's why most of the people can't know...it has to come on its own. But also, if you don't forgive Harold, I may never be able to return to my death...I would never leave Crest Hill County."

Benny's eyes glanced down and locked into Jason's magnificently blue orbs. "Yes Jason...yes, I know, and that's why I can never forgive him."

For the first time in a long time, Jason felt shock, for all the things he was able to foretell, THIS, he never saw coming.

Part IV

Lisa was not prepared for this last apparition. She was not prepared for her past to sneak up behind her like this. She was not prepared for a day with no real sleep in sight. She was not prepared for shame.

Alex Winford was very young when he'd met Lisa – so young in fact, that Lisa had a most difficult time remembering him. She'd been only a teenager at the time, and in the midst of her junior prom, waiting to be asked out by several of the men at her school; none of them however, quite like Alex Winford. No one was quite like Alex. He was part of that invisible group of people, the unwanted, the nerdy, and the quiet. He never made himself quite known – and yet everyone had known him.

This afternoon he'd come to Lisa's door, the last of the ghosts it seemed. She felt as if she had become a part of some macabre 'Christmas Carol' play, and just like that production, the last visit appears to be the most dramatic.

Alex was sitting next to her. He had been allowed to appear older than he actually was - a handsome man, very dark hair cut just above the ears, appearing in his mid-30's; an age very close to her own. Smooth ivory features, high cheeks bones, lean build, with the most striking gray eyes she had ever seen. He would have made a most beautiful man had he made it to late adulthood.

As fate would have it, he never did, and ended up on the bathroom floor of his parent's home, with a bottle of whiskey and an assortment of pills in his possession. His death, although painful, was still a determined one. His fight to the afterlife was the greatest battle he'd ever won.

Lisa, unfortunately, had been a part of that despair, that death.

"I don't know what to say, Alex. I had no idea I treated you so badly, "Lisa said, after having to digest Alex's news."

"He nodded. "Yea, it was pretty bad, and it was the end of my last bit of self-esteem."

She gulped. How had she been so horrible, to a person that would have grown up to look like this? He told her that she'd been so occupied by the popular boys that she mistreated those who were not; and she could recall ignoring the less popular crowd. Not very *Christian*-like at all.

"That's why I was brought back here, Lisa, to remind you of how you treated others, in hopes to give you answers on why some men treated you the way they did, "Alex explained.

"Are you saying these things are happening because of karma?"

"Not quite. Karma doesn't work on the collective, or in groups, so what this town is experiencing is a little more than karma."

"Then what is it Alex? What's happening to me, to this town? Is the world coming to an end? Am I being visited by ghosts of my past because I have done something? When is this nightmare going to end, when?" She stopped. She could tell she was very tired, and also becoming very agitated. Whatever these spirits were, why couldn't they come to bring her good news?

"I know this has become very unnerving," he said.

She felt her forehead, "Yes, it has. I don't know what God expects me to do."

Alex glanced at the front door, "Well, Lisa, it will be over very soon," and then he turned to look at Lisa again. "I am to be the last spirit to visit you."

She thought she'd misunderstood him. "What? Are you serious? Is this whole affair over?"

"Only for you – in a sense," he said. "The pain caused by you, and the pain you caused, has seemed to come full circle.

She leaned forward, her head dropped like an iron weight into her propped hands. "I don't understand what is happening? What happens to the rest of the town?"

"You were chosen Lisa, as not only being the first to discover how to cleanse this town, but also to spread that solution to others. You are not to act alone, but you must act now."

"Alex, you are speaking in riddles."

He placed a hand on her back, "Yes, I suppose I am, and for that I am sorry"

She looked up at him, with eyes that glistened with unshed tears. "Why can't you tell me what I am supposed to do? Can't you tell me anything?"

He was silent for a moment, and then took a deep breath. "Tomorrow morning something frightening will occur. There will be great anguish spread across this town. The church will be filled with grief. The pastor will be called there and great demands will be asked of him. You Lisa, must head there. You must tell him everything you've experienced. He will receive a revelation. You must then leave the church, and visit as many homes as possible – and many you will – for the people will need your calm spirit, they will need your gift so that they will not be afraid. This is why you were chosen above all others."

"Is the world coming to an end, Alex? Are we…"

He lowered his eyes and smirked. "This is not the Rapture, Lisa. Believe me."

She didn't share in the amusement. "Then, is God angry with us?"

He stared into her eyes. "That Lisa is a very good question, a *very* good question. What do you think?" He asked, reaching out his hand.

She took it without afterthought. "I think He might be. God isolates a city or people that He needs to deal with harshly. From Noah to Moses, to Sodom and Gomorrah, he ostracizes the evil, and within that evil, certain individuals are chosen to warn or reveal a way of escape. The choices we make can determine if a people or city will live, or burn and disappear forever."

He gently squeezed her hand. "Yes, I couldn't have said it better myself."

"But am I right, Alex? Is God planning on destroying us if we do not heed this…this…warning?"

"I can't tell you that, Lisa. He rarely foretells a plan."

"Then maybe you can tell me something else," she asked, her voice rather low.

He looked at her curiously. Beneath his hands he could feel her pulse race, her skin suddenly become moist, fingers shaking. This question was obviously a hard one for her. "Sure, Lisa. Sure, I can answer something."

"How is it for you, Alex? How is it for you now, wherever you are in the afterlife? When life itself is killing you, does God forgive you if you kill yourself?"

He could feel the deep concern of her questions. It was deeper than the universe itself. He didn't know if he should answer her at all. Her emotions had been shattered for years, between her church position, boyfriends, and her inability to have kids, and her own personal conflict with her spirituality in a town that is not as spiritually connected as her."

He began slowly, considering he would not see her again. In a small way, he wished he could. She had changed very much than the woman he remembered, who hurt him, who took his friendship as a token, or as a charm to show others how compassionate she could be. It brought her much attention, many men, and although she would never know it, it brought her trouble in her relationships. She attracted the person she herself personified.

"Yes, I did tell you that my death was painful, and it was, but it was nothing compared to the pain I was going through. The death came slowly. I could feel my body dying, falling away, as if my skin was being punched and separated – a cookie cutter. After the overdose finally began to take its toll, I wished I could take it all back, but that was in my mind; in my body I was trapped, laying on that floor for the longest time. I could eventually feel my skin unhook itself from my muscles, a feeling I thought came from the drugs.

"I hadn't realized then that I had already died."

Lisa found it hard to speak, "And was there pain at that point? Was there any suffering once you crossed over?"

Alex thought for a moment. "No, I suppose there wasn't. The pain had become something else. Something I can't quite describe. I can only say it is akin to the sensation you get when you are in a warm pool, and you step out into the cold – your body goes through a quickening that lets you know you have gone from one element to another."

Lisa lowered her head; ashamed. "I'm so sorry about that Alex. I know your parents must have suffered greatly. It must have been a shock for them to see you there, beyond anyone's help."

"My father was the first to see me," Alex recalled, his tone casual. "He reached for me, but I hadn't felt him touch me, and then, somehow, he reached *inside* of me, and pulled up my limp body...leaving my spirit, my soul, behind on that bathroom floor."

She inhaled; side eyed, startled, and her first instinct was to take a cautionary step back. "How long had you lain there?"

"Three days," he said. "Three days, to finally accept, and to understand what had happened to me."

"And then?" she asked intently,

"I realized the road that led me to that point of reflection, and many emotions passed through me for the last time: guilt, anger, regret, loss...shame."

"When were you able to move?"

"At the moment I came into the acceptance of my death."

Lisa, in her enthralled excitement, leaned forward at such an arch, she nearly tipped over. "Is this where you finally went to the Seat of Judgment, and faced our Lord and Savior, to give you a decision to your eternal home – be it Heaven or Hell? What did you see beyond the light? Is there really a light? Or is it the Glory of our God pulling you even..."

"Lisa!" Alex intoned, reaching out to grip her shoulder. "You ask too much, and you know it. The Seat of Judgment is a memory I was not allowed to retain, and our fates were not decided so quickly."

"Not decided? After death, there is the Judgment. It happens quickly. Are the lines that long at the Gates of Heaven that people have to take a number? The Bible says that..."

"Stop it, Lisa," voice stern but relaxed. "The Bible does not contain all the answers of an afterlife, nor should it."

She looked away realizing that asking such questions would be a compromise of the beliefs she held dear. Faith was strengthened by a belief in the unknown. She didn't need to know these things; all she needed to do was to believe.

"You are afraid of your part in my death," Alex said, sensing her discomfort. "You could have acted in no other fashion, Lisa. I no longer blame you or hold you accountable for my life. I've forgiven you."

Her lips quivered.

"You however, are going to have to forgive yourself. Can you do that Lisa. Can you say it?"

She looked oddly at him, as if she was unsure of his statement. She waited for him to continue, to explain himself.

"Forgive yourself, Lisa. You must forgive yourself."

His eyes upon her were so intense, that she found herself taking a deep breath, and upon her exhale she said, at almost a whisper, "*Lisa...Lisa...I forgive you.*"

"Again," Alex said, and took a tiny step back.

She tried it, and said to herself, "Lisa, I forgive you. I forgive you for how you treated Alex."

"Again." He took another step back, just inches from the front door.

"I forgive you Lisa, for treating Alex as you did. His death was not your fault, but your actions were faulty. You...I...I... didn't know what I had done...I didn't know it would cause other men to treat me bad. I have forgiven them for making me feel unworthy, and I forgive myself."

Alex smiled, as he reached behind himself, and touched the door's handle. "Just make sure you never do that to another human being, Lisa. Don't let your status at church treat the sinner as beneath you. Every life that comes into your life is a life that can be shaped by you."

She was close to tears. "I understand, Alex, and I will be aware."

"Wonderful," he said, as he began to open the door, "And now, I have to leave you."

"What!"

"You have your instructions to see the Pastor in the morning. Do not delay. Do not be distracted by what you hear."

"Hear?" she questioned, but pondered on it no further. "Okay. I will not be distracted by what I hear." She began to approach him, seeing that he wanted to open the door, and attempted to assist him.

But Alex decided to continue to step backwards, until he was actually walking through it, "Good bye, Lisa." Then he was gone, the door continued to swing ajar.

She ran for it, and swung it open, "Thanks..."

But no one was there, except a very dark town, and something crawling along the street like unwelcomed vermin.

...the mist had suddenly become as thick as she could remember it every being, and it was entering Crest Hill County as if on a mission.

Chapter 16

Part I

The screams began, and somewhere in Crest Hill County, the hairs of a caterpillar curled against the sound.

Tilly awoke with a start; the distant sound that charged her from beneath her slumber quickly became a fading memory, leaving her groggily between dreamscape and reality. She pried her eyes open, and stared at the curtains that covered her windows – windows that had an odd glow behind them as if the faceplate to the street lights had broken loose again. She shook her beating head from a most difficult sleep, wondering if the screams she'd just heard were real.

As her vision sharpened, she noticed why her sleep had been so difficult: she was still wearing the same clothes she had on when she returned from the Morning Glory Cemetery. The Cemetery! She had come home from the cemetery. Her body had been so tired and emotionally drained, that all she could think about was lying down. She wanted to forget what was *not* coming back: Carl and Nathan (her Grandpa), frozen by the mist.

Another scream

This time she heard it in all its shrilled overtones, and it was enough to bolt her out of bed and towards her curtains. She threw back the thick purple fabric, and leaned closer to the window – and at once, she thrust her head back at what she immediately saw. Out beyond the yellow-orange of the horizon, as it crept slowly up the hill, was a mist so thick, so staggered, so smoky-white, that the town below appeared to be burning.

Her door burst open, and she spun around breathlessly.

"You heard the screams, I see," said Ella, rushing towards the center of the room, stopping when she peered at the exposed window. "Its glow is so bright."

"What's happening Ella?"

Ella's eyes remained fixed on the town, watching as day slipped into night. She also tried to understand this unexplained sweatiness within her palms, the quickened pulsations of her flesh, the rushed menagerie of her mind as it began to calculate her next move – and realized with a start, that her body was having feelings of *anxiety*. Her brain was slow to tell her this because her actual birth had been short; her flesh had been so new, that she was unfamiliar with these *feelings*. She had not known that the feelings of the flesh could be so strong…so frightening.

Tilly took a seat at her computer desk, elbows slightly nudging her laptop, as she rested her forehead in the cups of her hands. She could smell her own raw scent of sweat and dirt, while her fingers wrapped themselves about her dry hair. She held back heaves of anguish that clung to her throat like tree sap. "Is Grandpa going to die, Ella?"

"I don't know, Tilly. I don't know how much time we really have at this point."

Tilly wanted to hate Ella for her useless answer. She wanted to know if her Grandpa was going to come back – *she had wanted to know that the moment Mark was asked to check around the area of the church when Nathan first came up missing. Mark came back alone.*

She hugged her child closer to her body, as if the mist could reach beyond the window to seize him. The mist appeared to enjoy the taste of the men in her life.

"It's the mist, isn't it Ella? It has chosen this town, and now it's choosing its victims."

Ella gazed at Tilly, the glow from her laptop, the darkness from her lacquered desk, and the shifting light within the room, exposed Tilly's panic. "It is the mist," Ella offered, "And we're all victims, because the mist is attracted to despair, to pain, to guilt and grief; and there is a certain allure for those who've carried such emotions the longest."

"I see," Tilly said, looking back at the opened window. "You said 'we' are victims. Does that mean the living and the dead, because you're looking just as scared as the rest of us?"

Ella hugged herself, fighting back a slight chill that pricked her skin. "It's the emotions, Tilly. I am not used to feeling these emotions, and despite my desire to stop their reactions on my body, I am failing. The scary thing is, is that my body is winning. It likes to be here Tilly, and I am not quite sure where that leaves me, the real me, the *inner* me…"

Another scream cut through the wind.

Tilly turned to look out unto the town, trying to locate the shouts, find a direction of the chaos, but couldn't. "The sound is moving, isn't it?"

Ella walked towards the window, pressing her hand against the glass. "It is. The mist carries the sound around like a toy, making sure the whole town is aware of what's happening."

When Ella pulled her hand back from the glass, Tilly noticed it left a slight band of moisture. "Is the mist affecting you as well?"

Ella examined the sweat in her trembling palm – and curled her fingers against it, trying to subdue it. She walked towards Tilly, and sat on the bed.

"It's my body, Tilly," she said, eyes cast towards the floor. "The longer it remains on earth, the more it is exposed to human emotions, and feelings. My spirit wants to return home, but my flesh is forcing it, willing it to stay here."

Tilly rose from her desk to sit beside Ella. She saw the danger, not for them, but for everyone in Crest Hill. "Are you saying the more you stay here, the stronger your flesh becomes, and your spirit will eventually be trapped in its own skin, this new skin that you were given in order to exist here?"

"Like a butterfly trapped in its cocoon."

Or like an actual human, Tilly thought, as she nudged herself closer towards Ella, and rested her hand upon hers, feeling the nervousness, and waited.

The shaking soon receded.

"Thank you, Tilly. I feel better." Ella said, exhaling.

"We exist for one another."

"Yes," Ella said, "And actually, although you may not have realized it, but you are calmer too. It is one of the effects of the mist."

Tilly assessed this for a moment, and realized that it was true. She felt her anxiety abate. "Is this some kind of nerve gas, causing a slow paralysis in our bodies?"

Ella laughed slightly. "No, that can be caused I believe as a result of too much television. But the calming effect of the mist is for your protection. Can you imagine what would happen if people's true fears surfaced in a town where the dead walked, and a strange mist made living statues of its citizens? Some people, at the site of a dead relative, whom they would have rather have remained dead, could possibly try to re-kill those that had already died; only to be driven insane when they resurrected themselves once again."

Tilly chuckled at the thought, "I can see where that would cause a lot of confusion."

Ella went to close the curtains. "Yes it can, Tilly," she exhaled, in a body that knew no breath. "Tilly…I believe it's time for you to meet and embrace your child."

Now it was Tilly's hands that revealed tension. "But we have met."

Ella looked over her shoulder, "You destroyed a life, Tilly. You and Carl may have agreed to have it done, but there was guilt and remorse associated with that decision, from both of you."

She wasn't sure how to respond, especially to a once-shameful deed that she had simply outgrown. Even so, it still ached from time to time, because it became an act she could never speak of, a hidden scar that was forever bleeding.

But what Ella was asking her to do, was to discuss that deed to the actual victim herself. How do you tell your child that you murdered them? "I'm afraid to do this, Ella. More afraid than you can know."

Ella went to leave the room, but stopped in the threshold to address Tilly. "Of course, you're afraid, Tilly. How else are you to know, that it is the right thing to do?"

++++++

When the door opened some 12-minutes later, Ella stood there holding her son. She brought the child closer, her steps very deliberate, very sure – the footfalls of a woman that was mission-bound.

Their eyes locked together the moment she reached for him, and she knew in her heart that this was her son, unborn...she had stopped breathing.

Ella cupped one of Tilly's hands as she held the child. "Just talk with him, Tilly," she then pressed a finger into one of the lad's dimpled cheeks. "And be careful."

"I'll be very careful. We'll be sitting safely right here on my bed."

"No," Ella spoke calmly, an edge lacing her words. "You have to be careful with more than just your actions, Tilly. This child is from a place you have yet to experience. Communication may surprise you."

The look Tilly exhibited gave Ella the permission she needed to continue.

"This is no ordinary child Tilly, because despite your actions, despite his death, he has continued to live without you. His flesh has remained that of a child, while his knowledge far amasses your own, so don't let his uncomprehending appearance dismay you, for at times he understands more than your ability to convey – and yet sadly, you will always be a stranger to him."

Tilly looked down at her child, Kenneth, his large watchful eyes mirrored-reflections of his great-grandmother Jenna's. They drew the courage from her like dried fruit.

Ella placed a thin finger across Tilly's lips. "Let the words come on their own."

The child cooed in her arms, and Tilly extended a finger towards his

face. He reached up to grab it, and she was startled at how tight the grip was –
and also the warmth of the finger; as if true life were running through him.
"Warm?" she mumbled. "What happens if you both remain here too long Ella?"

Ella reached out to touch the child's forehead, and she too was
surprised by the warmness to his skin. "This child, as with all of us, are once
again being reborn, and once reborn, the flesh has a strong yearning to live.
The soul knows that life continues so it wants to fly; the flesh knows that life
must end, so it remains grounded. Both will fight to preserve its existence."

"How long can such a fight last?"

Ella looked away, "Eventually, the soul will stop fighting to escape the
walls of the flesh – and Crest Hill County will become its final resting home,
its purgatory. Heaven for it will die, and the flesh will continue to live on
here."

Tilly was speechless.

Ella turned towards Tilly's door. "Jenna is about to awaken – I need to
get to her. She's going to realize that Nathan is not there and panic."

Tilly made a motion towards the door, "Should we both go over..."

Ella stood in the doorway, bracing her hands against the rim, "You're
going nowhere, Tilly. The best way you can help your Grandpa and Grandma is
by telling your child why you did what you did. The larger the truth, the
weaker the resistance; so tell the truth and the easier it will become."

And in a flash, Ella was out the door, closing it firmly behind her.

And Tilly was in the middle of the room, slowly motioning back to
where her bed was.

And then she heard a noise, as if the air conditioning was running at a
very low speed, and after glancing at the closed vent, Tilly realized it had been
her breathing all along.

Part II

At the first scream, Pastor Luther Reynolds fell to his knees. He
prayed, while his heart jack-rabbited in his chest. It was a distant scream, one
so blood curdling, he froze for a moment, unable to move, and a second later
he had rolled out of the bed, his knees hitting the floor smartly; he ignored the
sudden pain, pressing his hands together in immediate solace.

He prayed for answers. He prayed this was a dream. He prayed for himself. Then he stopped. Silence commanded the room once again. He opened his eyes. Slowly, hoping some spiritual apparition had not suddenly materialized; at this point, he wished for a sign of any sort.

The bedroom was empty, Mildred having opted for one of the guest rooms on the main floor. He welcomed her decision to sleep elsewhere, because he'd had enough unanswered questions to deal with, than to have to be subjected to her constant Q&A sessions.

He stood, and looked around the room. The sun had barely begun to rise onto this new day, but as it did, he could begin to see the mess around him. His desk was a mess, the church was a mess, this town was in a mess, and the people within were looking towards him for some spiritual guidance. But who did he have to guide him?

He felt he'd been getting close to an answer. Crest Hill County was a town that refused to release some of its grief. Grief is sometimes a by-product of hate, of resentment, envy, guilt, and even selfishness. Many of those very reasons can be a sin in the eyes of God. But usually there is someone that has the answer, someone that has been sent on a mission, a monarch, a hero, a savior imbued with the answers to guide a confused people out of perplexity, and to a solution…to freedom.

Luther knew he was not that person, and for the life of him, he couldn't imagine who would be.

Another scream lit the air.

The sound of a police siren

Luther ran towards the window and opened it with a force that rattled the glass. He could see the mist was seeping into town like some enormous octopus stretching out its tentacles. *Why was there so much screaming? What was happening?*

Suddenly his bedroom door flung open.

"Did you hear that?" Mildred said, standing at the door, rollers in her head, and one dangling loosely from a strand of frayed hair like a bungee cord. She stood alien-like in a robe of translucent purple, eyes wide, neck craned. "I heard screaming."

"I heard it too," Luther said. "I'm not sure what it's about."

"Of course you're not," she said, walking into the room. "You're just standing there looking stupid as usual."

He held his tongue as he watched this purple-roller-wearing-behemoth brush past him toward its own personal vanity. She huffed, and thrust open one of the top drawers, pulling out her personal phonebook.

"And who are you expecting to call? "Luther asked, as he reached out towards his bedpost where his robe hung, and donned it over his tee shirt and boxers.

"I'm calling Tyler Banes, the head of Police Dispatch. I know it's gotten crazy in this town, but people still have jobs to do…" she said, then directed herself to the phone conversation, "…yea, yea, can you just put Tyler on the phone or do I have to walk up there myself…yes, oh, hello Tyler..." she began to pace the floor.

Luther was still lost in his own thoughts, when his wife suddenly hung up the phone and ran towards the window.

"Oh my God, when did all this fog show up?"

"I believe this morning," Luther said, moving in her direction.

She turned to face him, her disjointed roller snapping loose. "Tyler said this mist is dangerous, causing people to become unconscious. The small surviving staff at the station is practically useless to handle any emergency, and they are still unable to contact any of the neighboring towns."

"Did he know where the screams were coming from?" Luther asked, peering over Mildred's shoulder. He glimpsed the mist, the surrounding town, the road leading up to his home, and a car that appeared to be heading in their direction. He leaned closer.

Mildred felt his touch and looked back at him, momentarily. He hadn't realized his closeness, as he focused beyond the window, the breathing of his chest pushing her shoulder slightly. The window wasn't fully closed, and a soft breeze flowed through it, tickling up past her chin, and nudging the hairs on his. She glanced at his double-chin, the underside slightly riddled with tiny hair bumps from a bad day of shaving. His nose flared, his ever-moist eyes batted slowly (a trait she'd always found attractive – made him seem sensitive). He continued to look past her, not even to seem to notice that she was there – when many years ago, he could not stop looking.

She brushed past him, her shoulder barreling into his chest. A perturbed sigh escaped her.

Luther looked back at her, a hand placed lightly on his chest. She marched to the center of the room and stopped. He could almost smell the anger on her; as distinct as the over-excessive perfume she donned. In his ear, another siren blared, but his focus became Mildred. He had not been focused on her for quite some time, but now, as the morning sun cast its shadow across her back – her *quivering* back – he could tell that her thoughts were elsewhere, and not on matters of rising mist, undead brothers, screams, or police reports. He knew what it was, and knew that now was the time to confront it.

Mildred was about to walk out of the room, but she was suddenly at the end of a rope she hadn't realized lay noosed about her neck. It had been so long since she'd been close to that man; the sliver of warmth that had always stood between them in bed had become fable. Her solace had been in her town status, her financial worth, and her *post*-dead brother – and she had gotten used to them because a certain woman had come to town and captured what was once hers...her husband.

Feelings she had long forgotten were like quicksand to her steps, and she fiddled with the remaining rollers in her head, and could sense Luther moving in closer to her – sensing her trapped state. She held up a hand to stop him. "Why Luther? *Why her!"* she managed to say before spinning around.

"Mildred-?" His words suddenly became lost in her look.

"I know I haven't been the best wife, Luther. I know that, but this town is your wife now, the living and the dead are your wife now, and they need you…" She paused to look deeply in his eyes, "Even though you still mourn for your mistress. And still I can remember a time when Maya wasn't there, a time when we actually existed without her, but something happened. I really don't know what it was, but when Maya slid into this town, something slid out."

Suddenly the doorbell rang.

Luther stood unmoved, but not unaffected. That speech revealed the tiniest flicker of the Mildred he'd fallen in love with so many years ago. A flicker that let him know she cared to be curious. Unfortunately, that flicker would need a lot more light to burn through the crust around his heart. For a man who could speak on inspiration, he now could find no words.

The doorbell rang again.

Mildred exhaled. "I'll get it."

Luther watched as she went beyond the doorway, heard her footsteps, the door being unlatched, low voices in quick conversation. When he looked at the doorway again, he saw Mildred entering, followed by Eric. The look on his face was frightening.

"What's going on Eric?" Luther said immediately, his mobility returning.

Eric ran his fingers through his tussled hair. His eyes darted nervously between Mildred and Pastor Reynolds, before resting upon the latter. "We haven't much time I'm afraid. You've seen the mist?"

"I'll say we have," Mildred said. "What's happening out there? The cloud cover is so thick. We might as well be a coastal town."

Eric's eyes jumped to the floor, his actions very sketchy. "Soon it will take hold of every citizen in Crest Hill County."

"What will? What are you talking about boy," Luther demanded.

"The mist. The mist is going to come into this town, and a great change will happen. Have you both noticed how little your body has been demanding food lately?"

They were both silent. They hadn't...until now.

"This is a poisoning isn't it, Eric," Mildred said, holding fast to her stomach. "I can only imagine why we are being scorned," she boldly glanced at Luther, "Certain sins cannot go unpunished."

Eric stepped between the two, his attention upon his sister, "This has nothing to do with what you are thinking Mildred," then he turned to face Luther, "But there is something *you* must do Pastor Reynolds."

Sweat started to bead across Luther's forehead.

"You must head to the church, Pastor Reynolds. Lisa is there, and she has many of the answers you are seeking. You must get dressed and leave now."

The church bell rang.

Luther stared at Eric for a long time, before he spun on his heels to dress, as Eric and Mildred went downstairs. Pastor Reynolds returned fully dressed; a crisp white shirt, black slacks, and a black blazer. "I am ready."

Eric smiled, and then opened the door. "I know you are."

Nothing was said, as Luther left. The mist had pulled back a bit along the driveway, but Luther was quickly swallowed up in it, and the sound of the engine and the spherical headlights faded away into nothingness.

Eric closed the door, and Mildred stared ghostly at its wooden hide. "Will he be fine, Eric?"

Eric stepped up and placed his hands on her shoulders. She was shaking. "He should be fine, Mildred. Where is Timothy?"

"What?"

"Timothy. Where is his room? The mist is going to be getting stronger now that emotions are high in this town, and Timothy is still holding onto his emotional hate of me. That hate can be like a magnet."

Mildred looked over her shoulder, "He's in the guest room near the end of the hallway."

"Let's go," Eric said sternly, and moved past Mildred, gently tugging at her arm.

They reached the door, and Mildred stood horrified. Eric pulled her closer. He too stood in silent terror, because from under the closed door flowed tumbling billows of mist.

Part III

Jason was troubled.

Being troubled was something Jason's body had forgotten how to feel, until about 30 minutes ago.

The church bell rang.

Fear joined Trouble, and both riddled his flesh.

It was a cool morning, and the water along the river pulled at the banks and drew in a collection of dirt, twigs, and food debris. Jason sat near the banks soft ground, his heavy feet pushing up small pebbles and rock through the choppy earth. His body was drawn to the tranquility of this place, the serenity; which he also realized allowed his mind to think uncluttered.

Harold had killed him.

If he were still alive, this would have disturbed and angered him, but that deed, that most evil act, had somehow been a freeing one. Jason could no longer be angry at a life cut short, just as a premature child could be angry for being born too early. The trouble of his mind stemmed from Benny.

Benny was not going to stop loving him. He was not going to forgive Harold. He was not going to allow him to be free. Jason's flesh would be drawn into this world, banishing him from the hereafter. If Benny forgave Harold, if Benny would accept his death…there would be a chance of victory for them all. Jason knew Benny would not.

So Jason remained troubled.

Jason also was very aware of the mist.

It floated around him now; thin trails of smoke, almost invisible in the bright sun. It resembled the light spray of a hot spring, only heavier and drier.

He ran his fingers through it; the feel of it chalky, with a noticeable weight. He rubbed his palms together, and the texture of it was like wet sandpaper. The mist was growing stronger in both volume and structure.

A sudden noise of crushed underbrush: twigs snapping, leafs crumpled, dirt sifted. Harold was approaching, and even though he was more than a few minutes away, Jason could sense him as if he were standing directly behind him.

A most uneven triangle, the three of them were; He, Harold, and Benny - A triangle experienced by many in this town. A triangle Benny was not willing to sacrifice, by the very statement he made in the salon...

"What are you saying, Benny?" Jason had questioned, staring closely at Benny's lips, to be sure that the words he had just heard had come from the lips he was now seeing.

"You heard me, Jason. I'm not letting you go," Benny said, casually cleaning his nails with the edge of his teeth.

"You don't know what you're saying," Jason pleaded.

Benny nodded, as if confirming his own thoughts, "Oh yes, I know exactly what I'm saying. If *me,* forgiving Harold means *me,* losing you a second time, then *my* decision becomes a no-brainer. I choose you."

Jason began pacing the floor, arms swung absently about him. "You can't do that, Benny. You don't have the right to make such a decision. I don't belong here. This is not my final resting place. This is no longer my home."

"And yet it is. We've both been given a second chance to have a second life again, Jason, and I, for one, plan on taking advantage of the chance."

He doesn't get it, Jason thought. *He really doesn't get it.*

"This isn't about you, Benny," Jason began, "This whole town is involved. You can't make a decision like that, which involves more than yourself. Why would you do such a thing?"

Benny stopped looking at his nails, and remained still. His look was a question, but his reply was direct, "Why? Because I love you, Jason, and I want to keep on loving you as long as I can."

"But I have died, Benny. Can't you realize that? The time for loving me has passed. The days of me actually making love are gone."

"Simple semantics," he said unexpectedly, and spit a nail bit from his mouth unto the floor.

Jason could only remember looking at that nail, separated now and dying; but once belonging to a living and breathing human being. Jason felt just like that nail, and that feeling of fear slowly crept up his spine.

"Hello Harold," Jason said, without turning, "I'm glad you could make it."

Harold stood there, looking at Jason as he knelt near the river's bank, the mist creating an endless cloak around him. He was not alarmed that Jason was aware of his arrival; it was after all, Jason who called him in the first place to meet him outside of town. He had not told him where, but Harold had the feeling that wherever he decided to park his car, and stroll to, that Jason would somehow be there.

"I hope the drive outside of town didn't scare you. Not many are allowed to leave, unless of course the un-living have invited them too."

Harold eased closer, looking down upon this blond angel fallen to earth...that is of course if he came from that direction. But Jason being...Jason, could only end up where the streets were paved with gold. "No. The drive was fine, despite my fear of traveling at near zero visibility."

"You were not alone in your guidance here," Jason simply said. He stood, continuing to toss pebbles into the river.

"I heard the church bell ring. What's going on there? Do you know? Is it a part of this fog we are having?"

"Harold. I didn't call you here to talk about church bells, or fog. I called you here to clear up a few thing...and to ask for your help."

"My help? You need help from the man that killed you? I thought all your troubles would be over after that."

He looked over his shoulder to glance at Harold. The man looked tired; skin stretched and dry, his blue jeans wrinkled, his cotton polo un-tucked and blotchy. He wore open toe sandals that looked to have been trying to slip from beneath his feet. "No Harold. My troubles seem only to be starting."

Harold waited.

"Benny is refusing to acknowledge my death, and if he can't do that, if he can't let me go...then it is here I will have to stay."

"I thought he was okay with your death?" Harold said. "It gave us the opportunity to be together without any interference. I don't understand."

"And neither do I," Jason said, as he began to walk past Harold with locked eyes, "And yet there is another thing I am troubled with, which involves you."

Harold watched Jason stroll out for a distance into the consuming mist, then stop. "What is it, Jason? What is this thing you want from me?"

Jason could hear the frustration in Harold's tone, the exhaustion. "Why did you kill me, Harold? I need to know why you had to perform such a final act. What could have pushed you to think you had such an authority over another human beings existence?"

This line of questioning Harold was *not* prepared for. But he answered it as if it were something he could not wait to expel.

"I killed you because I hated you, Jason."

And you still do, Jason thought. "...hated me for what?" Jason pursued. "It had to be for something more than me being a threat to your so called affair with a man that was still my lover."

Harold backed up a little, until he was stopped by the bark of a large maple tree. He crossed his arms there, looking up at its limbs, while the mist swirled around its gnarled fingers like an old woman reaching out towards the waters. "I hated you because I knew Benny continued to love you. I hated you because no matter what I gave him, it would pale next to you. I hated you for your blue eyes, your blond hair, your perfect lips, your regal height. I hated my mind for constantly having an image of you and him. I hated you for not seeing his needs."

Harold stopped, staring at Jason. His eyes were hard, unforgiving, and it was then that Jason realized, the healing would have to start with him. "So what do you have to say to me, Harold," Jason said, reaching down to run his fingers through the brush, gathering up a few loose pebbles.

"Saying something to you? What are you talking about?"

Jason would have to have him realize this on his own, so he tossed the pebble in his direction. It landed near his feet. "You kill me because you were jealous of what you *thought* Benny was feeling towards me?"

"Thought," Harold questioned, as he kicked at the spot where the pebble was tossed. "I knew he was..."

Jason tossed another pebble; this one was aimed a little higher, close to Harold's knee. "No. No that is not quite right Harold. You were the one sleeping with Benny, you were the one sneaking out with him, and you were the one he left me for. You killed me because you *thought* Benny didn't love you."

"Well, he still talked about you all the time. He still loved you..."

Jason tossed another pebble, stepping closer to Harold, "No you are wrong."

The pebble hit his thigh this time. "What are you doing?"

Jason ignored him, and continued, "You were wrong Harold. You killed me when you were still winning. Benny had history with me, so of course he would talk about me, about as much as he talked about his mother in Florida. I am sure he talked about me about as much as his favorite porn star..."

"Tommy Fildinger," they both said together.

"You're weak for what you did, Harold. You had the prize, and still you hated," Jason said, tossing another pebble, this one landing on Harold's belly.

Harold tried to move, but his actions were slowed somehow, and he could feel the mist getting thicker around him. "He didn't deserve to love you, to think about you...what's going on here?" he said, fear lining his throat.

"Didn't deserve to love me? What kind of statement is that? How can you control what a person loves? Oh, that's right...you kill them. Is that what you do?"

Harold tried to step to the side of the tree, but his back was pressed to it, and his attempt to move away only caused him to slide against it, as if his body was attached to the very bark. "What did you bring me out here for?"

"You killed me Harold. You killed me for what? I brought you out here to find out why you killed me. If Benny was guilty for thinking about me, and you were guilty for stealing him away from me, then what was I guilty of to such a degree that you had to kill me?"

"I..." Harold began, but the question caused him to think. He was scared now about the way the mist was reacting, and he was also afraid of Jason as he continued to approach. "I don't know. I want to get out of here? Are you going to try to kill me out here? Is that why you brought me?"

Jason laughed. He had not done that since being here, and it felt good. "Kill you? Kill you? What would the dead gain by killing the living? I want to know what I had done to you that deserved you killing me?"

Another pebble. It hit the forehead.

Harold pulled his arm up to protect his face, but it was as strained effort, as the mist tugged at his hand, pulling it back in the opposite direction. He could feel himself growing frantic, his neck inching forward, his eyes looking back up into the tree, wishing it were really alive, wishing it would reach down and pluck him from this nightmare. "Benny doesn't love you!"

Jason came closer to Harold; he could smell the fear radiating from his skin. "You know that is a lie. You know that is more of a lie than all the lies that you have been telling yourself. Why don't you start telling the truth for a change?"

Then Jason reached out to touch Harold.

An instant calm surrounded him, and Harold slowed in his actions, even though he was unaware of the mist folding in around him like a slowly masking cocoon. "I killed you...but maybe I shouldn't have. I was afraid of losing Benny to you, so I did the easiest thing, when I saw you on the street that day, as you stopped to look at some papers in your briefcase. I was across the street, and it was dark, there was no one else around, and there was construction going on around the corner, so I knew...well I thought, how nice it would be to have you out of the picture. Before I knew it my car was heading in your direction, and I did nothing to stop it. I just made myself believe that it was the right thing to do."

He could see that the mist was moving away from him, but Harold had not figured out the connection.

"So why did you kill me Harold?" Jason said, as he rubbed Harold's shoulder, and lowered his own voice.

"There is no reason, Jason. No reason at all really. I guess I did it because I could, because I was scared, because I was not you."

Then the mist moved away.

Jason moved his arm back. It was as close to an apology that Harold would confess – as close as was needed. Jason needed Harold to realize who the real enemy was, in order to ask the man for another favor.

"And now we need to go see Benny. I need you to help me; to help him realize the consequences of his own decision. Benny is trying to lock us both in a past that needs to move on. He is trying to love both of us, be with both of us, and hold on to both of us."

"He's trying to repeat the same mistake he made when you were alive. He never made a choice because of what I did," Harold said, finally moving away from the tree.

"And he is trying to not make the same choice again; but destiny is demanding that he does. Otherwise, this mist is not going to be moved, by any means. Selfishness too can be a great sin, and it is one that is easily justified by the one being selfish."

Harold took a deep breath. "What is it you want me to do?"

Part IV

Another scream hit the air, and Jenna listened to it. She thought the sound was originating from within her own skull, breaking free from her own day-mares. It wasn't. The sound was beyond her, and as she stared at the ceiling, watching the sun push the shadows within the room away, she reached her arm out habitually and realized why the coldness of her bed was not something that struck her as being familiar.

She realized that her husband was not at her side... then remembered why.

Jenna gritted her teeth against the pain this realization caused. She clenched her fist, and the sheets that fell to her fingers were crushed. She felt a tightening in her stomach, and saw the eyes of Nathan in every picture on the wall, and on her vanity of him; staring back at her, accusing her, condemning her. She had caused him to go out into that mist. She caused it, because she could not forgive him for killing her child. He was not the father, and so she took it for granted that he had no fatherly feelings for the only daughter he really knew. She didn't perceive that he really loved Ella; and that he regarded that accidental death...as well...accidental. But she had been wrong, and now Nathan was gone.

Another scream.

Jenna jumped in her bed, her neck turning towards her closed windows. The curtains were parted, and she wasn't sure, but it appeared as if there was a fog bank swimming directly underneath her sill, and the town below appeared as if it were floating in a cup of hot soup.

"Mom!" a voice beckoned to her.

Jenna looked at her door in time to see Ella entering. Her steps were quick, and her dark eyes wide. "Ella?" she said, getting her mind together quickly, "Ella. What is it?"

Her minds still a bit foggy, Ella thought. She had thrust in upon her too quickly. "How are you doing? A lot is about to happen, Mom, and..."

"Is that why I hear screaming outside, even though I am miles from town?" Jenna asked, her eyes still looking out her window.

"That's right," Ella said, easing herself unto Jenna's bed, and running her fingers across the soft and colorful quilt she had laid there, which was covered in a barrage of geometric shapes.

"The quilt is your grandmother's," Jenna found herself saying, her head tilting forward slightly, the wedge in her throat being pushed aside for the moment.

Ella looked up at Jenna, the rays of the sun slid slowly across the bed, reflected in the mirrors and family pictures that lined the walls of this room. She picked up the edge of the quilt; the thick tight feel of the cotton had immense weight to it despite its light appearance. "It's quite beautiful."

Jenna hunched up on her elbows, seeing Ella's long fingers as a direct result of her own mother's DNA; Matilda Jenkins, a woman whose blood ran thick as molasses. "Yea, your grandmother managed to produce some beautiful things, despite the mule that lived within her soul."

Ella looked up at her mother, and there was pain behind the pupils – cloudy pupils that reflected years of memories, years of experience, years of training and being trained. "What was she like?" She asked. Ella knew Jenna was afraid of her memories, but she also knew, it was a history she had been robbed of.

Jenna swung her feet to the floor, her eyes continuing to divert to the window in front her. She noticed that the sun was rising. Maybe she could do this without pain. "Your grandmother, Matilda Jenkins, was a most cantankerous woman. Very staunch, very reserved. She wasn't very liked, but she was loved in her honesty...much like most of the townspeople regarded me these days; but age gives your mouth permission that the youth just aren't allowed to have," she said with a smile.

"Did she always make beautiful things?"

Jenna looked down at the quilt. It was quite beautiful. It was one of the many things she kept from her mother, but seldom associated with her. "She always loved her knitting. It kept her busy, since dad was such a business man. Verdel Jenkins. That was your grandfather."

"And my sister, my twin sister, what about her?"

"Stella. Taller than you and thick boned. She favors Tilly very much. But you both share the same eyes, the same bone structure in the face, the same smile, and the same way you lean forward, as if always ready for the unknown. She is a very beautiful woman, Ella. I wish you would have met her. It is good to see her in you – it was how I knew you were mine."

"I saw the recognition in your soul," Ella said.

Jenna instinctively reached her hand out to Ella, and Ella took it. "I am glad you are here," she said without thought, "Your sister, was light skinned, sort of the shade of hot caramel. She's traveling the world right now with her fiancé. She was always traveling, always dating one man or another, always searching," Jenna stopped for a moment, and swallowed thickly. "I have always believed that she was spending her life looking for something to replace the hole that was left by you. I never told her that she had a twin sister; because of the shame I'd felt, of the fact that she regarded Nathan as her own dad, and also because I didn't want her to look for you...and from what I know now, she would have never found you."

Ella wasn't sure what to say as the proceeding silence filled the room, and they both looked out the window as the thinning mist spread itself even further across the town, like steam from a piping hot meal.

She could feel Jenna glance at her, and then return her gaze back out the window. They were enjoying the joy, the solitude, the being of being. Then Ella heard sobs.

"I want my husband back, Ella. I want this to be over. I want to tell Nathan I'm sorry. I'm sorry for what I've done to you, my family, myself. What am I to do Ella? I can't handle this. Is there any way to make it just stop? How can we all get over our pasts, when this mist is bringing our pasts back to us?" Jenna said, turning to look at her daughter.

A scream suddenly jolted them both, and it came from inside the house.

It came from Tilly.

Both Ella and Jenna, ran the short length of the hallway into her room. When Ella thrust the door open, she was stunned to see Tilly standing over Kenneth, who was partially wrapped in his blanket, silent. He barely moved when Jenna rushed past them both.

"What happened in here?!" Jenna said, nearing the child.

"Don't touch him!" Tilly shouted, and her eyes batted as if she'd been brought out of some strange hypnosis.

Jenna jumped back, and then looked at her grandchild, "What are you talking about. You put the child on the floor! What is wrong with you?"

"No," Ella interrupted, as she slipped past the hunched-over form of Jenna, and scooped up the child. She looked at it very closely, wrapping the child back up as best as she could. "It's okay, Tilly. It's okay." There was a slight grin on her face.

Tilly took a step back as Ella neared her. "No it is not. You don't know what has happened."

Ella looked up at this scared woman, "It isn't, you're right...but it will be."

"I don't understand," Jenna said. "What happened to Kenneth?"

Ella turned towards her, and there was a pause, then she began to speak slowly, "Mom, I need you to come over here, but what I am about to show you may shock you a little." She then turned her attention to Tilly, "And I want you to remain calm, Tilly. I know what happened, and I am sorry I didn't tell you that sometimes this is what occurs...when you are doing everything right."

"Right? Are you saying I caused this...that...the...my god, it felt like Jell-O."

"My goodness, what did the child do?" Jenna asked.

Ella waited until Jenna was close to her, yet kept her eyes on Tilly – reassuring eyes. She then took a tiny step back, and while they all watched, she turned a corner of the blanket away from Kenneth, until his head and shoulders were exposed, and only the straps of his tiny blue jumpsuit were showing. "You must have really poured your heart out to this child, and was beginning to forgive yourself for what happened," and then she brought up an index finger, and directed it at one of Kenneth's dimples, "Because even under the blanket, I can feel his lightness, but I can also feel where parts of him...well, are just not there anymore," and she placed a finger on one of his cheeks, but slowly, every slowly, she pressed it, "But when one as young as him, is ready to go back to his afterlife," she then plunged her finger forward, and the skin moved back, gave way, and the finger slid in as easy as if Kenneth was composed of cake batter, "This is what happens." And then she brought her finger up, and the skin seamed back together.

"Oh my God!" Jenna said, reaching for the child. Then she stopped. "What is happening to us?"

Ella looked at her. "Tilly is very close to saying goodbye to Kenneth. She is so close to allowing him to return back to his own life."

"But I can't. I just got used to seeing him. Can't I just talk with him a little more? I promise I won't let all of this freak me out anymore," Tilly pleaded, as she reached out her arms towards her child.

Ella retched her arms away from Tilly, "No. No you can't!" her voice rising. "You have made your choice, and there is no turning back at this time. You have to not only allow this child you killed...and I stress, you KILLED, back into your life, but you also have to allow him to be gone from your life. You have to move on, just as this town has to move on, otherwise it will lay here stagnant, and useless."

"I don't know if I can, Ella. I don't know if I want to," Tilly said.

Ella could hear the declaration, but there was a timid tone to it. She believed that Tilly could, given enough time, but there was another more pressing issue. "It won't matter at this point Tilly, because you can't do it alone. Even if Tilly were to do her part, I don't think it will be enough right now."

"And why is that?" Jenna asked, her eyes meeting that of Kenneth's.

"Because Tilly was only part of this union," she said, pulling the corners of the blanket back up towards the child's chin. "We need the assistant of Carl."

"But...," and Tilly was unable to finish the statement.

Jenna helped her, "Carl is frozen by the mist Ella. How can he do anything? What happens if he never does anything?"

She looked away from them both, her eyes veering down towards Kenneth, but her mind crawling with that emotion known as *fear.* "I don't know Mom. I really don't know."

Chapter 17

Part I

Lisa could stand it no longer and quickly pulled over to the side of the road. Her hands gripped the steering wheel so tight, that she could feel the perspiration growing beneath her fingertips.

The screams.

She'd been hearing the shouts ever since she braved herself to step outside the house – and into the mist. That first step was a most challenging one as she opened her door. The sun just moving beyond the crest of the town, the air was cool, crisp, and the mist thin, light, and her heart, beat fast and furious.

Alex had told her to get to the church. She thought that would be an easy directive to initiate; and it would have been if she had not had something else happened to her.

VISIONS

She began to have visions most strange in nature, most alluring, and extremely odd. They came in waves, not visually, but on a more physical realm. Emotions and stories, told to her in quick bands of noise and color. She could not really explain it, except to say that it resembled perhaps a level of intuition she was not familiar with.

She'd felt it when she'd passed the Stampton's home. A flash came to her that their daughter was found in the bed, frozen. The mother had tried to revive her, in a room she at first thought had been on fire, filled with smoke, but it had been the mist, taking on a very thick look and feel. When Tamera Stampton rushed towards her daughter's bed, the thickness of the mist dissipated, as quickly as if a window had suddenly been opened.

Then the vision left her.

From that one moment, Lisa realized there was something more to this mist that went beyond normality. It could somehow change; its makeup moved in and out as if it breathed – thinner on the inhale, thicker on the exhale.

She continued, not quite sure what had happened, or how she was able to perceive such things, or what such perception meant. In this action, this blind obedience, she hoped for an answer.

Then there was another scream.

She looked out across the town, the sight of Crest Hill County loomed in the distance, and the scatter of housetops flowed like the pieces of a Monopoly board game. She pressed her lids very close together, confusion enveloping her senses. That scream – it was nowhere near her. She knew it! Yet she'd heard it as if it had come over her radio, directly within her reach. How was that possible? She looked out there again, the shadow of thinly spanned cloud-cover moved across the town. As the sun interceded with sparks of brightness, Lisa was able to see the mist reaching out across the land like the slivers of a broken spider web trailing in the wind.

Then another vision came.

Donna Putman had awoken to a room filled with smoke too. She'd sat up too quickly and felt lightheaded. Her eyes, although cloudy, did not sting. Her lungs felt cooled, not raw. She had been caught in a real fire once as a child, and that traumatizing memory had never broke the bond of her cortex. This incident, immediately confused her, and her actions followed suite. She shook her husband who lay beside her, with a simple bend of her knee. Nothing. She called his name. Nothing. Then the smoke got the best of her, and she rolled to the floor, her nightgown enshrining her legs, and she tumbled a little harder than intended.

Her wrist smarted on the landing, but her instincts remained intact. Darryl slept like a log, and there was not enough smoke to choke him – she hoped. Wouldn't the man, no matter how hard his sleep, still awake to a coughing fit in a room filled with smoke, she wondered. But this was Darryl, and she was still very much surprised at a lot of his mannerisms. So before crawling to see about him, while she was still conscience, she edged towards the door, and felt it. Odd. It wasn't hot. She bent closer to the floorboards, trying to look underneath. No light. She was at once struck dumbfound, and her mouth hung open, on the precipice of yelling FIRE! She breathed in slowly, testing, filtering the air around her. No heat, and her lungs acted as if there was nothing in the air at all.

Then she called her husband's name.

Nothing. That was odd.

She yelled it softly.

Heard nothing. Except the beating of her heart, translating down her arm, and thudding at her palms as it pressed into the floor. She crawled to him, looking up at this sleeping giant from the edge of the bed, and reached out to shake his arm. It was like touching an icy baseball bat.

That is when she screamed.

That is when Lisa's vision ended, and caused such a stir in her, that she had to pull the car over to access what had just happened. It was as if what she had envisioned had been projected against the very mist she was trying to navigate through. It was a vision she not only saw, but felt...and just as Donna's heart raced, hers did as well.

She veered her car back onto the street. She was not sure why she was told to go to the church, but as she neared it, she noticed only a few more cars on the street besides her own. It was like a ghost town. She crawled into the church's parking lot, and rounded its driveway towards the back. She was a bit startled to notice the Pastor's car was nowhere in sight; and he was the main reason for her being here.

The back of the church was not designed as a parking lot, although a lot of the church staff would still park there, creating one. When Lisa stopped her car amidst the trampled grass and soil, she noticed the mist had cleared, and she was able to see the rear of the church, where there on its stairs sat Earl. If not for his constant breathing and the jagged peering of his eyes, she would have thought him a mannequin. His head rested on the wooden handrail.

"What's happening around here, Earl?" She asked as she neared him.

"Wha-?" he said with a start. His eyes quickly swam around in his head, and then ran the course along Lisa's white slip-ons, her cuffed jeans, and her pale-yellow blouse; until it reached her face, which was frequently being slapped across the forehead by loose strands of her golden hair. "Lisa, I thought I would get here a little early, having seen the crowds we've had here of late. But it hasn't been too bad today for some reason."

She eased down beside him. "You look as tired as I feel," she said, reaching out to loosen the collar of his dress shirt; a beautiful shade of purple. "Why didn't you just rest inside?"

He shrugged. "Don't know. Came out here to see the sun rise I guess, and then saw the mist in the distance, and how it seems to be easing this way, and it was funny, because suddenly a powerful sleep took me over."

"Really?" she questioned, looking up around her, the mist hovering about them like white chalk smeared against a blackboard. She reached out towards the strands that wafted near them, watching it swirl harmlessly away from her grasping hands, but as it traveled along her palm it felt as if something was pushing up against it.

Earl watched her, mesmerized at her actions. "Much thicker than it was at Maya's service. Sometimes you can even feel it."

"Yea, I did notice that it looked a bit heavy," she said, looking curiously at this odd substance, which acted and appeared like no other type of mist, or fog, or anything that she had known before. She noticed a large mass of it close to her shoulder, and struck out to grasp it in her hands. Before it dissipated however, she felt a grittiness to it, and then it was gone. What exactly is this, she thought.

"And what brings you here, Lisa? Noticed you weren't here yesterday either. I hope you were able to get some rest..." Earl began to say, but a yarn sucked up the tail-end of his words.

She dropped her arm, and looked at her car; a simple beige Honda. Beyond it was the expanse of the church yard, and two smaller buildings that held the nursery, and a cafeteria (which sometimes subbed for children's Bible Study), and for a moment she could picture Maya in there, teaching those little cherubs one week, and on nice days, trotting them to the grass outside – to the horror of the parents who dreaded grass stains and bug play – only to have her return their munchkins in pristine condition; both of attire and of mind. And on very hot days, behind the cafeteria, was a fountain where she would tell them the most amazing stories of her homeland, and how their faith was practiced around the world. Lisa missed her.

"I'm supposed to be meeting Pastor Reynolds out here," Lisa finally said, turning to look at Earl, only to suddenly notice the amount of stubble cascaded across his jaws, the pulled skin under his eyes, and his tousled hair; many strands having already escaped the band that formed his ponytail. Even his eyelashes looked wilted and exhausted. She realized the tension in this town was affecting everyone.

"Is the Pastor supposed to be coming? It would be a good day, considering this is the lightest crowd we've had."

She glanced back at the church's rear doors, which stood slightly ajar.

"Yea, I noticed there weren't that many cars out there in the lot, and usually I can hear the prayers streaming past the doors and down the road."

"Do you think this means everything is starting to right itself again, Lisa? I don't think this town can take much more. People are scared, I can feel it, but we're also becoming very complacent about all of this."

"You've noticed that too?" She'd been thinking the same thing. "Yea, with our town trapped in this situation and our future uncertain, with the added fact that no one on the outside appears to know we are in danger, and us really not knowing what to do, I believe complacent is just the right word for this, Earl."

"And yet, do you still feel scared deep down inside?"

"Shitless Earl. I am scared shitless."

Part II

Mildred stepped back, as Eric forced his arm into Tommy's door, and when she could hear the crunch of the wood on contact, she cringed, and grabbed her own arm. She could see that the door was not locked, but it was as if the mist that filtered inside and under the door, was somehow butting itself against it. He pressed himself against it again, losing none of his vigor – and on this attempt, the door flung open, and the mist mysteriously began to recede.

"Timothy!" Mildred said, rushing into the room, fanning at the fumes as if parting a silk curtain. "Timothy, are you okay?"

Eric wasn't as hindered by the mist as Mildred seemed to be, and he could clearly see his son, on the far side of the bed; one leg hanging over the edge – but extended, stiffly, into the air as if he were kicking at the window in his sleep and the leg froze there. His eyes were closed, and as Eric moved around the bed, he reached out towards Timothy, and scooped his arm under the boy's torso, pushing him back unto the center of the bed, and easing his leg down. "Timothy, can you hear me?" He looked up to see Mildred clasping her mouth with both hands, not sure if she was trying to stop breathing, or trying to stop from screaming.

"It's okay Mildred. The mist is thinning out, and you're in no danger of breathing it," Eric said, sensing her distress.

She looked at him stunned, thought about inquiring of his extra sensory perception, but slowly untwined her fingers instead. She looked around the room, and could now see the full screen television on the wall, the clear glass stereo system beneath it, an amour to the far left wall next to the bathroom, and the pictures of large cities across the United States: Chicago, New York, St. Louis...and others, tacked to the walls. It was then that she was brave enough to inhale.

"Is he going to be okay?" Mildred almost whispered, as her eyes finally focused on Timothy; who was dressed in his black silk white-striped pajamas, which seemed so very, very still. She slowly lowered herself to sit at the foot of the bed, stroking the child's leg, grateful of the warmth coming from his ankles and feet.

"He's going to be okay, Mildred," Eric said, reaching up to brush a hand across the deep brown curls of his hair. It was then that his eyes began to bat a little, and his neck turned slightly. He was rousing.

His eyelids flung open, and he focused in on Mildred. "What's going on here? I thought I smelled smoke a minute ago...or did I see smoke?" He looked out his window past his father, at the swaying mist outside his window that looked as if his aunt's home had took a leap into the clouds. Is there a fire...was there a fire?"

"No Timothy, there wasn't a fire. The mist is getting stronger. Some very strange things are happening in Crest Hill County," Mildred said, her hands nervously clasped in her lap.

"It's coming to claim the people of this town...and we got to you just in time." Eric said, standing up to close the curtain.

"What?" Timothy said?"

Eric sat back on the bed, shaking his head, and looking up at Mildred, "We stopped the mist from putting you in a deep sleep. I can't explain it all now. We just need to know that you are okay."

Timothy nodded that he was.

"Claim? Are you saying the mist is coming to claim people? What does that mean Eric? How can cloud formations created by an exchange of heat and cold masses, come to claim anyone? What is going on?"

Eric looked at Timothy, and internally weighed what he was about to say. "Mildred, this is not just mist, it comes from what is happening in this town. There has been too much death, too much hate, and quite frankly not enough forgiveness. If this town does not learn to forgive its past, then it *becomes* the past."

Mildred looked at him, her eyes unmoving, but she was finally getting what he was talking about, she was finally seeing the revelation of his words. "I don't believe you."

Eric leaned back slightly, as if to take a better look at his sister. "Yes you do," he said, and folded his arms. "You believe me, but you also are beginning to not care."

Part III

"Benny, you have to listen," Jason tried to interject.

"You just don't realize the opportunity that has been presented to us. This is our chance to start over," his tone began to lessen.

"No...No it's not, Benny. I've had my time on earth. We all have our time. The opportunity has passed."

"How can you say that it has passed, when you are here *now*? And if I understand you correctly, this whole town, if we don't do anything, will be able to live as we are, forever...to live with each other for all eternity."

Jason watched Benny move in closer to him, the scent of his skin was strong, warm, and on a certain level dangerous. Benny reached out towards him, slowly this time, grasping the collars of his shirt in his nimble fingers, rubbing them as if testing its fibers.

"No, Benny. You must not do this," Jason pleaded.

"Do what?" his Cheshire-grin returning.

Jason could see the denial within Benny's green eyes, smell the seduction on his breath, and hear the rapid movement of the blood in his veins.

"Do this, Benny. I can't let you do this, to me, to this town."

"But soon, it will be like this forever. Soon, through some cosmic magic, we'll all be transported to a place where we can enjoy each other forever. That is what will happen, isn't it?" Benny asked, moving in closer.

"Yes...and no," Jason replied, his body feeling very nervous. He could not lie, as bad as he wanted to, he just could not, and yet he could not reveal the entire truth either.

"Then I will favor on the side of yes," Benny said, his arms having slid along Jason's shoulders, their lips but inches apart.

He leaned forward slightly.

Jason closed his eyes just as Benny's lips touched his. The sadness that followed, and ran through his body, was indescribable.

Jason spoke, his mouth continuing to brush along Benny's," This isn't right, Benny."

"Just shut up and kiss me," Benny said, pressing his face closer.

"I'm sorry, Benny," Jason whispered.

"Sorry for what, babe?" Benny whispered back.

"For this..."

And suddenly, Benny could feel his neck pivoting forward slightly, Jason's lips getting softer, and the firmness of his shoulder falling away.

Benny opened his eyes quickly, looking into Jason...or for a moment, it seemed he was looking through Jason. "No, Jason!" He shouted, as he swung out his arms, and tried to brace Jason, to grab him around the waist, but his arms met him around the hips, and continued to fall into him, as if he were made of Silly-Puddy. "You can't leave me like this, Jason!" Benny continued, looking upon Jason, his skin taking on a chalky, sandy tone. His lover was literally breaking apart before his eyes. "Don't leave me now, not now!"

"Sadly," Jason replied, before his body lost all solidity, "I will be back. You have unfortunately seen to that."

And then, in a cloud of dust and color, Jason was gone.

And Benny collapsed on his bed, breaking into a pool of salty tears.

Part IV

The area behind Jenna's home was very spacious, with a gazebo surrounded by a lush flower garden. Behind the gazebo was a short limestone walkway leading to a marble fountain near a tiny pond filled with the most exquisite Japanese gold fish.

Jenna took a deep breath; the scent of magnolias, azaleas, daffodils, marigolds, and water lily's saturated her senses. She let the soft sounds of the distant pond, the lilt of the adjacent birds, the rustle of the nearby trees, and the almost silent whoosh of air passing through her lungs fill her ears, her space.

There was sweetness to the air, very light, not quite associated with the surrounding flora. It was tender to her many senses, and she welcomed it. The taste; it was like *honey*.

With her eyes closed, she listened, as a pair of sensible shoes trailed cautiously up the gazebo stairs. She could hear them pause, their steps heading in her direction, but their path diverted, faded, as they strolled opposite her. She could hear the stretching of the wood as they sat on the gazebo bench.

"Yes, Ella," Jenna said, her eyes remaining closed.

"Are you...okay?" came the timid voice.

"No," Jenna replied bluntly.

"We were concerned by the way you stormed out of the house."

"That wasn't a storm, Ella. That was a stride," Jenna said, inhaling slowly. "That scent...do you-"

"It's associated with the mist, Mom," Ella replied.

Jenna opened her eyes. "Really? Why did I bother to ask? Every question comes back to the mist."

"It only smells like that up here, where the mist has not traveled very much. The scent is the lure," Ella said, hands pressed between her thighs, her eyes downcast.

"I really don't want to hear anymore, Ella," and with that Jenna closed her eyes again. "I'm tired of all this bad news. I want my husband back."

"I know you do," Ella said, her voice sullen. "But it's not over yet, Mom. Nathan still has a chance."

Another answer she didn't want to hear.

Another answer filled with bad news.

Another answer that posed many more questions.

"Tell me, Ella, what happens if we can't get Nathan back? What happens then?"

Ella's eyes widened.

Jenna continued, "Am I supposed to lose my husband forever? Is he to die because of his guilt? I don't understand all of this Ella, and I don't think I will no matter how many times you explain it."

Ella kept her silence. She was still contemplating the first question Jenna posed.

"I just want to know what happens in the end, Ella, my deceased daughter. What's going to happen to my lifeless-looking husband? What's going to happen to my granddaughter's aborted child-come-to-life? What's going to happen to you? What happens to Carl? What happens to this town? What happens to my life?" She then opened her eyes.

"You would live, Mom," Ella said, she kept her eyes unblinking in Jenna's direction. "You would live, Tilly would live...Nathan would live."

"Nathan would live?" Jenna repeated.

"Yes Mom, Nathan would live," Ella said, and let Jenna think on this, let her soul truly understand this.

"I'm sorry," Jenna said, with an angry voice. She looked skyward, past the intricate design of the gazebo, and array of African Violets twisted through its frame, and managed to calm herself. "I didn't mean to raise my voice, Ella."

"No one ever does, Mom – and yet they do."

She nodded at her daughter's truth. "We live – we all live. Is that what you're telling me?"

Ella felt nervous. She had not really known this feeling, because in the human sense, she had not really lived. As she tried to concentrate on herself, on what she was feeling, a new feeling registered throughout her flesh: fear.

She didn't like it.

"Is that what you're saying, Ella?" Jenna persisted.

Ella snapped back to the present. Her flesh was giving her signals that things may have already gone too far. She was becoming human (to a being from the afterlife, this was equal to death).

"Yes, that is what I'm saying. Many people, who were cast under the spell of the mist, will return back into this present reality."

Jenna began to smile. "Well...isn't that good news? All we have to do is wait, and time will take care of itself."

Ella felt sadness. So many emotions rolling at the same time. How could the living deal with it? "No. Once the afflicted awake from their sleep, the town will be dead. The people will live, but the outside world will know you no longer. Crest Hill County will become your eternal purgatory."

The smile Jenna had radiated suddenly fell away. "Are you saying Crest Hill County will cease to exist?"

"Yes," Ella said. Jenna did not like the answer she was hearing.

"My God, that's horrible," Jenna proclaimed. "I have family outside of town: my daughter, your sister, Nathan's nieces and nephews, so many people. What will they think if we suddenly vanish? My daughter must remember that she has a mother...won't she?"

"Not really. There will be other memories, strange dreams they will have, and soon there will be no distinguishing of the two – of reality and dream. Other parts of their psyche will be affected, in ways that even I do not understand."

Jenna shook her head, her eyes looking in the direction of her feet. She wanted to scream, and could feel her throat constrict, keeping her high pitched shout locked behind her tongue and cheek. She soon found herself rising, "My God! I can't stand to hear any more of this, Ella. I can't stand it I'm telling you. Nothing but bad news – nothing but..." she paused, her words cut short by a throat that suddenly didn't work, and she looked up into the sky, as if the answer to her problems were written on the bottom of the clouds – clouds she was surprised to even see, as the mist broke and the sky was momentarily revealed.

"This is horrible, Ella. This is so much worse than death," Jenna said, lowering her skyward gaze, and turned to one of the closest railings, and froze there, looking out unto the pond area. "I'm scared. I'm really scared – and I'm so, so angry. I want this to be over."

Jenna could feel a hand rest on her back. "It will be, Mom, but it's going to have to start with your acceptance."

"My what? What should I be accepting?"

"Your great-grandchild," Ella said, rubbing Jenna's back. "You need to forget Nathan, no matter how hard it may seem. You have to concentrate on the living right now, and doing your part to stop what is happening in your town. You have to start forgiving Tilly."

A silence as thick as molasses hung in the air. "What are you saying, Ella? I don't have any angry feelings about my granddaughter. What am I supposed to be forgiving her about? I realize she had an abortion, and she didn't tell me, but I have already forgiven her for that."

"I am not talking about you forgiving Tilly because of her abortion," Ella said, and stopped for a minute, as she looked back at the house. "Tilly is in the kitchen, and she will be coming out here very soon with Kenneth. This will be the time to talk with her, understand her, and bury your feelings before this town is buried in theirs."

"What am I supposed to be forgiving her about, Ella?" Jenna repeated.

"About Carl."

And at that moment, Jenna realized that her teeth were starting to clench.

When she turned to look at the back of her home, she could see Tilly emerging from the back doors, carrying her child in her arms. "How did you know?"

Ella spoke softly, "I think your questions should be geared elsewhere.

"Hey Grandma," Tilly said, as she neared the gazebo. "Are you doing okay? I know things are crazy here, but-"

"Did you love him Tilly?"

Tilly paused at the bottom of the stairs, and cradled Kenneth in her arms. "Yes I did, Grandma," Tilly answered, taking on another step.

Jenna nodded. "Did he love you?"

She looked at her child before answering, "Yes he did…and still does."

"And…how did this happen, this love?"

"Four summers ago, when I was helping out at the cemetery. I was so scared then, being out there as night approached, and Carl had been so sweet in understanding that fear."

"Wouldn't you like to hold your grandchild while you talked?" Ella suggested, beckoning for Tilly to walk up the remaining steps.

Jenna was there with her arms out, "Why yes I would."

With a smile, Tilly handed Kenneth over.

"Tell me more," Jenna asked, rocking the child in her arms.

And as Tilly did, Ella could see that everything was going to be alright with them after all. And she too listened, to a saga of love that was very intense, very taboo, and very incredible.

If only Carl could be there to hear it.

PART V

The mist continued to travel from the Morning Glory Cemetery at a steady rate. It wafted throughout the town, parts of it very thick, parts of it very thin, some of it chalky, and some invisible to the naked eye. It remained level mostly; exploding upward like a solar burst from the sun.

The victims had become numerous by the time the sun came close to kissing the horizon. Many screams lit the wind, many tears caressed quivering cheeks, many prayers went up to individual Heavens, and many minds just didn't or couldn't comprehend.

Many tried to run away.

The roads that led out of town had slowly and quietly been stretched, pulling the town further and further away from the rest of civilization. Frightened citizens had gassed up their cars, and tried to speed out of town; but were met with two most disturbing occurrences: they were either so intrigued at the frozen animals along the road, that they too had become a victim themselves – not seeing the mist close in around them; or they would have noticed that the road had become so very, very long, and in some way had wrapped itself around, and before they knew it, that instead of heading *out* of town, they in fact, had been heading back *into* town.

One of these happenstances was about to happen to Pastor Luther Reynolds.

He had become overwhelmed. He truly did not know what to do. He only had an inkling of what was happening in Crest Hill County, and a little of what he was supposed to do. Finally, the answers were coming. His Bible studies had revealed much; the stories of David and his dying son, the story of Noah and the Arc, of Lot and his wife, of Moses and his People – stories that proved one must move on from grief, that a towns sins will destroy them whole, even if they were not aware of their wrong doing, even if they were not aware that they were just hurting themselves.

And then he began to think of Maya as he was heading towards the church, and he had to stop his car from the press within his mind. He was still longing for her, and trying to deal with that empty feeling inside. He felt so broken and alone, like shattered pieces of glass.

And as he sat in his car thinking…another thought had come to him. A though about the mist, and what its purpose was, and he was on the edge of finding out…

…until the sweet scent of honey had come to him; reminding him vaguely of a perfume that Maya had once worn.

Then he noticed the mist surrounding him, and he stared at it, trying to gauge its makeup, its movement, its ability to almost maneuver on its own accord. He took a deep breath – the sweet scent came at him again, and he closed his eyes, soothing himself, and when he opened his eyes again, something flashed before him, and he could have sworn, not far from his car, just beyond the glass, that he saw something traveling within the mist.

It swarmed, thick, as if the mist itself was wrapped around an object.

It became darker.

It jerked in its movements; like an arm waving.

He felt mesmerized, relaxed, and his body didn't want to move; didn't want to even roll down the window to investigate.

He hadn't even noticed that the mist had somehow seeped into his car; thin lines that fell in and out of his nostrils, caressed his ears, embraced his form.

His breath was slowed, and the honey scent filled him. He was not aware that darkness was surrounding him, and he could no longer move; nor that his eyes had grown heavy, and that he was heading into a most deep sleep.

Of the many victims to befall the mist he never thought that he would be one.

Chapter 18

Part I

Pastor Luther Reynolds missed it.

He saw a part of it, if only for a moment; the spark that formed, the hint of light, the melding darkness that appeared to take shape, take substance, become alive.

Pastor Luther Reynolds missed it.

He missed the sound, like the flapping of angel's wings lifted by a song – as if a thousand violins had been playing all at once.

If Pastor Reynolds had been aware, if his eyes had looked a little deeper, he would have noticed the mist was taking on a much too familiar shape.

Fingers. They appeared to come out of nowhere and hovered in midair, like some detached dream come to life. They wiggled, grasping at nothing, and soon developed into an arm.

…and that into a shoulder

…and that into a torso

…and that into a form that dropped from the air.

Pastor Reynolds had parked at the rear of one of the city's parking lots. There were no other cars near him, no other people. So no one could witness these events, could witness this woman as she lifted herself up, her naked form pulling in more mist, surrounding herself, until she was completely cloaked – and then it took on an intense color scheme, changing its makeup, becoming much more than mere mist, mere smoke, and transformed into a material that became clothing, draped gently upon this most delicate of female forms. A white blouse accented by a peach dress of amazing folds and fluidity, that the fabric seemed alive.

Then eyes opened.

Nostrils inhaled.

Arms stretched.

...and Maya became alive – once again. It was a feeling she'd missed if only briefly.

She moved, glided almost, towards Pastor Reynold's car. She saw him beyond her own reflection, cast in his driver's side window. Looking at him, she had never wanted more, than to be able to shed a tear. She reached out her hand towards the smooth cold glass, and her ivory fingers pressed against it; and it gave way, like a latex glove, and then popped to let her through. She reached out to rub the back of her hand across Luther's forehead – as he slept. She caressed his skin; felt the roughness of his jaws – he'd slept very little since her death, the sags under the eyes, and the layers of wrinkles pushing upon his eyebrows. He had been saddled with too large a burden, in too small a town.

She ran her fingers through his hair; the smoothness of his small curls tickled the skin underneath. It needed cutting. And then she touched his heart; actually reached in beyond his skin to embrace her hands around it, and she rested it there, feeling him once again.

She pulled away, and took a step back. She had to remember why she was there, and to resist the wanton desires of her flesh. It was strong, her skin, it had only just arrived back in Crest Hill County, and she could feel it yearning to live again. It wanted to love Luther again; more completely than she was allowed to do when alive. She looked at her reflection in the window again, their images so close to each other; overlapping, pressed together, the lips very close – a superimposed image that should have been theirs to keep.

She turned away. The reason she was here was to finish the job that Luther had just failed – in no real fault of his own – for his own grief for her, this town, his in-laws, and even his wife, weighed heavily upon him. He just chose the wrong moment to reflect, the wrong moment to mourn; and as the mist began to take hold of him, the demise of Crest Hill County became more evident.

She had been summoned as the town's final hope.

So without looking back, Maya walked away, the deep curls of her slightly reddish hair danced around her forehead, and her look was determined, as she altered her focus, and concentrated on the job at hand. There was a lot of work ahead of her, a lot of causalities of the mist, a lot of the dead being confronted, a lot of the living in a state of denial...and the sweet scent of honey was thick in the air, so very thick.

The first person she had to see was one she had avoided in life, and succeeded in death.

She had to confront, Mildred Ross Reynolds.

Part II

Mildred ran her fingers through the warm water of her bath. She made a few phone calls to cancel the women's monthly prayer meeting – it was just a technicality really, many could not come, and many more wouldn't even answer their phone. She really felt a little forward asking such a mundane request in such a moment of calamity, but since they would all be banished in this town, living eternally together, she might as well return to her First Lady duties, since she'll be doing them *forever*.

Luther had not called all afternoon, so she figured he was stuck at the church, saving souls, or doing whatever holy thing he tended to always do. Tilly had not called either, and seeing that they were nearing the start of another week, it only stood to reason that she would not be offering her services this week. *Well, let's hope she gets her act together by next week,* Mildred thought. *There was so much furniture that still needed to be dusted.*

Mildred let her black silk robe fall to gather at her ankles. She rubbed her hands along her body, taking note of any new folds or dimples that may have arrived; the specter of age was slowly becoming an unwelcomed companion. She lifted her leg on the ledge of the Jacuzzi tub, the steam wafting up to meet her, the sound of the bubbles echoed off her mirror-lined walls, the toilet and duvet, the glass shower, and the tiled floors. She let her foot slip, and it eased towards the water, its titillating warmth and serenity a welcome call to her. Her toes dipped under the jets, and soon her leg followed, the deep contrast against the tub made her dark skin look that much darker.

Soon, she eased her full self beneath the water, its liquid fingers easing their way into the muscles beyond her flesh. Tranquility; that is what she was finally feeling - an escape.

As she became lost in this sensation; her neck leaning back on one of the many headrests that lined the tub – the doorbell rang.

She ignored it.

Then it rang again.

If they didn't have a key –they shouldn't be at the door, she thought.

She told Luther many times to surround the house with a security gate, an electric fence, a battalion of ravenous pit bulls – something. But Luther always tried to maintain an open door policy with his flock; she knew it was a method he used to keep a closed door policy with her.

She could feel the tension ooze from her pores as if her muscles had turned to syrup. She was finally okay with what was going on in this town. True – she would not leave, but it was also true, that the things she loved would be hers' forever: her brother, and her power. The latter she was truly looking forward to.

Again, the doorbell rang.

It startled her this time, and as her arms slipped from beneath her, she fell beneath the water for a brief moment. When she surfaced, she had become a lot hotter than the water that surrounded her. Without even a thought, she stood up, grabbed a towel, patted herself dry, flung on her robe, slipped inside her house shoes, stormed downstairs, and reached the front door.

A timid knock rang out.

She took in a tentative breath.

Then she opened the door, hurriedly and angrily.

"What the hell do you-" she paused. Stopped.

"Hello Mildred."

She slammed the door shut.

"No!" Mildred exclaimed. "No, this can't be happening. No, she cannot be back – dear God, anyone but her!"

She pressed her back against the door, the grooves of the wood cut into her flesh. She closed her eyes, and began to pray in tongues; her lips moving faster than a helicopter's blades.

The doorbell rang again, and this time it was followed by that timid rapping.

Mildred prayed faster. "Go away!" she found herself shouting, her body shaking suddenly.

"You know I can't do that Mildred," said Maya, voice calm.

Mildred opened her eyes. She looked up at her ceiling, the tall cathedral shaped dome of it, and the thin concave skylight that shone the stars so beautifully at night. She looked at her paintings, etched in faraway places, and wished she was anywhere but here.

"We need to talk, Mildred. I need you to open this door," said Maya, her tone very direct.

"No!" I won't believe you're here. Go away!" Mildred said frantically. She brought her hands up to clasp over her ears. That voice. She'd had hoped to never encounter the likes of that voice ever again.

"We have to talk about Luther."

Even with her hands about her ears, that woman's voice still rang through. Was this to be her Hell, and would she have to endure a lifetime of living in the shadow of Maya? She would rather that the Lord take her now! "I'm not going to talk to you. I refuse to!" Mildred said, and walked away from the door. She would just continue to drown out the noise of the doorbell and that woman's voice, in a cacophony of jet bubbles emitted from her tub. She, with her head held high, started for the winding staircase that led to the upstairs bathroom; a trail of water following her like sludge from a snail.

She only made it to the third step, before a voice called out to her.

"Mildred!"

Slowly she spun around. "Shit!" she proclaimed, as the vision of Maya fell across her sight, and the shock of it caused her to slip and lose her footing. Her legs flung out before, and she twisted to grab the handrail. She hung there, closed her eyes, and mumbled, "Why is this happening to me, Lord?" It was the closest she had come to her God in a very long time.

Maya said nothing, as she watched Mildred right herself.

Mildred pulled herself up, and stared at Maya – a person she had last seen in a position of defeat; eyes closed in death, body snatched of its soul. Now, as she looked at this woman, she saw billowing hair, glowing skin in the light of the fireplace, a white flowing blouse with sleeves that stopped at the elbows, and a hem that cascaded about her ankles; which were covered in the most stunning golden slip-ons. *No wings*, Mildred thought. Thank God there were no wings – she would not be able to handle a vision such as that. But she did look rather angelic, and that upset Mildred. *A whore in God's Kingdom? It was not possible.*

"I am not an angel, Mildred," Maya said.

A whore that could also sense her thoughts, Mildred pondered. "Of course not…demons rarely are," she replied, standing at the foot of the stairs now, one hand remained on the railing, the other defiantly pressed into her hip.

Maya shook her head. "I'm so glad to see you haven't changed."

"Death suites you well, Maya," she exhaled…then slowly inhaled, letting her mind settle for a moment. "Now that you've displayed your skill for walking through walls and reading minds, why don't you display your agility for getting the hell out of my house?"

Now *that* made Maya smile. If there was one truism here, it lay in the fact that Maya, under any circumstance, would not have been brought back from the dead because of any grieving exhibited by Mildred. "Luther has been caught up by the mist, Mildred," Maya decided getting right to the point was going to be the best strategy.

"What?" Mildred said, and the reality of her words had taken her momentarily off guard. "Caught?"

"Yes," Maya said, taking a small step forward. "He had been on his way to church, but pulled over for a moment, in a section of town where the mist was very thick. It overtook him."

Mildred brought her hands to her mouth. "It killed him?" She found she could hardly get the words past her throat.

"No, nothing like that. He's asleep, Mildred," Maya explained.

"Like Timothy was today?"

Maya nodded, "Yes, much like what had happened to Timothy, but Timothy was able to wake up thanks to you and Eric."

Mildred let this information sink in for a moment. "How would you know about what happened to Timothy?"

Maya could see a level of hate and resentment in Mildred that was very deep. It was hard for her to realize they alone would end up being the town's only hope. Two opposites flung together.

"I know a great many things Mildred; some I can reveal, others I cannot. God is quite angry at this town. The consequences that this town has brought upon itself are going to become even more severe than it is now. As in the story of Moses, and their wandering in the desert for 40 years…Crest Hill County too is about to be banished to an even longer journey."

"What do you know about God, Maya? You said you were no angel, then how are you to be gifted with all this foresight?"

"Mildred, no one is going to be an angel when they die. Have you not been listening to your husband's sermons? Do you not read? Angels were created long before man, so they are not the same thing, nor are angels superior to man. Man is just confined by the flesh, and man has a soul. Have you heard of any angel having a soul – a unique part of itself that still lives on in the same light of …" then Maya suddenly pounded a fist in her palm. "I did not come here to discuss the logistics of the afterlife with you. We have to work together if we want to save this town to-"

"You need me?" Mildred interrupted.

The hate was growing thicker, Maya noted. "Yes. I need you."

"Then keep on needing, Maya. I don't need you. I don't want you to even be here. Do you have any idea what you have done to me, to my husband, to this town? Go back to wherever it is you came from, because I'm going back to my bath before the water gets any colder," and with that, Mildred spun on heels, and headed back up the stairs…

…But something held her ankle, and when she looked down to see what it was, she noticed a cloud of smoke wafting up from the bottom stair; thick and churning, and there was a roughness to it, a chalkiness she could feel coursing along her skin…and it was holding her. Its appearance was very similar, resembling the mist outside, as if a chunk of it had been snatched off as easily as a piece of cotton candy. She looked back at Maya, and said nothing.

"Why are you doing this, Mildred? Do you hate me that much, even in my death?"

"Yes. Yes I do."

"But, why? Of all the things I know, this comprehension has eluded me the most. What have I done?"

Mildred didn't respond, and only stared down at her ankles, while giving an upward glance in Maya's direction.

"I'm sorry," Maya said, looking down at Mildred's foot. The cloud slowly vanished. "I just need to understand why you wish to contribute to a town's annihilation, just because of your hatred of me; of something that is now in the past; something that can remain in the past with your help."

"But what about the pain, Maya?"

"I'm sorry?"

Mildred began down the stars again, her hands rolled up, her body stiff, her eyes unblinking. "…the pain Maya. How can you say what happened in the past, can remain there, when each time I roll over in my bed and look into Luther's eyes, I see you there. That pain happens each and every day, Maya – not in the past, but always in my present."

"Yes, I can sense that from you, and unfortunately Mildred, there are no easy answers."

She stepped closer to Maya, slowly but determinedly, "Well, I need some easy answers. I need what you obviously cannot give. I need a peace of mind to know that my husband is mine. I need him sometimes to just forget you, Maya. Can you do that for me?"

"Yes. Yes I can, Mildred," Maya said, as Mildred walked right up to her, the warmth from her breath was amazingly wet.

Mildred smiled. "Great, then tell me what I must do."

"I'll meet you here in the morning. Be ready to go to the church with me that afternoon. I have other people to visit at this time, but I want to spend that morning talking with you."

"Talking to me?"

"Yes, it's obvious you have some things to get off your chest, and I have some things to tell you."

"And what could you possibly have to tell me?" Mildred said.

"How to possible keep your man, Mildred. What else."

Part III

She knows, Maya thought, even before she had a chance to venture within the vicinity of Erica's neighborhood, she could feel that the woman was expecting her, and she was plotting a most devious plan – one which Maya was not privileged to know yet.

Erica was her best friend – they had always had a connection that was deeper than flesh, than even spiritual; it stood on a level of chemistry that was unnamed in the charts of the periodic table. It was and would always be beyond this world.

Maya was travelling with amazing speed; the way most of the undead were now allowed to travel; as if they floated, instead of walked, along the pavement. Small explosive bursts that opened holes within the mist, allowed them to span miles at a time. This was satisfying, but now, Maya wished she could get there in the twinkling of an eye.

She was told, by no means verbal, that Erica too, was getting a little too comfortable, a little to satisfied with the way things were. Maya was brought back so that everyone would know the truth, and then, if after that, they began to feel the same; if they still wanted the eternity they so desired, then they would have it.

Maya walked up the stairs to the mobile home and found the door ajar. A scent, most evil, most conniving, came out of that house, like something suddenly let loose that had been contained for a millennium.

Maya opened the door. Every light in the house was on, and at the tiny kitchen table, sat Erica, her back facing the door, the scent of hot chocolate escaped within the air – a sweet scent Maya was used to. Hot chocolate was always Erica's favorite treat.

"Hello, Maya," Erica responded, still standing in the door's threshold, the dawn's night winds pushing at her back, causing her clothes to flutter just a bit.

"I see you're quite at home since I've left."

"Funny, it's been as though you'd just gone up to Chicago for a week's getaway."

"If only I had travelled such a short distance," Maya responded. She slowly closed the door.

"I knew you would finally come," Erica said, as she paused to take a sip from her cup. It was long and drawn out. "You always seemed to show up when things looked their worst."

"I take it things have gotten pretty bad in town since my death?" Maya asked, taking a quick look around. She couldn't remember ever seeing Erica's home look so meticulously clean.

Erica turned around in her seat, "Things couldn't be better, Maya." She said, and a tiny smile appeared on her stolid features.

Yes, she was tired. Not her flesh, but her soul. Maya could see it as if she had been made of glass. "This can't go on, Erica. You can't keep doing this…this family thing. You know that don't you? You know what's at stake."

She pivoted slightly, to grab her cup, and hold it in her hands. "I know Maya, but seeing you here can only mean that God has brought my family back to me. I'm happy again."

"Then I'm sorry, because sadness is sure to follow," Maya said, but could already see her words had no meaning. She decided to try a different approach. "Have you missed me?"

Erica stood, placed her cup on the table, and remained there staring a Maya for what seemed like hours. Her voice came out brash and choppy – a combination of anger and guilt, "Yes, yes Maya, I have missed you as I would miss my lips if I had no mouth."

And before Erica could say another word Maya stepped up to her…and wrapped her arms around her best friend. Maya felt Erica's arms come around to hold her too, and a bit of the evil began to ebb. Not many in Crest Hill County have lost as much as she had. All that she had loved had gone, leaving her with such a craving for affection, which a thousand rivers of emotions could not quench. She felt for her friend – because she would suffer the most when this would be all over, and yet be the strongest for it.

"Can I have some hot chocolate, old friend," Maya said, her lips barely moving.

And without as much as a wink, Erica went to prepare it.

Maya sat and enjoyed the hot chocolate. She allowed her body, for one moment, to taste, to feel, to enjoy what was given to her. She appeared to breath, to blink, to swallow – not for survival, but so that the living would not be alarmed at their lack of human mannerisms. She allowed her flesh to act on its own accord…and it enjoyed this momentary control. She enjoyed the taste of the chocolate, the tiny marshmallows as their softness and sweetness embraced her lips and tongue, and she enjoyed the warmth the cup emitted against the inside of her palms. She relaxed.

"Where's Eric?" Maya asked.

Erica glanced at her. She knew the niceties had come to an end. "Sleeping in his room. Where else would he be?"

The tone was very protective, Maya noted. "You mean he is in his room *feigning* sleep, for your sake of course, since the dead have little need for sleep."

"I meant what I said. He is *sleeping*." Erica said, and tilted her empty cup back against her lips, then slapped it back down on the table, and stood. "I'm going to make another cup," her eyes focused entirely on the cup, "You want some graham crackers with yours?"

She is in total denial, Maya thought. *A dead man was in her bed, and she wasn't dealing with it.* "Sure. Graham crackers sound nice." Maya said, holding back another barrage of questions that she would have to wait to ask. She could not sense Eric at home now, as well as Timothy – somehow, Maya knew that their whereabouts was going to be an answer she would rather not hear.

As Erica began to pull condiments from her cupboards, she asked, "So what brings you here to Earth Maya? Is it Luther? Have you seen him yet?" Then she turned with a smile, "Does Mildred know you're here?"

Maya regarded this without response. *Too much goading*, she thought, so very unlike Erica at all. She decided to remain on the direct approach. "I came back because Luther is in danger…you all are in danger, Erica."

Erica spun round too fast. She held a bag of marshmallows in her hand, and when she turned back around to look at Maya again, they flung across the room like exploding stars. "Damned!" she spat, her hands still reaching out in a vain hope of trying to catch the spongy missiles. "What has happened to Luther?"

As Erica bent to clean up the mess, Maya stood and walked in her direction, past her, and to the other end of the kitchen where she knew the broom and dustpan were. "Get off the floor Erica, and use these."

She grabbed for the cleaning items, and began to sweep. "Is he dead? Is that why you are here, to tell me this?"

Maya reached out towards the dustpan when the sweeping was done, and dumped the remains in the trashcan near the door. She could hear Erica heading back to the counter where her cup remained. She began to pour chocolate powder in the cup, and set the eye on her stove for the hot water. "No. He is not dead, but he has gone through something your son experienced while at Mildred's house. The mist almost claimed him. Your sister-in-law managed to wake him. Luther was not so lucky."

"What!" Erica said. "Eric said nothing when he came home with Timothy? Are you sure? You've only just arrived here. How do you know these things?"

Maya exhaled – a habit at most – and moved towards the eating table. She rested a hand on one of the wooden chairs. "I know a lot of things, Erica, and don't have time to explain them. The mist has gotten thicker, a fact you have not been noticing, because of your…family concerns. It filled up the room Timothy was in, and Eric sensed this, and saved him."

"You mean to tell me that my son, my only son, almost died and Eric neglected to tell me this?"

"He was never in any real danger, Erica."

"I don't give a fuck if he was in any real danger or not…there was a chance that he was. Do you not know how much I have lost, Maya?" her voice a restrained hostility.

Maya sat quietly, watching as Erica spun in the direction of the stove and snatched the kettle from it before it had a chance to ring out, then poured its contents into her cup, "Of course I know what you have lost Erica. I'm one of those things."

Her anger fell back a few beats.

She finished filling her cup, and with red cheeks, walked towards Maya, placed her cup on the table, and in one slow motion, grabbed Maya's – taking it back to the counter to refill it with both water and chocolate. "Yes, you are right." She was shaking when she brought the cup back to the table. "I can't take this Maya. I can't take all of this anymore. I just can't."

"Is that why you are plotting and planning, Erica. Is that why selfish thoughts not of your nature are consuming you?"

Her features went solid.

"Whatever are you talking about, Maya?" Erica said, her composure changing from water to flour.

Maya leaned over the table, her sandy locks bounced across her forehead, her eyes stared unblinking – she had even forget to continue to breath, or at least to feign it, "Erica. I love you – God knows I do – but playtime is over. I don't know what you've been thinking, or what you've been planning, but I know a part of it has to do with killing, for lack of a better word, Eric! You are also somehow, keeping this little plot away from your son Timothy."

Erica's stone features fell away, melted like warmed ice, and something different appeared. Something Maya could not quite describe. It was a sort of pulling away – as if Erica had just drawn back a curtain on this show she was performing, and the house lights had suddenly come on.

Maya felt fear. It caught her off guard for a moment. She'd forgotten it so quickly, had become so used to being without it that it felt more like a slight chill against her skin. But she remembered it as soon as it came. Erica did have a plan, and it was one that went totally against her character…

…this is what frightened Maya the most.

You're right, Maya," Erica said, maneuvering her seat back towards the table. She slowly reached out to grab a cracker, and finally take a sip of her hot chocolate. "Yes Maya. I do have a crazy little plan, from all of the info Eric managed to tell me about what was about to happen to this town."

As everyone is about to have their *dead* tell them, Maya thought. Everyone is starting to find out these truths at the same time. She didn't want to ask her next question, but she did, "What have you suddenly discovered, my dear old friend?"

She appeared to take her time on this; chewing on the words like the graham cracker in her mouth. "The dead, Maya. I was thinking about the dead, and what happens to them. When you talked about Luther – you didn't seem very alarmed. You said he would be okay."

Maya hesitated, but answered, "Yes. Eventually when this is all over, he will be okay. He will be trapped however, in Crest Hill County, forever."

Erica nodded, as if this had been common knowledge. "Eric told me that he and my baby belonged in the afterlife, it was fate, or God, or destiny that sent them there. That my being able to forgive them, or even to forgive myself, would be enough to at least send Eric Jr. back. He said that Timothy hated him, and in order for his father to go back, that Timothy would have to forgive too. Once Timothy really loved him, forgave him, it would be as if Eric had never existed at all. If however, he did not forgive him, then he would remain here, and Crest Hill County would only exist to us, but to the rest of the world, it would vanish."

Maya was stunned. "It would appear that Eric has said too much."

"Is it true, Maya? Is that how this can all end?" Erica asked, with her lips at a half-smile.

Maya was torn. There was a battle raging within her at the moment she realized that Erica knew the truth – or at least all the truth she was willing to disclose – and that Maya was bound to answer. But instead of saying what was pushing against her soul, charging to be set free, she said, "I'm not going to say."

Erica smiled even more than before. "So it is true!" she turned away, and a little chortle escaped her throat. "It is good to see that even after death; we still continue to know each other."

"Even so, Erica – what are you thinking? Do you want to have things remain as they are?"

Erica looked away from Maya, and in the direction of her bedroom at the end of a long hallway. "If it means being with my child a little more, then yes Maya. Yes, I would rather risk this place, to get a little of what I've lost."

"And what about your husband? What about Eric?"

"I still don't forgive him for running out on me, but I didn't know he had died. Now my son is grieving for a father we both never really knew, and a brother who died too young. I only care about him. If what Eric told me is true, the act of Mildred and Timothy will set Eric free. This means I can live with my baby in this new Crest Hill County, and never have to worry about him dying again. We all will now have a choice, right now, to decide about who we want to live, and who we want to die. It is amazing! And with any luck, Timothy or Mildred will rid me of Eric…forever!"

"But why are you thinking like this Erica?" She couldn't believe she was actually having this conversation with a woman regarded as her best friend. She didn't know her anymore at all.

"Because I want a choice, Maya. I don't want God, I don't want my husband, I don't want my friends, to ever make the choice to leave me again. I just don't want to go through that any more in my life."

Maya was afraid to speak anymore. She was genuinely afraid to continue with this dialogue – a dialogue that delved deeper and deeper into avenues she didn't want to go. Erica had unearthed a most dangerous truth and a most dangerous lie all at the same time.

"Erica. Where are your husband and son?" Maya said sternly. She needed to know this answer quickly (because she knew they weren't in the house).

Another smile. "Why, I sent them out to bond Maya…to finally start to forgive each other of course."

Part IV

She had to leave it alone.

Erica had recognized a most dangerous secret.

Erica had recognized the power of choice.

The universe itself was founded upon choice; whether it was "Let There Be Light," or through The Bang Theory – elements came together for a reason, directed by an unknown. Choice was the gift possessed by humans, for which the Heavens were denied. So in the end, Maya was able to make her own choice, and to move on.

But for now, her attention needed to be directed to another pressing matter: the assisting of a fellow deceased, and helping them to handle the avalanche of emotions that their flesh was subjugated to.

Jason happened to be in desperate need of her help.

He too had lost much: his life and his lover – due to a simple lie and an act of desperation. Benny had come at him with such blatant raw emotion, such inebriated lust, such unhinged power, that Jason could no longer exist in the same space with him. He was slowly being pulled back into the living – this pseudo living – and it felt as if his dead flesh and his living soul were being fused back together with a welding rod. He hurt in a way he could not remember.

"Jason?" Maya said to the back of the head that sat bathed in shadow. She watched it move slightly, saying nothing.

She eased up behind him, the spray from the water erupted in a cool sensation around them. It was a feeling that was as close to the afterlife as she had felt all day. She reached out towards him, her hands resting lightly on his shoulders. She pressed them slightly, feeling a jumble of emotions as if a current had passed between them.

"What is happening, Maya?" he said, pain and despair knotted in his throat.

"The end of all things," she responded.

"Feels like the end of me," he said, leaning his head to one side, resting it lightly upon Maya's wrist. "The tears won't come."

"Of course not Jason, you're dead. Tears only flow for the living."

"And the pain?"

"That can be felt by those both dead or alive…regrettably."

The subtle splash of the fountain filled the night air. The silence was so still, Maya realized, as if the walls of a grave were being pulled up around the city.

"Have I failed? Is that why you're back? Have many of us failed, so that God has brought down his favorite missionary?"

She stopped rubbing his shoulder, and leaned forward across the bench, resting her elbows along the back of it. Her face was next to Jason's; their common beauty and likeness, made them look like siblings or lovers. "No one has failed, Jason. It is the pull of the flesh and the soul; a battle that has gone on for eons. For you, it has just reached its limit, that's all. Your flesh is longing to be alive again, because it was snatched from this earth without ever reaching its purpose. It is angry, and it sees the opportunity to live, and to be loved. It can feel Benny's love; a love that had never really diminished, even in his affair with Harold. It is very, very strong."

"Yes, it is, and it scares me. Should it? I've been dead much longer than you? Should I not be able to resist, stand my ground, and save Benny, save this town?"

"Perhaps, but in the afterlife Jason, you know time means nothing. Time is a way by which life and death are measured. For us, our time was up when we died. In Benny's case, he has never been afraid of you, he wants you alive – he has always in some sense, knew you would be back. This is very odd, because now he may never let you go."

"But he has chosen Harold. He cheated with Harold. He conspired with Harold. How can he profess to love me?"

"He only *thought* he loved Harold," Maya said. "He really only thought he could love Harold as much as you. The greatest deception Benny committed was the one he perpetrated upon himself."

Jason turned to look at Maya, her soft gray eyes like a pelt of animal fur. "So what can we do, Maya? Are we to do anything – or do we just want to see what he does? Do we hope he will finally…let me go?"

She smiled at Jason, a reassurance. "No, we need to visit Benny, together. Tomorrow I am hoping to guide this town back to its senses, but tonight, I need to get my friends there. Benny is at the verge of obsession, but it can be stemmed," then she appeared to take in a deep breath. "Take my hand."

And he did.

Then a second later, a melding of mist surrounded them like ants, and in another second…they were gone…

…they reappeared in front of Benny's condo.

Maya knocked lightly – while Jason stood aloof behind her.

A latch was unhinged, the door opened, and there was a sudden loss of oxygen, as if all the breathable air in the corridor had suddenly been suctioned out. Benny stood there in the threshold, and the skin on his face had gone from wrinkled annoyance, to a stance of wonder.

"No! I don't believe it!" he said, and before Maya had any time to react, Benny sprung on her like a broken rubber band, and embraced her to the point of smothering. "You're back! It's all going to be perfect now," and then he cried.

Maya shuddered; within herself, and from Benny's sudden outburst. It was also as she suspected; that Benny's love was a very strong thing – she could almost feel it drain the death right out of her, and awaken her flesh. She craned her neck back, clearing her lips of Benny's flayed copper hair. "Hello Benny."

He held onto her shoulders as he took a step back, awed in his observance of her, "You look amazing, much better than I have ever seen you. The afterglow of the afterlife has done you well," and then he looked beyond her. "And I see you have brought the Calvary."

"You could say that," Maya said. "May we come in?"

"Of course, you can…what is it, midnight now? Time flies when you're planning your future you know," Benny said, as he led them inside.

Maya stood next to the sofa, while Benny closed the door, and Jason took a seat. She could tell that both of them were in serious trouble, and very worn, "Benny, have you been sleeping well?"

Benny wore nothing but a black t-shirt and jeans; his feet in a pair of sandals, stood out very shiny and pedicured, "With all the excitement in town, of course not." He turned to look at Jason, giving him a wink, "Isn't that right baby?"

Maya watched Jason; his agony was quite transparent. She would have to hurry and get him out of here.

"So how is life with the Big G, Maya? You gorge yourself on milk and honey up there?"

She was appalled; but it being a forgotten emotion, she wasn't sure what her response should be, "The afterlife is what the afterlife is, Benny. You will have your time there at some point, so don't rush it?"

"Always with the elusive answers, Maya," Benny said, as he pranced past her, and into the kitchen, where he opened the refrigerator. "And you baby, what has been happening?"

This was directed at Jason, and Maya placed an index finger to her lips to thwart his response. Some things needed very little reply.

"I know you are a little worn form your journey from the everlasting, Maya, but I think I have something that will ease the tension from both of you," he said, returning to them both with a box of Turtles Candy. He offered the open box to her first.

She took one, almost instinctively. It felt natural to do so.

He took a seat next to Jason, still keeping his attention on Maya, who was looking at the candy suspiciously. "Go on and take a bite; it's not like you have to worry about gaining any hips now that you're dead."

She reached down to fist him playfully on the shoulder, "You watch yourself. I am still a lady you know," and she popped the treat in her mouth. The chocolate was an immediate rush for her, and it charged through the sensations of her tongue like electric current.

She then watched Benny hand-feed Jason one of the chocolates, and there travelled another sort of electricity.

She had to close her eyes immediately, to decipher the spirit that roamed in this house. Benny's spirit was strong. It was as selfish as it was generous – and above all it was like a parasite that wanted to live among its host at any cost. Maya had to check herself, for as her memories wanted to relive its association with Benny, her soul had to remind her that such a union was far too late. She had died. He had lived. This had to end.

Then she opened her eyes again, and saw that Benny feeding him another chocolate.

"What are you doing, Benny?" Her tone was now a bit harsher, and she could see that Benny was aware of it.

"That's not a very Heavenly disposition, Maya," Benny responded, positioning his body in a way that was closer to Jason; the knees touched, the hand lowered closely to the thigh, the torso was pointed inward.

"What *are* you doing, Benny?" Jason replied, the tone slightly subdued, but strong. He continued to enjoy the Turtle, but the chew was much slower, his eyes glancing down at the hand that fed it.

Benny scooted back. "Yea, I think I know why we're having this little intervention," and then he looked intensely at Maya. "But would that have really brought you back Maya? Why are you here? Will you be staying along with Jason? Did Luther bring you back?"

She had to shake her head from all the questions. She leaned forward, reaching her hand out. "Can I have another one?" She asked.

Benny began to reach into the box of candy again.

"No," Maya interrupted, "I want Jason to give it to me."

Jason reached for the box, but Benny pulled it back a bit, staring up at Maya. He was clever, Maya noted, and he could guess there was a ruse afoot. But before he could try and guess what it may be, Jason pulled the box away from him, and stood up to offer Maya a candy.

Maya smiled, and took another piece. "Thank you, Jason," and before Jason could return to his seat, Maya reached out and grabbed his wrist, and pulled him away from the sofa, to stand opposite her. "Remain there. I think I may want another piece real soon," she said, keeping eye contact with him.

Benny leaned back on the sofa, and brushed his fingers across his chin, "What is that, some sort of Ethereal Mind Trance or something? Is that how we are going to play this?"

She matched his grin, "Yes Benny, that is how we are going to play this."

He glanced back at Jason, who looked at him, his eyes very lost, "I'm not letting him go, you know."

"I realize that the moment I saw him," Maya answered, too looking at Jason. "What are you hoping to accomplish, Benny? You know this is wrong."

His eyes still hung on Jason; there was a tinge of sadness there. "Yea, I know it is. Tell me something I don't know."

She leaned towards Jason, and simply opened her mouth. He placed a chocolate in it without hindrance. It was rather delicious, these little gooey-crunchy confections. "That you are a coward, Benny. Maybe that is something you didn't know."

His look was one of confusion. "I'm sorry. I don't get you, Maya."

This time Jason spoke, "I understand what she's saying," and took his eyes from Maya and clocked them at Benny. "She wants to know if you loved and missed me so much, why did you just not kill yourself, to be with me in the afterlife."

The question visibly shook him. It took him a minute to answer. "I've asked myself that question maybe a thousand times, Jason. But you know I'm not much of a gambling man, and the odds of there even being an afterlife was not a good enough guarantee for me. I needed to be assured of being with you – forever"

"But you know now, Benny. Would you kill yourself even now?" Jason asked.

"I don't have to Jason. You're here," Benny said.

"But would you?" Maya continued to prod, "Would you kill yourself now to save this town, or are you satisfied with killing Jason now, to save yourself from a little grief?"

Angry eyes pierced in her direction. "You were nicer when you were alive, Maya."

"No. I was only more empathetic, Benny. Our needs had been the same – to love those that could not love us back the way we wanted them too. It is a very selfish love, Benny. It causes whores to love their pimps, students to love their teachers, mistresses to love their masters, and you to love the dead. You deserve better for yourself than to be mired in a love that cannot grow. Jason deserves to be happy in the afterlife he had to die to get into…an afterlife that did not include you, Benny."

Benny stood. "Maybe you should be leaving Maya."

"Maybe I should," she said, as she reached a hand out in Jason's direction, where another chocolate was deposited, "But I'm not."

"What?" Benny said, alarmed.

She chewed more slowly. "I will leave and go as I please, Benny. This is how it works in the afterlife. But that time has not come, at least not naturally; but it is being forced upon Crest Hill County – the overlapping of the dead and the living, the afterlife and the human life, things that should have passed away, and the things that are still living. Good and evil, malice and merriment, none of these things were meant to exist in an eternity amongst their selves, especially where death would not be a factor. Death is the equalizer, Benny, and it has been banished before its appointed time."

"English, Maya!" Benny said, unnerved.

She smiled, and then licked her fingers of chocolate. "Of course – monologues do run deep when you have the time to give them I suppose. But what I am saying Benny, is have you thought about who will you be exiling yourself with? Love has blinded you into thinking that only you and Jason are going to coexist when this town dies. Have you forgotten about Harold?"

Honestly, he had not. "What about him?"

"Harold is going to hate you. Hate will continue to exist here in Crest Hill County. It will not be an afterlife of hugs and kisses, Benny. Like I said, malice and merriment will co-exist – a dog chasing its tail endlessly. Harold will hate you for your decision to love Jason, and he will be a fester on your skin you cannot peel away."

"I didn't realize this Maya," Jason said, "That there will be no check systems in place." Fear was in his tone.

She looked back at Jason, "You were not supposed to. There will be no escape for the living trapped in Crest Hill County. At one point, even death will only lead them back here, just as the roads out of this town are the same roads that lead back into it. But the real torture will be for Benny is that he will argue with you, he will eventually stop grieving for you, and the moment he does, you will be set free. Your afterlife is your destiny, and it is there you are destined to return, and Benny will live this circle he has drawn for himself, where he and Harold will go throughout eternity in a ribbon of hate and regret."

No one spoke. The truth had been revealed; a truth that may have come too late.

"Now, I think I will leave."

Benny looked at her, his eyes dashing in Jason's direction. He knew what would happen; that he could lose Jason for a second time after all, and yet he could not will himself to let go.

"You have a decision to make Benny, but very little time to make it. There will be a church service tomorrow, and I think you need to be there; if you can get your emotions in check. By tomorrow, what may have felt easy to do, will suddenly feel impossible." And then she turned to Jason, "And I need you to stay here for just a moment longer, then you must leave."

"Why does he have to leave? What have I done to him?" Benny questioned.

"You have loved him too much."

"But I-"

"Goodbye Benny. I hope to see you tomorrow afternoon at church," and without another word being said, a small column of smoke rose up from the floor, masked Maya, and as it whisked away…so did she.

Part V

Lisa Slept.

Maya watched her in the tranquil solitude of her home. Maya also knew that she slept uneasily. Her ghosts were gone, she handled everything in the perfect manner; meekness and forgiveness had become her allies of late. She had done very well.

Her uneasy rest was a result of not having seen Pastor Luther Reynolds come to the church. She waited there all night, in a state of fear and trepidation. Maya came here to ease her mind, sooth her thoughts, allow even her dreams to coast a little easier.

So she stood in the darkness, watching Lisa, her face grimacing in her sleep like the skin of a prune. Maya would not disturb her slumber. It was a blessing that in a town which slept so little, that Lisa had managed to obtain just a tiny bit of this most elusive pleasure.

Maya also stood here to give Lisa another blessing; and that was to provide her with some of the many answers that lay hidden in her heart since this whole ordeal began. It was the least that could be done by a woman who had not only gone through so much, but who had displayed such obedience, that it had been impressive, even on a heavenly scale.

Lisa's tiny head, surrounded by her golden locks, appeared to sink out of existence within her large pillows. Maya reached out towards her forehead. And pressed the center of it softly with her forefinger – knowing that it would send her deeper into slumber. She continued to press there, pushing harder, until her finger broke through the skin as if it had cracked through a flaky pie crust.

This didn't hurt Lisa, but it did establish a connection. This allowed them to speak to each other in that lost realm between awareness and dreamscape. This allowed Maya to tell her about what happened to Luther. Her facial features contorted wildly as this was communicated.

"Is he alive?" Lisa asked within her subconscious.

"Yes," Maya replied, moving her fingers around Lisa's skull as if she were pushing it through a bowl of wheat. "But he is in a deep sleep. The mist has been slowly transitioning people, getting them ready for a lifetime of death."

"But what about those, who have ghosts that are now gone? What about people like me?"

"Doesn't matter, Lisa. Your ghosts will stay gone, to continue in their afterlife. You however, will remain." Lisa understood. Her spirit seemed to be at peace with whatever happened.

"And what's the solution Maya? I am sure you were sent here to provide us with some sort of solution. God does not create such dire consequences without providing first a solution."

She's right, Maya thought. She could see now why Lisa was able to come through this faster than most, and why she was granted this most cherished slumber.

"Hopefully, the solution will arrive tomorrow. I want everyone to meet me at the church tomorrow afternoon. The mist is going to come in at its heaviest. There will be great fear. I need you to spread the word. I need you to go through the town as best as you can, to get people to the church."

"Will I be able to drive in the mist?"

"No. You will be walking. The mist will help you to travel faster. It will be like walking though cloudy corridors into people's lives. There will be chaos but you must get them to the church."

"I will do the best I can," Lisa said.

A pause.

"What's it like?" Lisa communicated.

The question caught Maya off guard, and she knew what Lisa was asking.

"It's more than you can imagine, Lisa. The colors, the feelings, and the spirits you encounter. It is so much more than the rewards that are preached at the pulpit.

"And…?" Lisa began, but stopped.

"No Lisa, I can't comment on that – you know that," Maya said, as she slowly began to pull her finger back.

"I know, I know, I suppose curiosity had gotten the better of me."

"As it does with many, but knowing the face of God is a reward that will be granted to a very few – even in the afterlife, and to understand it all – let alone describe it, is well beyond human understanding or the lifetime that is allotted to them."

There was laughter in Lisa's thoughts, "We are fast in wanting to know, but slow in the patience it takes."

Maya too found that humorous, and pulled her finger completely from Lisa's mind. "Yes, patience is very short for the living, as well as for the Spiritual – and if it has run out for both entities by tomorrow, then it will be much too late for Crest Hill County to turn back from their own Armageddon."

CHAPTER 19

Part I

Fear ran though the town, like an unchecked disease. The mist was thick, and many of the living became victims of its undulating murkiness.

There was also a heavy spirit of despair weighing upon the citizens of Crest Hill County. Everything was at a standstill. Many people slept, and could not be awakened. Many cried because they could not awaken those that slept. Many tried to move those that slept, but were quick to discover that forces beyond this world were holding them still; the mist weighed heavily within their feeble fleshly forms. They could not be moved.

The police, the ambulances, the doctors, could do nothing. Transportation was halted by near zero-visibility driving conditions.

Maya stood in front of Mildred's door, the mist was light around her house; its surface gritty and cool. It hid the sunlight away from the town, casting it in gray overtones. The town would fall under its spell, and in just little over a day, it would become unstoppable. There was a lot of work to be done, and it would begin now, once Maya knocked on this door, and finally confront the only woman she had ever known that would be considered her nemesis

Before Maya even had the opportunity to knock on the door, it suddenly opened; the swiftness of it rushed more of the mist inside the home, looking indifferent.

"Finally," Mildred said, stepping aside to let Maya in, and also taking note of the cloudiness behind her. "What's happening out here?"

"We have a lot of work to do in very little time, I'm afraid."

There was hesitation as she closed the door. She could feel no breeze, and the air was stilled – like death itself had swept past her welcome mat. It wasn't dissipating as quickly as it had when she saw these same cloudy plumes in Timothy's room. They buffeted along, crashing into each other – mingling and melding, shadows engulfing shadows, making the town seem like a fading projection against the sky.

"How did this happen, Maya?" She said, closing the door, a collection of smoke lingering at its edges. "What have you brought to this town?"

Maya was silent, and she took a step forward, Mildred could hear the soft feet sliding against her wooden floors. "It's happening faster than I thought," Maya whispered.

Mildred turned to look at this golden image – skin as smooth as painted glass, and could see Maya staring just above her head, where near the door…the mist still wafted. Mildred swung her hand at it, as if banishing a bad dream, "What is happening?" she said, but noticed that the mist clung to her on its edges, making her arm appear smoky. She jackknifed her arm again, swinging it wildly, stumbling back against Maya. The mist would not let her go, "What is this Maya? Dammit, let go of me!"

Maya reached out to grab Mildred's arm at the crook of her elbow, and brought her hand down until she reached her wrist. The mist seem to pull away as easily as a banana from its peel.

Mildred yanked her arm back, rubbing at the wrist, and stared at Maya for a swift cold minute, her eyes holding back actions she seemed hindered upon displaying, then in a jolt, she brushed past her and headed towards her liquor cabinet.

"We don't have time for that Mildred! You need to sit down and listen, and then we have to head out to the church."

Mildred didn't answer, and pulled out two crystal decanters; one containing a dark elixir, and the other a clear one – she mixed them both in a rock glass, and took a deep drink. She said nothing, her eyes roaming across the room at her many paintings. She exhaled, closed her eyes, and let the burn travel south past her throat. She took another long sip, finishing the glass, and casually brushed at the breast of her pin-striped suit, as the heels from her black pumps tapped a hollow sound against the floor.

Maya waited patiently.

"I'm going to die," Mildred said, reaching for the bottles again to refill her glass. "Dammit! I spend years putting up with Luther's desires for another woman, years pinning for my brothers return and distress because he left, years hating his weak-minded wife, years hating you, and just when I think I'm free – you die, and the world comes to a fucking, crashing, end! I hate you so much Maya."

Maya continued to watch, as Mildred indulged in her drink.

"I hate you for taking away my life."

And in that moment, before Maya was even aware of the end of Mildred's statement, there was a rush of hands, like duel windmills flapping in her direction. Maya couldn't believe it until it was occurring: Mildred was attacking her!

"I could fuckin' kill you, Maya. Why did you do this to me? I should have killed you, instead of you just dying. Why didn't you just stay alive, and simply run off with Luther, make me the hero, the victim, in all of this, and free me from this life of the mundane?" And as she said these things, her hands was slicing through the air, and pelting Maya along her arm, her face, her chest, and her head.

But Maya could see what was really happening, as Mildred's came very close to her, but never really touching. Maya's body was still new to Crest Hill County, and the essence of the afterlife still clung to her like a second skin; the glow that shielded her received the brunt of the attacks. Maya could see the anger in Mildred's eyes, as her shouts and accusations came out in a rush of warm air and spittle. She knew Mildred was not upset at her, but at the choices she had made.

Maya fell back against the curtains, parting them slightly. Mildred could see the cascading mist beyond the glass, and it gave her cause to lash out more violently. When Maya decided that it had gone on long enough, she thrust her body aside, and caught Mildred's wrists. She pressed the joints there and Mildred's arm fall limply to her.

"We don't have time for this, Mildred," Maya said, slowly pushing her back. At this close proximity, she could catch a revealing whiff of the liquor on Mildred's breath – and quickly realized that those two drinks had not been her first of the day.

Maya reached up to push Mildred to the sofa, where she collapsed as if her bones had turned to jelly…then she started to cry.

"This is not fair," Mildred shouted distressfully. "You both were wrong, and you both know it."

"Shut this up, Mildred!" Maya said, "Luther never cheated on you, he honored your marriage. You, however, had forgotten your vows to *honor* and *obey*. You neither honored nor obeyed *his* needs.

Mildred shifted back on the sofa, wiped her eyes, and sniffed. She looked up at Maya, who somehow offered her a tissue; even though there was no tissue box present. "Thank you," Mildred accepted.

"I need you at the church with me, Mildred. The congregation needs to see its First Lady take charge of this situation. They need you to honor them, since the Pastor cannot be there. They don't need to see an angry, jealous, upset First Lady – they need to see one that's go it together. They need to see the one that marched into my funeral as if she owned the damned church – because you do."

Maya took a second for Mildred to digest her words.

"So, tell me, Maya…how do I keep my husband?" Mildred managed, past veering eyes.

Maya could see the difficulty that Mildred was having with that simple question, and yet she could also feel the sincerity in it as well. So Maya took a small chance, with a seemingly innocent gesture and reached her hand out towards her.

Then waited.

Mildred eased forward, her shaky hands slowly reaching out to meet with Maya's. Maya squeezed those trembling fingers.

"Mildred, I will make this quick, but please listen first. We both know this whole ordeal has been tough, and in some ways has already killed us once, and is killing us again," and she paused there, as the power of her words began to work on her flesh, and a wave of sadness overcame her. She looked up at Mildred, who looked as tired on the outside, as she felt on the inside. She continued.

"Luther loves you, but he also misses you. He misses the woman he once married, that knew how to please him without wanting to be pleased herself. Power has corrupted you, and you have brought that from the church into your marriage…into your bedroom. You have lost your empathy, your ability to feel and react upon the pains of others. Get that part of you back, Mildred. That builds the trust that Luther needs. That will make him hear you again. That could get you the escape from this town that you so urgently require. I know you don't love Luther as you once did, and that you love the power he gives you more, but that kind of thinking has to stop, or you will lose him in whatever reality you end up in."

There was a slight pulling away.

"Not that you don't love him. It was still a marriage, although a broken one. But now that I am dead, you have to step up to the plate. You have to remember why you married this man when he barely had a church, and you barely had two dresses to wear. You have to stop wanting to escape. You have to stop wanting to escape your marriage through your brother also. He's dead, you can't go with him – you never really could – and you have to be your own person. My death, his death, gave you the chance to move on your own haunches, and start living the life you wanted to live – and fortunately with a man that still loves you. Take advantage of it Mildred. It is not your time to die, it was ours.

Silence.

Without a word, Mildred slid her hands from Maya's grip, and slowly began to stand. She eased from between the sofa and coffee table, and walked to the center of the room; her back to Maya. She said nothing, but the lilt in her shoulders, and the drop of her head, let Maya know she had accepted a most ugly truth, and a weight lifted from her like vapor.

Maya lifted herself from the coffee table.

"Okay Maya," Mildred said breaking the silence, "I will try that. I will try what you have said." Then she turned. "But what happens now?"

"We need to head for the church. Mildred closed her eyes, "Let's get started. Time is of the essence."

Maya moved to open the door, and the delicious scent rushed into the room, and caused Mildred to taste her lips. "Ignore it. It is a ruse by the mist to sway you," Maya said, but she could see the words barely reaching Mildred, so she leaned over to grab her hand; there was no more time for explanations. Once she touched Mildred, a column of smoke rose up to surrounded them, and carried them into the mist – and into a most dangerous rabbit hole.

Part II

After the first burst, for lack of a better word, Lisa was more exhausted mentally than she was physically. She could still feel her heart beating wildly, and she reserved to stand still, to stand silently for a moment, to both catch her breath and catch her sanity.

Travelling outside of her home was becoming an experience she was not prepared for. The mist was unbelievably thick, filled with a pallet of colors not found in most rainbows; from sparkling gold, to translucent silvers, shimmering whites, and ominous blacks, melding and coalescing within each other, as if they were *becoming* each other, frightened as well as fascinated her. And then to hear the soft screams, like a dying animal she could not see, echoing through town, alarmed her as well. All of this had happened while she stood at her opened door, wondering if she should even take that first step into destiny.

So, when she took that step, she closed her eyes.

Then the burst happened; a sound that clouded her ears as if someone had slapped them with open palms.

Something had gripped her shoulders, pushed at them, caused her to stumble just a bit, and then that same feeling ran down her spine. Her feet left the ground, and when she opened her eyes, she realized that she had been thrust a few yards from her front door; as it stood open revealing her dimly lit living room.

"Oh my God!" Lisa exclaimed, searching the ground around her as if it alone had transported her. She looked back at her home across the street and realized that she was on the corner of her block; the stop sign was only inches from her shoulder, as the mist continued to hide the view of the remaining homes along the street, their location revealed by their lighted windows. She thought it was dangerous to leave her door opened, and decided to walk back.

Pop! Another sound clapped her ears, and clouded her vision.

When she looked up, she was at least *two* blocks away – the light from her door cast a streaming glow on the sidewalk, and behind her was the glow of a few ATM machines belonging to the bank. "*I am being led towards the church, regardless of which way I travel,*" she realized, and then she heard the screams she had been hearing earlier, were growing stronger, "*Unless I am being led elsewhere first.*"

She looked around, and seemed to feel a little less frightened. The angels of God would have to surround her place and protect it, for there was little she could do about that now. She tried to locate the church past the amalgamation of hues saturated within this miasma of danger, folding in and out like a pair of cloudy lungs – and then there was something else…its scent: a honey-like sweetness that seemed to smother her, and purge her with hunger. She wanted so much to just stick out her tongue and taste it.

She temped herself and did so.

Her eyes widened. It was like the taste of sweet milk on the back of her throat, and she involuntarily swallowed. It was hard to resist the lull it had. It unnerved her, this calmness, this easiness, this want to nothing more than taste it again. She rolled her hands into fists, closed her mouth, and began to pray. Something *this* good could not be good at all. How many of the townspeople surrendered their will to this everlasting respite?

Another scream.

She could hear it so distinctly, and turned, just as the sun was starting to peer at the city; revealing the bright reflection of car tops, and lamp posts lining the streets. The roads appeared wet as they faded into a shadowy distance ahead of her, where she was able to see a few blocks to the movie marquee above the only movie theatre in Crest Hill County; its façade laden with minuscule bulbs. Behind the theatre, Lisa knew there were a small row of two-story apartments, and although she could not see them, she was aware that the scream came from there. She knew of only one couple that lived there – The Shreports – and that shrill was from the mother herself. Before she realized it, she was starting to run in that direction…

Pop!

…and suddenly found herself there! The mist had clouded her vision for a split moment, and when it cleared, she was in front of the apartment complex, the movie theatre now behind her. She could hear the sobs of a child, and looked up at the second story to Mary Shreport's window and saw the dimness of a light casting from within. Lisa kept her eyes fixed on it, her ears picking up voices that would normally be impossible for her to hear, and she took a tiny step forward.

Pop!

She was inside their apartment, standing in a hallway she had seen before with its large vases and silk flowers. The wall was lined with tiny shelves holding the statuettes from whatever sport her children had won. The hallway was filled with misty vapors, and through it, she discovered the family in Mary's, the mother's, room; and Alicia: *her seven year old daughter*, standing at the window, and their teenage son Gregory stood near the bed, trying to shake some life into what looked like their lifeless father, Henry.

"He's not waking up mom!" Gregory said, his face red with anguish. He had pajama bottoms on, and his tiny muscles seemed to swell as he tried to lift his father's arm. "I can't raise it!" he then stopped, staring away from his family, towards the door.

Mary looked in the same direction, her appearance as haggard as the cotton nightgown she wore. She jumped upon seeing Lisa, "Who are you!" she said clutching Alicia.

Gregory reached for the lamp on the nightstand, just as Lisa stepped into the room, "It's me, don't worry. Lisa…Lisa McConnell, from church."

Mary moved in front of her daughter towards Lisa. She glanced at Gregory heatedly, "Didn't I tell you to lock that front door, Gregory? We lock doors around here."

"I did mom," he said, placing the lamp back on the stand.

"Quiet," she said, brushing her hand at her son, "Lisa, why are you here? Can you help us a minute? Henry is not waking up, and we can't seem to get anyone on the phone. This fog is just everywhere, and I was going to have Henry go and find out how this fog was getting inside the apartment, but he wouldn't move. Did you bring your car? I think he's passed out for some reason, and we need to get him to the hospital. Do you know what's going on…?"

Lisa listened to Mary rattle on, and felt the woman clawing at her arm like a cat. "Mary, I'm not sure what's going on right now, but the hospital is not going to help Henry. I came here to tell you and others in town, that we have to be at the church this afternoon." Lisa could see from Mary's reaction, that this was not the right thing to say.

"What?" Mary said, backing away, as she took another look at Lisa. "Lisa I am asking for your help. We need to get my husband in either your car or mine. We need to get him some help. He's not waking up…I can't get an ambulance…I can't…"

"I heard you, Mary," Lisa said, managing a new sternness. "We can't help Henry here."

"What is she talking about mom?" Gregory said, shaking his father's shoulders.

"Excuse me?" Mary said, as she looked back at her husband and son. "Gregory, get around to where your father's feet are, and me and Lisa will handle his head."

Lisa reached out to Mary's shoulder, spinning her at a half turn, "Mary, I don't have time to discuss this with your right now. I know your husband needs help, but we can only do that by going to the church."

Mary's long face seemed to bunch up from the center, and she reached back to take Alicia's hand, who had been looking on silently…and *chewing*. "Lisa, I don't know what you are talking about, but I don't have time to go to church. My husband needs help, and not some prayer meeting. Can you understand that?"

Lisa looked at Mary, and darted her eyes around the room; the adjacent bathroom casting a light into it, and saw the slim trails of mist that rose just above their king-sized bed. She had to hurry, and reveal a few things in the process. "I understand you're afraid for your husband, but what is happening here is more than I can explain right now. Is there anyone else in the house?"

"Grandma was here yesterday," Alicia said, "But she went back to Heaven yesterday."

So, they accepted Grandma's death, Lisa thought that was good. The hard part was over for them; unfortunately, Henry still became subdued by the mist. Lisa got that. What she didn't get was Alicia's mannerisms. She had to give Mary some truth however, "Mary, your husband cannot be moved now that the mist has captured him. It must have gotten to him in his sleep. Can't you see it all around you? Soon there will be no place to hide from it. The One Star Church is the only sanctuary we have."

"I'm not leaving dad!" Gregory said, folding his pale limbs across his chest.

"You'll be coming back to him, but for now this is the only way we can help him," Lisa said, staring back at the angry eyes that beamed at her –

especially the drooping eyes of Alicia.

"I don't know what you're talking about Lisa, but if you're not going to help…"

Before Mary was able to finish her sentence, Alicia let out a deep sigh, stretched her arms towards the ceiling, and at that moment her knees buckled, and she was close to crashing to the floor, but Lisa rushed to her aid, embracing her just as her head went limp.

Mary knelt to the floor, and Gregory ran around the bed frame. "What happened," Mary asked, reaching out to pull at her daughter's arms.

"It's the mist. We have to get her to the bed," Lisa said, lifting the child. This is what was supposed to be done, Lisa realized, without knowing why. When Maya visited her in her dreams last night, she knew that some knowledge had been given her. The mist had taken over. Its taste like candy – chewable candy – causing a change in the body. It pushed the body between life and death, preparing it for its next stage. That process caused the body to become immobile; as if it were here and not here all at the same time. "Gregory we are going to need your help in lifting your sister."

"Why is she getting so heavy?" Mary said, as she took Lisa's lead, with Gregory's guidance, to lift Alicia and lay the child's upon the bed next to her father; their knees bent heavily at the effort.

"What's wrong with my baby, Lisa? What do you know about this?" Mary asked, as they eased Alicia's head on the pillow.

Dammit, Lisa thought, *if the grandmother had still been here, the family would not have succumbed to the mist so quickly*; there was no afterlife in this house, so the mist had become stronger. And this prompted Lisa to ask a question, "Mary, what happened before your mother left? What do you think changed between you two – and what caused her death?"

Mary seemed to be looking at her own eyebrows for the answer, nervous sweat beading around her spinning-top shaped head. "She died of a stroke, in the bathroom," Mary explained, "and a week before that we had a terrible argument about how I hated her telling me how to raise my kids, and that maybe I would take the kids over there when I felt she could handle them better," then she reached out to grab Gregory's hand, pulling him closer, "But that chance never came. One of the guards at her apartment called to tell me that she had hit the panic buzzer on the night she died, and they found her in the bathroom."

"But they forgave each other," Gregory stepped in, seeing the emotions welling up in his mother. He hugged her, leaning his head against her, and looked back at his sister on the bed next to his father, "Her and Alicia was playing only just two days ago – making pancake faces. I really didn't want her to leave."

"But I believe your mother knew she had to. It had become time to accept the truth. Isn't that right Mary?" Lisa asked

There was wetness in Mary's eyes, "Yes. I felt better about her dying, once she let me know she hadn't taken me seriously. The next morning, yesterday, she was gone."

Lisa walked to the back of the room, near the bathroom, where there was less of the vapors, and beckoned for the family to join her. She was beginning to suspect something very horrible, "The mist is getting stronger, Mary, and for now it seems the only safe place may be the church. I was told, and by no human, to get as many families as I could to the church – what happens then, I don't know. But as long as you are awake, and presently living, we have to go. I can't tell you more than that, I'm sorry."

"What are you talking about? We can't just leave Dad and Alicia here? What if something happens to the house? Mom, what is she talking about?" Gregory asked.

His mother looked down at him; affection in her eyes, "She is trying to tell us that we have to get to the church in order to wake your father and sister." Then she looked in Lisa's direction, "How do we do this, Lisa?"

Lisa looked around, but she didn't really know the answer to that. She thought being away from the mist would bring some sort of sign.

"Mom!" Gregory said in a panic, as he pointed down at his mother's feet. The mist had gathered there in large billowy clouds, clinging to her ankles. Gregory pulled at his mother, but as he did, he nearly stumbled, for the same clouds were also clinging to him.

Lisa stared in dismay at how fast this substance formed, swelled, and swirled around them, and before she even had a chance to take a step in their direction, it had already amassed up towards their torso.

"Lisa! Is this it? Are we going to the church?" Mary said, fear was in her eyes, but having seen her mother come back from the dead, fear was more a companion that an enemy.

Lisa believed that Mary could be right. "Yes, I think so, Mary." But Mary had already accepted that it was, and that acceptance, had transferred to her son as well, and the mist swallowed them whole, lifted, reached the ceiling, and in an instance, went through it.

Then they were gone.

Lisa looked on in awe – as the sun finally began to fill the room with ambient light. "All they had to do was *believe*; how simple it all seemed now."

Part III

Mildred stepped back from the curtain. "I can't do this, Maya," she said, looking out at the church pews – as it began to slowly fill up with people, who seemed to come in on small cloud bursts. A moment ago, some of the Shreport family arrived, still in their sleepwear – as most appeared to be – looking dazed and confused.

"You have to Mildred. We both have a lot of work to accomplish, and it has to be done very quickly. Before long, the mist is going to overtake the church, and if that happens, then we all die."

Mildred didn't want to hear this truth; it had become an ocean of information drowning her ears. She let the curtain fall, and addressed Maya – who despite the method of travel, looked well preserved. Lisa was a wreck.

The journey was short, but what her mind endured was boggling. Maya had told her what to expect, but when the subjective met reality, she realized why even God himself was faceless in description. Her body had shot through the mist like a catapult, pushing her past neighborhoods and buildings that were miles apart; before she could get her bearings on where she was at, the television switched channels, and she was elsewhere. One moment she was floating above the city, held up by a means she could not perceive, the next she was on the ground, looking out at what appeared to be a city built from a dream; where images hovered in midair or remained poised like mannequins. A boy walking his dog, both of them in midstride, was close enough for her to reach out and touch, but fear held her back. Having seen many of the dead buried in her profession, she wondered if they too were alive. It made her even more frightened to be traveling within the very thing that was petrifying a whole town. She dreaded the thought that if she died along this journey (indeed if she was not dead already), how would she even know?

And the scent of honey was strong, and the mist tasted of the sweet milk her mother gave her as a child. It was so pure and unrelenting, that all she wanted to do was to open her mouth and take it all into her senses. Regardless of the dangers posed by Maya against doing so, she struggled with this almost irresistible urge. How could Crest Hill County hope to survive, when the taste of death was so delicious?

Then she reached the back of the church, and a sad sight met her: Earl was there, sitting on the steps, leaning against the handrail, one arm in the air, with his mouth opened mid-yarn. Frozen. Without thinking, she ran to him, and attempted to pull him up before it was too late – until Maya pulled her back. She crumbled right there in a tight ball on the worn grass, not knowing if she should scream or cry.

And now, they were inside the church, and she was expected to prepare the most unusual sermon ever prepared in the halls of the One Star Baptist Church – a sermon she had neither written nor memorized. This was the job of her husband, to speak to the desperate masses here in search for answers, not hers.

"Is Lisa expected to bring the whole town into this church? Must I wait for everyone before I begin?" Mildred asked, as she pulled at her collar; her neck now lined with sweat.

"In part," Maya explained, as she leaned past Mildred, to also take a look at the throng of arrivals. "Lisa is not the only one who is assisting us in this endeavor; nor is everyone going to gather within these church walls. There are eleven others out there, for many in this town have faith, but not of this kind God still helps his children: sinner, saint, or those in between. There will be a gathering at the local high school, and maybe another venue or two, but that isn't important," and she let the heavy curtain fall back into place as she addressed Mildred, "The mist is going to allow you to be heard and seen by them all, as long as we can get many to these safe havens as we can, before the mist gets stronger."

Mildred could see Maya's lips moving, but understood very little. "I don't see that we have enough time. The town is already covered to the point where you can barely walk down the street – or barely see it. How long do we have Maya?"

"I can't answer that Mildred. All I know is it is better to try, than to submit."

"But I thought-" Mildred began, but Maya quickly interrupted.

Maya placed a hand on Mildred's shoulder. "There is a delicate balance happening right now; one where the mist is claiming victims, placing them in a permanent on-hold state – and another where the townspeople have to be strong enough to let go of their friends and family that may have died.

The grief in this town is very thick, and the mist represents a part of that grief – it feeds off of it – and it becomes clever. The mist will soon claim other members, like Luther, which will cause you to feel yet more grief, more fear, more doubt, and in turn it grows stronger.

"But there is hope, if we can get the town to believe, to have faith, that once they have accepted death, grief, guilt, and themselves, that the mist will begin to diminish."

Mildred closed her eyes, trying to ascertain what meaning Maya was trying to relay to her. "So we bring together those that are victims of both grief and sorrow, in hopes that we can convince them to finally let go of the very thing that has caused it? To do this for a whole town, in let's say, a few hours? " Maya nodded, and Mildred pulled back her hand. "Are you out of your mind? No one is capable of such a thing; to first grieve, and then a second later, to let go, and to feel nothing."

Maya sighed. She could feel the frustration even within herself. "Yes, I know, but what I am asking of this town is to accomplish something that is beyond being human – I need them to become something more than that."

Mildred spun back towards the curtain, and parted it slightly again, looking out at the congregation, the grieved, the sad-eyed and bent-lipped, the confused and the crying. "My God, you ask for the impossible," she whispered loudly, and deep in her heart, she wished Luther was here. She missed him terribly now.

"I wish also, that you had had time to prepare a little speech for these people; for your words will have to be your only tool to persuade them of not only their plight, but also of their duty; all while the mist gets heavier around them, threatening to take them out one by one. They have to believe a woman they have long hated is actually telling them the truth."

"There has to be another way, another person, something."

Maya lowered her head, and took a step back, "I'm afraid not, Mildred. You're going to have to trust that you'll say the right thing, because this situation isn't going to get any better, and more victims will succumb to this mist, and the world outside will slowly forget about a Crest Hill County, or a church named Morning Glory, or a woman named Mildred. Tomorrow is no longer an option for any of us."

Mildred listened to these words; weighing heavier than gravity itself. So many years she ran from duties like this – acts of selfless inspiration and motivation – and now it had been thrust upon her. She looked beyond Maya, past the short walkway beyond the stage, where a few simple steps led down to a suspended tangle of curtain ropes, past the baptismal pools sitting propped against one wall, beyond the small row of dressing rooms, through a short hallway of smaller offices, down a few stairs, and towards the back where she knew a larger lounging area was, where just to the right was Luther's office – hers was within, past a sliding door at the rear. She could imagine herself running past all of that, and locking herself in that room with the wall mounted television, mini-bar, and chaise lounge. She could imagine herself shutting all of this from her mind.

Instead she took a deep breath as her body shook in short, erratic, spasms. She could not remember experiencing so much emotional traffic. But despite it all, she thrust her hand past that curtain; the brilliant light from the sanctuary glazed her vision momentarily, and she stepped out onto the wooden stage.

If eyes had been daggers, she would have been dead.

The murmurs throughout the congregation started to rise in volume like popcorn bursts – its sound came as questions: "What is she doing here? Where is the Pastor? What happened to Lisa? Oh God, not Mildred…" and although these probes stemmed her pace just a bit, she continued towards the lone mic that loomed at the edge of the stage just beyond the podium – and in her mesmerized state, she overstepped and her chin butted against the steel, causing an audio feedback that pierced the air.

She took a step back, wiped her sweat from the mic, and cleared her throat. The last kernel popped as the room became silent.

Mildred trained her attention to the large doors at the front of the church – as they constantly swung open to let in more people who had managed to make it through the mist. As the door opened, she could see that ominous vapor, hanging just before the parking lot, much too close, looming there like an animal. She remembered how it grabbed her when she stood in the doorway of her home; the sticky feel of it, the way it clung to her like wet sand, its swiftness – the church would have no time to react if it chose to assail them like that, suffocating them in its scent and taste, until everyone surrendered to a most delicious demise.

She began.

"Hello, congregation," her voice cracked, as words and tone were severed upon exit. She pressed her lips together, trying to ease the rush of anxiety rattling her nerves. She remembered Maya mentioning that the church was not the only place that would hear her – her image would be somehow projected to many others in other edifices. "I also want to give a warm greeting to those who I understand are at the school, and many others of you who may be hearing me now elsewhere.

"I know you are wondering what is happening in this town. Many of you are looking for answers, many are looking for a solution, and many quite frankly, are looking for some rotten tomatoes to fling this way."

There was a slight chuckle scattered throughout the crowd. She tried to smile, but ended up just wetting her lips.

"Many of you are also wondering why Pastor Reynolds is not up here," and she took a moment for the crowd to engage her words, and to keep back a sudden flood of her own tears. "He is in danger."

The popcorn grew louder.

She quickly spoke again, "We are all in danger," and she locked the fingers of her nervously swinging hands in front of her. "This danger is not from the many dead that have risen, nor the secrets that have surfaced with them, nor from the mist that is slowly engulfing our town…the danger comes from us.

"I know the name you once gave me, The Bitch of The Pulpit," and she could hear a voice regale that she *still was*, and she had to laugh slightly at that herself. "Well, nothing has changed! But what I am bitching about now *is* me. Sometimes, when you have checked the faults of everyone around you, you have to ultimately check yourself."

A small surge of *Amen's* went out.

"We all have a tiny bitch in us, just waiting for someone else to push that button," and she paused as a dark skinned girl of about twelve-years old came towards the stage. She reached her hand out, and in it was a bottle of water. Mildred smiled, and lowered herself to take the cool plastic in her hands. "Thanks," she said, before taking a sip.

"You're welcome, First Lady," said the child, with a smile that seemed to too large for her face.

Mildred smiled back, and then faced the mic again. "That tiny bitch can come in many forms – and God can supply answers to dealing with it. If it is a Lonely Bitch eating you into depression, then you can be supplied a spouse. If it is a Drug Bitch pushing you into a destructive solitude, then He can provide you with the support group you never imagined. If it is a Food Bitch swelling you into a bloated mess, then He can cause the refrigerator to suddenly go out."

Slight laughter.

Mildred then lowered her voice; her eyes cast at the stage, "But here in this town, we have been dealing with a Grieving Bitch. Grief is a funny thing, because so many other bitches can come out of it. Guilt, Shame, Anger, Depression, can all come from the passing of a loved one; and even the not-so-loved. Sometimes you grieve for the loss of a loved one, and sometimes you grieve from the guilt of sending a loved one to the grave. God is not sure how to handle a Bitch like this, because it is not caused by anything we lack as human beings; it is a by-product from being detached from a human spirit. We are all connected in this world, and there is pain when that attachment is broken. It can paralyze us if we let it. It can cause us to turn inward. It can cause us to stop moving, to stop accomplishing, and it can not only stop us from enjoying what our higher power can bless us with, but also stops us from blessing the world through Him.

"Today that has to end; or Crest Hill County will be dealt with severely and permanently. God is very angry today!"

From behind the curtain, Maya watched; she smiled. She could see the hate begin to slide away from Mildred, and an understanding wash over her. In a flood of light and color, her words banded out across the congregation like a spray – melding and bonding with the emotions of others – causing some to really listen to her; and in turn, their emotions rippled out.

Maya saw what was happening, but it was not happening fast enough. She would have to walk out unto that stage, and initiate her role in all of this; a thing many would not understand, and many would fear. She wished there was any other way, but as she lifted her head slightly, she remembered the emotion of panic…because the scent of honey and the taste of sweet milk, became very strong in the air…very, very strong.

Part IV

Eric paced throughout the house, thinking that he would just have to try again this morning; try to mend the broken relationship with his son, Timothy.

They had been out last night for a casual drive – the mist seeming to clear a decent path on the road. Timothy was on edge, as he fingered the vents on the dashboard. The day he walked out on his wife and children, was very fresh in his son's mind. He tried talking to his son, discuss the latest pop songs, the new dances, anything. Timothy only replied with grunts and whimpers.

When they returned to the house, Timothy snapped his seatbelt loose, flung open the door, ran into the house, and locked himself in his room. Eric remained in his seat as a rush of feelings overwhelmed him to the point of sorrow. Erica came out to him, dressed in nothing more than a tank top and baggy jeans (his jeans), and reassured him that she would talk to their son later, and assure him that she had forgiven his father, and he should do the same.

He strode from the truck like spilled molasses, and allowed his wife to guide him up the stairs. As soon as she opened the door, something struck him. *Maya had been here*!

He could feel the remnants of her spirit as a scent on the air; a warm, slow-moving scent that lingered before fading. That meant there was some heated altercation at the time of her visit. Erica mentioned nothing of it the entire evening, and soon she and his son was fast asleep, while he sat at the kitchen table, looking beyond the window at the ever-curling mist spinning its thin haze along the midnight skies. Does the thinness mean the bulk of it has already moved within the center of town? Does it only mean because he was here, that it wasn't as strong? Does it mean that most of the townspeople in this part of town now slept the eternal sleep? With Maya having had returned to the living, it had to all mean something. Maya was never to have returned.

Eric sat there staring at the mist, until late night surrendered to early morning; and the mist seemed to grow stronger. He walked outside, toward the back of the house, and sat on his son's tire swing; the air crisp against his skin, the mist lifted and fell with greater velocity, and homes once viewed only a few yards away, had become lost to its whiteness. If he still possessed a heart, it would have surely been beating out of his chest. This mist was crashing upon the town like a tsunami, and its momentum could only mean that they had failed. No wonder his flesh was coming alive with feeling and emotions. Soon, he would forget what death was like, and his flesh would once again be the ruler of his soul. This made him very, very, sad.

Then he heard the screams.

It frightened him, for that sound could only mean that the mist was lashing out at the city; it was strong enough to claim many, to silence them, to sentence them to their fate. The sound caused him to cower to the ground, covering his ears to escape the resonance; and for a moment – he actually fell asleep.

That is why he paced the floor so frantically this morning, waiting for his son to get dressed, while the others slept; because this drive may very well be his last chance to get it right with his son, to lift the shadow of hatred, and replace it with a cloak of forgiveness.

Then, he would be able to confront his sister Mildred, for her hate of him ran very dark.

The door to Timothy's room finally opened, and the young man stepped out in a large button-down shirt which draped to his knees; the front of which was covered entirely by some splashy embroidered design. His jeans were dark, the ends folded up against his gym shoes – both also garnished in colorful stitching and patchwork. If not for the curls of brown hair that fell past the shade of his hat, Eric would have to question the young teenager emerging from the room as his son. But he knew that face. He also knew the disposition: with his dragging feet, limp shoulders, and lowered head. Without so much as a word, Timothy walked past his father and out the door.

The silence remained as they headed out on the road. Although they were heading nowhere in particular, Eric was pleased.

"Why do you hate me, Timothy?" Eric asked, as he realized that small talk was of no interest to a young man thrust suddenly into adult situations. "Is it because I left your mother?"

After a moment of hesitation, he answered, "No."

Eric wasn't expecting that answer, but he proceeded along the same mode of inquiry, "Then why do you hate me so much, Timothy?"

Timothy huffed through his nostrils, as if reluctantly giving in to the act of conversation, "I hate you for not being there for me."

Eric didn't reply. There was nothing he could say about his selfish act of abandonment – for his wanting a world of adventure at their expense. "Go on Timothy. It's all right."

Timothy uncrossed his arms, and looked up nervously at his father past the brim of his hat. His eyes were intense, and his lips pressed close against each other, "I hate you for not helping me with my geography homework this year. I hate you for not telling me how to talk to Maria Buckley, who keeps tossing skipping rocks at me. I hate you for not trying to beat my high score on my *Grand Theft Auto* game. I hate you for not being there to talk to me when my little brother died."

He stopped there, and Eric continued to watch the road ahead being swallowed up by the hood of his car. "You're right, Timothy. I would hate myself for that too."

Timothy looked curiously at his father. "You would?"

Eric nodded. "Yep, I would hate me too. I wish I could have done all those great things with you. I'm gonna miss those things. I was scared, Timothy. I was scared when I left you and your mother, believe me I was, but that kind of fear can scare you so much, that you just don't know what to do to stop it."

"You're supposed to just talk to an adult," Timothy replied, as he kicked his feet under the dashboard. "That's what I remember you telling me to do when I was scared about something. Why can't you just follow your own advice?"

And so the little man can speak, Eric thought, looking at the crossness of his sons eyes – the expression was at least an expression of s*omething!* "I tried following that advice once Timothy, but I waited too long to listen to myself, I guess."

"I guess," Timothy repeated, pulling the bib of his cap down even further on his head, as he turned to glance out the window at his own reflection.

"Maria Buckley...I would say she likes you."

"*What?*" Timothy spoke, turning to look at his father questioningly.

Eric leaned his shoulders back; confidence rising in him. "It's obvious that Maria Buckley likes you, that's *what*."

"She does not!" he said, tone laced with embarrassment.

"Does so," Eric affirmed with smiling lips. He could hear his son's feet bounce faster against the underside of the glove compartment panel – there was more gaiety in it this time – so he ignored it, and watched the road open up to him, and the mist revealing a town vacant of life. Many shops closed, drawn curtains on the city banks, car wash gated, homes silent but harboring moving shadows behind their drapes.

Then there was of course, the screaming.

"How do you know she likes me?" Timothy asked.

He glanced at his son, as he continued into town. Timothy appeared not to notice the human wailing that blew through the wind. "Those aren't stones she's throwing at you, they are hardened kisses."

The feet kicking stopped. "She don't like me...and I know what stones feel like."

Eric could feel something of the old resentful Timothy shed away a little. He could also feel something changing within himself suddenly; like a tiny itch at the back of his neck. "Girls are like that sometimes. She wants to get your attention."

"Even after I called her a stupid girl?"

"Especially, after calling her a stupid girl," Eric said, noticing they were passing by the towns partially renovated strip mall; he remembered the scent of the pizza place was always strong here. There was no scent today.

"Well, I still think she's stupid," Timothy said, as he reached into his pocket to pull out a small black plastic device.

Eric glanced at it just in time to see it light up with a small television screen, and the name PlayStation was displayed on its front. "Is that some sort of game? Is that the one you wanted me to play with you?"

Timothy looked at his father, and slowly shook his head, then returned his eyes back on his game, "No, this is too small. I was talking about the big one at home. "

"I'm sure I could still beat that high score of yours at home," Eric said, still amazed at the desertedness of the town.

"Against Resident Evil? I doubt it, but it would have been fun seeing you try though. You don't know how to fight zombies."

"Well, they're dead, I'm dead, so what's the difference?"

"You're funny," Timothy said, smiling slightly.

Then Eric felt it again; that itching. He looked at his son, who had been staring at him, but suddenly veered his eyes away, "You wanna play later, when we get back home today?"

"I guess," Eric replied playfully.

"I kick dead folk butt, whether they are trying to take over a planet, or driving a pickup truck."

The itch returned.

Eric then realized what he was feeling.

He was feeling forgiveness.

Timothy was starting to forgive him, and the by-product of that was the itching, and as Eric noticed his hands on the steering wheel, the lightness of them, he realized that more was happening besides the miniscule sensations traveling along his flesh.

"And you know what else dad?"

"What was that Timothy?"

"I'm sorry I yelled at you earlier."

There was a short silence, as they both seemed to take in this new bonding. Eric looked at his arms, and they rippled a bit, and dark patches were beginning to appear – his skin was looking almost *opaque*. Without realizing it, Timothy was freeing him!

"I was just mad caused I missed you being around the house. Mom doesn't talk to me like you used to. Eric Jr. was always her favorite."

Eric had always thought that was the case with his wife, he pondered, just as he was passing by one of the town's high schools. Unlike the other parking lots in town, this one was nearly full – and he could feel that inside were many more people than the amount of cars reflected. He could not figure out what sort of gathering would be happening there.

Then he felt the presence of Maya, and he knew.

She was gathering the town for one last try at saving it. He didn't have much time himself, and maybe that's why he didn't get a reading on what was happening; his own personal agenda with his son was happening.

"Dad!" Timothy said, alarmed. He had dropped his game in his lap, and was pushing back on his seat, holding the strap of his seatbelt tightly. "What's happening to you?"

Eric pulled the car over when he noticed the skin of his fingers, and how the color was changing from an oak brown, to something more muddled; a mixture of sorts, as if his flesh were covered in tiny glass bubbles. "I may be going back home, Timothy."

"And this is how God does it, by ringing your body?"

Eric suppressed his laughter. "No. I'm afraid; this is his way of slowly taking me back."

Timothy let go of the strap; his hands shaking. "No! Not again. You can't leave again!"

"It has to be this way, Timothy," Eric said, although he could see a bit of Timothy's resentment returning, he knew it would be alright.

"But what about our game? I won't let you go."

Eric knew the weakness of that last statement, and felt for his son. "I am not leaving yet, and we will have plenty of time for you to beat me at your own game"

Timothy quickly wiped away a tear, as if he didn't want his dad to see it. "When does it happen then? When do you leave?"

I really don't know, Timothy," Eric said, until he could think of something better to say. He started the truck up again, and as he pulled away from the curb, he began to generate an idea. "When do you kids start learning to drive these days?"

There was a slight hesitation before Timothy answered, "About sixteen, I guess."

"Well, that's a shame," Eric said, as he eased slowly down the street. "When you get back to school, the guys are gonna be jealous to find out that you've learned to drive before they did."

"Huh?" Timothy questioned, as he began to withdraw once more, folding his arms. "But I can't drive yet."

"Take your seat belt off."

"You're still driving. I'm not supposed to do that," Timothy replied.

Eric looked at his son, and sensed his fear. "It will be okay, I promise. I am going really, really slow…nothing like the speed this truck was doing when your brother was in the car."

Timothy was silent.

"You can trust me Timothy. I won't let anything happen to you." There continued a short silence. "Remember us zombies have special abilities that you living folks just don't have."

Timothy glanced in his father's direction, and realized that while his father was talking to him, while the truck was moving, that his dad's eyes had not moved from looking directly at him.

"Trust me Timothy."

And as Timothy looked out at the road, the vehicle not teetering in the least, the direction was straight, slow, and cautious; all the while Eric's eyes were not on the road – and Timothy realized that yes, yes indeed, there was nothing to do but trust this man.

And with that, he unhinged his seatbelt.

"Now slide over next to me," Eric said, the tingling in his body had doubled in its intensity. His spirit was fighting against his flesh now, yearning to be free.

Timothy idled up next to his father; despite his instincts telling him to unlock the door, dip into this crazy fog, and run the hell away – he didn't…he wouldn't. The very thought of running away was such an ugly thing to him now. "What are you gonna do?" He asked, as he sat on the division that separated his seat from his father's.

"I really won't be doing anything, but I do want you to lean in closer, and try to grab the wheel here by placing your hand over mine. Do it really,

really slow, do you understand?"

"I do," Timothy said, looking up at his father, who finally relinquished his sideward gaze, and began to look once again back upon the road. He reached out with one hand, attempting to grab his father's hand, encase his own around the thick knuckles and slightly hairy fingers, of a man who digits looked like slivers of browned toast. But as he tried to place his hand atop his father's, something happened.

His hand passed though!

He jerked it back, and nearly jumped to the other side of the seat. "What the hell!"

"Listen, don't be scared," Eric said quickly. "This is what's supposed to happen, Timothy. Just think of me as a ghost, not a scary one, but just one that happens to be your dad."

Timothy didn't know if he wanted to think that way – or if he even wanted to hear it at all.

"Now try it again," Eric said, his voice almost pleading. "Try it again, and scoot all the way over this time. Close your eyes if you think that would help, but be brave, son. I need that from you. Be brave."

And so, he did. Timothy closed his eyes, moved over, reached out his hand, and grabbed the steering wheel. His body felt strange, as if there was a snap of coolness touching his skin, like pieces of cooled cotton rolling over him, and on the other side of that cotton, was warmth like heated oil. Still, he continued to slide over into his father's seat, his hands gripping the steering wheel tighter this time, the feel of the his father's fingers was like leather. He pried open one eye, to watch the misty plumes buffet against the windshield, like an aircraft breaking the cumulus. It both frightened and excited him.

"Are you okay?" came his father's voice.

"Yea, this is cool…" he started to say, thinking for some reason, that his father may have materialized in the seat next to him, and the voice he heard, was not afar, but coming from within him – speaking his thoughts. So he opened his eyes fully, and what he saw he could not register past his own senses.

He lay *inside* his father, as if he had slipped into gelatin.

"Don't think, just keep driving. I can guide your hands," Eric said, as the car made a gradual turn down a street. "I want to spend this time teaching you how to drive, if you'll let me."

Timothy continued to look out at the road, his feet moving within his father's, barely touching the pedal, yet through his father's legs, it felt as if he was. It was as if he'd suddenly had his father's weight, his father's height, and his father's reflexes. "I'll let you," Timothy finally said.

"Great. Next destination…home," Eric said. He was glad for this moment. It could not have been any better, for it was almost near its end…the end would come when Mildred finally forgave him.

For now, he was lost in the act of teaching his eldest son to drive.

Part V

Maya watched Mildred though the separation in the curtain.

The sermon was good. She had never known that Mildred retained such a fire for the gospel – but then again, perhaps that inferno had always lain within her, fueled by her need and her greed.

But today there was a change.

Today there would be many changes for the people in this town. Maya understood now, that her purpose on earth had come to its end when she died – and from there another purpose had begun. She had always been the example of controversy. A young girl, born of a white European mother and coloured Afrikan father. She had always been the butt of ridicule; a curse in some eyes.

Kids taunted her at school, not sure how to treat her once they'd suspected her heritage. The black kids were scared of her, as if she were a cleverly disguised spy, and the white kids were distant from her as if her genes were somehow contagious and dirty. *Johannesburg* was not a place used to change in this era; they feared what they could not label.

When she was older, college wasn't that much different. The young men and women at the *University of Witwatersrand* were like most kids in the universities around the world; distrusting of what they couldn't pigeonhole. Maya had a tough time even defining herself during these trying times, as if she could feel the two races of her past course through her veins like ice water. During the family gatherings, especially the "Summer Christmas", she would look out at the many shades of her family tree, smelling the meat simmer on the outdoor brille, and be subdued in a trance that had always felt surreal – as if she were watching the telly in 3D.

That was why being a missionary had become her hidden passion; her chance at being a part of something great, to be a part of God's bigger plan, and to make a difference to those who also felt discarded. She began feeding the poor in her city, gaining their trust, watching as her steady white hands met their dark shaky one. At first, she was scorned – as if she were trying to make heaven-points by catering to the poor…and then they heard of her parents. She was slowly respected. The look of arrogance they thought she'd displayed past her cloudy eyes, was recognized as pain, a shared pain.

The difference with Maya, was that she made no excuses for her shared race, and stood up for the coloured's as well as her white people – her love or hate was not skin based. This gave her the ability to become a world missionary, spreading the Word, and standing on the Truth, all truth. Instead of crumbling through ridicule, she took it as a chance to educate the ignorant.

Then she arrived in the United States.

They too were not ready for the different. The *United* States; had always seemed a misnomer. Many of the Blacks in the States barely knew where Africa was on the map, not to mention that there could be white Afrikaans flourishing on its southern most coast. Some knew of the racial prejudice that nearly crippled that nation – had seemed so similar to their own struggle, only difference was that in Africa, the children didn't have to read it in a history book. The wounds were still very fresh. America seemed to close itself off from the slavery of other countries, as easily as its very own history.

She was thwarted by a nation which appeared so divided; where wealth and poverty would lead you to believe that two whole countries meshed onto one soil. Then her travels took her to Crest Hill County – where her life would change.

She fell in love with the quaintness of this roadside town, and once she set foot on the soil, there was a sense of home that she had never felt – but had long since missed. There was a pull on her that would not go away. Her missionary church was on their way to *Bowling,* Illinois, when they passed through Crest Hill, and it was the utter diversity of the town that caused her team to make a stopover that lasted a few short days. It was also the powerful presence of God dwelling in that place – and a pastor of immense anointing that caused her full spirit to skip a beat. Pastor Reynolds had captured her before she had even known his name.

Sitting in his church one Sunday, she could not stop looking at him, not stop being amazed at his congregation, not stop feeling a warmth like a blanket enveloping her; sooth her, calm her, ease her…and at the same time, frighten her. She could feel a grief like non other shrouded underneath this place like an invisible film. *A town enslaved within itself;* is what she remembered thinking. Even before the rumor had reached her ears about the loss this town took when the school bus exploded, she knew she would be unable to leave. Crest Hill County would need her. It would need her to loosen this sorrow, which clung to these borders like tacked gum on the bottom of a shoe. Most towns grew out of their grief, but Crest Hill County was drowning in it.

Finally, when she reached the gravesite of the town, she then realized that she would never leave. The rows of tombstones were like an endless parade of dominos stuck in the sand. She stared out at that land, with Carl standing silently behind her, and he spoke only once when he laid a soft hand on her shoulder, "You are home."

Yes, she was. She was taken in by one of the mothers of the group she traveled with, and which when she transitioned, she was able to pass the home unto her. She found a purpose in the church as the piano player and taught the Sunday school – the children loved her. Mildred was another story. The resentment was quick, and the scorn she exhibited to Luther was intense; she was on him like a thumb to ground sugar; and Maya grew closer to him like sugar on Maya's tongue.

And the people of this town were drawn to her story, her struggles, and her victories. They were stories like none they had ever heard, and it made them forget their problems for a moment, their grief, their sorrow.

It had only been hidden, until her death, where it resurged like pressed oil, only to bubble up through the earth. She had only died little over a week ago, and the town had taken back its sorrow two-fold. It was Heaven's way of saying, "They are fooling themselves of the healing, because they are only licking the wound."

And now…

…Mildred was nearing the end of her speech, and it was time they were once again reunited with a grief they thought had passed. She took a few steps forward, parted the curtain, and stepped out onto the stage.

A most heavy stillness filled the church.

It was of no surprise to Maya; considering she had only died little more than a week ago.

She could feel the intense heat in the room as it tickled her skin, and she sensed many eyes discovering her. She walked up closer behind Mildred, who noticed a lull in the shared voiced in the room, and realized Maya had entered the stage.

Mildred began to step aside to allow Maya the mike, but Maya held her shoulder – and Mildred stood her ground.

"Hello everyone," Maya began, amazingly her voice carried throughout the room. "Many of you know who I am, and many do not. I am Maya Ohlms. I died little more than a week ago. I am here to try and save this town.

She paused.

A wind blew past the church doors.

Someone coughed.

Pockets of voices began to rumble.

A few cried aloud.

"Many of you in this room have either lost someone because of death, or are losing them because of what appears to be a most forced slumber that paralyzes the body. It is not a normal slumber. It is the deep sleep of impending death."

More murmurs.

Deep sighs of surprise.

"Many of your loved ones are frozen in a state that appears very unnatural, and you're scared, don't be. The answer lies in your loved ones that are still here. The risen dead that may be standing right by your side. I am going to ask you to come up to this stage, grab this mike, and to let them go. I am going to ask you to forgive them. I am going to ask you to say goodbye. In many cases, I am going to ask you to forgive yourself – for your thoughts have not always been pure, and many of your actions have resulted in the death you see before you. This will be your last moment to give and get respect – for this will be the only chance that the deceased will hear what you have to say."

Silence again.

"Today is the last day you will have to do this. The mist outside, is so much more than you may think. It wants you to die – the living and the dead – coexisting in this town forever, while shutting you off from the rest of the world. That world will soon forget you, and you will be neither dead nor alive to them. You will simply not exist.

Fear.

"I want you to exist. I want you to exist. I want you to want to exist. I want you to understand that it is you who are able to push back this mist. It will soon seep into this church, the school, wherever you hear the sound of my voice, and capture you all."

She tried not to cause a panic, but the crowd began to lose control, to back away, to stop listening, and some attempted – tested – the strength of the doors; calculating how fast they would have to run.

"Stop!" Maya shouted, her arms calmly at her sides, but her voice shook the walls. The lights flickered. Knees began to bend, to surrender to prayer. She lowered her tone. "You can't escape this…and for that I am sorry. There is no place left to run. You have run from your pain for the last time. Your purpose in life is being stopped by your grief in the now. If you stop your purpose, you stop your existence. The more of you that step up to this mic, and speak from your heart…the freer you will be, and the closer you will come to freeing this town. "So who will be the first?"

And for a moment not a foot moved…until the shuffle of one.

Maya looked down to see a tiny Hispanic woman slowly edging her way towards the stage, her eyes focused on the staircase as if that were her only destination, as if no one else was in her way. Her body shook like a winded flag, and as the press of bodies released her from their shadowy cloak, Maya began to recognize this frail woman; Rosy Aguilla was her name. Her daughter had returned from the grave: Franchesca Aguilla, who drowned in the river just outside of town when she and her friends had decided to create a makeshift raft - it was no match for the river on that cold winter night. Franchesca was a beautiful child, only twenty-six when she died; eyes large and full of expression, with a lean grace about her as if she only attracted good. She now stood behind Rosy, guiding her mother's steps, as if her mother hadn't walked since her death. But this was their bond, their routine, their way of justifying the idea that they needed each other.

She must have just now realized the truth.

Rosy wore, as she most often did, the color of her name, and now she was donned in a flowing pink dress that billowed around her lean frame like a rose turned upside-down. Francesca shed tears, running down fresh makeup, as she ascended the steps in a stunning black dress. These two came outfitted for their last goodbye.

There were tears in Rosie's eyes as she reached for the mike stand, and pulled it towards her. She was much shorter than Mildred, so Mildred lowered the stand to meet Rosie's needs. Rosy continued to allow her tears to flow across her cheeks, as if they had been flowing for so long that she had become numb to their existence.

She sighed, long and heavy, and closed her eyes. "This is very hard," she said. "My husband died a while ago, but left my wonderful Francesca as a gift to me in my final chance for motherhood." She opened her eyes to look at her daughter, "It hurts to see you at this time *miha*, because I love you so much, I have missed you so much, and I suppose I will be missing you greatly once again."

She paused, and Francesca nodded her acknowledgement.

"You're doing great, Rosy," Maya said, handing the woman a glass of water – where no glass had appeared before.

She sipped. "I don't know if I can do this."

"Of course you can," Maya assured. "Just keep looking at your daughter. Just keep remembering that she'll be the first awaiting your entrance into the afterlife. This is only the beginning of your journey together. You're doing great."

Rosy smiled, and locked her eyes on her daughter. "I guess all that I have to say now to my wonderful daughter is…" and on this last part she choked a little, but the words managed to spray out in the tiniest audible tone, "…is goodbye."

Then someone screamed.

Maya looked to the front of the church, and there was a swelling of mist at the door, as if it had seeped through the wood. People were pressing against each other to back away – the dead however, stood their ground, as fear…actual fear, was registered too in their faces.

Rosy inhaled, but not from what was happening at the front of the church, but from what was happening to her daughter. Her skin seemed to buckle, the pores to get bigger, and her skin tone to become translucent. "You will be fine back in Heaven, my child," Rosy said through a tight throat.

"Yes, I will be *mi madre*," Francesca said, fanning out her dress. "I will always love you," were the last words she said…before she disappeared.

Rosy looked up at Maya, her eyes yearning yet free, "Is she forever gone?"

"Yes, until you meet again when it is your time."

She lowered her head; her shoulders shaking. "Thank you for ending this pain." Rosy said, and then left the stage.

Then slowly, another person came up…

…and then another.

…and then another.

…and then Maya walked up to the mic, because the time had come.

She'd positioned herself to speak – but a scream erupted through the air, shaking the very paint on the roof. It was quickly followed by another one just as menacing, just as jarring.

Maya didn't have to ask questions to see what had happened, because as she looked out amongst the back pew she could see that the mist had eased its way through the framing of the door, and was swelling within the church; four members had already been engulfed in its smoky grip, as others crowded away from it in terror.

"Oh my God! The end is near!" One man near the door screamed, and in his hysteria, he pushed past the parishioners, pulled the door open, and ran out into the mist.

"No!" shouted Maya, her arms reaching out as if that very act were enough to pull the man back – it didn't. As her arm lowered in defeat, she whispered, "You'll die…you'll die."

But she knew it was far too late once an individual was caught in the thick of it…to survive, to see, to move, to think – all these reactions would collide and confuse like a house of mirrors. She could feel the energy from the crowd; unhindered, unchecked, untamed – they all seemed to want to rush into the unknown too.

"Move closer to the stage everyone – crowd in," Maya's voiced boomed through the air. "Everyone within the sound of my voice, here and everywhere, do not go into the mist, do not let its temptation tease you, do not be fooled by its seemingly innocent taste and smell – it will eventually kill you if you succumb to it. Keep your eyes on me."

And they did. Maya then lowered her head, and things began to change.

Her body began to glow, and move, and seemed to pull away from itself as if it were made of elastic. It stretched and pulled, until there sounded a…SNAP!

And two Maya's appeared where one once stood.

The congregation was in awe.

"Devilment!" someone shouted.

The Maya near the mic held up her hand. "No, that is not the case – this is God's will.

"I know this looks very odd to some, very frightening to many, and very miraculous to others, but this has to be done. Many in this town will begin to awaken as more of you come up here to confess. They will be confused, they will be scared, but worse of all, they will still be dwelling in the mist. I have to guide them away from it, transport them to safer dwellings, allow the spirits of this town to once again be strong, and cause the mist to fall back. So many of me are needed to accomplish this task, and from this point onward, that is what you are going to see."

And she paused, holding tight to her stomach, as her body went through yet another transformation, and another Maya appeared and disappeared before the people's eyes.

"But the mist is strong. It will want to fight back. It too will want to survive…for it is of a being most familiar, yet a stranger to us all. Now hurry…who will step up to the mic next?"

Slowly another person walked up.

Mildred managed to ask Maya, "Are you afraid?"

Maya smiled. "No, Mildred, I am not. Are you?"

She seemed to think about this. "I am not sure what I feel."

"That's good enough for me."

Chapter 20

Part 1

Lisa

She was tired.

More tired than she had every felt in her life.

Home after home, family after family, speech after speech – it became harder and harder to convince people of the situation that the town was in, harder to tell them what was affecting their mesmerized loved-one, and harder and harder to get them to accept it and get out of the house to be transported to the church, or to the school, or to wherever. She was very tired from the effort of the communication, and the effort it took to travel through the mist, and again she was transported through the mist and found herself in front of yet another door.

It was unlocked.

Inside, smoke had filled the hallways and many of the rooms. There was a sunken living room, and Lisa could see a baby grand piano sitting in the center on a small stage, surrounded by walls where there hung intricate oriental rugs.

Lisa stared at the tiny billowing clouds that buffeted along the floor, where in the center sat a large white sofa, glass coffee table, a 60inch flat-screen television, and the homeowner: Rodney Dixon – a man of brown skin and short curly hair, who was now sitting on the floor, his body leaning towards the edge of the sofa where his wife lay; Shelly Dixon, a beautiful woman now in a deep sleep. She was very petite, with dark skin, and a tiny band of curls wrapped about her head like copper coils. Rodney was sobbing heavily, as he sat there rubbing his wife's arm, and it stilled Lisa, moved her, and also brought back the memory of Shelly's sister; Lorraine Ashby – and the horrible timing of her death.

It was a simple tale of a loving couple who met in high school, destined to be married. It was also the tale of devoted sisters, who loved each other; each of them yearned for the others happiness. That tale took a swift turn when Rodney and Shelly finally were about to wed, and Ashby decided to tie tin cans to the couple's car at the onset of the wedding, and the accident occurred. She was a tall, pretty girl, with thick lips and large eyes; a fawn in human form. Her body suddenly going into convulsions at that moment a car was coming. To have a wedding and a funeral in the same month was devastating. The aneurism would have ended her anyway, but the car hitting her ended her beauty.

Lisa remained silent as she looked at Dixon coaxing his wife. She also noted the amount of mist in the apartment, which seemed quite a lot. This meant that the departed Lorrain must have left, and the mist overtook her sister.

Lisa decided that she had stood aloof enough and began to descend the steps into the living room, when she heard a voice at her rear.

"Lisa? Lisa don't go down there just yet."

When Lisa turned around, it was as if a door had smacked her in the face; Lorraine was alive, and standing directly behind her – through a mist as thick as a white wall.

The dead could repel the mist, and yet for Lorraine…it didn't!

It was surely a sign of the end.

Benny

He looked into Jason's deep blue eyes, and watched a trickle of sweat dance from his forehead, and across his thin blonde eyebrow. It was surprising to see that the dead could get so nervous. Of course, Benny thought, he too might have been nervous at the proposal he just issued his deceased lover:

Benny wanted just one long kiss from Jason, before attempting to let him go.

Jason was opposed to such a request, because it would solve nothing; either Benny forgave and forgot him, or he didn't – it was just that simple. But apprehension turned to curiosity, which was then followed by a human longing that Jason had forgot existed. So Jason agreed, and now stood waiting, with mouth pursed and eyes anticipating, for a kiss whose meaning and memory he had long forgotten.

"You look scared, Jason. You have kissed me before, so there is nothing to fear," Benny said, stepping closer.

"I'm not afraid Benny," his quivering voice lied. "I just want you to keep your word."

Benny advanced closer and gently reached up to touch Jason's shoulder. "Don't worry, I'll keep my word," and he moved his hand from Jason's shoulder, gliding it along his neck, and resting it just under his chin. The skin was amazingly smooth, and slightly cool. "But maybe fear is valid, because a kiss can be a powerful thing."

Jason believed this to be true too.

"Do you remember the first time we kissed?" Benny said, as his fingers left the underside of Jason's chin, travelled up and caressed the edge of his bottom lip, "We were on that cruise ship, with the wind coming off the ocean and tussling our hair. We wore it long back then, and I felt caught up in some live-Hollywood movie. People were all around us, talking, asking directions, playing games, with children running and screaming."

"And you turned around and shouted, 'Can the world just be silent for a moment!'. It was the funniest thing," Jason said, eyes glancing aloft as his mind reeled back into that recollection. "We had just met maybe two hours, and I thought you were insane, but all the more attractive."

"And it worked. The world became totally silent for us," Benny said, using his other hand to pull at the buttons on Jason's shirt."

"It did seem that way." Jason lowered his eyes to stare into Benny's.

"It was amazing," Benny said, slipping a finger past one of the buttons on Jason's shirt to feel hair on his chest.

Jason felt that he should reach up and pull his fingers away, but he ached for the warmth and the connection. He found himself breathing heavily through lungs that no longer needed air...but all the same took his breath away.

"Do you know how much I've missed you Jason? Do you have any idea?" He smiled, looking up at Jason, his fingers undoing a few more buttons until his full chest was exposed. He inched in closer, "Of course you know...you've always known." He then moved his hands down further, past his ribs, past his torso, past his hips, to rest on a spot were sunlight rarely visited. Something stirred. "I can feel that you have missed me too."

He was becoming more human, Jason feared. There was a slight movement of his member that surprised him; and he allowed the feeling to course through him, massage the underside of his flesh. Benny edged closer. Jason could feel his breath fall against his mouth, teasing him, causing such a hunger that Jason could no longer remain unmoved; and he pushed himself forward slightly to press his lips against Benny's. Hunger satiated.

Benny flung his arms up and around the neck of Benny – and just like the boat – the world disappeared in a vacuum where only they existed. Then Benny closed his eyes, his lips burning, his body hot, and suddenly, unexpectedly, his shoulders began to bear down as if a great weight had saddled them...and that pressure caused him to realize that he was being pulled away.

To his alarm he was being flung to the floor, and when he reopened *his* eyes, there were another pair staring back at him; one with goggles and a mask, the smell of dirt and dust infused his nostrils, as he looked at a man who was donned in boots and a rain coat. "Oh my God!"

"Be calm," Jason said, from behind this stranger. "It is Harold."

"Harold?" Benny repeated, scuttling back on his heels.

There was no response from this person, who only reached up to his face – amidst the sound of metal unsnapping, and rubber pulling. The mask was cast aside, and yes, there stood Harold before him, his face a twisted mess, and his hair a matted cast against his forehead.

"Harold!" Jason said, running past them both, "You left the door open."

And before Jason had a chance to close it, Benny could see the horror that lay beyond his threshold: the mist had gathered in the hallway to such a degree, that the very walls of the corridor were hidden. Then the door closed.

"What the hell is wrong with you Benny? Did I see what I thought I saw...again!?" Harold asked, as he began to take off his rain slicker.

"What are you doing here?" Jason asked. He walked past Harold to face him, but kept an eye on Benny, who appeared to be in shock, perhaps at what he saw in the hallway.

Harold turned his poison towards Jason, "What do you mean, what am I doing here? I am alive, I am his lover, I have the key, and I belong here!" He turned back to Benny, stepping up to him, and gently bringing him to his feet. He leaned in to speak to him, "What sort of spell has this zombie put on you, Benny? Have you even taken a look outside your window? Do you know what is happening around Crest Hill County? I thought he was trying to get back to

Hell, or wherever he came from, and I find you here locking lips with him. This is disgusting, Benny. Snap out of this."

Benny shook his head, and leaned back against the wall. "I don't want to hear anything from you Harold," he shockingly said, and pushed Harold squarely in the chest. "This is your fault you know. How dare you come in here demanding answers…demanding anything."

"Benny!" Jason said, stepping up between the two of them. "We can't accomplish anything this way."

Benny swung his arm out, knocking Jason aside, "No. I want him out of here. I want this killer to leave my house," he said, and rushed at Harold again.

Harold tried his best to fend off Benny's advancing blows; unsuccessful attempts to grapple his wrists, "I'm trying to help you, Benny."

"Then help yourself to the door. Get out," Benny said, as he reached out to take hold of Benny with one rapid hand movement, and with another was able to reopen the door.

"Benny, I'm sure we can talk about this together," Jason pleaded from behind. He was still dealing with the blow he had taken from Benny, and rubbed at it – there was pain there. Pain was something he hadn't had to deal with in a very long time.

Benny was like a wild animal; clawing and pushing Harold back toward the hallway. "I'm tired of all this talking. I am tired of all this thinking. I can't take this anymore."

"Benny. The fog out there! I can't go out there!"

"I don't want to hear it. How dare you use your key to barge in on us. This was to be something special," and then Benny did another unexpected thing…he punched Harold in the stomach.

Harold doubled-over, stunned, and was about to fall forward, but to his dismay and unbelief, the strands of mist behind him seemed to snag at his arms, pulling him in that direction, and before he knew it, he was back in the hallway – unmasked!

Benny closed the door.

He also ignored the frantic knocking that followed.

"What's happened to you Benny?" Jason said, rushing towards the door.

Benny held up his fists, and there was genuine fear in Jason as he looked upon those mallets. "Don't you dare! Let him stay out there. Let him go back home where he should have been in the first place."

"Didn't you see the hallway, Benny? The mist is out there. It's covered the whole town. Harold can't go back home," Jason said, bravely stepping forward, and pushing Benny aside.

The knocking had stopped.

As Jason opened the door to look into the hallway, Benny went over to the windows at the far end of the condo, and through them, he could see just how thick this mist had become; folding and meshing like a sky filled with whip cream.

"Benny, get over here!" Jason yelled from behind.

Benny ran back towards the door; Jason was just outside of it, kneeling down. On the floor was a pair of boots, mud caked and black – Harold had fallen. "What's wrong with him?"

But Benny could answer that with his own eyes, as he saw the petrified form of Harold just lying there, horror in his opened eyes, his hand out and fist balled in his last attempt at knocking, the mist seeming to cocoon around him.

"The mist…" Jason began, "…has captured him. This is very serious. Without the dead near him, the powers of the mist can become very strong."

"Well, drag him back inside!" Benny pleaded.

Jason stood. "It's much too late for that, Benny."

Then silently, and slowly, Jason nudged Benny back into the house, and gradually closed the door.

Jenna Reed

She sat quietly, with the taste of sweet bread cookies melting around her tongue. As she reached for more tea, she looked up at the other women sitting with her at the table: Ella – her deceased daughter, Tilly – her living granddaughter, and Kenneth – Tilly's deceased child and her grandson.

"Would you like some tea also?" Jenna asked, holding up the teapot. "There's plenty in here."

Tilly smiled nervously, "No grandma, I'm fine."

Ella sat next to Tilly, and knew that statement rang true. They were all fine. There was an encapsulated lull that infused their space. But beyond their space is what Ella was most concerned with, for outside she could feel the mist growing stronger, building in mass, a determined thing that was bent upon entry into this household.

"When is this going to be over, Ella," Tilly said, rubbing the forehead of her son as it snuggled against her bosom; his tiny hands grasped lovingly at the black tank top she wore.

"I don't exactly know, Tilly," Ella said, "A battle is happening out there; between the living and the dead, between resentment and forgiveness, between the spiritual and the fleshly, and I am not sure how it will all turn out."

"Let those that fight, fight, as long as we are safe in here," Jenna said, sipping at her tea, and unbeknownst to everyone, she had filled another cup, and was handing it to Tilly. "Here, I know you don't need it now, but it will be good for your nerves."

Tilly took the cup, and placed it on the table before her. "Thanks Grandma."

"You're welcome, baby," she replied, her eyes and voice longing, languid.

Then suddenly there was a violent knocking at the door. It was a forceful sound as if something of great weight had been thrown at it.

"I think we need to get out of this kitchen," Ella said, moving back in her seat and eyeing the door.

"What is it?" Tilly asked.

The door began to rattle at its hinges, and a definite scratching could be heard against its surface.

"Is the smoke causing that?" Tilly said then stood.

Jenna moved back in her seat. "I don't like what is going on here Ella."

Ella looked at the edges of the door, and she could see the ethereal threads of the mist sliding past the molding. "The mist is trying to get in I'm afraid. We have to leave this room and head towards the center of the house where we will be the safest.

As they began to move, a blaring light radiated around the door, then it flew open, and a plume of smoke billowed forward, and a body fell through, and unto the floor.

Jenna looked, but could not believe, "Maya?!"

Maya quickly rose to her feet, the whiteness of her dress melded and blended with the surrounding mist – and slowly separated as her garment took on more shape, its gold trim more detailed in its intricacies. She took a moment to see who was in the room, and rushed in their direction. "Ella is right. You all will be safer if you head towards the center of the house."

They all started to move from the kitchen, and into the hallway, but Jenna found her feet as resistant as her mind. "What are you doing here, Maya? Why are you alive for God's sake?"

Maya stopped, "I have been brought back to revive those that are sleeping. I don't have much time to explain all that is going on, but I do need you three to be safe. The mist is claiming more victims that I can awaken."

Maya pressed her palm against Jenna's back. She kept her ground. "Who Maya, are you going to awaken? I don't understand."

Maya looked back, and could see that the kitchen table was already being engulfed by the mist. "I'm going to awaken Nathan."

Jenna clasped her hands in front of her mouth. "What?"

"My goodness…that will be great," Tilly said, her eyes a convergence of tears and fear. "Isn't that great, Ella?"

Ella looked into Maya's eyes as she responded, "Yes, it is Tilly, but there are many more victims being claimed every second. Nathan could only be coming back to a condemned town."

"Everyone must stay in the hallway. Ella's presence will keep the mist at bay, but I have to leave now."

"Don't worry, I'll keep everyone safe, Maya, "Ella said, as she draped her arms around Tilly, and began to crouch unto the floor.

Then without a word, Maya began to walk back into the living room, letting her body be captured by the mist, as it pulled at her, drawing her slowly away…

…and that is also when Jenna found her body nervously tightening up, tension welling in her limbs. "I can't let this happen without me being there," she whispered.

Ella could sense something odd in Jenna's statement. "Mother, are you okay?"

She turned towards her daughter, tears in her eyes, "I can't stay here. I have to go with her." And once Jenna spoke those word; before Ella had a chance to react, she bounded on her feet, and ran towards Maya, and at the very moment she was about to disappear, Jenna reached out to touch the hem of her dress.

"No!" Ella yelled, but it was too late…Jenna was gone.

Erica

She knew she was being a bitch…but then again, she felt she had every right to be one.

"Erica, you have to listen to me," Eric pleaded, as he stood in the doorway of Erica's bedroom. His body, his flesh, his very existence was about to become a most distant memory; for as his son forgave him, his body responded – by slowly fading away, until at this instant, he looked quite unmistakably transparent.

Erica smiled, for this was playing out just as she had wanted it to. "I don't have to listen to anything," she said, while casually sitting back in her tiny loveseat, legs stretched out towards her bed, while she playfully fingered a bowl of popcorn in her lap. "Why don't you just close my door, and disappear."

"That's not funny, Erica," Eric said, while glancing between his reposed wife, and his 5-year old son – who sat on the bed, red overalls and stripped t-shirt, as he gleefully played some sort of pop-up game where he hit small animals back into the hole that their random heads protruded from. "Do you really hate me that much?"

She plucked a finger-full of popcorn in her mouth, and answered while chewing, "Everything is not always about you, Eric. Timothy was the one that was angry at you for leaving, and from what I can see, things are beginning to heal between you two. I believe the only reason you are still here, is that you have a few things to hash out with your sister. After that…*au revoir*," and she continued shoveling more kernels in her mouth.

She was right, he thought as he examined his hands – they were like a cloudy mass with protruding digits extending from them. But he knew what Erica was trying to achieve, and felt powerless against it. "Yes, my sister may be the very thing that sends me back to my afterlife – but it is still not right of you to desire that to happen, so you can continue to feel guilty about Eric Jr. here; so you can continue to force him to be with you for as long as you wish. I know it has always been your intent to have him back in your life."

She closed her eyes, and reached out to her side, where a small radio had been stationed on her dresser. She turned up the music slightly; her head swaying leisurely. "Yep, you have figured it all out my dearly departed…or shall I say *departing*, husband. While I did miss you during your vanishing act, I also desperately needed my son. This way, I have a little piece of you in him, and all of him with me. I will have my family back," she paused, opening her eyes, and swinging her feet to the floor. "You are now permitted to get the hell out!"

"You can't let this happen..." Eric said weakly, his tone trailing off in defeat.

Erica smiled, stood, and placed her half-empty bowl on the bed. "Well suite yourself," she said, heading in Eric's direction. "I'm thirsty from all this popcorn, and need a glass of water," then without even flinching, she continued to walk towards Eric...and subsequently, directly *through* him. "But I suggest you stop standing there looking stupid, and spend these last moments you may have with your oldest son – you remember, the one you were actually brought back here for."

Eric lowered his head. He could not believe how easily she dismissed him, walked right through him, and erased him from her life. He felt a small amount of pain at not only what she was able to do, but also from the pain he must have caused her. Then without a word, he turned on his heal just as Erica was returning. She walked through him again, and he felt something, a tiny spark, a yearning, before Erica turned to close the door. Shutting him away.

With Eric gone from her sight, the amber glow from the window caught her attention; and the macabre thickness of the mist beyond. She sipped at her glass, mesmerized in its swirling accumulation, and thought the next thing she heard had surfaced from her imagination...

...there was a voice calling her name.

"Are you back for another try, Eric?"

"I am afraid it is not Eric that beckons you this time," said the deep voice, its tone slow and drawn out.

She turned, and saw her son sitting on the bed, the hammer for the game he'd been playing was discarded, and his arms were laced across his chest, with eyes that were very intense – very adult-like.

"Eric Jr?" she questioned.

"Yes mother, it is time that you cease with these unorthodox games you persist in playing, and fully understand what is at stake here."

Erica hadn't even noticed when she dropped her glass.

Mildred

Stood back upon the stage, and prayed.

She prayed until her mind felt pressed, as if all the hope of the world, all her fears, all the questions and answers she had about what was going on in town, were pushing through her conscience mind and coming out of her mouth in only a whimper and a cry.

The mist had fell through the church doors a moment ago, and the scene that had unfolded was like something from the Bible itself. Shouts, screams, bodies pressed together, and total confusion had taken over the people here.

But as Mildred looked out, the heat causing sweat to roll into her eyes, she watched in awe at two things she could not understand: One was Maya – who stood also on the stage, her body stretching and splitting until there would be two Maya's – the second Maya vanishing away from sight.

"What is happening to you?" Mildred asked, turning back to look out unto the crowd, the mist climbing like an ivy along the walls of the church.

"I am trying to save this town as fast as I can, Mildred," Maya said, sweat rolling along her cheeks, her hair losing its former golden beauty to fall flat about her face. "I need to awaken those that have fallen asleep but haven't had a chance to mourn and forgive their loved ones."

Mildred was not sure how to respond, what to say, what to do…this had become a very complicated situation indeed; but she was starting to see what was happening, as groups of parishioners crowded the stage, clawing hands reaching for her ankles, the mike stand, horded along the stairs.

Alfred Wynn came to the stage. His wispy gray hair flew about his head like thin tendrils of a sea creature. His skin was withered and wrinkled, with a deep bronze color from years of professional swimming. He was 92 years old. He assisted in the suicide death of his wife, stricken with lung cancer. He could never forgive himself for feeding her the pills, then overdosing them in her favorite foods, then taping the plastic bag to her head.

His wife, Sylvia Wynn, stood at the foot of the stairs, smiling at him. Her hair stood wild and tall on her head. She held fast to the brooch pinned to the nape of her dress; it held a picture of them on their first date at Coney Island.

When Alfred stepped up to the mike, Mildred noted a stillness to the mist. She watched the back of the church. Alfred was a few inches from her on the stairs below. Behind him she watched who slept on the floor, succumbing to the mist's ability to lull one with a feeling of calm, saturating their sensory with delights of childhood memories and tastes, until the coma-like effects took hold.

But now, the mist had stopped, not moving beyond the second-to-last pew…it was as if it waited for Alfred to speak.

"It was so hard to see you go Sylvia," Alfred said, moving wisps of hair away from his forehead with a flick of his fingers. "And even harder to see you go a second time. We never got to take that trip to Florida like we wanted."

Mildred saw the mist move back slightly.

"I know Al," Sylvia replied, lowering her head, searching the floor for a moment. She looked up, "But we had our fun, we had other trips, we had a lot more than some beach in Florida."

He tried to smile, his eyes diverted by the movement around his wife; the line of dead and undead behind her. "I know that now."

"And believe me, there are many more exciting places to see together on this side. I have seen some amazing things. I will wait for you, guide you, amaze you...but promise me that you will take your time to enjoy what you have here – bring me back some stories of wonder."

Al's grin widened, his eyelids pressed back the tears that soothed his gray lashes. He didn't speak right away, although his mouth formed many silent words. When an audible sentence did manage to fall forth, it came at a slow stammer, "Thank you Sylvia...I love you. Goodbye for now."

And then the tears fell, clouding his vision, masking the miracle of Sylvia, as she slowly vanished from sight.

And the mist began to churn once again, but its steps, its progress, had been halted...and that was the second thing Mildred learned: the mist was weakened by the truth, by the living finally letting go of its dead.

But in her silent thoughts, another scream lit the air, and she looked back at the church doors, to see a child laying on the second row of pews, his cherub-like features stilled, as a swirl of clouds fumed from him, forcing him into that everlasting sleep; the mother being pulled back, and her deceased mother joining her as they stood back in line awaiting their turn to say their goodbyes.

"Keep moving," Mildred yelled, hurrying another man to the stage, as he began to speak to his dead, twin sons. "We haven't much time."

And as he spoke, the mist had moved to the third row of pews, but was once again stilled as forgiveness took to the mike.

Chapter 21

Part I

Lisa

She could not believe this. The mist was moving into the living room at such a rate, that it appeared frighteningly human. Lorraine was holding her, with arms so strong that she felt crushed by the embrace. Lorraine, *deceased* Lorraine, was in the same room as the mist – a thing that was not supposed to be, because in the presence of the dead, the mist gets weaker. But here it was, as strong as ever.

Lorraine stood near her sleeping sister, Shelly, with saddened eyes and body; her head bowed, shoulders dropped. Shame and helplessness weighed heavily against her. Shelly didn't have a chance to be forgiven by Lorraine, to mourn her, to say her goodbye's, so Lorraine remained, denied her chance to return to her afterlife. Rodney too was in a weakened state, kneeling next to Shelly, stroking her hair; his eyes were closed, as his lips whispered an inaudible prayer.

Lisa watched them both, ached for their separate pains. The mist was strong in its spell, and only one person could lift her from this ethereal slumber: Maya Olms. She should have been here by now. She should have been here to awaken Shelly and transport them to the safe haven within the church. Unless…that sanctuary was no longer safe.

"What do we do, Lisa," Rodney said, weakly. His eyes lay fixed on his wife, while his fingers traveled a course through Shelly's hair, along her nose, glided against her shoulders, where they met with her fingers. He intertwined them. "She carried so much guilt around about Lorraine. It must have felt like a dead third-arm or something."

Lorraine stepped closer; the mist parting from her like a satin curtain, "Yea, She has held that guilt inside for a very long time.

"She blamed herself for asking you to go out there to tie those cans to the back of the car," Rodney said, looking up at Lorraine. "She could have – none of us could have – known what was going to happen. The preacher had just finished with his blessings, before anyone heard the screeching of the car, and then the shouts from outside." He paused for a moment, catching his breath. "I'm still trying to make all of this real: my living wife sleeping as if dead, my dead sister-in-law standing here alive, you materializing in my living room like the Grimm Reaper, bringing this mist on your coattail. And now you are telling me that the only way to save Shelly is for another dead woman to come here, one that barely knew either of us, to wake her. This cannot be happening. Who has the right to say that our town is grieving too much? Who has that right?"

Lisa didn't reply. She paced. She had no answers. The mist, the dead, the citizens of Crest Hill County, Maya, everyone – we are all one body being eaten alive by grief.

Rodney looked away from Shelly, and stood. "When is Maya supposed to be here!" he said, frustrated.

Lisa looked up towards the ceiling, "I don't know Rodney, I really don't. Maya's absence must mean that there are many in town that have fallen asleep, and that will cause the mist to become stronger – because grief only gets heavier if it is not lifted. And if that happens, then I don't think even Lorraine will be able to stem its growth, and it could overtake us all."

"Are you prepared for that Lisa?" Lorraine said, as her gown was being buffeted by the clumps of mist. "Are you prepared for the chance that this mist could win, could fill up this living room, and could send you to a sleep as if in death? Are you ready to die Lisa?"

Her heart thudded faster behind her ribcage. She bit nervously at her lips. She knew the afterlife held a Heaven for her, a life with a new form, new flesh, and everlasting joy. Death was not something to be forged of fear and foreboding to her…and yet, "No Lorraine. No, I'm not ready at all."

Jenna

It had happened so fast, that in the time it took for Jenna to blink and inhale, she was instantly propelled from home and catapulted into a stream of billowy white streaks, blinding bands of light, and in the distance a darkness so deep, so infinite, that its size and distance were indistinguishable. And at arm's length there flowed a white gown of such majesty, that it appeared to be made of light itself; attached around a woman who had not seen her yet, had not known that Jenna had reached out to her – touching the hem of her clothes, the clothes of Maya Olms.

Jenna tried to scream, but she seemed to be travelling faster that the syllables could not be dispelled, so she kept silent, and allowed herself to be coiled with Maya on this journey and prayed they didn't hit anything.

Then the cloudiness of the walls seemed to dissipate, the lights pulled away, the darkness broke apart, and through it Jenna could recognize flashes of the familiar, but something was wrong, different somehow, and then she realized that she was travelling *above* Crest Hill County, a few feet higher than some of the homes. The evening had placed its murky film in the air, streetlights were roused from their morning naps; eyes beaming. Amidst the lights, the streets were empty, except for a few people, frozen, captured by the mist in mid-movement: jogging, walking their dog, napping on a park bench, or standing in mid-conversation with another. And below them, crawling like a python through the grass was the mist, thick enough to reflect light, tall enough to swallow a young child. The town was dead already.

And then Jenna notices tombstones. The sign of the Morning Glory Cemetery eased past her vision, as she travelled over the ground's uneven hills and scattered trees. She suddenly remembered who she left here, and before she could think, she spoke, "Are we going to save Nathan?"

The motion ceased, and a rush of cold wind seared across Jenna's cheek, while her insides pressed to one side like eggs in a tilted skillet, and Maya spun around, her eyes questioningly wide. "Jenna? What are you…?"

Jenna rubbed her arms at the icy feel of needles against her flesh, and let her insides settle a bit, while she looked up at Maya, "I tried to speak to you before, but once I touched you, and you took flight, I couldn't get my words out."

Maya reached out to squeeze Jenna's arm, feeling the warmth return, "I'm glad you survived the journey, and managed to cling to my essence."

"So are you?" Jenna said, unmoved.

A slight grin registered along Maya's fair skin. "Yes I am. Carl as well," she said, spinning on her heels and began to walk.

Jenna caught up to her, and motioned around in her path. She made eye contact, and her palms came together at her lips, as if her words were secrets. "I want to be there when you awaken Nathan. I want to be the first thing he sees."

Maya cupped a hand under Jenna's arm, and they slowly rose a few inches from the ground. They moved together along the landscape, the mist coursed around them untouched. "Eventually, Jenna. He won't be able to see you at first. The world remains unaltered to him, as if caught in a painting, and I'll have to ease him back into this world, this ciaos, with a few mental guides."

"I get that. I just want him to know that I don't blame him for Ella's death. He was scared. It was an accident. I'm sure he died a little too when it happened, and I didn't realize that. He's been living with that agony all this time," she gripped Maya's arm with her other hand. "One thing I've learned from all of this is that it is best to forgive the ones you love, before they are not there to love anymore."

"That is the ultimate lesson we hope is learned by everyone, Jenna," and slowly they began to descend, and Jenna realized they were getting closer to where Nathan was. "When I begin to awaken Nathan, I'll have to ask you to turn around, to close your eyes. I'll guide Nathan to you when he's ready."

"But why," Jenna said, her voice laced with fright. "Why can't I be there to see him, or to see you bring him back?"

Maya almost laughed, but held it to a smile. "Because that's how a miracle works Jenna."

++++++

Where they were going, Jenna could only guess, for the mist wrapped around them like a bubbling lava-cloud, she was so mesmerized at the way it moved that she drew back several times. She was so sidetracked that when she came upon a dark obtrusion barring her path, she nearly sidestepped it, until she realized it was Nathan.

He stood there like a dream, pulled from the clouds as if birthed from its loins. His eyes were opened, mouth agape, chin up, neck exposed, the skin brown, hairy, and as loose as a sock with worn elastic. She stepped up to him, wanting to see his breath, wanting his chest to rise and fall, wanting the thick artery in his neck to beat. But he remained still, so…

"…quiet. He's so quiet, Maya."

"Yes, he is. He's not here Jenna. He's not anywhere yet."

She reached out to touch him, afraid he would fall, as he leaned against a bench, one hand in his pocket – as he looked out with pressed eyebrows, and a pushed-up nose – the last expression he had when she blamed him for their daughter's death. She could see his anger, and his pain. "I'm so sorry, Nathan," she said as she caressed her fingers along his cheeks, feeling the bristles of the tiny unshaven hairs there, and cupped his chin in her hands, staring at those thick lips, that open mouth.

Then she felt Maya's fingers, as they pulled her hands slowly away. "I'm going to need you to turn around now, Jenna. Time propels him. And us."

She stepped back, glancing at Maya, then back at Nathan, not wanting to let him out of her vision again. But she managed it, and stared into the whiteness, and chewed on her anguish like cud.

Maya was quick, as she touched Nathan's face, the skin glowed beneath the fingertips, melding some areas like putty, while lightening other's, enough to view parts of his skull. She reached her other hand towards his torso, feeling along his ribcage, touching his hips. Jenna flinched. There was stiffening, as if she could sense her man being touched by another. Maya pushed her fingers into his skin as if it were a bowl of soup. She did the same to his torso, dipping beneath his clothes and skin.

She stopped. She called Jenna's name.

As she faced them both, she found a sight that perplexed her. Instead of Nathan and Maya being there; there was Nathan, Maya, and a smaller version of Maya to the right, as if she were a twin, except a few feet shorter. Jenna tried to understand what she was seeing, the smell of milk and honey clouded her perceptions, and she panicked, pushing at the mist, "What happened to you," she asked, arms fanning wildly, "What have you done to Nathan? Are you dying too?" she began to look around, as if trying to find a direction to escape.

In an instance, the shorter Maya vanished, and the original Maya moved with a swiftness in Jenna's direction, gripping her arm, "It's okay, Jenna. It's okay. The mist has you distracted, come be near your husband."

She pulled timidly against her, "What is this Maya? There were two of you. Who was that other woman? I don't understand."

That was a part of my spirit, Jenna. It is not as strong as me, because it comes from me. I can't awaken everyone on my own, Jenna – and as a spirit I don't have to. I can be many places at the same time. With enough people rousing from sleep, the stronger I become, I can split myself into myself. In fact, I am the spirit form of the original spirit which is still at the church. But you don't need to know that. That small form is going to assist Lisa, who is acting as a messenger for me..."

Maya's voice faded, when Jenna saw a rumpled Nathan lying on the ground, face wet, eyes cast aloof. "What's happened to him?" She said, moving past Maya, to kneel beside him, her hands unsure whether to touch him, move him, or hold him.

"He'll be fine. He should be coming-round very soon. I just hope it goes as well for the others."

"What do you mean? Aren't you going to wake Carl now?"

Maya looked worried. "There is a balance Jenna, and the stronger the mist, the deeper the sleep. The more I awaken the weaker the mist becomes – but its sleep is powerful, it can travel in the hiding places of this town, find many more people than I. At some point, I won't have the power to wake anyone. That is why I have to find them, wake them, and protect them. It is only I that can do that. But I am not sure if Carl can be awakened."

"But why?" Jenna asked. Nathan began to stir.

"Because I had hoped that the church would be a good haven, and people could have a trusted place to confess, or bid farewell to their loved ones," then Maya walked a few feet beyond Jenna. "But unfortunately, at the church, the mist has claimed them all."

Benny

He thought he wanted this, but regret always comes too late.

The mist had slowly seeped in under the door, the sides of the window, the cracks in the walls, and was inching its way up his bed, as he cowered in his bedroom. He crouched atop the covers, the door was opened, and beyond it he could see Jason, sitting on the corner of the sofa, appearing lost, and a little scared. He loved that man, but was that love worth him dying too? He would have him forever in this new afterlife – but what about the rest of his life?

He continued to ponder this as the mist crept up his bed, snatching away the last of the fresh clean air that had once been very prevalent in this house. Instinctively, he began to hyperventilate. He watched as Jason just sat there staring into space, the thickness of the mist saturated his features. It was as if he floated in a cloud. There were no tears in his eyes, but Benny could see that his once-dead lover really wanted them to flow.

Harold too would not be as lucky. Benny had run into the hallway, trying to pull him inside. His efforts had been futile. Harold's body was incredibly heavy. Immovable.

It was Jason who managed to drag him back into the house as more mist entered.

And now, all he could think about were the graham cookies his mother treated him to as a child; drizzled in honey with a glass of cold milk to wash it all down. This recollection was unrelenting. He could swear it was a scent brought on by the mist. Was that possible? It grew stronger as the mist grew closer, thicker, as it edged its way up the covers, stealing its way across his bed – the scent and memories of his past literally overwhelming him into a most unnatural state of calm.

His back pressed against the headrest. "Jason! What's going on!" he shouted, grabbing a pillow and attempting to fan it out against the mist.

"We're being transported to the other side, Benny. It's over. This town is being drawn out of the minds and memories of the world."

Benny could not reply – but he'd already known that this is what was happening. Yet although there was fear in him, as if his flesh were trying to find a way to flee from his bones; his soul had accepted its fate. It had relinquished itself – and so Benny stayed crouched on his bed, the mist tickling the toes of his feet, kissing them, sucking on them, reminding him of the many other lovers he's known that have also done the very same thing. It relaxed him a little – as did the memories of his mother's treat of honey grahams and milk. Funny…he could actually taste them now…

Erica

"Mom, I'm scared!" Timothy said, as he sat on the edge of the tub, inside of the bathroom within her bedroom.

Erica looked up at him, as she sat crouched on the floor, her back to the door. She had stuffed towels along the bottom edge of the door, and fastened masking tape along its borders, in a failed attempt at keeping the streams of mist from seeping in.

"I know you're scared, Timothy. I'm trying to figure out what to do," Erica said, racking her fingers through her hair. She also pulled at her tank-top, which was sticking to her in a light film of sweat.

"I wish dad was here," Timothy whispered, as he kicked the tile floor in frustration; a streak from his gym shoes marred the surface.

She didn't say anything about it. In a small sense, she wished his dad had been here too. But his dad *was* here...but he'd completely vanished minutes ago.

A knock rang out on the opposite side of the door. Erica jumped.

"Mother, you need to stop this foolishness. You need to get out of there. The mist will claim you – and you have still not released me!"

Erica crammed the palms of her hands against her ears. That voice. That adult voice; was coming out of her toddler son. A five-year old sounding like a twenty-five-year-old. "Go away, whoever you are. You are not my son!" She shouted, scooting her legs against the floor, pressing her back against the frame.

"Mom, listen to him!" Timothy blared, his fists raised. He shook them. "You have to listen to him. I don't want to die here."

"Shut up Timothy. No one is going to die!" Erica shouted back hysterically. She looked up at Timothy – his expression dumbfounded. She realized the utter absurdity of that statement in these times – but it was the only one that seemed right at the moment.

"My brother is right, mom," came the voice from beyond the door.

"Why are you talking to me? Bring me my son back," Erica demanded, and in her turmoil, she reached back to bare her fist against the door.

"I am back, but you have to let me go. You can't let this town die. You can't allow my brother to live his life shorter than destined. This is not fair to anyone, including you."

She couldn't reply. She did want Timothy to grow up, get married, come home and have some of her home cooking as he brought a grandchild to her lap. Be she didn't want that now. She wanted her baby back. She wanted more time with Eric Jr. "It's not fair that...I killed you."

There was silence; A long silence. Then slowly, Eric Jr. spoke, his voice somehow a bit younger now, "But it was my time. It was just my time. You can't keep blaming yourself, mom."

"But I can't *not* keep blaming myself," she said, her voice stammering. She brought a hand over her eyes, as tears flowed heavily along her cheeks.

Timothy ran to her, and simply wrapped his arms around her shoulder. "You have to mom. You have to let my little brother go. I miss him. I love him too. But I want to grow up to enjoy the life that he missed. I know why dad disappeared. I know that aunt Mildred was linked with him somehow, and his going back was a good thing. He was trying to save this town. He was trying to save us all. Now it's your turn," he lowered his head, shaking it as if he ran out of enough grown-up words to express himself.

Mildred must have forgiven Eric for something – they were linked somehow, and through Mildred, he was allowed to go home. She must have finally forgiven him. Could it have all been that simple?

"Mom! The fumes are seeping in around you. Come over here," Timothy beckoned, as he leaned against the rim of the tub.

She crawled closer to him, the mist swelling behind her, lightly masking the floor beneath them. She was trembling. Her mind was wandering, her thoughts chaotic.

Timothy could feel her body shaking beneath him, her head resting against his torso, her eyes closed in a blanket of tears. He reached out to wipe them away, but their stream was too continuous.

"Don't give up on her, Timothy. She is all that you have. She will need you to help her, whatever the outcome."

He nodded. "I will do my best," he said, and could taste a sweetness against his pallet that disturbed him because of its suddenness – and also caused him to instinctively swallow. It was a milky taste.

Then something thudded against the door. A most sudden and loud noise that bolted Timothy's attention.

"Eric Jr.?" Timothy called out. "Is everything okay out there?"

"I'm still here, and everything is not okay, Timothy."

"Why? What's happening out there?"

"It's not out here. It's in there. Mom has fallen asleep. The mist has taken her...and soon it will take you."

Timothy looked down at his mother, and tapped her shoulder, then shook it. She didn't sound asleep, but she appeared motionless all the same. "Mom?" he said, and that sweet taste welled within his throat again.

"It's over, Timothy. I'll be seeing you on the other side soon..."

And Eric Jr.'s words trailed off in Timothy's ears, as his eyes drew heavy, and his tongue lapped up the sugary honeyed taste that filled his mouth...and the darkness finally claimed him.

Chapter 22

Part I

Jenna

Jenna cried. She remained on her knees and found that all she could do was cry. Through her blurred vision, she saw the many forms of Maya bounding about the cemetery grounds; gliding, floating, running; seen one minute, then off into the mist they went – all a little different in their appearance than the one that brought her here.

She wiped her tears. Nathan continued to sleep as she ran a finger across his eyebrow. "Shouldn't he be waking up faster? I see so many forms of you running around, so am I to assume they will be enough to wake everyone? Will this nightmare end?"

Maya looked around. "I don't know, Jenna. There are so many. And only minutes ago, the elementary school was overrun by the mist. They will all have to be moved away from it, so they can forgive their loved ones, and weaken the mist's effect, but the odds are against us. Even you are in danger the longer you stay here.

Jenna was afraid of that. The taste of sugar filled her mouth with every inhale. She tried to ignore it, hold her breath a little longer, resist her involuntary reaction to swallow, but it was hard. "Are we going back to the house? Nathan has to say goodbye to Ella, and she has to forgive him."

"His sleep is deep, just as Carl's was. He can't make the journey until he is fully roused, and even then, there has to be enough people awoke and enough dead gone, so he doesn't succumb to sleep again." And deep within her, Maya sensed the battle was already over. Soon Nathan's body would become lighter, as it begins its transformation into limbo. She watched silently as Jenna unconsciously smacked her lips.

The mist could be so alluring despite one's resistance.

Benny

He hugged his pillows. His breathing had slowed. He could barely see with the mist in his room. His head lobbed. He hungered for milk and cookies. Strange.

"I'm sorry I failed you," said Jason from the living room.

Benny wanted to answer, but his throat felt tight. His mind was hazy, occupied. He gripped his pillow tighter, his back pushed flush against the headrest. He blinked, and his eyes felt as if the lids were going in slow motion. He looked into the mist, its growing array of colors, and he could sense there was more to it than first appeared.

He could swear that it pulsated, throbbed, breathed. It was as if he were looking more at an orgasmic response than of an ethereal one.

"What is going on with this mist, Jason?" Benny asked, leaning his head back against his headrest.

"Don't worry, Benny, you'll soon find out when we get to the other side.

Benny inhaled deeply, as the wavy swirl of clouds churned in and out of his mouth. "When is that supposed to be?"

"Any moment now, Benny…any moment now."

Lisa

She was now alone, and she prayed.

Rodney still lay on the floor, staring at nothing. Lorraine lay across from him, alive but silent; fear in her eyes – an emotional state that was getting ever easier to recognize. Lisa sat on the floor next to Rodney, her hand holding the still palm of Shelly's; who slept.

The mist was all around them, as if the house was on fire, and Lisa could not find a reason to communicate, to move, to think, and so she prayed. Prayed almost at a whisper, for every soul whose name she could remember, as they journeyed to a place caught between life and death. She even prayed for Lorraine, whose soul had once reached its destination – in hopes that this new one would be a tolerable one.

She coughed, as if the mist had been choking her, when in fact it held no weight. It however, left a trace aroma of cake, or brittle, or even cookies – and on the back of her tongue was the thickness of milk. She swallowed these puffs of vapor as if it were dessert. And she found her perspective thrown just a bit, and the coagulation of this floating substance put her in a trance-like state, lulling her, relaxing her.

She allowed it.

She desired it.

She gave herself up to it.

Then she realized suddenly…that she had stopped praying.

Tilly

No one answered the phone at Mark's place, and to be frank, Tilly didn't care. She absently continued to guide her fingers along the pliable flesh of her child.

The infant's color was slowly coming back.

Ella sat cross-legged across from Tilly, watching her, saying nothing, but saddened at the events unfolding around her. They were all dying, and there was nothing left to do but wait. The sadness however, did not come from the realized fact that they could no longer run from the mist, but their willingness to take it in and out of their bodies so easily now. Surrender.

Also, Tilly was second-guessing her readiness to give up being with her son. She felt closer to him, and maybe in this new afterlife, they would be closer.

Ella could sense the connection. The strength of the mist had lowered her will to let go. Tilly was already readying herself for a new life with her son – but she had yet to understand the connotations of the word FOREVER.

"Can you taste that?" Tilly asked, with a tone more rhetorical than directional.

Ella looked away. "No, but I know what you speak of."

Tilly smiled. "Why so sad, Ella. It's going to be great on the other side. No death, eternal life, a chance to be with our loved ones."

Ella could feel the sensation of tears well up along her eyelashes. "I don't take failure very well, Tilly, and no matter how you look at this, God had another plan for this town, a life for his town, and it has failed."

"God is a god of love, Ella. I'm sure he will understand," she said, returning her attention back to her son. "Will the air smell like this all the time in the place we're heading?"

"I'm not sure Tilly. Why smell and taste when you're dead – if not for just the purpose of pleasure?"

"Sure," Tilly answered, not really listening. "I think I'll go and take a nap. I'm suddenly tired."

"Go take a nap," Ella said, holding her head up as her tears dropped, "I'll wake you when we reach our destination."

"Oh, how nice of you. Thanks Aunt Ella."

"Sure, anything for family."

Mildred

All she hoped for was that there was no pain.

Maya stood near the back of the stage; there was nothing more for her to do. She had done her best, Mildred thought, as her own throat began to lock up, and her mind floated in a haze. She was still holding onto the mike, as if it were a lifeline, her last connection to this world.

She was informed that the school was frozen. People had run up to the stage as fast as they could, saying goodbye to their loved ones and forgiving past sins, but they forgot: forgiveness comes from the heart. You must truly believe on the inside, before anything can change on the outside. In conclusion, it had not been enough.

Mildred peered out at the church, her vision filled with tears, sweat, and smoke. Her chest would not stop heaving as she looked at those people gathered against the center pews, like discarded mannequins in the basement of some department store.

And soon she would be among them.

Her arms began to stiffen, and her vision was fading in and out. Voices echoed in her mind, like a-thousand voices screaming. Inside, she too was screaming. What was the magic number that would have turned this whole thing around? How many people did they need to come forward to lessen the mist in the tiniest bit? She glanced at Maya, and gave a half-grin. This had been the first time in a long time, that Mildred had not considered her the would-be mistress to her husband. What had really killed Maya, she wondered – and then a most disturbing feeling overwhelmed her; *maybe Maya's death had something to do with her*. She would ask her on the other side. It was too late to think about that now. Instead she turned back towards the mike, and thought about her brother, and how their relationship had changed, how she no longer resented him for leaving her in this town – for now, she loved the town of Crest Hill County; a town and a county all in one. She leaned into the mike, hoping that somewhere he would hear her, and whispered, "Can't wait to see you on the other side, Eric. Love you. Miss you. Forgive you…"

…and that's when her world went blank.

Chapter 23

Part I

Flash

Pastor Luther Reynolds saw a flash.

It seemed to have appeared within his mind – and yet he somehow had seen it through his eyes.

Flash!

There it was again; images, visions, prophecy. Something was happening to him – something extraordinary. Something he could not explain. A melting away perhaps.

He couldn't move; not that he wanted to, because there was a sense of relaxation about him that he could not explain. It was a sensation that went deeper than his soul.

He was still in his car, he at least was aware of that – and he was surrounded by ghosts…he surmised. There was death all around him. Deep and intense mourning; it saddened him.

Flash!

The mist. He remembered. It was folding back on his memory like an egg in batter, the recollections appearing again and again – yellow flashes of recall: Crest Hill County, the oil truck, the explosion, the destruction of two school busses, children dying, the town in devastation, fear, death, sorrow…

…Maya.

Mildred.

The Mist.

Beyond his windshield, he could see nothing. His breathing was rapid. There was a great fear welling up in him, coupled with that synonymous feeling of tranquility.

Flash!

Then it happened.

He finally guessed what the mist actually was.

Part II

Sweat.

It sheathed Lisa like a liquid film along her body.

The smell of milk and honey was still there …along with the mist.

Her mouth felt pasty, and she ran a finger around her tongue trying to rid herself of the taste, but it was to no avail. She had become more concerned with the way her hair matted atop her head and along the back of her neck. She ran a hand along the nape of her neck and shoulders; it was like wet thread.

Something has happened – she thought, and took an astonishing look around. She realized at once, that she sat in the living room of Rodney and Shelly…but she was alone.

Fear took hold of her, and she scuttled across the floor like a beachcombing crab. A quick shout lodged in her throat, pressing at it, pushing, but was too wedged to escape her lips.

There was less mist, she noticed. There was an abundance of light in the room, as she noticed the sun hanging just above the horizon. How much time had passed? Was the town now detached from the rest of the world and this was the start of the new day that would become their new life.

"Dear God, what has happened," she spoke towards the ceiling, as she attempted to rise, her knees staggering at the attempt.

"It is over," said a voice to her ears.

She spun around, her eyes squinting past the tiny flight of stairs that led from the sunken living room, and into the light haze that the mist offered. Within this opaqueness, there was a figure, male in form; and he stepped into view…

Part III

Benny awoke in his bed.

His body was shaking. He was curled up in a fetal position, two pillows wrapped in his arms. He quickly sat up to look over at his window.

Jason was standing between the curtains, looking out at the mist. Its billowy form glowing, casting shadows within the room.

"Is it over?" Benny asked Jason, as he stretched an arm out to examine himself. "I appear to be my same old self."

"Don't worry Benny, you are," Jason said, his focus still out the window.

Benny took in a slow deep breath. Was he now considered dead? According to Jason, when the town had crossed over, the life he used to live, the people he used to know would cease to exist. He stared at the back of Jason – the man he loved, and whom he now would spend an eternity with. He was starting to have some serious regrets about this whole decision.

"What happens to you, Jason? Do we just wait till the mist is gone? Is the town going to gather for some sort of meeting, or a list of instructions?"

Jason slowly turned to face Benny. "There is something I must tell you, Benny."

Benny's eyes widened, and he propped himself up on his pillows, and slid his feet to the edge of the bed. He didn't like the tone of Jason's voice. "What is it?"

"Harold has been taken."

Benny was confused. "Taken? What do you mean?"

"It was something that had to be done," Jason said, head lowered.

Benny rushed from his room, dashed through the living room, and flung open the front door. "Harold!" he shouted, but the hallway was empty. Taken. Harold was taken. He spun back around towards the living room, and was startled to see Jason standing in the middle of it.

"Have a seat Benny. There is much to discuss."

Part IV

Jenna didn't dream

She thought she would have at least dreamed, before the darkness took hold of her. But there were no dreams, and yet, when she felt her shoulders being tussled, and darkness gave way to euphoria, she could tell she had slept but a short time.

She could feel her body lying at an angle, as if she were leaning against something – something hard and soft all at the same time. Her vision was quite blurry, as if she wore glasses smeared with oil. She felt very tired, her arms too fatigued to even feel the space around her.

"Don't worry, I've got you," came a voice blowing at her ear.

"Nathan?"

"Yes, old lady, it's me," and he pulled her closer to him, closer to his soft hardness.

She smiled, feeling his embrace, strength slowly returning to her limbs. She lifted an arm to touch his face. "I'm so sorry Nathan, about what I said, and I…"

He squeezed her tighter, shaking her just a bit. "Don't talk about that now. Everything has worked itself out."

She blinked a few times. Her vision was slowly being returned. She leaned her head back against him, letting her mind wander for a moment. This moment reminded her of when she awoke in his arms after that horrible incident at the basketball court. *Nathan, always there for me*, she thought. She took comfort in that.

"Your eyesight and strength will return in a minute. Just relax," said Maya, standing near.

"Is it over?" Jenna asked; her constricted features reminiscent of a spongy walnut.

"I'll say it is," Nathan said, wiping a sheath of moisture from his face and neck.

"What's it going to be like, Maya? Will things be very different?" Jenna questioned.

Maya smiled. "Not very, as you will observe once you take a good look around."

And Jenna did, seeing nothing out of the ordinary. The mist was diminished, and she was beginning to see the slight gradations in the terrain as hills and walkways came into view. She could walk those and many of the paths and streets within Crest Hill County a bit more safely now. She was curious about the stamina she must have been granted, or was her body to remain in its aged mobility – certainly that would not be the case. She would live forever, have cheated an uncertain death, and sickness and disease was sure to be no more. For a person of her age, this was a blessed course of events, and her life's experiences weren't cut short for it.

And then the oddness came into view.

She saw Maya in the distance – a much leaner model – her body inches from the earth, as she glided around a curve and out of view. And behind her, another Maya – shorter in stature – had simply looked to the heavens and suddenly became a streak of white bound towards the sky. And two more sat on a bench to her right a few yards away, their bodies seamed together like glue, until they split into two separate beings…two separate Maya's (though slightly younger).

"I don't understand," Jenna said, pulling away from Nathan. "What's happened?"

Maya nodded in Nathan's direction, "Will you explain it to her, Nathan. I have to leave."

He bobbed his head, and then pulled Jenna closer to him, "Let's sit over here," he said, indicating a bench amidst a small rose garden atop a hill to their left.

She staggered in her walk towards the sitting area; the reality of the situation dashed her hopes at eternal life. "We're still on Earth, aren't we? We haven't crossed over?"

He looked bemused. "Did you want to cross over, Jenna? Denying Tilly her chance at adulthood, and Ella her afterlife back?"

She brushed her fingers across the pedals of the roses before sitting. Yes, she was disappointed. "I suppose, Nathan. But we've lived our life, most of our family and friends have gone. And soon we will be, and one of us is going to have to mourn for the other, and be alone until their time comes." She exhaled, "I don't want to imagine that time, old man. I don't want to have to endure that pain."

He wrapped an arm around her shoulder, feeling her breathing grow faster, seeing her lips curl inward as she attempted to swallow past a tightening throat. "I know. It would be a great transition to our lives, our own private heaven, but we are not alone in this, Jenna. The reason we are going through all of this is so we can understand that death will happen, mourning will happen, but living starts only once – and we can still do that."

She snuggled up closer against him. Silent.

"The church had a breakthrough that turned the tables," he paused for a moment, searching for words, then continued, "People realized that a mike wasn't needed to forgive their loved ones, or even to say goodbye. I think the town can be saved, Jenna. Isn't that great?"

Silence again.

Part V

Luther knew Him by so many names:

Jehovah
Jehovah Jara
The Almighty
Allah
The Great I Am
Messiah
Alpha and Omega
The Rose of Sharon
Lilly in the Valley
Yahweh
Father…
…and of course, there was …GOD.

When Luther sat in his car, prior to that overpowering scent of milk and honey engulfing his every sense, miring him in abysmal slumber; he had been contemplating the Mist.

He thought about its arrival into town, a mysterious substance, which wasn't wet or dry, and could not have propelled from the river or been produced from low-lying clouds. For it moved with purpose. He wasn't one to fall into digressive streams of superstitious assumptions, but he believed there was a spiritual event happening. And for him, the dissecting of spiritual occurrences would have to begin with the Bible. So he mulled over this mist, and found there was something of similar makeup in one of the events of the Old Testament.

He remembered there was a cloud that led a certain people through the desert in Egypt by day as they too were headed towards a promised land. It also went in line with the raising of the dead – for only one other had accomplished the task numerously; which made the nature of the spiritual being a certainty. For evil spirits could not raise the dead (and if they did, he was certain no good would come out of it beyond a zombie-like creature). He then looked out at the mist with a different understanding, and marveled. The Mist was in fact God, Himself. And as is his custom, He revealed himself only after isolating the people he was trying to help. That is when Luther drifted off into that semi-darkness; eyes wide.

Now he had awakened, and was sitting on the trunk of his car, watching as the mist faded along the horizon, breaking up the sun rays into a stream of multi-colored waves…and he listened. He listened while a small voice played back what had happened to him, and what was yet to come to pass in the small town of Crest Hill County – it would make for some great sermons.

But there were a few questions he found himself asking.

"You said there are people waking the town. Who woke me up?"

"It wasn't a human that came to you, but a spiritual form of my being – they were the vessel, but I roused you through them," bellowed this tranquil voice on the edges of the wind.

"How long before we can resume our lives as normal?"

"Normality is a state of mind, as my creations transcend such minimalism. Crest Hill County and the people thereof, will resume their destinies by morning. Time has slowed beyond its borders, so that your time of little over a week has passed by in only a few minutes to everyone else."

"It's going to be hard for a whole town to pretend this time hasn't happened. They will talk, brag, and spread the word of this miracle."

"None will hear of these days, for I will bridle the tongues of those that attempt. Soon, even those who experienced this thing, will have forgotten in time."

"I believed the mist too strong when it finally caught me. What caused things to turn around so quickly?"

"Your wife, Luther. Mildred was the tipping point when she healed of her brother.

Part VI

There was darkness.

That was the first thing, and the last thing she could recall.

It was more than a darkness that caused her not to see – that, by design, is what darkness did. It was a darkness that she could feel, like a skin of ice zipped tightly around her.

"Close your eyes everyone!" was the very last statement she could recall. Her voice the only thing she could hear. Her throat was closing. Her time was short. She remembered the last thing she had said. "Close your eyes and forgive in your hearts. If you can still hear me, start now…you don't need an announcement, you don't need a mic, you don't need a voice…because God reads minds, hearts, and your spirit. If you have breath in you, if you have sight in your eyes, if your mind is busy, then let it be busy forgiving, understanding, letting go, and bidding ado." Then she could feel the coolness of the mist fall past her throat, offering her a sweetness that surprised her, and she swallowed, and at once could feel the effects of weariness. Shadows covered her vision, and for a moment, she forgot to breath, and her mind fell into a dreamlike darkness.

Time passed.

Then a pinhole of light fumed in the void.

Then she inhaled.

Darkness was pushed back into bands of gray.

She *burped*!

Her neck began to move, and in her vision, she saw Maya; smiling, and saying, 'Good work, Mildred.'"

And while Maya stood there, her arms folded, head tilted – and she began to split in two.

…again, two more…

…and again…

…and again.

The mist lifted slightly.

Then Mildred looked out at the congregation. Everyone's eyes were closed. She thought they had not survived the depths of slumber the mist had burdened them with…until…

…she saw that their lips were moving, and praying, without ceasing.

This touched the core of her soul, and she thought how proud Luther would have been. They were forgiving in their hearts.

Part VII

Lisa was beginning to relax.

Rodney had really given her a scare – standing there shadowed by the mist. She'd thought Jesus Himself had come to greet her, and all she could think about was how much of a mess she looked.

But it had only been Rodney, reaching out his hand towards her, the fingers long and dark, and she hesitated before resting her palm in his, worried at how easy it would be for him to crush hers. But he took her gently, as if those digits were made of chocolate cookie dough, and led her through the house, and into the kitchen, where the mist had thinned out to soft entrails. "I made you a sandwich," he said, directing his eyes at the crystal plate and the tall sandwich atop."

Until then, she'd forgotten how hungry she'd been. "Thank you," she muttered.

Rodney stood nearest the sink and rubbed at the perspiration at the back of his dark neck, which seemed to soak into his newly donned t-shirt. "This has been a crazy couple of days," he said, eyes wandering.

Lisa bit into her sandwich, and her tongue savored the ham, provolone, turkey, tomato, and Hollandaise sauce as if it were a new thing. "I was out for a minute, I suppose?"

"Very much so, but that woman who used to live in town showed up…you know, that white South African woman who did piano at the church…"

"Maya, yes of course."

"Well, she touched her face for a few seconds after waking me up, and Shelly jumped right up and started hugging Lorraine. A few tears and heartfelt words later, Lorraine vanished back to where she came…" his voice trailed in emotion.

Lisa placed her sandwich back on the plate, and reached up to embrace Rodney, "It's okay, Rodney. You've been through an ordeal…we all have."

"But I still miss her, Lisa. Everyone gave their sweet goodbyes, but we're still gonna miss Lorraine very much."

"And yet we all must travel the same road as she, just with the different off-ramps. She did some good while she was here, and I'm sure she has assured her sister that no one is to blame. Now you two have a chance to prove to her that her efforts weren't wasted," Lisa explained, pulling back from him. "And you're gonna do that; enjoy the bride that Lorraine obviously believed would be right for you."

Rodney grinned at that.

"Now where is Shelly?" Lisa asked, motioning back towards her sandwich.

"Taking a shower upstairs," Rodney said, and as if on que, the water could be heard.

"Great timing," she said between bites, "You two were destined."

He folded his arms, and looked beyond Lisa's shoulder, out beyond a pair of ceiling-to-floor windows, as the sky took on an orange hue, "Yea…I guess we were."

Part VIII

"Mom!"

Erica thought that word had come from her own mind, until she saw Timothy staring at her, his cold tiny hands jarring her shoulders.

"Mom!" he repeated, as he swung his head about staring at everything in the bathroom, "Can't you see? It's not here anymore."

Erica's head swelled and ached as if she were suffering from a hangover; even her tongue felt dry and pasty, "What happened?"

"I don't know," Timothy said, hoisting his shoulders up and down, "All I know is, it felt like someone touching me, then I opened my eyes, and tried to wake you, but nothing worked."

That's when Erica looked down and could feel that her face was dripping from the chin, a whistle lay between her thighs, her acrylic back scrubber lay broken beside the tub, and one of her shoes were off. "Where is my shoe, Timothy?"

"I tried to tickle you awake, but nothing was working, so I just waited."

"And where is Eric Jr.?"

The bouncing shoulders again. "I don't know. I haven't heard anyone all this time."

She flung her elbow along the top of the tub's edge, and hoisted her disoriented body up to her knees, "We have to go out there and see."

"Are we sure we want to do that? I'm a little scared of him," Timothy said, staring back at the door, then at his mother.

She managed to sit on the edge of the tub, "I know, but that's only because he's lived a lot longer in that body than most babies should. But we have to make sure he's okay."

"What bad could happen to him?"

Good point, Erica thought. He was deceased.

Timothy closed his eyes, and took a deep breath, "But seeing that I'm the man in the family, I'll go out there," he said, hoisting his arm across his mother's back, as support while she stood.

Such a little-man he was becoming. I'll have to say goodbye to this one someday too. The thought saddened her, and instinctively she gripped his chin in her palm, and turned him towards her. She stared for a moment at those copper eyes, smooth reddish skin, a splatter of pre-stubble along his jaws, cheeks round, sculpted, as if there were a grown man pushing his way out. "You okay mom?" he managed to ask without lower jaw mobility. She released him. "Sure I am. Let's go."

She was okay now. She has had the child, teenager, and future man with her all along. If she wanted to experience the best moments with Timothy, she had to stop wanting him to fill the void that was left. She watched Timothy slowly open the door, and no longer felt the fear and grief of missing her son, of having him expire too soon for her – and if they must live together again then so be it. She would still love him, but she would love the time with Timothy also. And as Timothy guided her within her bedroom, she could see a tiny indentation in her bed that was slowly lifting, and the faint giggle of Eric Jr. came to her ears, and for the first time, in a long time...

...she was happy.

Part IX

Benny lifted his head.

"None of this is your fault," Jason explained, as he stood in the center of the living room, hands locked unto his hips. "Harold has brought this unto himself."

Benny eased towards the edge of the sofa, reaching his hand out to pull another tissue from the dispenser. "And what about my hand in all of this? What about my lying. What about the guilt I feel for your death, and Harold's demise."

Jason lowered his head, but lifted his eyes to stare solemnly at Benny.

"That Benny…is your punishment."

And what a torturous punishment it was, he thought. Guilt; that may be a thing worse than what was handed to Harold. "And this is what has been decreed by The Great and Powerful Almighty. Is this what He wants?"

"Wants? It is already done."

Tears; for him and Harold. The unending extinction that Crest Hill County was to have received from the rest of the world, is the very punishment placed upon Harold, to experience alone. Deemed Forgotten; is what Jason said it was called. Harold would continue to live, but those around him would continually forget him as the months went by. No matter where he lived, who he met, the relationships he amassed, each person involved would eventually and simply, forget who he was. God was not in the business of taking the lives of others, but he had managed a way to take others out of your life.

"And you say that eventually, I will forget him too? We'll meet, and he'll simply be a stranger to me?"

"Yes. He'll know you, but you won't know him."

The thought frightened Benny. To be in the world, to make a mark in your life that was created with invisible ink. You would have to change banks, residents, and jobs endlessly – only to have to begin anew. "Eventually dying along," he whispered aloud.

"Yes," Jason assured, as he sat on the edge of the table top. "That means the salon is yours. Harold has already moved from his apartment, he decided against saying goodbye to his family and a few friends, because their memories of him were taken first – only you retain his existence for a time.

He could think on this no further, "And what happens to you Jason?"

"I'll be leaving soon myself. Our time has come to an end for a second time, I'm afraid."

He leaned in to embrace his old lover, "But this time, I'm a happier man, and I'm happy for you."

Jason ran his fingers through Benny's hair, "I know…I know."

Part X

"So, what happens now?" Mildred asked of Maya, whom she could sense behind her. Ahead, Mildred watched as people began to pour from the church – the mist floated in slender ribbons above them.

"That's a good question, Mildred," Maya replied. It was true, the fight seemed over. The undead were leaving, and the living had found a way to move on past their grief. But there was one more confrontation that needed handling; one more bit of truth that Maya found difficult to speak of – concerning she and her.

"Overnight," Maya continued, "The town will begin to catch up to the outside world. The mist will move away, and as it goes so will I. There is no need for further confessions, the town has healed."

"And what about me?" Mildred asked.

Maya searched that question. There was a change in Mildred. She had lived a life of ego and greed. But this sacrifice, this act of helping others, had quickened her spirit anew. "Keep the way you are Mildred. For the first time, you actually cared about the people in this town, and they didn't need to give you anything in return. Remember that you're all connected. You and Luther are connected through marriage, and your selfish ways must not continue. He'll want more of your time; I'm no longer there as a distraction for you both – so you need to build the bond between you, because who is to say another Maya-type won't come along with less seasonal intentions."

Mildred kicked the ground, "I have a lot to learn about being a wife, don't I?"

"You have a lot to learn about being human," she said, and reached for Mildred's hand. "There will be a lot of people with questions, a lot of scared people coming here for guidance, a lot of people still grieved. Your husband won't be able to handle it all; he still mourns for me."

Mildred squeezed Maya's hand, "Guess I'm gonna miss you a little too when you go."

"Yes, you will," Maya confirmed, and then she reached around to grab her other hand, forcing Mildred to look into Maya's sky-blue orbs. "There is something else I have to tell you. Something that Luther is going to discover soon too. Something that may bring a moment of discourse between you both."

A knot wedged in Mildred's throat, "And what is that?"

"It has to do with the last time we spoke. The time we had a discussion about me and Luther, and your demands that I stay away. It has to do with how I died.

It has to do with how you killed me."

And this statement stunned Mildred, but past her nervousness and fear, she listened to one last confession that would change her life.

Chapter 24

Luther had never driven this fast in all his life (well there may have been a few times – like the time he went to visit Maya upon discovering of her death).

Funny the full circle that life spins.

His experience with God, was still with him, as if he were thrust into an illusion, and the questions he asked…then it hit him! There were many he did not: *How was the universe created? Were there any other lifeforms in the cosmos? Did He have a brother? Does he pray…and to whom?*

He'd asked none of those, and just as they had done in Biblical times, his fear and reverence had overtaken the selfishness of his own curiosities, that he blindly listened and kept questions at bay.

Then his phone rang.

That is when he knew the world of Crest Hill County was reeling back to a state of normalcy. Tilly was the first to contact him, telling him her ordeal, and that her son had gone along with Ella, back to the afterlife after seeing her Grandmother whisked off in a cloud of smoke. She assured him that by next Monday, she would be able to go back to working for them. He laughed at this, and told her to take a vacation, and start preparing for her next semester in college. Then he questioned her about Jenna's sudden vanishing, and got the shock of his life.

"…why, Maya had come, spoke to us, and while Jenna was trying to get her attention, somehow got whisked off along with her."

"Maya?" he heard himself say.

What Tilly responded with was lost to his thoughts as his hand suddenly got heavier, and he realized he had disconnected from her. Maya? Maya had come back? How? When? Why had God not told him *this*?

And then Lisa called.

She was heading home after what sounded like the most trying of times for her in these last few hours, because of the duties that were appointed of her through...Maya!

Then Erica called. And Maya's name was mentioned again.

He frantically called Mildred. And not only had she seen her too, but she went on to explain the happenings at the church; the church he had been heading to before the mist came and swallowed him up in euphoria, and how she and Maya had both managed the people at church. Hours upon hours they spent together. But up until a few moments ago, she had...vanished! Gone. Left. Departed, and Luther felt sick. His phone slipped from his hands, and his knees met the ground. He shook his head, his throat choked with his saliva, his eyes blurred with tears, his hands molded into huge ball bearings; to which he pounding against the ground. "Why! Why God had you not told me this!" he shouted into the pavement. He tried to regain himself, but his hips were attached to limbs of crumpled paper, and he could not rise. He heaved, as if there were not enough oxygen in the air, and grasped at his throat.

And then he got angry.

He rubbed those bearings against his pained eyes, drying them, and stood as best he could on his weakened legs, and forced himself into his car, and his foot against the accelerator. And he drove. He pushed that car to its limit, as he watched a town pass by him at a blur; its terrain desolate, its sound silent, its hues muddy, and kept pushing it.

Maya's house was just outside of town. If that is where she died, maybe that is where he could see her. "Why did you leave without seeing me?" he questioned distressed. "You were here. I am here. This can't be happening. You come here, and not see me. You know how much I have missed you. Am I to be tested along with this town? Where is my relief?" Then he rolled down his window, as he noticed the mist still loomed in the air, slightly thicker than in town, and he breathed in deeply; somehow in hopes of breathing her in too. "How can you leave without saying goodbye?"

The taste came back to his tongue, slightly off, fading from his senses as quickly as he could swallow. So he pulled his car over, and ran out into a grassy field, and began to inhale and exhale at a violent rate. "Don't leave me, Maya!" he said, suddenly hyperventilating. "Where are you?!"

And then something brushed against his cheek.

He turned, but nothing was there. He spun around again, and lost balance, and fell to the wet grass on hands and knees.

Another brush.

This time he slowly lifted himself, and looked towards the heavens. Within the mist he noticed a darkening, as if a column of smoke had risen and clung in the air, and this darkness slowly approached him. He closed his eyes.

He could feel a softness, a mass, pushing against his cheeks, his chin, along the back of his neck...

"Maya?" he whispered.

"Yes," she replied.

He felt faint, and instinctively opened his eyes. The mist had taken on a shape, a womanly shape, Maya's shape. He stood swiftly, and tried to hug its form.

It dissipated.

"Hello Luther," said the voice again.

Luther turned to look behind him, and the form had reassembled.

"Hello Maya," he said, with a choked voice. He unwrapped his arms, and took a step forward. "How are you?"

The voice laughed, and Luther realized the banality of the question. Still however, she answered, "I'm fine Luther. I'm fine."

"Of course you are," he responded with a smile. "I'm not sure what to say."

The shape moved closer to him; reached out towards him. "I miss you would be fine."

"I miss you," he repeated.

"I'm sorry that I was unable to see you, Luther. I know that you're hurting – I know this all too well, but it will pass, as all things must."

"I truly hope that in this, you are right, Maya. I truly do."

"I am."

"And what if I don't want it to pass? What if I want to hold on to this...this...miracle within my heart?"

The form reached out to Luther, and brushed a hand across his cheek. "As a pastor you know, it's not always what you want. This plan is bigger than you or I." Then the form became more solid, the touch more flesh-like, and she lifted his chin. "We all want to hold onto a miracle; even I. But an end has to come, sooner or later."

Color began to form in the apparition. Hues; the blue of an eye, the crimson strands of hair, the pinkness of skin. Breath left his lungs, and his eyes forgot to blink. He was caught in a vacuum, and the only words he was able to form came from some deep recess within his soul, "I love-"

She placed a finger across his lips. "I know."

He reached up to grab her wrist, and this time she accepted it. "Then before you leave, maybe you can grant me another small miracle."

Her face was there. It smiled. It nodded. It understood. And slowly she eased forward, watching as his eyes closed, his lips pouted, and in one final gesture, she kissed him.

If he were butter, he would have melted.

And then she released him, and the hurt returned – as if a wound had opened up.

He opened his eyes.

"I have to leave now Luther."

He understood, and there were no words he could utter. So he watched the colors fade back, the image become more fluid, and the cloud of mist lift back into the sky. "I will always love you, Luther. Remember that."

He smiled.

"And your wife…Mildred is a changed woman. I think you will be pleased."

"Maya?" he managed to dispel through clenched vocal cords.

"Yes?"

"How did you die? They say you may have simply had a heart attack, but there were no signs of that."

"In a sense they were right, Luther."

And then her form travelled ever skyward, splitting into loose vapors, towards the sunset. And as it did, Maya's voice came back to him one final time.

"And to answer your question, Luther…I died of a broken heart."

THE END